Desolation Salvation

Alan W. Thompson

All Scripture quotations, unless otherwise indicated, are from The Project Gutenberg EBook of The King James Bible - www.gutenberg.org (Release Date: March 2, 2011 [EBook #10]).

Translations from English to Latin, or any other language, were provided by Google Translate. The translation from Hebrew to English was achieved leveraging the phonetic translation available of the King James Version of the Bible on Blue Letter Bible (blueletterbible.org).

First Edition, September 2021

Contents

Contents

Preface

I would like to thank everyone who helped make Creation Abomination and Abomination Desolation such a huge success. Many of you shared your enjoyment of these books on social media, through email, and even by visiting me at various events. While I enjoy the writing experience, I absolutely love the opportunity to interact with and talk to each of you. Your support in purchasing both Creation Abomination and Abomination Desolation has helped to give me the encouragement to finish the third book, and by sharing reviews, you have helped increase these books' overall visibility. Thank you for everything you have done, and I can't wait to hear how much you enjoy Desolation Salvation.

Writing the Creation Abomination book series has been a challenging but very rewarding process. I originally had the idea for Creation Abomination back in 1995. At that time, I had written a detailed outline of the book, but then I let it sit on the shelf, collecting dust for many years. Then, I was inspired in 2010 to write the book and I started work, both researching and writing. I spent a considerable amount of time doing research, as I wanted this to be as realistic and plausible as possible, but with a supernatural twist.

Desolation Salvation is the culmination of over eleven years of effort. I'd like to acknowledge the friends and family who have helped motivate me throughout this entire process.

CHAPTER 1

Catastrophe

(September 10, 2019 - The Story So Far...)

As the group silently walked through one of the curved openings, the immense underside of the elegant dome covering the shrine came into full view. The entire area of the cupola was bejeweled with thousands of intricately placed tiles, reflecting elegant symmetry and charm. Directly beneath the ornate ceiling lay exposed earth and the actual rock that the building's name referred to, protected by a waist high barrier enclosing the entire area. Their tour leader motioned for the group to stand together off to one side, close to the barrier that shielded the ground from visitors being able to walk upon it.

"I wanted to give you just a little bit of information about this shrine, but we need to keep our voices low so as not to detract from the reverent atmosphere," Menashe whispered. "This structure was built in ninety-two A.D., on the site of the Second Temple that was destroyed during the siege of Jerusalem by Rome in seventy A.D. As you can see, the building is in an octagonal shape, and is capped at the center by a dome approximately sixty-five feet in diameter. This allows for an ambulatorium, or circular walkway, to encompass the holy rock you see in front of you, which is also called the foundation stone. Muslims believe this to be the exact spot where Muhammad ascended into Heaven. For Jews, it is believed to be where God started His creation of the world, where Abraham almost sacrificed his son Isaac, and later, the site of the location of the Holy of Holies. Without a doubt, it has significant religious importance to both people of both faiths."

Menashe then led the group off to a far corner of the room, continuing to inform them about the history and significance of the building. Roughly fifteen minutes later, they had completed their tour and left by the same door through which they had entered before.

"That was absolutely stunning!" Tara exclaimed. "I'm so glad we were able to go inside!"

"Yes, thank you Menashe," Rich concurred. "This has been a wonderful experience so far."

"I'm happy you are enjoying yourselves. Come, let's walk toward the east side of the site to take a look at the construction site of the new Temple on the Mount."

The group walked about halfway toward a large, protective fence surrounding the area, and paused.

"I think this is about as close as we can get while still being able to see some of the actual structure. While the peace accord has paved the way for the rebuilding of the Jewish Temple here on the Temple Mount, there were many concessions that needed to be agreed upon for it to move forward. For example, even with Jerusalem being recognized as the capital of Israel, the Marwani Mosque and the Dome of the Rock have enormous spiritual significance for Muslims. As such, part of the agreement stipulated that these remained under the control of the Islamic Awqaf Department of Archaeological Tourism. It was through that compromise that Israel was given permission to rebuild their temple, as long as the footprint of the structure remained within the original perimeter walls. As you can see, they haven't wasted any time."

"They certainly haven't," William agreed. "It looks like the exterior walls are nearly complete and it's only been about six weeks since the peace treaty was finalized."

"Yes, they are moving quickly," Menashe agreed. "However, I recently heard it would likely take a couple of months beyond the initial projection of one year to complete construction, due to some delays in procuring materials. With that said, things are definitely moving forward nicely. Anyway, why don't we make our way over to the Western Wall next?" he suggested. "There are so many incredible sites to see, all in this relatively small location."

Following their guide, the party started walking back toward the Dome of the Rock. Walking alongside Menashe, Ariel was quietly engaged in a conversation which was not audible to the rest of their group. Roughly three minutes later, they found themselves casually strolling around the other side of the shrine toward the Western Wall, which lay roughly five hundred feet in a southwest direction. Ariel was now walking directly next to Rich, and William thought to himself that their angelic protector and his father-in-law would actually make a pretty good couple. No sooner had the thought entered his mind, though, Ariel turned her head and glanced back at him, arching her eyebrow in an almost knowing manner, as if she had read his thoughts. William immediately flushed a deep shade of crimson in response, to which Ariel quickly flashed a mischievous smile.

"What's that all about?" Tara inquired in a hushed tone.

"Oh, nothing," he quietly lied, not wanting to disclose to his wife what he had just been contemplating about her father.

Still following the Tzaddik, the group was now approximately two hundred feet from the large barrier on the west side of the location. Without any warning, their chaperone suddenly stopped and stared at the ground about twenty feet to his immediate left. Leaving Ariel's side, Rich walked over to join him.

"What is it?" he probed.

"I'm not sure," Menashe replied. "I thought that..."

Cutting himself off mid-sentence, their newfound companion sharply pointed at a dark shadow lying on the ground.

"Right there," he declared, *"did you see that?"*

"See what? I don't see anything except for some shade."

"Look closer!" Menashe directed.

Starring at the ground, Rich strained to see anything of significance that would justify the odd behavior his friend was exhibiting. The next moment, Rich's head jerked back slightly, and he let out an audible gasp.

"You *saw* it, yes?" their guide pressed.

"I did!" he testified. "It looked like the shape somehow shifted slightly."

"I noticed it about one minute ago. At first, I just thought it was only a shadow, but then I realized it was pacing our group off to the side!"

Tara, who had been holding William's hand, instinctively tightened her grip as a heightened sense of alarm swept over the party. That is, everyone except Ariel, who simply stood facing Menashe with an expression of serenity on her visage. The Tzaddik shifted his eyes to meet her gaze, and their heavenly guardian simply nodded in response, almost as if she were giving him permission.

Menashe then took two deliberate steps toward the dim outline on the ground and withdrew a small book from the front pocket of the jacket he was wearing. Holding the book tightly between his thumb and forefinger of his right hand, he raised it above his head.

"Zulluwth tetrapous,"[1] he boldly declared. *"Apenanti naqab 'Adonay, yalak!"*[2]

[1] Vile beast.

[2] In the name of God, depart!

Immediately the shadow seemed to shimmer, almost as if it were vibrating, then it shattered in upon itself, dissolving into the earth and leaving only the light of the Sun on the ground in its place.

"What was *that?*" Tara gasped. "The shadow seemed to almost explode!"

"At least we know your talisman is working," Ariel observed, "otherwise, you wouldn't have been able to see what just occurred."

"But what was it?" she pressed.

"That was a scout of the Adversary. I think it's time we leave now. Menashe, why don't you pick a place for us to get some dinner?"

"Of course," the man somberly replied.

About ten minutes later, the five of them were seated in an SUV and were just starting to pull out of a parking lot close to the historic location. The radio was tuned to a local station that was playing some traditional religious music.

"This will be a visit to the Temple Mount I will remember for many years to come," Rich wryly stipulated. "Why can't we just have a normal day?"

The next moment, the music precipitously cut off, and an ear-piercing tone erupted from the speakers. Everyone in the area immediately recognized it as the ubiquitous notification of an emergency alert. As the tone was still sounding inside the vehicle, sirens immediately started to blare all over the city of Jerusalem.

"You don't think it's a missile attack?" William blurted out in a panicked tone.

About ten seconds later, with the sirens still blasting, the alert signal on the radio stopped.

"The following is an emergency announcement," a male voice conveyed through the speakers. "Please wait for an official announcement and instructions."

The radio was then silent for almost thirty seconds. Menashe pulled off to the side of the road, so everyone would be able to focus on what was occurring. Then, the same male voice came back on, speaking in perfect, yet heavily accented English.

"This is not a test. This is an official notification of a natural disaster that has just occurred. Only ten minutes ago, we received word that a large asteroid impacted the Earth in the South Pacific Ocean, striking the Arafura Sea, just off the coast of Australia. The impact of this object has caused catastrophic destruction to the region. From the limited information we know at this point, the following countries have been severely impacted by this devastating event: Australia, New Zealand, New Guinea, and parts of Indonesia. Furthermore, the United Nations has issued warnings of what will likely be tremendous tidal waves from Malaysia up to the Sea of Okhotsk off the coast of Russia, to the islands across the Pacific Ocean, the coast of South America, Central America, and the West Coast of the United States. The government is asking everyone to return to their homes, and that we all pray for the safety and well-being of those who have already been afflicted by this disaster, and those who will be impacted in the near future. We will share more information as it becomes available."

Turning to face Ariel, Rich placed his hand delicately on top of hers and stared somberly into her eyes.

"The first angel sounded, and there followed hail and fire mingled with blood, and they were cast upon the Earth," he softly stated.

Without saying a word, Ariel placed her free hand on top of his, and looked up into Rich's face. A single tear slowly rolled down her alabaster cheek.

Roughly one thousand eight hundred miles to the Northwest of Jerusalem in the town of Meyrin, Switzerland, just on the outskirts of Geneva, a small silver Audi pulled into an open parking space in front of a large, grey two-story structure. A woman with a dark complexion and naturally beautiful hair, which was woven into intricate weaves wrapped closely to her head, hopped out of the driver's side of the car, quickly shutting the door behind her. Bending over slightly, she peered impatiently through the window at her passenger, who was casually relaxing in his seat.

"Lucien, ne reste pas assis là,"[3] she called in a French accent, "on va être en retard!"[4]

"Ouais, ouais,"[5] the man replied as he climbed out of the car. "Je sais. Ils ne commenceront pas sans nous!"[6]

With both hands extended slightly in front of her, palms facing up, the woman cast a decidedly annoyed glare at the man and elevated herself to her full height, a good three inches taller than him.

A smirk appeared on the smaller man's face, and he began to lightly chuckle.

[3] Lucien, don't just sit there.

[4] We're going to be late!

[5] Yeah, yeah.

[6] I know. They aren't going to start without us!

“D'accord. Ne t’affoles pas!”[7]

“Tu es impossible!”[8] she called back over her shoulder as she spun around and started making her way toward the entrance of the building.

Within just a few steps, the man had caught up to her and the two of them continued across the pavement, striding into the lobby of a relatively insignificant looking building through two large sliding glass doors.

An older gentleman, likely in his late sixties, looked up at the two from behind a small security desk as they entered into the vestibule.

“Bonjour, Éric,”[9] the woman announced.

“Bonjour, Donella. Comment était le déjeuner? Tu ferais mieux dépêcher revenir là-bas. Sont sur le point de commencer.”[10]

Without replying, Donella and Lucien made their way to a turnstile located off to the right of the desk and passed through after swiping their security badges. A moment later, the two of them walked quickly down a short hallway connecting Building 156 six with Building 157, where the main control room for the Large Hadron Collider was housed at the CERN laboratory.

At the far end of the hallway sat a large stainless-steel door with a security keypad to the right, adjacent to the frame. As the pair came within approximately fifteen feet of the doorway, a deep, rumbling bellow reverberated down the hallway and throughout the entire building.

[7] Ok. Don’t get your knickers in a twist.

[8] You’re impossible.

[9] Hello, Eric.

[10] Hello, Donella. How was lunch? You’d better hurry back there. They’re just about to begin.

"Ils ont commencé sans nous!"[11] cried Lucien.

But before Donella could respond, the floor beneath their feet lurched sharply to the side, causing them to collide and fall unceremoniously to the floor. The ground continued to shake violently for the next thirty seconds as if a major fault line had been triggered, along with the low blustering thunder of earth and steel being tossed to and fro. Then, just as abruptly as it had begun, all movement and noise ceased, leaving both colleagues lying prostrate on the concrete surface.

"Mais bon sang, qu'est-ce qui ce passe?!"[12] Donella blurted out with a bewildered expression on her face.

Without saying anything, Lucien pushed himself up off the floor to a standing position, then reached down to offer a helping hand to his teammate. Just as he was starting to assist her back to her feet, a deafening bang erupted from the steel door at the end of the corridor. Lucien was startled to the point that he lost his grip on Donella's hand, and she slipped back down on to the concrete surface with a distinct thud.

Looking back toward the source of the noise, Lucien's breath caught, completely caught off guard by the spectacle unfolding before his eyes.

A thick, putrid haze was starting to slowly percolate out from between the sides of the door and frame. Rather than drifting into the air as one would expect of smoke, it started to coalesce back upon itself, appearing as if it was crawling along the surface of the casing. As the volume of opaque fog increased, thick tendrils of vapor emanated outward along the entire perimeter of the door, almost in a web-like

[11] They started without us!

[12] What the hell's going on?!

pattern, crawling along the walls until it reached the corners of the passageway. At this point, the dense mist consolidated at the outermost edge, and the shadowy fumes darkened further in a sinister process that exuded hatred and evil.

"Qu…qu'est-ce qui se passe?"[13] Donella stuttered.

Before Lucien could respond, a bright flash radiated from a crack in the door, and the surface of the aperture seemed to fall inward upon itself as if it were plunging backward into an unseen room. As it plummeted further and further down into what appeared to be almost another reality, light seemed to bleed away from the surface, leaving an obsidian colored, multifaceted exterior. The lack of light was so stark that the muddy vapor along the edges of the web-like roiling coils looked light grey in comparison.

"Allez!"[14] Lucien screamed, taking a step back toward Donella with his hand extended downward. "On doit sortir!"[15]

Just then, an immediate and intense sensation of heat caused them both to snap their heads back and stare at the freshly materialized dark abyss. A deep, reddish hue of light began to emanate from the center of the pernicious portal, accompanied by a deep, guttural growl from an unseen entity. As the intensity of the light increased, the two onlookers could make out the faint outline of massive stalagmites and stalactites scattered sporadically throughout the interior of what appeared to be a massive subterranean chamber. Occasional flashes of fire flickered in the background, licking upward into the air as the putrid

[13] What's happening?

[14] Come on!

[15] We've got to get out of here!

smell of sulfur filled their nostrils. A faint crunching sound could be heard at somewhat regular intervals, gradually increasing in volume, intimating that the source of the vibration was drawing closer.

Frozen in absolute fear, neither of the associates were able to move, even in the slightest. Lucien then let out an audible gasp as he perceived a colossal shadow growing across the interior of the cavern, closing in on the opening leading into their world. As the murky outline widened, a horrific beast revealed itself.

Two pairs of gnarled horns sat atop the grotesquely broad head of the insidious creature. The first set curled back and upward from just behind the monster's temples, only to then curl straight back down and around to the front, before arching back again and off to the sides. The other two extruded from just above the outer edge of the eye sockets, angling back and ending in razor sharp points. The creature's head was covered by a thick, textured dark layer of skin, pocked with wrinkles and scars. On the side of its head were two small slits where ears should have been. The face of the succubus was just as fearsome to behold. Rather than skin covering its visage, an almost exoskeleton-like structure framed its features, protruding from the surface by at least two inches. It had massive, sunken sockets housing two large, crimson-colored eyes, and a broad, almost bull-like nose flung thick mucus across the room as it drew in and expelled air. Two rows of knife-like teeth were barely visible beneath what looked to be a lipless mouth that stretched across from ear-to-ear.

Holding up the massive head was a short, muscular neck with thick, twisted veins curling beneath the surface. A set of broad, powerful shoulders branched out to either side of the heavily muscled torso, which looked to be four feet across. Clumps of wiry, black hair covered its enormous chest, which rippled rhythmically as it flexed its massive tendons. Powerful, protracted arms hung down to just below the fiend's knees, where the sinewy extremities ended in vile, jagged claws. In contrast to its abnormally small waist, a pair of burly, ripped legs extended down toward knees which bent awkwardly backward upon themselves. A set of powerful calves angled forward from the knees, ending in horse-like hooves that churned up clumps of ground with each advance.

Shifting her gaze up to head, Donella locked eyes with this demonic savage. Sensing the terror in its prey, its horrific maw curled upward in a depraved grimace. It became apparent that the two halves of the opening were still connected in several locations by blistering skin, and as the gruesome mouth widened further, large tears began to appear on the creature's face, and revolting black fluid freely flowed from the fissures.

The malignant barbarian now stood at the threshold between the two realities, leveling a horrendous glare at its prey. Without any warning, the beast lifted its head and let out a terrifying howl. Then, it took a deliberate step across the boundary into their world, reached forward with its abominable paw, and grabbed Lucien, wholly enveloping the screaming man within its grasp.

Donella let out an ear-piercing scream, but it was to no avail, as the demon drew the helpless man back into its realm. Immediately, Lucien's skin began to dissolve as his body came in contact with the intense heat. Twice the height of its prey, the demon easily held him three feet above the ground. Without any delay, it dangled the defenseless man upside down by one of his legs, and after taking hold of the other, it forcefully pulled the two extremities of the quivering soul apart, tearing its victim in half. Seemingly satisfied at the outcome, it cast the two halves of the lifeless carcass roughly onto the ground, as an atrocious cackle burst from lungs. Donella stared aghast, but her eyes widened even further as she saw, just behind this maniacal creature, thousands of other demons all making their way toward the portal.

On the verge of hysteria, she screwed her eyes shut and shrieked a second time, preparing for what she knew was going to be her end. Then, without any warning, all sensation of heat was gone, along with the fetid smell of burning flesh.

The next moment, the sound of a large stainless-steel door slamming into the wall broke the silence, and Donella immediately opened her eyes to find several of her co-workers staring at her as she sat on the floor. She was shaking so much that it looked as if she was having a seizure. Huge streams of tears streaked across her face, and her clothes were sodden with sweat.

"Qu'est ce qui s'est passé? Nous vous avons entendu crier,"[16] one of her associates asked in a very concerned tone of voice.

Her body still convulsing, Donella stared blankly at the group surrounding her.

One of the men knelt down on the floor, and as he placed his hand cautiously on her shoulder, the frightened woman shifted her gaze to meet his. She stared silently into his eyes for almost a full thirty seconds without breathing or making a sound.

[16] What happened? We heard you screaming.

"Donella, qu'est-ce qui ne va pas?"[17]

The next instant, she audibly gasped for breath, and started to wildly look around the corridor.

"Donella, que s'est-il passé?"[18]

Returning her attention back to the man, Donella's breathing began to slow as she consciously attempted to control her emotions. After a few moments, she finally responded.

"Je ... je ... " she stammered, then paused. "Où est Lucien?"[19]

[17] Donella, what's wrong?

[18] Donella, what happened?

[19] Where is Lucien?

CHAPTER 2

Preternatural

(September 10, 2021)

It was just after eight o'clock in the evening, and the Sun had already made its descent over the horizon in the West. The sky was alive with vibrant hues of pink and orange, creating a watercolor canvas for the large billowy clouds intermittently placed throughout the stratosphere. A small, light-colored structure was set back from a dirt road running adjacent to the property. The dwelling itself sat on a plateau that was mostly devoid of foliage, except for a few smaller bushes here and there. A wooden overhang extended out from the side of the home by eight feet, encircling the entire residence, and a total of three nondescript lawn chairs lay on the porch off to the right of the front entry. To the left of the building, a dusty SUV was parked beneath a flimsy looking roof that bowed slightly in the middle. With the sky quickly darkening, the illumination from a light cascading through a small window on the front door seemed to intensify with every passing moment.

The interior of the modest residence comprised a large, single room containing a small seating area, a kitchen with a dining table and four chairs, and a sleeping area consisting of a double sized bed and two smaller cots. Two men were sitting across from each other at the dining table, engaged in a conversation as they casually picked at a small plate of bread and grapes. Positioned on the couch was a large, burly man, in his late fifties or early sixties. He was lying back against the cushions with his feet extended onto a low-lying rectangular table positioned directly in front of the sofa. His thick forearms were comfortably crossed across his barrel chest, and he gazed through eyeglasses at a picture on the laptop computer just to the side of his feet. An antique looking, horse-drawn buggy clattered down a dark cobbled street. An old, gaunt man with a scraggly beard steered the cart expertly, holding the reigns loosely in his grip. He wore a tatty black suit that gave him a look of an embalmer at a mortuary. Located directly behind the elevated bench on which he sat, was a low-lying flat area, with a large rectangular coffin situated in the middle. The somewhat eerie sound of a pipe organ was coming from the computer along with the rhythmic ‘clip-clop’ of the horse’s hooves on stone.

“How much longer are you going to watch that trash?” William called over to the larger man.

“This is actually quite interesting,” Rich replied. “Besides, there’s a story coming up that I think you’ll find interesting.”

“What exactly are you watching?” the man sitting across from William inquired.

“It’s a show that investigates *real* paranormal phenomena.”

“Oh, *actual* supernatural activities? Like the ghost tours you can pay for in most older cities in the United States?” William responded with more than a hint of banter.

“This is a documented event that happened in St. Augustine, Florida,” Rich countered. “Besides, I would think *you* would be more likely to believe in this than anyone else...given your history.”

“Yeah, well, I think I’ve had my fill of transcendental events.”

William paused for a moment but despite himself, he relented to his curiosity.

"Ok, what's the next story?"

A broad grinned creased the large man's face, and a distinct air of satisfaction crept across his countenance.

"They're going to be talking about the Large Hadron Collider in France. Apparently, when the Collider was turned on for the first time back in 2008, a series of supernatural events began to occur, both in and outside the facility."

Just as Rich finished his sentence, he glanced back at the small screen.

"Here we go," he enthusiastically remarked. "They're about to start the feature."

Standing up from his seat, William made his way over the couch to join Rich.

"Alright, scoot over and make some space."

Without a word, Rich pulled his feet off of the table and slid over to his right, making room for William, then placed his feet back on the wooden stand situated in front of the sofa.

"Our next story takes us to the border of France and Switzerland, where the European Organization for Nuclear Research, known as CERN, is located. Founded in 1954, CERN originally focused on the study of atomic nuclei, but shifted direction shortly after to study the interactions between subatomic particles. While there have been multiple scientific breakthroughs in the nearly seventy years since it was founded, their most renowned accomplishment came exactly thirteen years ago to the day - September 10, 2008 - when the world largest particle accelerator was turned on for the first time. This is where our story begins."

"This should be good," William interjected.

"Quiet!" Rich complained. "I want to hear what they're saying."

With a smirk on his face, William let out a lighthearted chuckle and returned his attention back to the program.

"The Large Hadron Collider, or LHC," a male voice with a thick British accent began, "is comprised of a twenty-seven-kilometer ring of hundreds of superconducting magnets at an average depth of 92 meters beneath the surface. Two high-energy particle beams hurtle in opposite directions at velocities approaching the speed of light in a vacuum contained in two separate hollow rings. After attaining maximum speed, these beams are guided by a series of electromagnets until they are racing through the same tube. As these particles whizz past each other in such close proximity at ridiculously high speeds, the inevitable occurs - a collision. During this head-on encounter, a massive amount of energy is released, as the protons and neutrons are broken down into hundreds of sub-atomic particles. The combination of particles colliding at almost the speed of light, and the consequential release of energy, is the focus of our report."

"Since the LHC was turned on, there have been a string of supernatural incidents reported by scientists and local residents alike. The earliest event was recorded on November 20, 2009, with the first successful collision of hydrogen atoms."

The image on the screen changed and showed a middle-aged woman with olive-colored skin and long, dark hair, wearing a white lab coat and sitting on a chair facing the camera. While she spoke in French, a voice over made the translation into English.

"Roughly three days after the first successful experiment, I saw something that wasn't normal. I was in my office working on procedures for an upcoming test, when something caught my attention out of the corner of my eye. As I looked across my desk to the opposite side of the room, the wall seemed to shimmer and became translucent, almost as if it was dematerializing. That's when my head started to hurt, and my vision blurred. I closed my eyes for a moment, and when I reopened them, the surface of the wall looked to be covered by a thick sheet of wavy glass that made it difficult to clearly see through it. After a moment, I was able to make out shapes and colors on the other side, and then..."

The woman briefly paused, obviously distraught by the memory of what she was describing.

"...And then, I realized a shadow on the other side was moving toward the opening in the wall. As it got closer to the hazy aperture, I could make out that it was a creature of some sort, until finally, it was standing directly in front of the glass and seemed to be peering at me. It reached forward with its hand, and the instant its palm touched the barrier, an ear-piercing shriek shattered the silence, sending a chill up and down my spine. I covered my eyes with my hands and turned away from this frightful image, thinking my life was about to end. But then, a few moments passed, then a few more. Finally, I worked up the courage to look back at the wall, but the vision was completely gone."

The image changed, and this time, a dark-skinned man was on screen, sitting on a sofa with his legs crossed. Again, the language was translated by the voice over as the man began his account.

"Back in 2011, I stayed late one evening to finish up a report I was writing for a recently completed test. It was just past midnight, and there was no one else at the facility as far as I knew – except, of course, for security personnel and cleaning staff. Well, I was sitting at my desk typing on my keyboard, when I suddenly became aware of a reddish light source coming from behind me, and I felt the sensation of heat on my back. When I turned around to see where it was coming from, I was astonished by what I saw. Floating in the air, about one meter above the ground, was a gateway or portal of some kind, leading to what appeared to be another location, or possibly another dimension. The fissure itself looked to be collapsing upon itself, but before it completely disappeared, I was able to make out a massive, cavernous chamber, with rock structures hanging down from the ceiling and reaching upward from the floor. I saw bursts of flames erupting from the surface of some rocks, and a large lake of fire about twenty meters from my location. Then, the illusion completely vanished, and I was left there, staring at an empty room."

Once again, the image changed, and now a gaunt, elderly woman with short, grey hair was sitting on a cushioned chair facing the camera. The familiar voice continued in the translation as she related her story.

"In the summer of 2017, I decided to take my dog, Titou, for a walk in the evening, at around seven o'clock. My family owns a small farm over off *Chemin de la Cascade Boulevard*, not far from the CERN facility. Each evening, we take the same route along the southern edge of the campus, and this was no different."

She paused for a moment as tears began to well up in her eyes.

"I tell you what happened," she finally groaned. "They took my poor Titou, they did. This creature appeared out of thin air and grabbed her in its claws. There was nothing I could do!" she cried. "I tried to save her, but it was just too strong...pulled the leash right out of my hands, it did. Then, it crawled back into its hole and disappeared just as quickly as it had arrived."

The display changed again, this time showing aerial footage from a drone over the CERN buildings. The same British accent continued to narrate the next part of the story.

"This is but a small handful of the reported incidents which have occurred at this laboratory since the launch of the LHC. There have been over one hundred similarly documented occurrences, coming from employees and local residents alike, and an untold number which have never been shared. There is one common thread that exists in all of these incidents, though: none of them have ever been captured on video. But while no actual proof exists, and no one has been able to come up with a plausible explanation, one scientist has come forward with a controversial theory."

This time, the image on the screen was filled with a man in his early sixties, standing behind a lectern at the head of a large auditorium. He had long, white, wavy hair that stretched back from an exaggerated widow's peak at least five inches, its unruliness suggesting it had never been combed. He wore thick, black-rimmed glasses, and despite his age, the skin on his face looked abnormally taut, almost as if he had been the victim of bad plastic surgery. Describing his lab coat as white would have been a stretch, given the fact that it looked as it hadn't seen the inside of the washing machine for at least a year. He wore a whitish colored shirt with a plain brown tie and black slacks. As he stood facing the audience in the lecture hall, the words 'Peter Essers, Physicist and Expert on String Theory' appeared at the bottom of the screen.

"We must acknowledge the existence of other dimensions than our own," he began in a Swedish accent. "In fact, I believe we have literally proven their presence right here at CERN. Everyone has heard talk of these fantastical experiences that can't be explained. Visions of creatures or beings not of this world. Physical manifestations and interactions which defy logic. I tell you, the Large Hadron Collider itself is confirming alternate dimensions, and creating a pathway from our reality to theirs. You see, the massive amount of energy that is released when protons are split into hundreds of subatomic particles, like quarks and gluons, is literally bending, or more accurately, *pinching* the space-time continuum. This distortion contorts the very fabric of our reality into a compressed point that then pierces into another dimension."

Several jeers erupted from the crowd, who were clearly contesting his comments. A rather rotund man sitting in the front row of the room stood up and actually shook his fist at him.

"Please, please," Doctor Essers implored, "hear me out. We have seen numerous *events* occur since the Large Hadron Collider was activated, but this pales in comparison to what has occurred since September 10, 2019. You see, that was the date the *Télos* asteroid plunged into the sea to the north of Australia. On that same day, and every day since, the number of paranormal instances at the Hadron has skyrocketed to at least ten times what had been reported previously. Now, many of you will say that these two events are not connected, but it is my assertion that they are, and I can prove it."

The lights in the auditorium dimmed slightly as the man turned to face the image on the large screen behind him. On the canvas was a map of northern Australia, with a specific point in the Arafura Sea designated with a large black "X."

"You see, this point here marks the impact location of that calamitous event two years ago. Now, if you determine the antipode, or exact location opposite this point on the other side of the globe," he continued as the image of the earth began to turn on its axis until it paused at a point in the Atlantic Ocean, "it ends up here, roughly one thousand kilometers off the coast of Brazil."

"This proves nothing," the husky man in the front row called out.

"But it does," he countered. "In 2016, scientists documented how large low-shear-velocity provinces - or, in simpler terms - gigantic blobs of ancient rock, comprised roughly ten per cent of the earth's mantle. Until this time, we couldn't explain how the shockwaves from massive earthquakes occurring on one side of the planet could be detected in locations dramatically different from the antipode of the epicenter. But now, we have advanced our knowledge and understand how these large provinces affect shockwaves. Working with the Seismological Laboratory at Caltech, we have recreated the impact of the meteor, taking into account the amount of energy released, along with the deflection of energy waves due to this ancient rock."

The image on the screen shifted to show a three-dimensional view of Earth, but with a transparent surface. Scattered throughout the lower mantle of the representation were massive areas of dark red earth.

"These darkened areas represent the large low-shear-velocity provinces. Now, watch what happens as the *Télos* collides with Earth."

The room was absolutely silent as the spaceborne object swept in from the right and slammed into the ocean just above the Australian continent. Immediately, shockwaves depicted by bright yellow lines started to emanate outward from ground zero in all directions. As they traveled across the planet, the color of these bands changed to a bright orange to differentiate them from the surface waves. These carrot-colored contours then began to reach down beneath the surface, traveling in what appeared to be a uniform pattern. Then, as they came into contact with the dark red areas of the mantle, the started to bend sharply at almost a forty-five-degree angle from their path. As they continued to traverse through the core and out the other side, it was apparent that they were now aimed at Europe. Within a matter of seconds, the waves narrowed and seemed to be being guided, with almost laser-like precision, to the eastern edge of France. The next moment, they intersected the surface, with the primary focus hitting just to the west of the small town of Meyrin, Switzerland.

A cacophony immediately ensued, part gasps and part exclamations of surprise. As the lights slowly brightened, the image recentered back on Doctor Essers, who was standing triumphantly, his arms crossed firmly across his chest and a satisfied smile firmly planted on his face. He waited a moment for the crowd to quiet down, then continued.

"It is my conclusion that these two events are inextricably linked. The occurrence of supernatural events at CERN are directly attributable to the Hadron Collider. The increase in these paranormal activities coincides with, and is a result of, the horrible disaster of the *Télos* asteroid. String theory stipulates that there are a total of ten different dimensions. It is my firm belief that we have unknowingly opened up a gateway into one of these dimensions. In fact, it is my suspicion that we have mistakenly and unintentionally opened up a portal into the very realm of hell."

The on-screen image changed again, this time revealing the narrator, who was standing in front of the main CERN campus sign with his hands neatly interlaced in front of his torso. His visage exuded excitement as he addressed the camera.

"This may well be one of the first scientifically supported instances of paranormal activity. We will keep you posted with further updates as we learn more about this incredible story here in Merwin, Switzerland."

With a look of utter disbelief, William turned to stare into the face of his father-in-law.

"What does this mean?" he wondered.

After taking a deep breath, Rich finally responded.

"Hell from beneath is moved for thee to meet thee at thy coming: it stirreth up the dead for thee, even all the chief ones of the earth; it hath raised up from their thrones all the kings of the nations."

CHAPTER 3

Problematic

Reaching forward, Rich firmly closed the lid of his laptop, and settled back onto the sofa with his arms folded across his chest. Pursing his lips, he took a long, deep breath in through his nostrils, held it momentarily, then noisily exhaled.

"Well," he began, "I guess it figures. I mean, why not? Why shouldn't there be a gateway that brings demons directly into our world? It's not like we're having to contend with enough of these evil creatures as it is already!"

Menashe stood up from the dining table and dragged a chair to the opposite side of the coffee table so he could join in the conversation with the other two men.

"Don't jump to any conclusions," he cautioned. "For all we know, this is purely conjecture. It's more likely science fiction than science fact."

"It does kind of all make sense though," said William. "I mean, it was right around the time the Hadron came online that everything started to hit the fan. In fact, the six clone children were *born*," he spat with a disgusted expression on his face, "right before CERN turned the machine on for the first time. It can't just be a coincidence."

"Ok," Menashe pushed back, "if they're connected, then why did the number of paranormal events increase when the *Télos* asteroid impacted the earth?"

"The energy!" Rich blurted out.

"Exactly what I was thinking," William agreed. "The amount of energy discharged when a massive rock traveling at thousands of miles per hour slams into the earth has got to be staggering. I'd wager it would be even larger than the amount required to split protons into subatomic particles. And if those seismic surges all converged on a location where the fabric of space and time had been degraded…"

"It might damage it to the point that malignant spirits could come into our reality more easily and with greater frequency," Menashe acknowledged. "That would help to explain why there has been such a dramatic increase in the number of supernatural happenings."

The three men sat for a moment, pondering the implications of this conclusion. Finally, Menashe stood up from his chair, paced back and forth for a moment, then spun to face his companions.

"Ok, so let's just pretend for a moment this is accurate. That the Large Collider has somehow opened up an express lane to hell. How can we be certain these things are all linked? And that the connection is important?"

Pinching his chin, Rich stared at the floor in a thoughtful manner. After a moment, he started to slowly shake his head back and forth.

"To be honest," he began, "I don't know. I guess there could be other realities. My religious training - and my heart - tell me that heaven and hell exist, but I'm definitely not an expert. I have no idea if they're in an alternate dimension, or just somewhere really far away from Earth."

He then cast a speculative glance at William, who shrugged his shoulders in response.

"Don't ask me; this is your area of expertise."

"I'm at a bit of a loss," Rich admitted. "It sounds like they could be connected, but I truly don't know enough about this topic. And definitely not enough to conclude if and how these occurrences might affect future events."

Menashe slowly started to raise his hand with his index finger extended, almost as if he were a student asking for permission from to speak. Rich raised his eyebrows in response.

"Out with it," he shrugged.

"I might know someone we could talk to who possesses a significant amount about this topic."

Menashe paused for a moment and stared at both the men on the sofa.

"Well, go on then!" Rich barked in an exasperated tone.

"Her name is Widad Nazari and she's an Ulama."

"An Ulama?" Rich probed.

"Yes. An Ulama is a scholar who is very well respected as an expert in Islamic doctrine and law. She is also an authority on the topics of preexistence and the afterlife."

"I didn't know Islamic beliefs incorporated these ideas?"

"They definitely do. In fact, they're a core conviction in their faith."

"You seemed hesitant to bring her up," Rich pressed. "Why?"

"Well, she is somewhat of a recluse. In fact, there really isn't any way to get a hold of her, except by going to see her in person."

"Doesn't she have a phone?" Rich prodded.

"As a matter of fact, no. She normally doesn't make any direct contact with the outside world. We would have to go and visit her directly."

"Why is that an issue?" William interjected.

"Well, we can't just hop in the car and drive over to her house. She lives in Mecca."

"Mecca, as in *Saudi Arabia*, Mecca?" Rich said with a groan.

"The very same."

Menashe paused for a moment, averting his eyes anxiously off to the side of the room.

"There's something you're not telling us," Rich continued to press.

Returning his gaze back to the two men, Menashe took a deep breath and began to speak.

"You see," he began, "Widad is a very well respected Ulama. Actually, she is often sought out for counsel by other Islamic religious leaders. So much so, she has taken up permanent residence at the Masjid al-Haram."

"What's that?" William inquired.

"It's the Great Mosque in Mecca, the most sacred site in Islam. Located in the center of the Mosque is Kaaba, the most important Muslim pilgrimage site. Over two million people visit it every year."

"So, what's the catch?" William asked.

"You have to be Muslim to even enter Mecca," Menashe answered in a flat tone.

"I see," Rich laughed. "Well, that might present a problem."

CHAPTER 4

Coercion

(Seven Days Later)

The United Nations office was just fifteen minutes from the CERN facility in Meyrin, Switzerland, half a mile from Lake Geneva. It was an impressive complex of several massive buildings centered around a large primary structure, interconnected by a series of large hallways. In one of the largest edifices, an enormous, circular conference room was housed, where delegates from all around the world would meet to debate critical topics. The broad room was over one hundred feet in diameter, with six rows of seating situated in front of semi-circular desks, which rippled out from the center point in a distinct pattern. With three quarters of the floor containing delegates in their curved accommodation, the remaining floor space remained mostly clear, except for a single, arched desk against the far wall, with seating for the ten individuals that presided over meetings.

Today, the United Nations Economic and Social Council, or ECOSOC, was in session to discuss the best strategy to deal with the impact of COVID-21, a new, more contagious variant of the initial strain. All fifty-four members of ECOSOC were present, along with a small handful of support personnel, all of whom were scattered throughout the room to allow for social distancing. Even with all of these individuals in the room, at least seventy seats were unoccupied. At the head of the room, occupying the seat of leadership, sat the President of the council, Emilohi Adebayo, the delegate from Nigeria. In the chair immediately to the right of the president was Global

President Elect Doctor Koenraad Schmidt, and to his left sat Akira Kim, the Director General of the World Health Organization. Arranged around the perimeter of the room at regular intervals stood a number of darkly clothed soldiers, exuding animosity as blatant as the automatic rifles slung on their shoulders.

A significant amount of dissonance resonated throughout the chamber as various members were literally shouting across the room at other delegates, waving their arms in an animated manner. It truly was a chaotic scene.

"Please everyone, please," President Adebayo implored, "there must be order. We must quiet down so each representative's voice can be heard."

While the room didn't fall completely silent, there was a noticeable decline in both the number and volume of voices. President Adebayo threw a hesitant glance toward Schmidt, who gave only a very slight nod in response. The next moment, the Global President Elect stood from his chair and silently raised his hand above his head. As he did so, the room fell virtually silent as all the delegates directed their attention to the head of the room and retook their seats.

"President," Schmidt huffed, "the floor is yours."

"I…umm…" she spluttered. "Thank you."

Taking a deep breath, Adebayo straightened her suit jacket by pulling down on the bottom front quarters, then readied herself to address the audience.

"Honorable delegates," she began, "we all know the challenge lying before us might seem insurmountable, but we must rise to the occasion for the good of all citizens of the planet. While there is not a single solution that will explicitly address every concern *your* nation is facing, it is critical that we consider them equally."

She paused for a moment as her words were translated for those delegates who didn't speak English, before proceeding.

"If there are no objections, I propose that the delegate from Brazil, the Honorable Antonio Siqueira, addresses the forum."

A relatively short man with a light complexion stood up in the second row of seating. He wore a steel-blue suit and a white collared shirt with the top two buttons undone.

"Thank you, Ms. President," he declared in a thick Portuguese accent. "Brazil has been hit particularly hard by the COVID-21 variant. And as you are aware, this is on top of the challenges we are still facing from the original COVID-19 strain. We have had nearly five hundred thousand deaths from the disease so far this year. Our hospitals are overrun, we are understaffed, and our medical supplies are almost non-existent. One of the biggest challenges we have is the accurate and reliable contact tracing of individuals who have been infected. This has created the nearly impossible situation of properly notifying and quarantining potentially exposed persons. We have tried different solutions to address this difficulty with less than perfect results. I believe that through better technology, we can monitor individuals more carefully to protect the safety of everyone."

"Well, you definitely need to get a better handle on this," a woman in her late thirties warned. "Argentina was able to handle this second variant without too much trouble until thousands of Brazilians started to flee from your country, bringing COVID-21 with them and spreading it throughout our population unchecked. In just a matter of months, we find ourselves in nearly the same dire situation as you. And this has completely derailed our economic recovery. We had just started to open up our borders again to tourism, and now both Europe and the United States have reinstated travel bans. Your *laughable* border controls have thrown our economy into a downward spiral."

"People are dying, and you're worried about tourism?" the envoy from Brazil sneered. "It won't matter how strong your economy is if there's no one left alive to benefit from it."

The representative from Argentina stood up from her seat and glared at the gentleman. The anger rising up within her was truly palpable, as she shook her fist at him in a threatening manner.

On the opposite side of the chamber, a dark-skinned man in his forties rose from his chair and glowered at both individuals. He stood a good six inches taller than the emissary from Brazil and looked quite angry.

"If any country has been economically destroyed by this pandemic," he said in a Caribbean inflection, "the Bahamas is at the top of the list. We've been under lockdown for over one-and-a-half years, and there doesn't seem to be any end in sight."

"Well, maybe if your country provided something useful, other than a sandy beach, you wouldn't be in such dire circumstances," Antonio retorted.

"Doing something *useful?*" he exclaimed. "Why doesn't Brazil do something beneficial with their citizens, like efficiently distributing the new vaccine?"

The next moment, dozens of delegates were standing and shouting at one another again. One man had turned around to argue with another delegate seated directly behind him, and was now leaning across his desk, forcefully poking him in the chest. All civility seemed to have been tossed aside as the level of aggression grew.

"Ladies and gentlemen, please...please, take your seats!" President Adebayo begged. "We won't accomplish anything this way!"

As the chaos continued throughout the assembly hall, Schmidt simply leaned back in his chair with his fingers interlaced across his abdomen, smugly surveying the scene. As he scrutinized the tumultuous debate, he became aware of an ominous presence in the room. Glancing to his right and slightly down, he saw what looked to be the silhouette of an obscured hand lightly resting on his arm. Seemingly in response to his recognition, the extremity began to lightly pat his bicep.

"*The time is right*," a rough, guttural hiss resonated in his head.

Without hesitating, Schmidt leaned closely over to President Adebayo, placing his mouth directly alongside the woman's ear.

"Don't you think *now* would be an opportune time to bring forward the idea of a single, global digital passport, for each and every citizen on the planet?"

Emilohi flinched as the final syllable reverberated in her eardrum.

"But Doctor Schmidt," she started to whisper, "I don't think we have the support..."

But she abruptly froze mid-sentence as Schmidt scowled at her menacingly.

"Of course," she relented with a slight tilt of her head. "I will make the suggestion."

Reaching across his body, Schmidt vigorously gripped the woman's upper arm, squeezing it to the point that her skin began to bulge slightly upwards between his flexed fingers.

"You'll do more than make the suggestion," he growled. "Make it happen!"

After being released, the woman merely nodded in acquiescence to Schmidt and stood up from her seat.

"*Ladies and gentlemen!*" she called out at the top of her lungs. "*That is enough*!"

The room instantly fell silent, and everyone stared at her in astonishment.

"You are behaving like children, and the world doesn't have time for you to grow up. Now, pipe down and take your seats!"

Remarkably, every person in the circular chamber quietly complied and stared expectantly at her. Without taking her seat, the President continued to address the crowd.

"These are stressful times," she called out, "but we do not have the luxury of wasting time bickering with each other. We must take action swiftly, and it must be decisive. I would like to bring to the floor for discussion, and approval, resolution number two-six-six-six. This resolution hereby reaffirms our commitment to the health and safety of every man, woman, and child on the planet, and commits to putting in place the necessary measures and technologies to ensure we are protecting everyone by whatever means possible. With this motion, I recommend the implementation of a new, global digital passport, to facilitate the accurate and timely contact tracing of individuals exposed to COVID-21. Furthermore, I advocate the use of technology for the precise tracking of individuals in every country throughout the entire world who have been vaccinated, and those that have not. And finally, by mandate of this resolution, any person not complying with this order will have restrictions placed on them, including their ability to travel freely, to work, to receive government assistance, and even buy and sell goods and services."

Discord immediately erupted from several of the attendees.

"This is absolutely absurd!" a large man jeered in an Italian accent.

"Outrageous!" another woman proclaimed.

Several other comments were thrown out from across the amphitheater as delegates expressed their opposition to the proposal. Finally, a slender, almost gaunt-looking man from Britain rose from his seat. His skin was extraordinarily pale, and his face looked as if it was permanently twisted in a sour expression.

"Ms. President," the man snorted in an English accent, "you have gone too far. What you are proposing is not only an extreme invasion of privacy, but it will give one governing body absolute awareness and knowledge of virtually every single person on the planet, where they go, and what they do. Do you not see the inherent danger with this level of surveillance?"

But before Emilohi could respond to his question, Doctor Schmidt stood up from his chair, locking eyes with the Englishman, who visibly flinched in response. He continued to stare at the man, without saying a word, until the delegate physically shrunk downward and retook his seat. Obviously satisfied with the other man's reaction, a brief smirk appeared on Schmidt's visage.

"It's Mr. Taylor, yes?" he scoffed in his thick, German accent.

"Umm...yes...President Elect," he faltered.

"I see," he mocked. "As I'm sure you know, we are living in extreme times, under acute conditions. And as the past dictates, severe measures are sometimes required for the greater good. I'm also sure you are aware of the fact that the mortality rate associated with this newest variant is claiming the life of fifty out of every one thousand people who fall ill to this pandemic. That's five percent of every man, woman and child who catches this fateful disease. And that rate jumps to over thirty percent for anyone whose symptoms require hospitalization. Furthermore, this variant is also highly contagious, and it is wreaking havoc across our communities!"

Having taken a moment to collect himself, the British envoy looked more confident of his position and leaned forward in his chair, locking eyes once again with Schmidt.

"You are stating the obvious. It is clear to me that your motivations are grounded in your desire for more power," he gruffly accused.

A thin smile of satisfaction creased Schmidt lips.

"*Finally, someone with a bit of a spine*," he thought to himself. "*He will make an excellent example.*"

"Please, go on," he encouraged.

"Oh, I'm definitely going to continue," he snapped. "Ever since the rededication of the Temple in Jerusalem, you have been hell bent on slowly diminishing the sovereignty of each and every nation of the world. And you do this under the guise of peace and safety. You have forced your will upon every citizen of this planet and brought an armed contingent into the very halls of the United Nations!" he shouted, gesturing to the soldiers in the room.

Schmidt paused and looked at the man in a speculative manner. A horrible smile crept across his face.

"Are you finished?" he challenged. "I see. Well, now it's my turn to talk."

Doctor Schmidt walked around the curved table and directly toward Mr. Taylor. Within a few seconds, he stood just on the other side of the table, glaring down at the other man, who had retaken his seat.

"So, if I'm hearing you correctly, you feel the order that has been instilled into our global community is undesirable? Hmm, I see. And what would you suggest? Allowing each nation to try and solve humanity's problems on their own? That hasn't worked out very well, has it? This *threat of force* you refer to," he virtually hissed, "is the only thing holding civilization together."

He turned and walked back to the center of the room, and as he came to a stop, he abruptly wheeled around to face the target of his verbal barrage. Then, he slowly cast his attention to one of the armed soldiers standing in the periphery of the auditorium.

"This potential menace," he attested, "is here for the safety and the security of every living soul. Any action they take," he warned as he purposely cast his gaze back to the delegate, "will be for the protection of the greater good."

Mr. Taylor visibly began to tremble as he realized the unveiled threat the President Elect had just directed toward him. After a hard swallow, he stood once again, but this time, his body language clearly showed deference to Schmidt.

"I apologize," he shuddered. "You are absolutely correct, and we must continue down this path."

"Excellent," Schmidt seethed in response. "What do you suggest?"

The British representative looked around the room helplessly for some sign of support, but when none of the other diplomats would even look at him, he carefully peered back at the President Elect, whose glower sent a chill down his spine.

"I...I...," he faltered. "I would like to call for a vote from the Economic and Social Council to support resolution two-six-six-six."

Radiating smug satisfaction, Schmidt turned back to face President Adebayo, who nodded in affirmation and stood up from her chair.

"Honorable delegates, I move to call for a vote on United Nations resolution two-six-six-six. Do I have a second?"

"I second the motion," Mr. Taylor quickly blurted out.

"It is moved and seconded that this council proceed with United Nations resolution two-six-six-six. All those in favor, say '*aye.*'"

With one accord, a thunderous affirmation echoed throughout the circular chamber.

"All those opposed, say '*no.*'"

The room fell dead silent.

"The ayes have it. Let the record show the vote is unanimous. This motion has been successfully carried and will now be passed onto the entire United Nations Council for ratification by all member nations."

Without a word, Schmidt clasped both of his hands behind his back, and slowly walked toward one of the exits at the head of the room. Four of the darkly clad guards fell into position closely behind him, and they all departed the assembly hall through a set of double doors.

CHAPTER 5

Precipice

(Two Weeks Later)

Just after seven o'clock in the evening, Rich, Menashe, and William found themselves sitting around a small, dining table in the home of their Jewish friend. Despite the fact that the Sun had nearly completed its daily pilgrimage across the sky, it was still relatively warm outside, with a temperature of just about eighty degrees Fahrenheit. The three men were actively engaged in a discussion about the best approach to travel from Jerusalem to Mecca.

"We'll definitely need to pick up a few supplies," Menashe advised. "And as you know, it's getting tougher and tougher to purchase anything in what might be deemed bulk quantities. The government is actively restricting citizens from hoarding any goods."

"That's the least of our problems," William countered. "If there are any items we can't purchase before we leave, we'll just pick them up on the way."

"Don't be so sure. Everyone is experiencing scarcity right now, and then there's always the issue of how to pay for it. Once we leave Jerusalem, the only prevailing currency to buy anything will be the US dollar, and its value keeps plummeting. At the rate prices are increasing, we might need a suitcase full of cash to buy anything."

The next moment, Menashe's cell phone began to vibrate on top of the counter. Reaching forward, he grasped his device to check the caller ID.

"It's my friend, Baruch, who lives in the United States. I haven't heard from him for weeks."

Holding the device to his ear, he answered the call.

"Chaver, Shah-vehr. Ma nishma?"[20]

Menashe sat listening to the words coming through his device, while the other two men stared silently at him.

"Hem karyanut tsadaq hoveh?"[21] he remarked after listening for a few moments, before pausing again as the voice on the other side responded to his question.

"Toda raba!"[22] he announced. "l'hit'raot."[23]

After turning his cell off, he anxiously looked at the other two men.

"What is it?" Rich queried.

"Grab the laptop and go to CNN.com. There's a news conference being broadcast from New York. They're expected to make an announcement on some new COVID-21 requirements."

Rich hopped up and retrieved the notebook from the stand in front of the sofa and opened it after rejoining the two men. Within a second, he had launched a browser and was navigating to the correct website.

"There," he finished, "let me switch to full screen."

"What about the audio?" William complained.

With a muffled grunt, the large man manipulated the mouse until sound began to emanate through the speakers.

"…and as you can see, large protest groups have gathered just outside of the U.N. building in Switzerland," a high-pitched male voice was saying. "A similar scene is taking place at most other United Nations buildings, and within capital cities across the globe, as individual rights organizations are protesting what they feel is too much

[20] Hello, friend. How are things?
[21] They're making an announcement now?
[22] Thank you!
[23] Goodbye.

control and regulation when it comes to personal freedoms."

The image on the screen changed to show a large line of darkly dressed soldiers standing in front of what looked to be the United Nations edifice in New York city. They were all holding large plastic riot shields and menacing steel batons, with an ominous looking submachinegun strapped on their shoulders. Facing off against this defensive line was a large group of men and women wearing facemasks and carrying protest signs.

"While tensions have been high, they greatest level of disquiet has been right here in New York City, where we expect the Director General of the World Health Organization to be making an announcement shortly, along with the Global President Elect."

"I don't have a good feeling about this," William cautioned.

"Alright, we're going to go live," the voice declared from the laptop. "We have just been informed that an official statement is about to be made."

The picture changed again to reflect a large briefing room inside the United Nations, and the all-too-familiar figure of Koenraad Schmidt making his way across the slightly raised platform. As he reached a small podium, several jeers erupted from the audience gathering within the auditorium. Without a word, he raised both hands above his shoulders until the crowd quieted down enough for him to be easily heard.

"Ladies and gentlemen, colleagues, and all citizens of this planet, it is my distinct pleasure to stand before you on this momentous day," he declared in a German accent. "I must apologize for Akira Kim, the head of the W.H.O., who was unable to participate in sharing this significant statement."

"Wasn't able to, or refused to accompany?" Rich said sarcastically.

"Be quiet!" William ordered. "We need to hear this."

The burly man exhaled audibly through his nostrils in response but remained quiet.

"As you are all aware," Schmidt carried on, "the world has been contending with multiple catastrophes over the last few years. First was the *Télos* asteroid impacting the earth on September 15, 2019, resulting in an estimated eighty million deaths. This was followed rapidly by the horrific COVID-19 pandemic which has claimed the lives of over four-and-a-half million souls to date. And then, just as the world started to pull itself out of the humanitarian and economic calamity that both disasters caused, we were struck with an even more pervasive and deadly epidemic in the form of COVID-21. While only four million cases have been reported in the three months since this strain was identified, this has translated to nearly a million deaths due to the dramatically increased mortality rate. Furthermore, the transmission rate of this new disease far exceeds that of COVID-19, making this one of the largest threats facing the world today."

"But fortunately, it isn't completely all doom and gloom. We have successfully verified that one of the COVID-19 vaccines is nearly ninety-two percent effective against this new strain. This further emphasizes how important it is to vaccinate every man, woman, and child on the planet as quickly as possible. It also highlights the necessity of accurately tracking that information, to dramatically slow the spread of this fatal plaque by whatever means possible."

"To that end, the United Nations has drafted a resolution modeled after the United States House Resolution six-six-

six-six, which was designed to authorize eligible entities to not only conduct testing, but to enable comprehensive contact tracing. While this resolution was ultimately defeated, its legacy lives on in United Nations Resolution two-six-six-six."

Schmidt paused for a moment to gaze around the briefing hall before continuing.

"It is my honor to publicly announce to the world that this crucial resolution has just been unanimously passed by all one-hundred-ninety-three member states of the United Nations council. While there are many, many details to share, I will divulge some of the most crucial elements with you now."

"With this new resolution, all inhabitants of Earth will now be tracked through a new, global digital health passport. To ensure one-hundred percent accuracy and compliance, digital wristbands leveraging Radio Frequency Identification will be provided to every nation to be distributed to their citizens. The information tracked on these life-saving devices will include name, nationality, government ID, whether or not the individual has received the correct COVID-21 vaccine, and the date of that vaccination. And to maximize the effectiveness of this resolution, we will also be tracking the exact location of every man, woman and child on the planet."

"This is completely bonkers!" William blurted out.

"While it will take some time to fully roll out the new health passport, we anticipate that we will have completed it within the next twelve months. As we work toward the go live date, we will immediately begin enforcing stricter rules and regulations to impede the transmission of this highly contagious variant. Any person not possessing their digital health passport will not be allowed to travel across country borders. We anticipate compliance with the tracking of vaccinations will become commonplace to protect everyone from this hideous disease. We look forward to the day when we can accurately and completely track all of humanity, their compliance with vaccination, and the law. To accomplish this, we will move towards a time in the not-too-distant future, when anyone without this proof of vaccination will be unable to function in society. This is the beginning of a new era. This digital future of ours ensures that you are able to travel, work, purchase goods, and function as a productive member of a truly global society. It is a bright future the lies ahead of us; one that will bring us further peace and prosperity."

Rich quietly closed the laptop and stared at the other two men with a bleak expression before speaking.

"And he causeth all, both small and great, rich and poor, free and bond, to receive a mark in their right hand, or in their foreheads: And that no man might buy or sell, save he that had the mark, or the name of the beast, or the number of his name."

"What does that mean?" Menashe shuddered.

"It means the end is near."

CHAPTER 6

Prelude

(Three Days Later)

Despite it being eleven thirty in the morning on a Monday, the city streets in Jerusalem were largely devoid of the hustle and bustle that would normally be taking place. There were relatively few cars on the road, and even fewer pedestrians walking on what were ordinarily crowded sidewalks. Other than a few small, billowy clouds that were scattered intermittently over the city, the Sun had almost completely climbed to its apex in the beautifully clear sky.

One of the automobiles on the road was a large grey SUV, which was making its way up Jaffa Street toward the large shopping district of Shuk Machane Yehuda. The occupants of the vehicle were riding in near complete silence, with their eyes constantly darting in all directions to try and spot any security stations or roadblocks. The mood in the city had soured greatly in the few days since the dramatic announcement by the United Nations.

Having made their way successfully to an almost completely empty public parking lot, Menashe pulled into an open space close to the exit and put the car into park.

"This should work just fine," he cheerfully relayed. "We'll need to walk from here to gather the few remaining supplies required for our journey."

As Menashe finished his sentence, William audibly exhaled through his nose, with an annoyed expression covering his face.

"What's bothering you?" Rich probed.

"Oh nothing," William lied. "I'm just not looking forward to being taken into custody by those abhorrent security forces, and then thrown in prison once they find out who we really are."

"I think you're overstating the risk. Besides," Rich continued, "I don't think Schmidt is worried about us anymore. In fact, ever since the confrontation at Cenetics, I don't think he's given us a second thought."

"Don't be so sure," William disagreed. "We still have a role to play in things, and I don't think Schmidt is the type of person that would easily forget about us. Let alone that *vile creature* he's working for."

Rich thought for a moment, then nodded his head in agreement.

"You're probably right. Besides, an ounce of prevention is worth a pound of cure."

A quizzical expression formed on Menashe's face. Without waiting for him to ask, Rich went ahead and explained.

"It means, better safe than sorry."

"Oh," Menashe offered with a slight coloring of his face. "Many of your colloquialisms are lost on me."

"Rest assured, my friend, your ability to understand and speak English far exceeds either of our abilities to try and comprehend Hebrew," Rich joked.

"Ok, we should start heading out," Menashe smiled.

Their small party exited the SUV and started making their way down the sidewalk towards their destination. Immediately on their right, adjacent to the pathway, sat a four-story concrete office building, and across the street were a couple of smaller retail shops with vibrantly colored canopies. Within a couple minutes, they were standing at the intersection of Ki'akh and Jaffa, waiting for the light to change to green so they could cross to the other side. Once they had made it across the street, they paused at the corner until the light changed again, then proceeded to traverse the pavement to the far corner.

"There's a camping store halfway up the block we need to stop at first," Menashe asserted. "We'll need to pick up a couple of sets of cooking gear, water bottles, a decent backpack, and a few other items."

As the men entered the store, it became painfully obvious they were the only customers present. Besides an elderly woman standing at the register, there was not another soul in the entire shop.

"Tzaharayim Tovim!"[24] the gray-haired woman enthusiastically greeted them.

"Shalom!"[25] smiled Menashe. "Eyn mal'shiyn kayom?"[26]

The woman pursed her lips momentarily and shook her head from side to side.

"Eyn achadiym,"[27] she answered with a bit of despair in her voice. "Sipek, hit'bonen b'erekh gam natan yada kal davar."[28]

"Toda Raba!"[29]

The three men perused the stored for a few minutes gathering up the required items from their list, then made their way to the register to check out. After they had paid in cash, the woman reached across the counter and grasped Menashe's hand with a surprisingly strong grip.

[24] Good afternoon!

[25] Hello!

[26] Not many shoppers today?

[27] Not for many weeks.

[28] Please, look around and let me know if you need anything

[29] Thank you!

"Mizhar!"[30] she warned them. "Chayal vkhl mkvm."[31]

Their Jewish companion simply nodded in response, then ushered the others out of the store.

"What was that about?" Rich pressed.

"She was warning us to be careful as there are a lot of soldiers out today. If we head back the way we came, I believe there is a store around the corner which should have camping knives in stock."

As they turned to walk to their right, they all froze and collectively held their breath.

Roughly one hundred feet away, a pair of troopers clad in black paramilitary uniforms stood next to the intersection they had initially crossed, carrying automatic rifles. They appeared to be in a deep conversation with one another, so they hadn't noticed the small group staring at them yet.

"Ah…I…don't think we want to go that direction," Rich stammered in a hushed tone.

"Neither do I," William agreed. "Let's head in the opposite direction."

Turning on their heels, the three of them started to quietly walk down the sidewalk away from the armed guards. But after no more than twenty steps, Menashe stopped abruptly as an expression of anxiety swept over his face.

"Zevel!"[32] he cursed.

"What's wrong, Menashe?" William asked with a note of concern in his voice.

"I can't believe I didn't remember!"

[30] Be careful!

[31] There are soldiers everywhere.

[32] Crap!

"Remember what?" Rich pressed.

Slowly shaking his head back and forth, Menashe exhaled loudly through his nose as he bit his bottom lip.

"That there's an Israeli police station roughly fifteen meters from where we are currently standing," he confessed.

"Oh shit!" Rich groaned.

"That's what I said," Menashe replied.

"What do we do?" Rich pleaded.

"There's isn't much we can do," Menashe admitted. "At least, not without drawing everyone's attention. We should just keep walking forward like everything is normal, and hope for the best."

As the three men continued to advance, they spotted what was most assuredly the precinct station. It was a relatively small stone structure, set back about five feet from the sidewalk. The entrance contained two glass exterior doors, with a navy-blue sticker of a six-pointed star surrounded by laurel leaves affixed to both of them.

Just as they were about to cross in front of it, one of the doors swiftly swung open and two officers dressed in standard police uniforms raced out of the building. They immediately started to run down the concrete path in the same direction that William and his companions had been walking, seemingly unaware of the stunned group.

Looking at his two friends, William shrugged his shoulders with a baffled expression.

"Let's just keep moving," Rich ordered.

As William started to walk in front of the glass entrance to the station house, he became acutely aware of the strong sensation of heat emanating from his chest. Conscious that something was amiss, he reached upward and felt warmth radiating from the amulet which hung on the necklace directly beneath his shirt. A sickening feeling of dread swept through his body, as he turned to peer in through the doors.

A woman in her mid-forties was sitting at a large desk located in the front of the building, dressed in the recognizable all-black uniforms of the President Elect's elite military force. Obviously absorbed in her work, she stared at a flat panel display sitting on the workspace, as her fingers feverishly floated over the keyboard. As William observed her, an intense feeling of nausea hit him, and his stomach lurched. Suddenly, the skin on the woman's face seemed to shift, almost as if there was something pulsating beneath the fleshy membrane. The next instant, the face of a demon-like entity appeared within the silhouette of the woman, and despite the fact that it lacked any eyes, it felt as if the creature was intently glaring back at William.

"We've got to move!" William enunciated. "*Now!*"

Without another word, he started to make his way across the road, leaving Menashe and Rich with no other choice but to follow. Upon reaching the other side, William headed down a narrow alley immediately across from the station at a rapid pace. Within a few moments, he was easily ten steps ahead of the other men, who had to nearly start running to keep up.

"Will!" Rich barked. "Stop for a second! What's going on?"

Stopping in his tracks, William spun around to face the other two men, then glanced off to his right, where an even narrower passageway was located.

"This way," he commanded as he exited the alley.

Rich looked helplessly at Menashe, who simply threw his hands up in response.

"I guess we follow," he shrugged.

Both men silently pursued William into the cramped corridor, which was no wider than twelve feet across. At the other end, forty feet away, the opening came to an abrupt dead end. Standing in the middle of the passageway, William motioned for the other two men to come closer.

"What the hell was that all about?" Rich protested. "I thought the idea was *not* to draw attention to ourselves."

"Just shut up and listen!" William panted. "I just had another vision. And the amulet..."

He paused for a moment, seemingly frozen, while the other two men quizzically stared at him.

"And the amulet what?" a high pitched, abrasive voice cackled from behind Rich and Menashe.

As the two men spun around to confront the unseen intruder, their hearts sunk.

Standing at the entrance to the narrow corridor was the female guard that William had seen back at the police station. She was dressed in a dark uniform and didn't appear to have a weapon of any type, except for the steel baton, which hung loosely by her side. Her fingers were interlaced in front of her waist, and she glared at the small group with a threatening expression.

"And the amulet *what?"* she repeated in a sinister tone.

When no one responded to his question, a vile sliver of a smile creased her angular face. As she started to walk forward, she released her hands and let them fall to her sides. Her arms seemed abnormally long and the tips of her fingers reaching the top of her knees. After a few steps, she paused, a mere five feet away from Menashe and Rich.

William, who was standing behind the other two men, frantically looked around to locate an escape path. The sides that formed the alleyway were the exterior walls of three-story apartment buildings, with only steel barred windows facing into the corridor. Realizing there was no way out, he turned back to face the officer and readied himself for battle.

Almost as if sensing his plan, a soft, almost growl-like snicker echoed from within her chest, accompanied by a sickening grimace. The corners of her mouth seemed to stretch out and up in a grossly abnormal fashion. Suddenly, the sides of the entity's mouth literally split open, and as the flesh tore, a horrid, seething black ooze started to percolate from the tears in the creature's face. As the putrid blood trickled onto its skin, flesh and muscle slowly began to dissolve and slide from the beast's form, almost as if they had been eaten away by a caustic acid. None of the men were able to move even an inch, seemingly hypnotized by the scene that was unfolding before them. As the seconds ticked away, every covering, from clothing to flesh, melted away from the creature, sliding down to the concrete road in a quivering mass.

With the metamorphosis complete, a dark, sinewy monster stood before the frightened group. It had a vampire bat-like head, with a lower jaw that hung six inches beneath the upper border of its horrible mouth. Long, fang-like teeth protruded from disgusting, black gums, with an obsidian discharge of drool running down its thin chin. It didn't appear to possess eyes or a nose, but a massive, protruding forehead curved from the top of its head down to its upper lip. Thin, almost delicate looking ears jutted out from either side of its head, ending in sharp points.

Its neck was elongated and connected to thin, sinewy shoulders that framed its form. Its leathery, muscular arms extended downward, with each skeletal hand displaying three long fingers that ended in razor sharp nails, from which the same acidic black liquid freely dripped. The torso of the beast narrowed down to a waist easily half the size of its chest, and its thin legs bent awkwardly backward to bony knees, only to then angle sharply forward and down to claw-like feet that seemed like they ought to belong on a bird of prey.

Immediately behind this malignant beast, the air started to thicken and swirl into an undulating black haze, and the view of the street became totally obscured, almost as if the men were looking at it through a multi-faceted prism. Despite being the middle of the day, all light began to retreat from their immediate area, and long shadows beneath the creature started to crawl across the ground, straining to reach the soon to be victims. A low rumble started to reverberate through the air, increasing in intensity like a locomotive drawing closer and closer.

As these events were unfolding, Menashe reached into his front pants pocket and fumbled for a moment, trying to grasp something. The next instant, he pulled his hand back out and placed a brass ring on the index finger of his right hand. Making a tight fist, he raised his hand high above his head and a small burst of light seemed to erupt from between his firmly squeezed fingers. As the light grew, the eyeless creature rotated its head and seemed to focus squarely on him. Its muscles and tendons then shifted and tensed as if it were trying to move, but to no avail.

Then, with his left hand stretched directly toward the demon, Menashe took a step forward.

"B'tokh 'elhiym shem, kilel atah!"[33]

[33] In God's name, I curse you!

The vile creature howled in pain, and while its muscles continued to contort beneath its skin, it was incapable of moving an inch.

Menashe took another step forward and continued.

"Mish'neh 'elhiym ratzah, zarak hachutzah atah!"[34]

The paralyzed demon shrieked in terror, and its ears quivered uncontrollably.

"Derekh' 'elhiym matzavah, nadah' olam atah!"[35]

Menashe was now standing directly in front of the monster, no less than one foot away. With absolute purpose, he lowered his fist until it was between his own face and the creature, and opened it with his palm facing inwards. With his left hand, he grasped the ring on his index finger and turned it one hundred and eighty degrees, so the symbol sitting atop the ring was facing him, too. Then, he slowly rotated his hand until his palm faced the demon, who desperately struggled to move out of its way. Without hesitation, Menashe forcefully extended his arm, and placed the symbol of the ring squarely on the center of its broad forehead.

The tough, wrinkled exterior covering the head of the beast immediately began to dissolve. Then, without warning, the demon disintegrated, collapsing upon itself, and completely disappeared from reality. At the same instant, Menashe was thrown backward past William and Rich, slamming into a large trash container at the back end of the alley.

Immediately, the thick haze that had been shrouding the passageway in darkness completely dissipated, and William and Rich rushed over to Menashe's lifeless body, which lay contorted on the ground.

[34] By God's will, I cast you out!

[35] Through God's strength, I banish you from the world!

CHAPTER 7

Correlation

As he knelt on the ground next to Menashe's unconscious body, Rich checked whether or not he could sense a pulse by placing his fingers directly beneath the other man's chin. After a brief moment, he looked up at William, who was hunched over the two of them with a distressed expression, and gave him an affirmative nod.

"Thank goodness!" he exclaimed in obvious relief. "Does he look like he suffered any injuries?"

After a moment of inspection, Rich gently touched a growing knot above the senseless man's temple.

"His head's probably going to throb for a while, but I don't see anything else.

The next moment, Menashe began to groan, his eyes fluttering for a second before completely opening.

"What..." he croaked, "what happened?"

As he attempted to sit upright, the larger man held him down by placing a hand on his chest.

"Easy there," he cautioned. "Take a moment before you try and move."

"I'm fine," Menashe huffed with a note of exasperation in his voice. "Let me up."

After removing his hand, Rich pushed himself upright with a slight grunt. He then extended his hand down to Menashe in an attempt to help him get to his feet.

"William, a little help?" he ordered more than asked.

"Of course," William offered as he reached down to assist.

Menashe gladly accepted both of the extended hands, and with surprisingly little effort, he quickly found himself standing upright. Immediately, he staggered forward as his head started to swoon, and if the other men hadn't still been holding him firmly in their grip, he would have fallen back to the ground.

"Take a moment to gather yourself," Rich directed.

"Yes, of course. Thank you."

Menashe took about thirty seconds to ensure he had his wits about him, then he gently pulled his arms back from his two companions who were still helping to support him.

"I'm good now," he advised.

"Excellent," William encouraged. "Do you think you can walk? We need to get away from here as quickly as possible, in case someone comes looking for that *thing*."

"Yes," Menashe agreed, "I should be fine now. I believe there is a small park at the far end of the alley."

"As long as it's in the opposite direction of that precinct, I don't really care where we go," William asserted.

Walking the short distance back to the primary passageway, the men paused, and Rich furtively stuck his head around the corner to ensure no one else was present.

"All clear," he disclosed.

As the three men emerged from the side corridor, they immediately turned to their right and started to walk briskly away from the police station. Within a matter of a couple minutes, they found themselves at a cross street containing no traffic. On the opposite corner of the intersection lay a small, but extraordinarily well kempt, neighborhood park.

"That's it," Menashe announced. "Let's make our way over there so I can sit down for a second."

The small group was able to easily traverse the street as no vehicles were visible in either direction. After reaching the other side, they made their way into the grounds and headed over to a park bench beneath a large shade tree. Upon reaching their destination, Menashe eased himself down with an audible 'oof.'

"Much better," he announced with a whoosh of breath. "Let's sit here for a moment before we head back to the car."

"Of course," William acquiesced, "but we can't stay here too long."

He glanced back toward the narrow alley from which they had just emerged, then looked back at his friend.

"What happened back there?" he gently coaxed. "I mean, how did you do that to…that creature?"

Without a word, Menashe raised his hand in front of him with his fingers slightly spread apart and his palm facing upward. With his other hand, he reached over and removed the golden ring and offered it to William.

"You're not the only one with an object imbued with power," he announced.

As he put the ring between his thumb and forefinger, he was surprised at how heavy the object was. He held it closer and started to slowly rotate the ring between his fingers until he could clearly see an intricate symbol located on the very top. The outer edge of the circular impression contained a total of twelve different symbols, evenly spaced apart. A slightly raised circle framed the emblems, encircling another design located in the center of the surface. The pattern was fairly simplistic, and almost resembled the balances a merchant would have used to measure the weights of goods at an ancient market.

"What's this?" he probed.

"It's called *The Seal of Solomon,"* he enunciated. "It is a signet ring attributed to King Solomon from Islamic tradition. But it's not just Islamic; it also has connections to the Jewish Kabbalah."

"You said it was infused with power?" Rich interrupted.

"Yes. I'm the one who consecrated it. The same day you, Ariel, and…" he paused for a moment as an expression of reverence swept across his face, "…and Tara first visited me at my home, I knew I was going to need additional strength if I were going to join your crusade. So, I decided I might as well arm myself with the most powerful object I had at my disposal."

"It's definitely powerful," William shuddered, thinking back to the horrible image of the demonic entity literally disintegrating into thin air. "Exactly how does it work?"

"It was originally given to King Solomon to command extradimensional life forms known as the *jinn*, both good and evil. As you saw, when wielded with authority, it not only controls, but can command any being that is normally hidden from our sight. However, in this case, the demon was actually visible."

As William and Menashe continued with their discussion, Rich found himself dwelling on the words Menashe had just shared.

"*I wonder if the jinn he mentioned are in fact demons from another dimension,*" he speculated silently, "*like they talked about on that show. And the creature that literally oozed out of that soldier. I wonder…*"

Suddenly, Rich felt like he had been struck by a thousand volts of electricity, as the answer to all the swirling thoughts in his mind became obvious.

"I think I've figured something out!" he shouted.

The other two men were visibility startled by his outburst and immediately turned their attention to him.

"Figured what out?" William coaxed.

"Figured out why Schmidt is so intent on protecting the Cenetics facility. I believe all the soldiers dressed in black are in fact clones created inside the laboratory. And as we just saw, each of those clones is possessed by an evil spirit. Satan is literally building an army here on Earth, in preparation for the end of the world. But it's not just a spiritual army; it's a physical one. One of shape and form...with actual bodies, and everything that comes along with it, including increased power and abilities. The demon that Menashe destroyed wasn't just a vision...it was actually in our physical reality."

"If that's true," Menashe offered, "then we've got to move with a real sense of urgency."

"Exactly," Rich agreed. "Things seem to be speeding up, and time is starting to run out."

The larger man paused for a moment, then looked at William with a concerned expression.

"What should we do?" he pressed.

William pursed his lips in thought, then turned to Menashe with an expectant look.

Simply nodding in response, Menashe stood up from the park bench.

"We must journey to Mecca as soon as possible. Don't ask me how I know this, but it is crucial that we speak with Widad. The clock is ticking."

CHAPTER 8

Conclave

(The Next Evening)

The night sky was nearly pitch-black as the waning Moon was only three days shy of its next new cycle. A heavily clouded sky amplified the somber mood, frequently shrouding the earth from the insignificant glimmer of illumination trickling down from above. At one in the morning, a deafening silence permeated the air, and it seemed that every living creature was slumbering or completely absent. The familiar smell of freshly fallen rain hung in the air, carried along by a light north-westerly breeze across the damp ground.

A moment later, the sound of tires on wet pavement interrupted the stillness, accompanied by the glare of headlamps from a dark, grey luxury car. The vehicle drove across a completely vacant parking lot situated in front of one of several large, four-story structures comprising the immense Cenetics research campus. After pulling into a space located close to the front entrance, the driver's side door opened, and the occupant exited into the chilly air. The sound of wood-heeled dress shoes echoed against the tall buildings, growing louder with each step as the owner drew closer to the entrance. Finally, the large, revolving glass doors began to spin, allowing the individual to make his way into the interior of the facility.

An older gentleman, easily seventy years of age, was visibly startled by the unexpected visitor, and he clumsily stood up from his chair behind a large security desk to confront the trespasser.

"Kann ich ihnen helfen?"[36] he challenged.

Ignoring the question, the intruder simply strode directly across the spacious lobby and approached the counter. As he neared the desk, the expression on the face of the security guard shifted from one of suspicion to one of recognition, mixed with deference.

"Arzt Schmidt. Ich habe dich nicht erkannt. Ich bin..."

"In English!" the other man rudely interrupted.

"I...I'm sorry," the older man stammered. "Doctor Schmidt, I didn't recognize you," he corrected himself.

Without responding, Schmidt flung a threatening glare at the elder watchman, who recoiled from his gaze, and abruptly sat back onto his swivel chair. With a satisfied expression, he walked over to the stainless-steel security turnstile and swiped his badge against the reader, which responded with a high-pitched chirp, signifying access had been granted. The next moment, two black barriers retracted within the opening, allowing Schmidt to pass through. He then started to make his way to the elevator on the opposite wall.

"Do you plan on staying long?" the guard cautiously inquired.

Without acknowledging the question, Schmidt sharply pressed the call button and the doors immediately slid apart in response. Immediately, he took two steps into the lift and turned on his heels with a miffed look in his eyes. The security guard simply stared at him as the elevator doors slowly glided back together.

While facing the closed doors of the elevator, Schmidt pulled the security badge from his pocket and brushed it against a small black covering located next to the call

[36] Can I help you?

buttons on the panel. Immediately, the sound of a quiet click came from the left side of the conveyor. Slowly turning toward the noise, he caught a glimpse of a small steel panel completing its path upward, revealing a single button contained within a hidden compartment. With an audible puff from his nostrils, he reached forward and pressed the red switch that sat at an angle inside the box.

This time, a much louder click reverberated through the elevator, followed by the light humming of an electric motor. The motion clearly indicated the conveyor was descending, despite the fact that the buttons on the main panel gave no indication of a basement being present. As the platform continued to lower, the top half of the back wall started to slide down, revealing a concealed glass window. Shifting his feet, Schmidt turned at the same instant the view through the aperture changed, revealing a spacious cavern of a room on the other side.

Leaning slightly forward, the man peered down through the window to a stone floor at least forty feet beneath his current position. He then shifted his gaze around to the sides of the room, taking in the flickering shadows being cast by flames oscillating from multiple torches that extended out from the perimeter walls. A grim look of satisfaction appeared on his visage as the lift descended the remainder of the way to ground level, where all motion ceased with an abrupt jolt. The sound behind him signified the doors had just opened, and after gripping his hands behind his back, he exited the lift, making his way back around the elevator shaft to enter the subterranean hall.

Located in the middle of the massive gallery, was a gargantuan circular stone table, six inches thick and at least thirty feet in diameter. The dark grey surface resembled a multi-faceted gem and was extraordinarily smooth. A slightly raised edge created a border around the perimeter, encircling a sizeable pentagram, whose points fell just shy of the boundary. Multiple three-foot-tall columns, resembling the thick, burly legs of a bull, complete with enormous hooves, supported the surface. A single, throne-like chair was positioned next to the table, possessing a high backing that extended at least five feet above the seat, ending in two large, curled stone horns. Directly in front of the cathedra sat an ancient looking mirror with golden decorative vines framing the reflective surface, as well as an ancient looking blade with a wooden handle.

After pausing for a moment to survey the room, Schmidt purposely walked toward the stone table and roughly took his seat on the high-backed throne. With an expression of pure disdain, he silently surveyed the room from side to side, until finally shifting his gaze to the archaic blade that lay flat on the surface next to the mirror. Without hesitation, he sprung up from his seat, grasped the handle of the knife, and scraped it across the palm of his other hand, inflicting a severe gash. Blood immediately oozed out from the damaged flesh and began to trickle down to his fingertips. After making a tight fist with his injured hand, he then thrust it upward toward the ceiling, extending his fingers outward. Fifteen feet above him, an elaborate chandelier, nearly half the size of the table, dangled in darkness. A total of thirty-nine gnarled extensions of what looked to be bone, reached outward from an enormous, black ring of iron affixed to the base of the candelabrum, and on the end of each osseous arm was an unlit, twisted candle. The massive light was suspended by three enormous black chains that connected to a single ring at the top of the chamber.

With his hand outstretched above him, blood slowly began to percolate down his forearm like tendrils of disease coursing toward his heart. The next instant, he jerked his hand downward, slamming it on the surface of the stone table with a loud clap. Instantly, all the torches on the perimeter walls erupted in a bright blaze of light. The once-clear surface of the mirror now appeared clouded, as if an obsidian ink was swirling in a counter-clockwise direction. With the palm of his hand still lying flat on the surface of the table, he then raised his other hand above his head and stared intently into the reflector.

"Audi vocem meam, magnanime Dominus!"[37] he hissed in a low tone.

A flicker of light momentarily appeared in the glass, but then disappeared just as quickly.

"Accipere sanguinem meum!"[38] he attested in a raspy cackle.

This time, a flame erupted from beneath the surface of the mirror. Then, another flash of fire arose, positioned behind the first.

"Ego fidelitatis in meque recipio!"[39] he howled.

Suddenly, each of the candles situated on the chandelier above burst into flames at least six inches in height. Despite the bright illumination emanating from the hanging fixture, the disposition of the cavern seemed to darken, as a dark burgundy, blood-like hue blanketed the chamber.

"Fero consumite viscera animae!"[40] he called out again and again as his eyes rolled back in his skull. *"Fero consumite viscera animae! Fero consumite viscera animae!"*

[37] Hear my voice, oh great Lord!

[38] Accept my blood!

[39] I pledge my allegiance!

[40] Consume my soul!

The next moment, flames literally belched from the surface of the reflector onto the table. As Schmidt turned his attention to the mirror, he gazed intently at the exterior, which seemed to wobble like ripples on a lake. Then, the charcoal clouds boiling on the surface dissipated, revealing a portal into the very bowels of hell. The next instant, the Father of All Lies, The Prince of Darkness, materialized in the gateway.

Peering back through the mirror was a horrible image. Two pairs of vile, deformed horns curled outward from either side of the head, framing a repulsively scarred face. Narrow, snake-like slits were centered on the skull where a nose should have been placed, and a ghastly pair of blood-red eyes sat at the bottom of sunken eye sockets. A horrifying set of razor-sharp teeth lined a lipless cavity with black, putrid saliva dribbling from the corners. A circular scar resembling a brand that had been seared into an animal's skin, was situated on Its forehead, containing eight runes at evenly spaced intervals on the outer edge. Contempt and hatred exuded from the horrific entity.

"Is everything proceeding as expected?" He growled.

"Yes, Father," Schmidt virtually whimpered. "The vote was successful, as You foretold."

"That is fortunate for you!" He threatened.

"Yes, Father. It is only a matter of time now, and we will be able to track every living soul on the planet. Leaders have committed to rolling out the global passport in one year, and then..."

Intense flames immediately erupted from the surface of the mirror, and the expression on the Devil's face should have destroyed Schmidt on the spot.

"That is unacceptable!" a thunderous voice reverberated throughout the cavernous chamber. *"We must move forward*

with all haste! It is time to unleash an evil that hasn't been seen on Earth for thousands of years!"

Visibly shaken, Schmidt took a brief moment to gather himself before addressing his Master once more.

"Yes, Father. What would you have me do?"

"You?" He incredulously asked, followed immediately by maniacal laughter.

"Yes, what can I do to help facilitate your plan?" he literally pleaded.

Leaning forward, the evil creature angled its head slightly downward until it was peering at Schmidt from beneath Its excessive brow, not saying a word. A few moments later, He leaned back to His original position with an ominous expression.

"You should focus only on the items I have entrusted you with…nothing more. I grow tired of your perpetual attempts to prove your worth to Me. Continue to do so, and you will find it to be of very little value."

Flinching in response, Schmidt knew he should not press the issue any further.

"Yes, Father. Your will," he announced. "How do you intend to accelerate things?"

"Don't worry yourself with these details!" He angrily boomed. *"I have already put things in motion to hasten my plans. Things will occur soon…very soon."*

CHAPTER 9

Contagion

(December 28, 2021)

Even though it was only two o'clock in the afternoon, the Sun was already well on its way toward the horizon, given the high latitude and close proximity to the north pole. Conditions for this time of year in the Western Siberia Plains normally meant ten to fifteen degrees Fahrenheit below zero. However, trends over the past decade had led to increasingly higher temperatures, and today was no exception. While the thermometer read a positive eight degrees Fahrenheit, the consistent ten-mile-per-hour breeze from the Northeast made it feel like it was closer to negative two.

This area of the Siberian plain was almost completely devoid of any human habitation. For the most part, it was flat with little to no topography to speak of, except for a gentle rise and fall of the terrain. Being so close to the Artic Ocean, roughly five hundred miles south of the Kara Sea, the ground was usually encapsulated in year-round permafrost, creating difficult conditions for productive farming. However, with temperatures on the rise the globe over, it was becoming more common that significant areas of the 1.2 million square miles of land comprising the western expanse were edging above freezing a couple months out of the year.

A thin layer of pure white snow lay over the gently rolling landscape, which consisted of a combination of vast, low-lying grass plains, juxtaposed with dense forests of spruce and pine trees. Alabaster powder relinquished its hold on the branches and fell silently to the ground below, dislodged by a combination of wind and gravity.

Stretching out at least three miles along the edge of an immense forest lay a vast field covered by a flawless blanket of snow, except for a single set of tracks leading across the expanse from another set of trees. It was a pristine scene, the kind one would expect to see in a traditional Norman Rockwell painting.

A pair of camouflaged hunters suddenly emerged from the tree line, dressed all in white. Both were clad from head to toe in frost-colored clothing, except for black boots that peeked out from beneath oversized ski pants. Their faces were covered by light silver neck gaiters, pulled up tightly beneath white rimmed goggles with grey lenses, and small puffs of frozen air drifted out from beneath their coverings with each exhale of breath.

"The tracks head this way," the shorter of the two men mumbled in a Russian accent.

The other man simply grunted in response.

For the next two minutes, they silently stalked across the hundred-yard clearing to the edge of the forest. Just before entering the brush, the larger man quickly held up his hand, signifying they should pause.

"Chto eto?"[41] his companion whispered in Russian.

With his hand still in the air, the hunter stood quietly, straining to catch an indication that their prey was close by. After another moment, he let out an exasperated sigh.

"It's nothing, Michail. Let's just keep moving."

"It's warmer than usual," Michail complained. "Far too warm if you ask me, Andrey."

"Why complain about something that makes our lives comfortable?" he countered.

Michail paused for a moment, then nodded his head in agreement.

[41] What is it?

"It feels wrong, though. As a boy, my father would take me hunting in this same area. It was so cold that his beard would freeze."

The large man chuckled, clearly trying to keep as quiet as possible.

"This is much nicer," Andrey countered while motioning to the surroundings. "I wish our gear was lighter though. I'm sweating like a boar."

The large man deliberately dug the heel of his boot into the snow, then twisted it back and forth. Satisfied with his effort, he removed his foot and pointed at the ground.

"I can actually dig into the earth. This is supposed to be permafrost!" he pointed out with a frown.

Without another word, both hunters started to make their way back into the forest, silently following the tracks. After walking for about five minutes, the large man once again signaled for them to stop. While looking at his friend, he silently pointed at his own eyes, then motioned out in front of them, off to the right. Standing in the snow next to a tree, a massive moose was slowly sauntering, stopping occasionally to bite at twigs and branches. He stood nearly seven feet from hoof to shoulder, and his head and impressive antlers rose to a height of nearly ten feet. He was a magnificent beast, easily over thirteen hundred pounds.

Michail looked like he was going to jump out of his jacket. As he started to reach back for the rifle slung on his back, Andrey quickly grabbed his shoulder and shook his index finger in front of his face from side to side. Then, he motioned over to their left, toward what looked to be a somewhat sizeable hill protruding up from the otherwise flat landscape.

"We'll have an advantage from the top of that hill," he whispered. "Then, when you miss, I'll get the kill shot before he gets away," he then added in a comical tone.

The smaller huntsman gave a quick nod of approval and the two of them started to covertly make their way over to the predominately treeless knoll on the left. As they silently climbed up the gentle rise, both men frequently looked back in the direction of their target to confirm it hadn't moved on. Roughly two minutes later, after reaching the crest of the ridge, they crouched together, gazing out toward the location of their prey.

"Posmotri na eto!"[42] Andrey beckoned with wide eyes, motioning out to the landscape in front of them.

They were now elevated forty-five feet above the ground, and from this vantage point, they could easily see more than eight miles in every direction, given the relatively sparse surroundings. The mound on which they currently stood looked to be the first of at least one dozen raised embankments stretching out to the horizon. Most of the hills were a bit shorter than the one on which they were situated, but at least two of them stood at an equal height.

"What's with the hills?" Michail wondered. "They weren't here before."

"I have no idea," Andrey commented in a perplexed tone of voice.

A moment later, he shrugged his shoulders and refocused his attention on the moose, which was still nonchalantly munching on branches.

"Ok, my friend. Show me how good your aim has become."

After lifting his goggles and resting them on top of his head, Michail pulled down his face mask and flashed a sly grin at his companion. He then sighted down toward his target and made a slight adjustment to his scope.

[42] Look at that!

"About one hundred meters?" he asked.

"One hundred and ten," Andrey countered.

Grunting in agreement, Michail made another adjustment to a dial on the side of his eyepiece. Then, positioning himself on one knee, he steadied the rifle and peered intently through the lens. Resting his finger flat against the body of the gun, he sighted his target. Once satisfied his shot was lined up correctly, he purposely threaded his index finger into the guard, placing it ever-so-lightly on top of the trigger. Finally, he took a deep, cleansing breath, and while slowly exhaling, he tugged very smoothly against the steel lever.

Immediately, a crack of thunder erupted through the air, as smoke and fire burst out of the barrel of the weapon. Then next instant, the massive animal fell to the ground, where it lay motionless.

"Otlichnyy vystrel!"[43] the bulkier hunter exclaimed.

Pushing himself up on his bent knee, Michail stood upright, eyes beaming, a wild grin spread across his face.

"You know, Michail, next time…"

Suddenly, a tremendous flash of light, accompanied by a deafening explosion, burst out from the ground directly beneath both men's feet. Earth and rock were hurled into the sky along with immense flames and blistering heat. Enormous chunks were thrown upward and outward from the ground in a colossal detonation, obliterating both men in an instant. The force from the blast heaved huge boulders at least five hundred feet up into the air, along with thick clouds of smoke and dust.

No more than five seconds later, a second eruption sliced into the sky from a hillside directly to the north, roughly

[43] Great shot!

half the size of the previous explosion. The aftermath, though, was devastatingly similar to the first eruption. Over the next three minutes, a series of detonations, like a carefully planned skyscraper demolition, ripped across the plains, emanating out across the landscape. In a relatively short period of time, an extraordinary amount of energy was released, throwing thousands of tons of earth, rock and dust up into the atmosphere.

It seemed as if each explosion was a volcanic eruption. However, there was a difference. There was no thick, billowing cloud of smoke and ash, no hot liquid rock being thrown into the air, and no living rivers of boiling fire flowing up out of the earth. Instead, there were thick trails of what looked to be floating wisps of cotton, similar to those that edge their way across the sky after blowing on a dandelion. But these tufts were not white. Instead, they were dark, vile, almost fiber-like particulates. These strands of blackened threads poured up and out of the ground in what seemed an interminable flow.

As the strands of haze spewed up into the atmosphere, they began to swirl and almost appeared to multiply in number. Before long, there were so many particles churning in the sky that the Sun itself darkened. As they reached higher and higher into the troposphere, they were drawn into high velocity air currents that carried them effortlessly to destinations unknown.

CHAPTER 10

Epidemic

(Fifteen Minutes Later)

The intensity of the daylight was starting to diminish as the Sun continued its downward slope toward the western horizon, and dark hues of purple and orange were beginning to materialize in the virtually cloudless sky. Along with the disappearing daylight, temperatures were quickly starting to fall, and the thermometer just dipped below zero degrees Fahrenheit for the first time that day. Adding to the chill, a stiff ten-mile-per-hour breeze was pushing down across the landscape from the North East.

In the center of a large, mostly flat plateau, sat a somewhat antiquated looking military base. Elena Petrov, First Lieutenant of the Russian Air Force, was tasked with monitoring the radar system from her seat in the traffic control tower overlooking the small Airbase of Aerodrom Sovetskiy. Located one hundred kilometers south of the Kara Sea in western Siberia, a busy day usually translated to a total of three of the four available aircraft landing and taking off. At that moment, there was only one under the control of the tower and it had just begun its final descent, passing beneath one thousand feet of elevation.

The flight control room, large enough for at least one dozen troops, was empty except for one other person. In stark contrast to the alert and focus being displayed by Petrov, Captain Gusev sat lazily in his chair, his arms crossed comfortably across his chest, his feet up on the desk, and a light wheeze emanating from beneath his blue hat, which lay over his eyes.

"Antonov twenty-two, you are clear for final approach on primary runway," the first lieutenant spoke into the receiver.

"Roger that," a male voice responded from a small speaker sitting on the table.

Leaning back in her chair, Elena then glanced over at her superior who was still lightly snoring, completely oblivious to what was going on.

"Chto za konskaya zadnitsa,"[44] she mumbled under her breath.

"Da…chto,"[45] the drowsy man grumbled as he started to stir.

"Nichego, ser. Prosto Antonov vot-vot prizemlitsya,"[46] she apologized, her face turning a crimson red.

Gusev, however, had already fallen back to sleep, acknowledging her comment with an abrupt snort and a soft exhale.

"Pridurok!"[47] she thought to herself indignantly.

She then turned her attention back to the airstrip that ran across the ground roughly two hundred feet from her current location, then at the aircraft that was gliding down for landing. The wings of the plane tilted slightly back and forth as the pilot made a final adjustment, and the next moment, the tires touched down on the pavement, accompanied by a puff of grey smoke from the two rear wheels.

At the same moment, a telephone to the side of the radar system rang loudly and abruptly. Captain Gusev, who had

[44] What a horse's ass.

[45] Huh…what?

[46] Nothing sir. Just that the Antonov is about to land.

[47] Moron.

slipped back into a deep slumber, lurched in his chair in reaction and fell back onto the floor in a clatter. The first lieutenant flashed a brief smile at the fumbling man, then turned to answer the call.

"First Lieutenant Petrov," she announced into the receiver.

As she sat listening to the voice on the other end, her facial expression shifted from little to no interest, to one that exuded grave concern. She then grabbed a sheet of paper and began to furiously write down the information being conveyed to her over the phone.

"Yes, sir. I understand. I will deploy unites immediately!" she stated sharply.

Petrov then hung the phone up, and without saying a word, she walked to the side of the room and slapped her hand on a red button located on a small electrical box. Immediately, a loud siren blared from two large speakers affixed on top of the traffic control tower, piercing the bracing air.

"Chto sluchilos'?"[48] the captain demanded.

"Bylo napadeniye!"[49]

The first lieutenant walked back to her workstation, grabbed the radio, and flicked a switch located on a dark black box. She then lifted the microphone to her mouth and depressed a vertical switch on the side.

"Air unit one. Report immediately to your aircraft. This is not a drill!" she barked sternly into the equipment.

Gusev and Petrov both walked over to the left side of the tower to peer out of the large windows on the wall. Off in the distance, they could see seven soldiers running out of a

48 What happened?

49 There's been an attack!

small barracks wearing flight suits, heading straight toward a massive aircraft located on a side runway. It had an enormous wingspan, with two herculean propellers located on either side of the fuselage. The front of the plane contained an upper flight deck on top of an all-windowed nosecone. Without hesitating, the airmen ran up a flight of stairs and disappeared into the aircraft.

Following closely behind the pilots were three support personnel, who took position around the plane to ready it for takeoff. Two of them removed large wheel chucks from the enormous tires, while the third stood directly in front of the plane with two orange batons held over his head. The next moment, he thrust both sticks out to either side of his body. The sound of powerful engines turning over emanated from the wings as the gigantic propellers started to spin up to speed.

"Flight control, this is Antonov thirty. We're ready for take off," a female voice with a thick Russian accent called out over the loudspeaker.

"Roger that, Antonov. Take off immediately. Flight plan uploaded to computer," Elena barked into the receiver.

The enormous Russian plane slowly began inching forward along the concrete. As the aircraft neared the main runway, the field serviceman ran off to the side of the plane, allowing it to freely roll onto the tarmac. The plane veered sharply to the left, then traveled along the path for approximately two minutes until it arrived at the end of the road, where it turned one hundred and eighty degrees and centered itself at the head of the airstrip. The pilot fully throttled both turbines and the plane surged forward, rumbling down the length of the runway, gaining more and more speed as it advanced. Petrov and her commander both watched as the enormous airplane zipped passed the control tower and gracefully lifted up off the ground and into the air.

Inside the spacious cockpit, seven personnel were all busily attending to their specific duties. The pilot was still forcefully pulling back on the control column so the aircraft would continue climbing to the desired height. To her left, the navigator was actively clicking away on his keyboard in order to confirm that the flight path had been accepted. Behind him, another flight officer was reading a message displayed on a small screen in front of her seat.

"Commander Zakharov, you're going to want to hear this," the officer reviewing the message called out to the pilot.

"Read it, Sergeant!" the pilot directed.

"Massive explosions detected in Siberia. Proceed immediately to sixty-three-point-four North, sixty-nine-point-nine East. Report observations."

The pilot's head immediately snapped in the direction of her comrade.

"Was it an attack?" the captain pressed.

"Unknown, sir. It doesn't say," she coolly replied.

Turning back to face forward, the aviator audibly exhaled through her nostrils.

"No point jumping to conclusions. Let's proceed to target," she simply stated.

As the aircraft leveled out at a cruising altitude of twenty thousand feet, the crew remained mostly silent during their journey, except for confirming the location and acknowledging commands. Everyone on the flight deck knew all too well their commander meant what she said, and she wouldn't tolerate any idle speculation about what actually happened and who had caused it.

The latitude and longitude coordinates specified a position approximately two-hundred-eighty miles to the southeast of the Russian airbase, which meant it would take just over thirty minutes to arrive at their current speed. Once they had attained their cruising altitude, they could already see a black haze out on the horizon, no doubt a result of the event they were investigating. After about twenty minutes of flight, it was clear that large sections of the forest were ablaze, dumping tons of smoke and debris into the atmosphere. And after a few more minutes, they were able to plainly see the amount of devastation strewn out on the landscape below, stretching over twenty square miles.

"Antonov to command. Come in, command. Over." Zakharov enunciated.

"This is command, Antonov. What do you see? Over." came the response through the speaker in the cockpit.

"Immense devastation. Large sections of forest are burning over thirty square kilometers. There is..."

Pausing for a moment, the pilot's eyes widened, dumbfounded at the scene below. After another moment, she continued with her report.

"There are multiple craters on the surface ranging in size from fifty to one-hundred and fifty meters. It looks like several meteors hit the earth."

The commander was staring intently at the destruction on ground below, when she realized there were thick columns of smoke extending upward from the center of the craters like the tendrils of a plant curving up a stick. There was substance to the almost web-like strands, and they seemed as if they were pulsating as they climbed up into the stratosphere.

"Commander, look out!" the co-pilot cried out.

Directly in front of the aircraft, an enormous column of soot and filth hung in the air. The width of the pillar looked to be over five hundred feet across, and the craft was quickly closing in on penetrating the side wall of the dark funnel.

"Hold on!" the pilot barked.

The next instant, the plane banked sharply to the right as the commander strenuously turned the plane on its side. Then, she pulled back on the stick with all her strength to try and avoid flying into the dark cloud.

"Help me?" she boomed.

The co-pilot grabbed the controls in front of him, yanking with all of his strength to try and evade the taint blocking the airplane's path. As the craft strongly veered, it looked as if they were going to successfully avoid flying into the dark haze altogether, but then disaster struck.

The wings and fuselage of the plane were wholly swallowed as they entered into the pillar of charcoal-colored smoke. Once inside the haze, it was impossible to see anything through the clear canopy covering the flight deck, and both pilots continued to energetically pull on the controls, trying to steer the plane out of the murk.

The next instant, they broke through the smoky atmosphere and were able to see again through the front window of the plane. However, unbeknownst to the crew, a thin, wispy trail of dingy smoke had somehow made its way in through the windows in the fuselage directly beneath the cockpit, and it was now slowly creeping its way along a set of steel stairs that led up from the lower deck.

"That was too close," the co-pilot stressed with a sigh. "I don't think..."

"Chto eto za zapakh?"[50] the navigator blurted out.

Turning to her left, she spotted the black vapor. The next moment, she gasped in amazement, as thin tendrils of the obsidian haze curled through the air, down her throat and into her lungs. Immediately, she began to cough uncontrollably.

"Maski!"[51] she gasped. "Naden' ... svoi ... maski!"[52]

The other six occupants on the flight deck immediately fumbled around for their masks. Four of them were able to secure them quickly and continued breathing normally. Regrettably, though, the other two were not as fortunate, and only secured their own masks after inhaling some of the foreign substance that had invaded the interior of the plane. Even with pure oxygen flowing into their lungs, each of the three aviators who had been exposed to the substance were virtually choking as they struggled to breath.

The pilot continued the sharp turn until the plane was heading in the opposite direction and started the return journey back to the Russian Air base. As the engines throttled to maximum speed, Zakharov looked back out of the window and observed thick, undulating columns of smoke climbing above the aircraft's current altitude into the upper stratosphere. Once attaining this height, they were caught in the high-level Siberian winds, blowing all the poisonous particles southward at speeds in excess of one hundred miles per hour.

[50] What's that smell?

[51] Masks!

[52] Put on...your...masks!

CHAPTER 11

Distress

(Early the Next Morning)

The deafening blast of emergency sirens abruptly jolted William from a deep sleep. He had already been precariously situated on a narrow cot, and the hasty movement caused him to awkwardly fall down to the floor of Menashe's home with a distinct thud. After quickly pushing himself into a seated position, he glanced over at his father-in-law, who was completely oblivious to the commotion and continued to snore loudly.

"Rich," William called out. *"Rich!"*

The bulky man showed absolutely no response.

"Unbelievable!" William complained.

The next moment, the door in the far corner of the room swung open, and Menashe ran out into the living area with a bewildered look on his face.

"What's going on?!" William barked.

"Get him up. Hurry!" he ordered as he made his way over to the laptop at the kitchen table.

Looking down at the comatose man, he shook his head and exhaled in frustration. He then lifted his foot and extended it toward the sleeping man, roughly shoving his shoulder.

"What the..." the groggy man exclaimed. "What the hell are you *doing?!"*

"Get up! *Hurry!*" William shouted. "Sirens are going off - it might be a missile attack."

Despite his broad girth, the rotund man was able to get up quickly from the mat on which he had been snoozing.

In the meantime, Menashe had opened the laptop, and was typing in the address for ILTV Israel News. After the page loaded, he clicked the link to view the 'Live Stream' and all three men stood around the table in a semicircle, staring intently at the browser. A moment later, the image flickered before displaying seven symbols centered on the screen with the word 'Attention' written in English beneath it.

The picture flickered again, this time revealing a woman in her mid-fifties sitting behind a small desk. She appeared to be consciously steadying herself, and after taking a deep breath, she looked into the camera with a steady, stern expression on her face.

"The following warning has just been issued by the President of Israel. An extremely hazardous event has occurred, and multiple countries have been impacted. We are advising all civilians to stay indoors for the next forty-eight hours while we ascertain the extent of this emergency and the threat to Israelis. In the western plains of Siberia, a natural disaster occurred less than twelve hours ago, threatening the lives of tens of millions of civilians. The following is what we know so far."

"At the beginning of 2021, mysterious craters started appearing sporadically throughout the desolate plains of Siberia, in the Western Peninsula. These holes vary in size from thirteen meters wide and forty meters deep, to as much as forty-five meters wide and up to one hundred fifty meters deep. While the interior walls of these formations are predominantly smooth, each of these pits has been surrounded by large chucks of dirt, rocks and other debris that appear to have been ejected out of the earth in some sort of violent reaction. Some of the boulders have been found upwards of one thousand meters from the focal point."

"Scientists have been examining these phenomena for the past six months and were initially perplexed by what was causing these aberrations in nature. Then in June, a small Russian field team were surveying the extended western plain by air and observed a number of large mounds extending upward from what is normally a flat, smooth area. At the time, they remarked that they resembled the bulging that we associate with volcanoes and the buildup of magma beneath the surface."

"The answer to the cause of these massive craters was finally discovered as scientists drilled into them and found considerable amounts of methane gas beneath the surface. Under normal conditions, methane would gradually make its way upward and be released in small, continuous quantities. However, the temperatures of Siberia, especially in this region, rarely rise above freezing for prolonged periods of time. On average, temperatures throughout this area range between ten and negative thirty degrees Celsius, depending on the time of year. This is the crux of the problem."

"As we all know, though, average temperatures around the globe have been gradually increasing over the past few decades. During 2020, for example, Siberia experienced a period of particularly high temperatures, including a high of thirty-eight degrees Celsius in the small town of Verkhoyansk, which has historically boasted the coldest temperatures on the planet of any permanently inhabited area. The result of these sustained hotter conditions has been wildfires and the loss of permafrost."

"Permafrost, sometimes measuring fifteen hundred meters in thickness, is a large subsurface of soil that stays frozen throughout the entire year, even when outside temperatures rise above freezing. As such, it creates an almost impenetrable barrier, trapping any gases that would normally be released to the atmosphere in massive pockets deep beneath the Earth's surface. There are multiple permafrost regions throughout Siberia that have been in a frozen state since the last Ice Age, over two point six million years ago. It is this loss of permafrost which scientists have identified as the culprit behind the formation of these spacious holes in the earth."

"When the last Ice Age began, thousands of animals and massive quantities of plants were trapped in the frozen earth, preserving and preventing this material from going through the natural process of decay. Unfortunately, as permafrost thaws quickly due to shifts in the climate, all the stored-up plant and animal material decays right along with it. As the frozen ground has thawed, the combination of massive quantities of naturally occurring methane, along with the release of enormous amounts of carbon dioxide and methane from decaying materials, has resulted in the formation of large areas of the earth being thrust upward. With no outside intervention, large fissures would ordinarily appear in the surface of these mounds, allowing trapped gases to escape. However, these bulging ridges are essentially a ticking time bomb, waiting for a random lightning strike or other force to set them off in a tremendous explosion."

"Twelve hours ago, at two p.m. Krasnoyarsk Time, an immense detonation occurred roughly eight hundred kilometers south of the Kara Sea in the arctic circle, resulting in shockwaves that were detected by seismometers four hundred kilometers away. Russian officials immediately dispatched an AN-30B surveillance aircraft to fly over the region, determine the source of the explosion, and to assess damage. Just over one hour later, that same plane made an emergency landing back at the Aerodrom Sovetskiy Airbase, and the entire flight crew was taken to a secure location by medical personnel in Hazmat suits for ongoing observation."

"A spokesperson for the Russian government has acknowledged that the aircraft reported flying into a thick cloud of smoke ascending from massive craters in the earth. Some of these fumes penetrated the cockpit, resulting in multiple members of the crew coughing and having difficulty breathing. With sixty minutes of their arrival at Aerodrom Sovetskiy, the medical team was able to ascertain that the entire flight team had been exposed to an aerosolized form of anthrax. Within four hours of the incident, Russian scientists declared that the specific nature of this bacteria doesn't match any strain currently on record and given the location of the explosion and nature of the permafrost, it is highly probable that the anthrax released into the atmosphere is a type that has been extinct for at least ten thousand years. This situation is grave, and a biohazard level four, the highest and most severe level, has been declared over southern Asia and the entire Middle East."

"Normally, anthrax is too heavy to travel very far, and would fall to earth from the upper atmosphere within thirty kilometers of the point of origin. However, this poison was aerosolized by the extreme heat of the explosion, making it exceptionally light, which allowed for its dispersal over great distances, depending on weather conditions. The high-speed Siberian winds are likely to carry this contamination well over three thousand kilometers to the south, threatening the lives of all who lie in its path."

"The following is a list of areas directly impacted by this pernicious toxin: Kazakhstan, Uzbekistan, areas surrounding the Caspian Sea, Iran, Afghanistan, Pakistan, and large areas of Western China as well as Northwest India. Local citizens have been alerted to this biohazard and every effort is being taken to try and preserve life. Disastrously, in vaporized form, this bacterium will cause widespread and devasting consequences for all humanity. Initial estimates place over five hundred million people in the destructive path of this lethal cloud."

"While we don't expect any of the fallout from this catastrophe to hit Israel, we are taking every possible precaution. Modern aerosolized anthrax can have upwards of a sixty percent mortality rate. Unfortunately, we have no idea how deadly this specific strain will be, or how it will affect humans and animals. We ask everyone who is listening to this broadcast to pray for all our brothers and sisters lying in the path of this calamity."

Slowly reaching forward, William closed the laptop and turned to look at his father-in-law.

"I can't believe this is happening," he nearly sobbed.

With a somber expression, Rich reached over and placed his hand on William's shoulder in a consoling manner.

"I'm afraid this is only the beginning."

CHAPTER 12

Surreptitious

(Two Weeks Later)

With the sun setting almost fifteen minutes earlier, twilight blanketed the outskirts of Jerusalem in a growing darkness, accompanied by a drop in temperature. Over the past two weeks, conditions had been running at least ten degrees cooler than normal, but that night, the thermometer had already dipped beneath forty degrees Fahrenheit.

Sitting behind the wheel of his silver SUV, Menashe was lightly humming a tune as he pulled onto the main highway leading away from downtown Jerusalem. Occupying the passenger seat, William stared blankly out onto the darkening roadside. Meanwhile, Rich was lying down in the back nursing an upset stomach.

"Oof!" he moaned from the rear of the vehicle.

"I guess you shouldn't have had that second helping of Skakshuka," Menashe chided him with a grin.

"Now you tell me," he lamented.

"I warned you how spicy it was," he countered.

"I didn't think it would be so fiery."

A couple beads of sweat rolled down Rich's ample forehead as he shifted his weight to get more comfortable.

"Umm...Menashe," the distressed man panted.

"What's wrong?"

"You might want to crack open a window," he sheepishly admitted.

"Really?!" William snapped.

"I'm sorry, it really isn't my fault."

Without a word, Menashe opened the two rear windows slightly to allow for fresh air to circulate, then closed both of them after a brief moment.

"That's going to have to be good enough. It too cold to keep them down any longer."

"Hey Rich," William pleaded, "how about you keep things bottled up until we get home?"

"I'll do my best, but we've still got about another forty-five minutes."

"Let me see if I can shorten that by a few minutes," Menashe joked as he pressed the accelerator down and the car surged forward slightly.

"Have you heard anything new today about the anthrax disaster?" William probed.

"Not much," Menashe replied. "Let me switch on the radio to see if they have an update."

Reaching forward, he depressed the volume button and the display lit up, with the letters 'BBC' prominently displayed on the small screen.

"Shifting topics," a voice announced from the speakers, "we're going to cut over to a live broadcast from an expert panel discussing the impact of the anthrax contagion. Representatives from the World Health Organization, the US Centers for Disease Control and Prevention, Public Health England and the Chinese Center for Disease Control, have convened in Munich to share information about the fallout and how we can best combat this horrible catastrophe."

"Thank you for joining us today," a man with a deep British accent commented. "With everything going on right now, I know it wasn't easy to attend in person. I would like for us to begin our conversation this evening with a discussion about the total number of impacted civilians throughout the affected regions."

"The numbers are astronomical," a woman with a raspy voice commented. "How can we have gotten our initial estimates so wrong?"

"Our initial projection was based on the assumption that the speed of the jet stream would have ranged somewhere between one hundred thirty and one hundred eighty kilometers per hour," a female voice articulated with a Spanish accent. "Unfortunately, that was not what occurred. Over the first three days since the outbreak of the toxin, high altitude winds have maintained an accelerated speed in excess of two hundred twenty-five kilometers per hour, sometimes reaching as high as three hundred kilometers. While this has helped to minimize fallout of the aerosolized poison over areas closer to ground zero, we must recognize that those regions were sparsely populated. The stronger-than-average air currents pushed the initial fallout zone at least five hundred kilometers further south than originally anticipated. And that…"

"And that," interrupted a female with an East Asian accent, "is the crux of the problem. The vigorous winds have resulted in an extension of the anthrax zone into some of the most heavily populated areas in Asia. It has pushed everything well beyond the borders of China and India."

"Doctor Fen Zhao makes an excellent point," the British moderator broke in. "Let's initially focus on China and then we will shift our attention to India."

"Thank you, Doctor Williams," Fen remarked. "For China, most of the population is concentrated in the eastern half of the country, so fortunately, the extension of the fallout zone did not significantly increase the death toll. The government of the People's Republic of China has reacted quickly and decisively to this crisis, and we have been very successful in transferring millions of citizens out of the impacted areas."

"In India, we have not fared so well," another man interrupted. "The extension of the affected zone by five hundred kilometers has had devasting effects on India. Our population is spread out relatively uniformly across our country, so every additional meter this contamination reaches, puts more and more lives at risk. The World Health Organization has determined the shifting of the fallout has nearly doubled the affected population from what was initially estimated to be five hundred and fifty million persons, to just under one billion."

"And that's just part of the equation we must consider," the moderator interjected. "In order for us to truly ascertain the impact of this calamity, we must factor in the mortality rate. Our initial estimate of fatalities for those exposed to this toxin was around sixty percent. But this was a completely unknown, never-before-seen strain. In fact, we now know that the lethality of this poison is staggering, claiming the lives of nearly eighty percent of those exposed."

"Given the increase in size of the geographically impacted area, and the substantially higher mortality rate, has anyone calculated how high the death toll could climb?" the man from India pressed. "And what we could have done to avoid this?"

"Let me address your second question first," the British moderator replied. "There really isn't much we could have done to minimize the impact of this event. Similar to the devastation we experienced from the *Télos* asteroid, we didn't have any warning. And even if we had had days of advance notification, where would people have gone? As for your first question," he continued, "I received an update this morning based on revised estimates."

The man paused for a moment, obviously collecting himself to deliver news that was extremely difficult to convey. Glancing down at his hands, which were resting on the table, he took a deep breath and stared directly into the camera.

"Based on our latest data, it looks like the death toll will climb as high as six hundred million, with nearly half of those lives lost coming from India."

There was complete silence from every member of the panel. As the camera shifted across the various participants, it paused momentarily on the gentleman from India, who now had large tears streaming freely down his cheeks.

"My God!" the woman from the Chinese Center for Disease Control exclaimed. "That's nearly twenty-five times the number killed by the Black Plague!"

"And we can only pray our estimates are wrong. One thing that is praiseworthy, is the response from all nations around the world, which has been astounding. Hundreds of thousands of pounds of medical supplies, antibiotics, oxygen, and everything in between have been sent to every impacted nation. In addition, all countries in the region that have not been adversely affected, are opening up their borders for any and all refuges. This is clearly the greatest disaster our world has ever faced, and we are going to be dealing with the impact for generations."

With a sigh, Menashe reached over and flipped the radio to off. Pursing his lips, he sat in silence for a moment until his expression changed to one displaying reluctant recognition.

“I hate to say this,” he admitted in a hushed tone, “but this may actually be to our advantage.”

Rich’s head immediately snapped up as he pushed himself into a seated position, a look of outrage emanating from his face. But before he could open his mouth to criticize the statement his companion had just made, Menashe quickly continued.

“Please don’t misunderstand me. I’m not saying millions of people dying is positive. It’s horrendous! Beyond dreadful. It is certainly the worst disaster to have ever stricken our planet. But the situation this has created is something we can benefit from.”

“Which is?” Rich challenged while biting the inside of his inner mouth to prevent further outburst.

“We have been struggling to determine how we were going to travel to Mecca to meet Widad. Before this catastrophe, it would have been nearly impossible for us to get from Israel to Saudi Arabia undetected, especially given all of the security measures and extra COVID restrictions.”

“And don’t forget the demonic entities trying to destroy us,” William added.

Rich sat quietly, allowing the words to wash over him.

“It’s a horrific situation,” William whispered reverently, “but we’ve got to keep moving forward, despite everything that is transpiring.”

“I know,” the hefty man relented. “It’s just so incredibly sad.”

“It truly is,” his son in law concurred, “but we must honor everyone who has lost their lives by maintaining our faith until the very end.”

The three men rode in silence for a few minutes, contemplating the cost to humanity. Finally, Menashe began to speak again.

"I've been looking into things over the past few days," he divulged. "It looks like the best way for us to get to Mecca will be to travel by sea. We should make plans to board a vessel at the Port of Haifa, traverse the Suez Canal, then make our way down the Red Sea to the port of Jeddah. From there, it will be a short car ride to Mecca, where we will finally be able to talk to my friend."

"That sounds like a good plan," Rich agreed. "How soon until we leave?"

"There's a barge leaving in three days that I should be able to secure us passage on. I'll attend to that tomorrow, while the two of you finalize packing. This should be an interesting voyage."

As the vehicle rolled down the dark roadway, an undetected, writhing, murky mist slid down from the rear corner and into the cargo area. For a moment, it roiled in an agitated manner on the floor, before physically forcing itself into a crack between the rear hatch and bumper. Then, it disappeared into the darkness of the night.

CHAPTER 13

Fissure

As the silver vehicle continued down the dark highway in an easterly direction, the black, murky entity fluctuated back and forth between a gaseous and solid form, suspended over the roadway. While it twisted and roiled in the air, the faint outline of an almost emaciated winged figured became visible, until it oscillated once more and became an amorphous frame. The indistinct haze continued in this manner until the automobile finally disappeared around a slight curve in the roadway, at which point all chaotic motion ceased, leaving behind an unnatural looking, hideous beast.

Standing in the middle of the asphalt was a gaunt creature, no more than five feet in height. The beast's head was extremely narrow, topped off by a pair a black, six-inch horns that looked to follow the slope of the forehead, arching backwards. A layer of thin, almost transparent skin lay tightly across a skull consisting of a prominent, broad brow, high cheek bones and an angular chin. A pair of crimson recessed eyes appeared to be indented into the beast's face by two inches, and vile black mucus slowly oozed from the sockets. An almost human-like nose was positioned squarely in the middle of its face, protruding by two inches to a sharp point. A thin, lipless maw arched downward in a disgusting grimace, and the point of six razor-sharp fangs jutted out from the bottom jawline.

The head of this fiend sat on top of an elongated neck, a full eight inches from its narrow torso. Taut skin covered its chest, and the detailed outline of bony ribs was easily visible. At the point where they connected at the center of its frame, a thick rectangular bone stuck out from beneath the skin, giving it an exoskeleton-like appearance. Long, thin, sinewy arms hung loosely by either side, extending down past its pelvis to the tops of its knees. Despite the slightness of the arms, the flexing sinews and tendons displayed great strength beneath the surface. An almost claw-like appendage at the end of each limb looked as if it could easily cut clean through a three-inch tree branch. Detailed abdominal muscles flexed along with the gently rising and falling ribcage as the hellion drew in air. Its legs appeared small and somewhat underdeveloped, as if they were seldom used as a means for movement.

Standing motionless in the roadway, the horrific demon simply stared down the dark highway at where the vehicle had driven. A thin smile split its hideous visage as an incomprehensible cackle crept out of its throat. It then slowly turned its head in the opposite direction, looking back up the highway toward Jerusalem.

"I will report," a seething cry announced.

The next moment, it became obvious why the legs of this entity appeared so underdeveloped, as a second pair of muscular arms extended outward from the back, revealing immense wings. Each airfoil stretched out on either side, and once fully extended, created a wingspan of at least ten feet across. The thin, unsubstantial skin covering the body of this beast was replaced by a tough, leathery-looking outer covering, and each appendage was tipped by a ghastly seven-inch sharpened hook.

With an ear-piercing screech, the beast launched itself into the air and began flying down the roadway toward the ancient city. A moment later, a pair of headlights appeared from the top of a gentle rise in the road, indicating that another car was heading directly for the creature. The instant the glow of illumination made contact with the winged fiend, it shrieked in pain. As it shifted its trajectory in response, it was now in near absolute darkness, flying on the side of the road in the direction of the offending vehicle. Each of the two converging objects should have easily slid past each other without any incidence. But for the driver of the oncoming vehicle, this would unfortunately not be the case.

At the last moment, the vile demon shifted its weight and angled itself directly at the automobile. Then, a fraction of a second before impacting with the vehicle, it changed course again, rotating almost ninety degrees on its axis, positioning its horrific, razor-sharp claw to pierce the front panel of the car. As the sharpened bone ripped through the steel exterior, it sounded like the engine of a locomotive being torn in half. Seemingly without meeting any resistance, the sharp edge created an incision along the full length of the vehicle. The next second, the car veered wildly in the opposite direction, careening off of the road and flipping end over end multiple times, until coming to an abrupt halt in the dirt.

The winged aggressor then angled upward into the air and twisted round to examine the damage it had inflicted. Upon arriving at the nearly destroyed car, it landed on the ground immediately next to the driver's side door, and with a repugnant smile, it slowly surveyed the gash it had torn into the side. It peered forward and stared in through the broken window at the lifeless body of a man, pausing while it acknowledged the jagged wound inflicted on his flesh. Then, glancing at its own barbed hook, it noted the blood of its prey still present on the surface. With a horrific smirk, it tilted its head, dabbing at the sanguine fluid with a snake-like tongue, savoring the moment.

The creature than let out an almost jubilant cry and took to the air again. With just a few flaps of its mighty wings, the demon soared up to a height of at least one hundred feet and started to accelerate in a straight line toward the glowing city. As it reached the outer edge of Jerusalem, it showed absolutely no sign of stopping. Within a matter of a few minutes, it had traversed the entire width of the capital and was now soaring at an even faster rate toward the Mediterranean Sea.

Within ten minutes, the demonic predator had reached the sea and was soaring fifty feet above the surface, following a precise north-westerly route, gliding over the water at an ever-quickening pace. Roughly fifteen minutes after reaching the Mediterranean, the coast of Cyprus was clearly visible off to the left, but within a matter of seconds, it had disappeared from view. A short while after came Turkey, then Bulgaria, Serbia, and finally, Germany.

As the winged beast drew closer to its destination, the speed with which the landscape was changing began to slow dramatically. A few moments later, it was coasting over a thickly forested area of Germany, surveying the landscape below for something specific. After finally spotting its target, it started to descend to a massive stone dome, covering an area of the ground at least seventy-five feet in diameter. As it reached the top of the concrete exterior, the demon appeared to change state for a moment, dissolving through the barrier into the interior space.

Once inside, it gently flapped its wings, hovering thirty feet in the air directly over a dark, vile pit full of bubbling sludge and taint. As it glanced to the far side, dozens of horrific demons, and other ungodly creatures were climbing up out of the ooze, then slowly crawling on the ground in a northerly direction.

Without hesitating, the hellion flapped its powerful wings, passed through the stone barrier a second time, and soared into the air to an altitude of four hundred feet. At this height, it was able to witness a stream of countless horrific creatures sluggishly making their way through the forest toward a faint glow on the horizon. With an ugly caw, the fiend began to make its own way toward the glimmer of light, flying directly above the procession of demons. As the creature flew above the line, it observed that the foliage in direct proximity to the hellish parade was diseased, dying, or completely dead. In addition, at uneven internals across the landscape, several enormous hulking demons were positioned to monitor the progress of the column, and if necessary, to inflict punishment for not moving quickly enough in the form of a barbed whip.

Within a minute, the winged imp arrived at the source of faint light, and the destination for all of these repugnant souls – the Cenetics campus.

Situated in a large clearing of the forest, it now comprised nearly twenty large buildings. Over the past few months, several structures had been constructed, extending the perimeter of the grounds out to the edge of the tree line. Situated at the front of the campus, adjacent to a large parking area, was a four-story building, easily four hundred by four hundred feet, capped by a massive concrete dome containing an oculus at its apex. As the line of demons drew close to the four-story structure, they began to slowly descend beneath the surface of the earth as if they were walking down an invisible ramp beneath the building.

Spotting the opening in the roof, the winged creature swooped down toward the aperture and penetrated the interior. Directly inside the structure, a large circular courtyard, approximately one hundred feet in diameter, was surrounded by a series of offices with windows facing into the area. Several trees were growing inside, reaching up nearly full four stories to the underside of the dome. Directly in the center of the space, a large, brass medallion with curious symbols etched into the surface was positioned on the ground. As the devilish being soared down through the trees, it made its way toward the golden seal, showing no signs of slowing. Before hitting the ground, the outline of thc beast shimmered and as it did, it easily slid down through the floor and into the earth.

Located beneath the structure was a colossal, underground circular cavern, with a massive stone table situated squarely in the middle. While a number of torches flickered along the perimeter of the room, a large chandelier hanging down from thick steel ring in the ceiling provided most of the illumination. As the evil spirit glided down to the floor sixty feet below, it recognized the individual casually resting on the high-backed concrete throne as his human master; someone he loathed and feared at the same time.

Ostensibly sensing its presence, Schmidt's head snapped upward to gaze at the corrupt creature making its way down from the ceiling above. As he locked eyes with the insignificant beast, his face exuded a flagrant enmity.

Landing a mere eight feet from its handler, the creature immediately scurried on all fours in a deferential manner, taking its position at Schmidt's feet and bowing its head in obedient submission. This nauseating display of meekness curdled Schmidt's disposition even further, and a look of disgust flashed across his face.

"Sephtis!" he accused. "Why are you here? I commanded you to keep close watch on the enemy, so we know what they are planning next!"

Remaining in a position of subjugation, Sephtis raised its head slightly in response, being certain to continue averting its eyes.

"My Lord," he cowered, "you know that I..."

Abruptly standing up, Schmidt struck the devilish fiend with a mace-like cudgel, sending it tumbling across the floor and into the side of the stone table. After righting itself on all fours, it momentarily looked as if it were about to launch an attack of its own, but it thought better of it and continued with an attitude of servitude.

"You know what?!" he boomed.

"My Lord, you know I would only come if I had valuable information to share. I dare not incur your displeasure or wrath, Lord."

Schmidt retook his seat with a self-satisfied expression on his face.

"Well," he fumed, *"get on with it!"*

"Yes, my Lord. I did exactly as you asked and watched the three humans you commanded me to, making certain not to be seen."

The creature paused for a moment, apparently collecting its thoughts before continuing.

"They have been planning a secret journey to the Islamic city of Mecca. This I know for certain. But the specifics of their trip have remained hidden to me. That is until today...this very evening."

Leaning back on his throne, Schmidt motioned for the demon to continue.

"Three days hence, they are planning to travel on a barge from the port of Haifa, down through the conduit of water, and straight to the city."

Sephtis glanced up at its master who appeared to be silently deliberating the news and formulating the next steps.

"If it meets with your approval," it offered in a reticent manner, "I will marshal the troops to meet our rivals as they travel to the seaport of Haifa. I will ensure that…"

Slamming his fist on the table, Schmidt abruptly cut Sephtis off and it recoiled in fear.

"You will do no such thing!" he howled. "The only thing you need to do is to go back to your spying! I have something special in mind that will eliminate this nuisance forever!"

Bowing rapidly, Sephtis backed away from the table without making any eye contact.

"Of course, Lord. Your will be done," it repeated over and over as it made its retreat.

Deep in thought, Schmidt seemed unaware of the creature's departure as it spread its wings outward and flew back up through the stone ceiling.

After standing motionless for thirty seconds, he turned to the archaic mirror resting on the table, seemingly contemplating whether or not to commune with his Master for approval. Then, picking up the ancient knife, he gripped it tightly in his hand and stared thoughtfully at the edge of the blade. The next instant, he cast it roughly across the stone surface.

"This is my time," he indignantly thought to himself. *"And this will be my glory!"*

As he turned away from the table, a slight flicker of light emanated from the mirror, almost as if a fleck of fire had momentarily appeared beneath the surface. But just as quickly as it had surfaced, it was gone.

CHAPTER 14

Summoning

(One Hour Later)

As the elevator climbed to the first level of the Cenetics facility, the occupant stared impatiently at the two stainless steel doors, almost as if he expected his glare to accelerate the process. A moment later, the motion of the lift ceased, and both barriers started to slide in opposite directions. As soon as the gap was wide enough, the man slithered out into the spacious lobby and started to make his way to the exit.

Sitting behind the security desk was the familiar face of the aged night guard who, without thinking, impulsively stood up and turned toward the visitor to address any needs they might have. However, as soon as he realized it was the none-too-friendly Doctor Schmidt, he retook his seat with a miffed expression on his face.

Without even glancing in the direction of the watchman, Schmidt quickly traversed the breadth of the foyer with lengthy strides. After a mere handful of seconds, he shoved his hands forcefully into the door, which immediately gave way.

"You have yourself a good evening," the sentry sarcastically called out.

As the door rotated around the center shaft, Schmidt glared back abhorrently at the guard through the glass, sending a shiver up and down his spine.

Having arrived on the opposite side of the exit, the chill night air blasted Schmidt's face as he stalked out onto the pavement and started making his way to the parking lot. Within thirty seconds, he had arrived at his dark grey sports car and hopped into the driver's seat. A few moments later, he was speeding down the entry road to the highway roughly two miles away. After about two minutes of driving down the main thoroughfare, he took his foot off the accelerator and retrieved a small remote control from his inside suit pocket. As the automobile decelerated, he glanced into the rearview mirror, ensuring no one was there to observe his actions. Despite it being one o'clock in the morning, he knew he needed to be cautious to ensure nothing would upset his plans.

Confident he was alone, he turned the lights off and allowed the car to crawl at a mere three miles per hour down the near pitch-black road. Despite the darkness of the environment, the repulsive man was somehow able to perceive all of his surroundings, as if the putridity that contaminated his soul gave him powers beyond that of any other living person. As he searched the side of the lane, he spotted the objective of his investigation. On the left side of the road, roughly ten feet in front of the vehicle, sat a diseased, rotting stump of an ancient black alder tree amongst a number of low-lying bushes and other shrubs. Audibly inhaling through his nostrils, a grotesque grin creased his face and his eyes narrowed into tiny slits.

The next moment, he pointed the small black remote in the direction of the fallen tree and depressed the button. Instantly, all the undergrowth on the forest floor began to slowly slide to the right of the infected timber, revealing a hidden lane that led back into the sinister looking woods. Without hesitation, he steered the car onto the barely visible dirt path and guided it toward an even deeper darkness. As soon as he had cleared the imperceptible barrier, he pressed the button on the control once more, and the ground cover slid back across the passage, completely obscuring the entrance.

For the next ten minutes, Schmidt slowly rolled through the trees deeper and deeper into the backwoods, with the headlights off to guard against any unwanted eyes spotting his advance. The darkness of the night completely cloaked the countless number of trees, which seemed to extend endlessly in every direction, and as the lane wound its way through the landscape, the surface became more uneven, resulting in the frequent jostling of the vehicle and its occupant.

Suddenly, Schmidt's car made its way into a large, circular clearing at least one hundred feet in diameter. A large, windowless concrete dome, easily three stories tall was situated in the center of the area, fifteen feet from the tree line, curving off in either direction following the timber line. Schmidt immediately slowed his vehicle and turned the steering wheel so he could park alongside the tall structure. After coming to a stop, he put the vehicle into park and exited through the driver's door. Seemingly oblivious to the brisk air beating against his cheeks, he began to probe his surroundings intently to confirm that he was in fact totally alone. With a satisfied nod, he made his way to the front of the vehicle and began walking alongside the cement barrier, actively searching the adjacent ground until he spotted a small, rectangular cover lying flush to the surface.

With a grunt, he knelt down beside the wall and began brushing the dirt and other debris off the stone lid. After prying the corner of the covering up from the earth, he tossed it to one side in a casual manner and leaned forward to peer into the opening. Located roughly six inches down within the earthen cavity was a stone lever, which he immediately grasped and pulled toward himself.

Instantly, a sharp metallic clanking noise could be heard from somewhere beneath the surface. The noise sounded like the turning metal sprockets of a piece of industrial equipment. The next moment, a circular pattern appeared on the top of the dirt approximately six feet in diameter, which then started to sink down into the ground. As the sphere of earth descended, a pie-shaped section, roughly ten inches in length on the outmost curve, split off from the larger portion six inches beneath the surface. This cycle repeated each time the larger section penetrated further into the earth, and after a few seconds, it became obvious it was forming a spiral staircase into the depths below.

As he stood at the edge of the first step, Doctor Schmidt created the outline of an ancient symbol in the air with his finger. As he traced a precise pattern, a deep figure began to shimmer with a reddish hue, revealing the meticulous sequence he had just created. Turning his hand over into a cupping form, an orb of crimson light appeared, floating just one inch above his palm, and he began his descent beneath the surface.

Strange symbols and images began to appear, covering the walls of the stairwell as they were revealed by the luminescence emanating from the mysterious sphere. After one full rotation around the center column, Schmidt found himself eight feet below the surface, standing in a small rectangular room, with a narrow doorway lying in the far wall. As he made his way across the small chamber, the orb slowly danced between his wrist and fingertips, as black flecks shimmered across the surface. As he approached the doorway, another stone lever became visible on the side of the opening. Without even glancing at the bar, he grasped the shaft, pulling it down firmly, and the next instant, the dirt stairway began to climb back to the surface, sealing him in an earthen tomb.

Standing at the entrance to the next room, he extended his hand straight through the doorway and gradually closed his fist. As his fingers drew close to the undulating sphere, the light began to dimmish, until it was fully extinguished within his repulsive clutch, abandoning Schmidt to an infinite void of sheer blackness. While standing in the lightless hollow, he closed his eyes and started to gently sway back and forth, his hands tightly clutched against his chest.

"Te rogamus tenebricosae sectae dominatus praepotens,"[53] he sibilated through clenched teeth. "Da mihi potestatem super atra inanis!"[54]

The ground beneath his feet began to vibrate, and a deep rumbling began to reverberate throughout the tiny subterranean room.

"Te rogamus tenebricosae sectae dominatus praepotens. Da mihi potestatem super atra inanis!" he chanted.

As he continued to recite the despicable words, the heaving of the earth intensified, and Schmidt's body began to violently convulse. His hands were clasped so tightly that the blood refused to flow through the ends of his pale fingers. Suddenly, the rocking motion ceased along with the shaking of his entire frame, leaving the evil man standing completely immobile in the darkness. The next instant, his eyelids began to haltingly crawl toward his brow, revealing jet black, soulless pupils, surrounded by a deep crimson glow.

Thrusting his hands out toward the cramped portal, he let loose a bestial growl as fire erupted from his palms, bathing the interior chamber in searing heat. As the blaze

[53] I beseech thee, powers of darkness.

[54] Give me authority over the black void!

subsided, an orange flickering remained in the adjacent room, and he stepped through the opening. Four archaic torches, protruding from curved walls, cast twisting shadows across the stone room, along with shimmering hues of reddish-orange flame. The circular chamber was twenty feet across and stretched upward ten feet to a rotunda-like ceiling. The walls were covered with prehistoric-looking paintings depicting scenes of unspeakable horrors. Hideous demons wielding crude weapons of destruction were standing victoriously over decapitated, lifeless bodies on the blood-soaked battlefield. Enormous cages, suspended from the ceiling of vast caverns, housed dozens of humans dangling precipitously over bubbling lakes of liquid fire. Men, women, and children alike were being exterminated on a grand scale.

An imposing, shard-like boulder stood vertically in the center of the room, next to a circular flight of stairs that spun down further into the interior of the earth. Schmidt quickly made his way over to the enormous stone fragment and began his descent down the primitive stairwell. As he descended each level, crude flambeaus spontaneously ignited, illuminating the twisting path. The sides of the circular staircase were covered with equally revolting imagery of vile scenes that would cause any sane mind to recoil in disgust.

After about two minutes, Schmidt reached the bottom of the staircase and made his way out into a considerably sized subterranean cavity at least eighty feet across and four stories tall. At the far edge of the cavern, lying to the west, a perfectly round opening of at least twelve feet in diameter had been bored into the surface of the wall, extending backward into solid rock as far as the eye could see.

Positioned on the ground, adjacent to the circular aperture, was a silver disk measuring twenty-five feet across, lying flat on the ground. Toward the edge of the metallic circle was a raised surface forming a thick band, followed by a flat space twelve inches across, bordered by yet another raised ring encircling the outermost edge. The smooth area centered in between the two elevated boundaries contained a total of thirty-three different runes etched into the metal material, evenly spaced around the entire perimeter.

With a determined expression, Schmidt walked up to the metallic disc, pausing at the outermost edge before stepping onto the surface. As he as he did, a viridian glow emanated from the entirety of the silver circle, and a light humming began to reverberate through the cave. Walking to the center of the disk, he began to trace a symbol in the air with his finger which, when completed, seemed to materialize as a hazy red figure. He turned thirty degrees to his right and repeated the process over and over, until after roughly sixty seconds, a total of eleven different semi-transparent runes shimmered around the evil man. The next moment, exactly eleven of the symbols positioned around the edge of the circular platform started to emit a crimson hue and the volume of the humming increased dramatically.

As Schmidt stared back into the burrowed tunnel, he became aware of a small pinpoint of light in the exact center, set back at quite a distance. The ray gradually increased in intensity as it drew closer, until it finally separated into five distinct beams of light, racing along the perimeter of the shaft and impacting an invisible barrier that separated the passageway from the cavernous room, where it grew tenfold in its brilliance. A flash of light instantly filled the room, and two red beams slowly reached outward across the opening, perfectly vertical to the ground from each of the five points. As they stretched across the expanse, it became obvious that they were on a path to connect with the lines originating from points on the opposite side of the circle. When all the beams had finally intersected with one another, they perfectly formed the nefarious symbol of a pentagram, which immediately turned a deep shade of crimson. The next instant, a metallic buzzing pierced the air and light began to race along the border of the circular opening where the points of the unholy star touched the perimeter, until they had completely enclosed the circle.

With a nod of grim satisfaction, Schmidt approached the massive glowing pentangle, stopping just short of the glowing surface. Taking a deep breath, he placed his left hand directly onto the shimmering façade, and his eyes rolled back into his skull.

"Ideo indigas imperfectasque spatio et tempore!"[55]

Schmidt's entire body immediately appeared to become translucent, and his form began to vacillate between solid and gaseous states. His hand then started to penetrate the pulsating barrier as his entire form was drawn through the luminous portal. As his arm infiltrated the surface further, its presence completely disappeared, as if it had been erased from existence. Finally, the exterior layer of the aperture began to engulf his torso, and with his face only mere inches from passing through, Schmidt closed his eyes. His body then completely disappeared, wholly absorbed by the mystical entrance.

Now traveling at a seemingly impossible speed, Schmidt hurtled in a perfectly straight line down the center of the

[55] Traverse space and time!

immense passageway, hovering four feet above the ground. While the walls whizzed past him at a nauseating pace, the effect of such a high rate of speed was completely absent on him. He appeared as if he was standing completely motionless, not a single hair out of place.

This spectacle continued over the next ten minutes as he traveled over four hundred and fifty miles through the surface of the earth. Finally, he began to slow down and a distant light designating the end of the mine became visible in the distance. In the time it took for Schmidt to fill his lungs with air, he now found himself standing directly in front of a transparent boundary identical to the one he had initially crossed. As he exhaled through his nostrils, he placed his hand on the barrier and his body instantly began to pass through. A moment later, he found himself standing on top of an identical silver disk inside of an enormous cavern. As he looked down at the metallic platform, he noticed that several glowing symbols located on the perimeter had started to dim in intensity, until they finally flickered off.

Shifting his gaze, Schmidt took in the immensity of the subterranean chamber in which he now stood. It was easily ten times the size as the one beneath the vile abyss located just outside the Cenetics facility. Colossal stalactites hung down from a ceiling looming one hundred feet above the floor. Many of these structures extended down some thirty to fifty feet, ending in sharpened points, where others attached with equally tremendous stalagmites reaching up from the floor. Multiple winged hellions were gliding through the air, dipping and curving around stone structures, while other infernal creatures crawled across stony surfaces. An almost unbearable heat permeated the entire cavern, and the putrid smell of brimstone hung heavily in the air.

A corrupt beast, easily twice the height of Schmidt, started to approach in a somewhat menacing manner. Schmidt, however, showed absolutely no concern or fear. In fact, he almost seemed bothered by the creature's presence.

"My Lord," the monster bellowed, "we didn't expect you. Is there something wrong? We barely had enough antimatter to complete your transfer through the gateway. If there..."

Schmidt abruptly raised his right hand and swung it in the direction of the maniacal fiend, with a slight twitch of his forefinger. In an instant, the air between the two shimmered and the beast was thrown backward, horns over feet, fifteen feet across the stone floor in a loud clatter.

"Nothing is wrong!" he virtually spat at the creature. "I know exactly what I'm doing! Know your place and do *only* as I say!"

"Yes, my Lord," the cowering demon mumbled. "Your will, my Lord."

Walking directly toward the creature, who was just now getting back onto his feet, Schmidt glared at him with a discourteous expression.

"You say we're almost out of antimatter, yes?"

"Yes, Lord," the demon relented with a look of chagrin on its face.

"Then we need to get more!" he boomed.

He paused for a moment, staring into the eyes of the beast, almost as if he was trying to read his mind. The demon just stared blankly at him in response.

"Move!" he commanded.

"But Lord," he complained, "we were nearly discovered the last time we spun up the machine. *Master* has commanded me that we should wait until we are ready to bring everyone through..."

The brute's voice caught halfway in its throat as Schmidt cast a hateful scowl that should have obliterated the soulless entity on the spot.

"At once, Lord," the creature acquiesced.

Without another word, it then scampered over to the side of the cavern, pausing in front of a smooth area on the wall, where it began to trace a symbol in the air. In response to its beckoning, the seemingly solid rock began to waiver, then completely disappeared, revealing an earthen hallway leading back approximately forty feet, where a dim light appeared to illuminate another room. Without hesitating, Schmidt strutted over to the opening and made his way down the passageway and out into what appeared to be a high-tech control room. As he walked into the room, the air that separated it from the tunnel shimmered and he appeared to dissolve through an invisible barrier.

Once on the other side of the opening, he began to scrutinize the area. A series of large screens reflecting different images of what appeared to be a highly technical apparatus were affixed to a long wall on the opposite side of the room. Two rows of tables covered by flat panels, keyboards, and a few pads of paper, were arrayed in a semi-circle facing the screens, stretching almost the full length of the area. Despite it being two o'clock in the morning, two scientists wearing white laboratory coats were located off to one side. One of them was sitting, furiously typing on a keyboard situated directly in front of him, while a woman was standing next to him, slightly bending forward so she could read the screen.

Almost immediately realizing that someone had entered the room, the woman spun toward him with a startled expression.

"Que fais-tu ici?"[56] she demanded. "Tu n'es pas censé être..."[57]

Her voice was abruptly cut off as Schmidt finished tracing a symbol in the air, and both researchers now seemed to be frozen in a trance-like state. With a look of satisfaction, he purposely walked over to the computer on which the male scientist had been working, and roughly pushed the man out of his chair and onto the floor. He stared momentarily at the individual lying in a heap on the ground, then took the recently vacated seat.

After taking a moment to orient himself, he brought up an application on the screen, and after a few quick keystrokes, a deep humming noise could be heard echoing throughout the facility. One of the images on the large screens hanging on the opposite wall flickered and was replaced by a picture of what looked to be a test tube encircled by three rings of steel, covered at either end by a circular steel cap. Within the tube was an orange, dowel-like structure extending inward from either end, and from the center of each surface, a thick gold wire protruded, nearly connecting with one another, leaving a very small space between both points.

The humming sound grew a little louder, accompanied by a thumping noise that reverberated throughout the entire room at a relatively slow cadence. The next moment, the speed of the beating quickened, until it was nearly impossible to discern when one sound ended and the next began.

[56] What are you doing here?

[57] You're not supposed to be...

Suddenly, a flicker of sustained light appeared on the screen in between the two wires. The brilliant flashing intensified in brightness over the next few moments before, without warning, the vibration and pounding ceased entirely.

A huge smile creased Schmidt's visage as he analyzed the undulating sphere of light suspended in the air between the tips of the wires. After striking a few buttons on the keyboard, the view zoomed in on what could only be described as vibrating light. As it drew in closer, the surface almost seemed to have a texture to it, ebbing and flowing in irregular patterns.

Jumping up from his seat, Schmidt stepped over the still-motionless man lying at his feet and walked over to a substantial steel door at the side of the room. After swinging the door outward, he entered a small area containing a large, metallic box situated in the middle of the room, with four thick steel prongs protruding from the surface. Thickly gauged wires extended from the ends of each spike, connecting to the base of a receptacle that housed the same glass tube displayed on the monitor. Identical to the image on the screen, a vibrant, dynamic light emanated from the container, casting shimmering patterns on the walls of the chamber.

Schmidt immediately grasped the tube, and after pulling it from its holder, he spun around to head back the way he had come. As he walked toward the rear of the room, he glanced at a poster on the wall with large letters emblazoned across the top: 'C.E.R.N.'

As Schmidt reemerged in the subterranean cavity, the same nefarious creature that had initially greeted him stood waiting, an almost worried expression on its face. Disgusted by the display of weakness, Schmidt shook his head, accompanied by an expression of antipathy that seethed from his visage. Walking directly over to the edge of the silver disk that lay on the stony floor, he paused before entering it and held his hand at his side with the palm facing down. With a twisting motion of his wrist, he turned his hand upward and raised it slightly.

In response to his command, a small section along the outer edge of the metal circle began to rise out of the floor. As it reached upward, it looked to be supported by a solid piece of steel, and upon reaching a height of four feet, the motion completely ceased. Etched on the surface of the steel pillar, the outline of a sun was depicted, with exaggerated beams of wavy light extending out from the perimeter. The symbol itself then began to twist and an opening appeared on the surface, allowing a small receptable to exit, exactly matching the one from which he had removed the glass tube just moments before.

After taking a deep breath, he then placed the end of the glass cylinder containing the undulating light into the opening and twisted it counterclockwise, locking it in place. Suddenly, all the runes on the perimeter of the disk burned a horribly deep crimson color, and the air directly above the metallic platform shimmered like heat from a fire. Next, a dark, thin, vertical line appeared, suspended directly over the center of the silver disk, which immediately split into two edges that raced outward from one another, revealing a gateway into the bottomless pits of hell.

The image that could be seen through the unholy aperture was truly harrowing. Dark, seething clouds of smoke crawled through the caustic atmosphere. The scorched sky was filled with horrific winged demons who looked to be searching for their next victim, with some of them already tightly clutching torn limbs and battered bodies. Barren, lifeless plains stretched out toward the horizon in all directions, with lakes of boiling fire sporadically placed across the landscape. Massive flames erupted from blistered rocks, along with smoke and searing heat from fissures in the earth. Abhorrent monstrosities painstakingly searched through the dying, dead, and decaying bodies littering the ground in an attempt to satiate their ravenous cravings. This truly was the most terrible, loathsome location known in existence.

Facing the horrific portal, Schmidt raised his right hand and drew the repulsive stench into his lungs.

"Creaturae noctis et dimittetur luminis, audi vocem meam,"[58] he intoned. "Serve voco te, regina magno mortis. Clientes Aosoth pariet!"[59]

Off in the distance, a shadowy entity materialized and started to make its way across the barren plains. As it drew closer to the portal, the figure appeared to be wearing a long gown, and stretching out from behind the being was a pair of enormous white wings, dragging on the ground. After a few moments, the fiendish creature was close enough to be clearly identifiable as female and, unlike many of the demons Schmidt had seen previously, this one had physical characteristics that one might perceive as beautiful. Short, tightly cropped black hair extended from her head, and she had a surprisingly delicate, alabaster face. Standing eight feet tall, she possessed a slender frame bordering on the

[58] Creatures of the night, forsaken of light, hear my voice.

[59] I call thee to serve, great queen of death. Bring forth your minions, Aosoth!

wrong side of anorexic, with exaggerated skeletal features protruding against her dress. As she walked onto the silver disk linking Earth's reality with the underworld, two jackal-like beasts sprinted forward, taking up position on either side of their master.

The imagery of a wretched landscape shimmered again, then completely vanished, leaving behind the evil mistress and her two snarling companions. After looking down at Schmidt, an insidious smile crawled across her face, erasing any semblance of beauty that might previously have been perceived. Standing fully upright, her hands positioned by her sides, she then fully extended her tremendous wings directly over her head to a height of twenty feet.

With a confident expression, Schmidt crooked a quizzical eyebrow and a vile smirk appeared on his face.

The towering succubus then retracted her wings, knelt down on one knee and bowed her head in deference to Schmidt. The next instant, she tilted her head upward, gazing at her master with fire burning forth from both eye sockets.

"My Lord," she seethed, "what is thy bidding?"

Schmidt simply looked at the heinous being with a grim smile.

"Aosoth, I have work for you to perform."

CHAPTER 15

Pilgrimage

(Three Days Later)

It was just after five o'clock and the Sun had just disappeared down through the eastern skyline over the sands of the Egyptian desert. Normally, the stratosphere would have been alive with vivid pinks and oranges, producing a magnificent amalgamation of pigments. Today, though, was largely dismal with a thick blanket of dreary clouds obscuring most of the sky.

In the midst of this sullen landscape, a colossal tanker was slowly gliding south through the Suez Canal to its ultimate destination in the Persian Gulf, where it would fill its bowels with rich crude oil. A gentle breeze blowing across the deck of the ship from the west brought a welcome gust of cool air to the three individuals standing on the port side of the bow as they stared out over the smooth dunes.

"It's hard to believe that earlier today we were just entering the canal at Port Said," Rich stated.

"Well, not really!" William complained. "We left from Haifa Port at four o'clock this morning which, if I remember correctly, meant we had to leave your house just after one-thirty am to make our departure time."

He paused for a moment, roughly rubbing his eyes with the palms of his hands, then turned to the third party of their group.

"Don't you think you could have reserved our transportation for a more *accommodating* time of day?"

"It was fortuitous to have secured anything at all," Menashe countered with a chuckle. "With all the refugees fleeing south from the anthrax contamination, we're lucky to have even found this one."

"Besides, Will," Rich chimed in, "you can't beat the sleeping arrangements!"

"I almost forgot," William groaned, "a ten-by twenty-windowless shoebox shared with thirty other evacuees."

"And that's why we're spending most of our time up on deck," the larger man smiled.

William shook his head in annoyance and glanced down at the water rushing past the side of the ship. Roughly twenty feet away, a broad, low-lying sandbar at least one thousand feet wide separated the southernly route through the aqueduct from the northernly passage. Letting out a deep sigh, he lazily hung both arms over the side rails of the transport, looking as if he would collapse if they weren't there to support his weight.

"Where exactly are we?" he whimpered.

Looking out across the starboard side of the ship, Menashe considered the buildings that were slowly sliding by as the ship progressed on its journey.

"Unless I'm wrong, that's the northern edge of the city of Ismailia, which would put us roughly one kilometer north of Timsah Lake. That's pretty much the halfway point through the canal, which would put us into the Gulf of Suez in around twelve hours."

"Shoot me now!" William griped.

"Come now," Menashe lightly chided, "this is an amazing journey with many unique landmarks to appreciate. For example, when we enter Timsah Lake, there is an amazing sculpture sitting close to the edge of the canal, known as the Egyptian Statue of Liberty. It should be coming into view fairly soon, if it isn't already."

Looking out from the bow of the ship, Menashe began to survey the shore of the sandy embankment the channel ran alongside. After a few moments, he motioned back to the other two men to join him by the railing.

"Right over there!" he affirmed, motioning in the direction of the breakwater off to the left. "You can just start to see the glow of lights reflecting off the statue.

"I *think* I can see it," Rich commented while straining his eyes. "But I can't be certain."

"It's right..." Menashe paused, seemingly distracted by something catching his eye in the distance.

"Right where?" Rich insisted.

Without averting his gaze, Menashe reached over and smacked William on the back.

"What was *that* for?"

"Over there," Menashe whispered, pointing toward the horizon.

"What? The ship?" William pressed.

"No! Up above the ship! Don't you see that dark haze in the sky drifting away from the it?"

"Yeah, I see it. What's the big deal?"

"It's moving against the wind!"

"Strange. What do you think it is?" William probed, furrowing his brow.

"I'm not sure," Menashe stated, "but it seems familiar to me somehow."

The three men watched the progress of the dingy fog, and as it started to make its way across the broad sandy shoal, William unconsciously reached up, laying his hand on his shirt directly over the talisman that hung around his neck. Suddenly, a bleak expression started to appear on his face, along with what could best be described as an air of recognition.

"Do you remember when we were touring the Temple Mount in Jerusalem?" William asked anxiously.

"Yes," replied Menashe. "That's when..."

He abruptly stopped speaking, and his expression shifted to one of stark realization.

"That's when what?!" Rich blurted out.

"That's when Menashe banished a vile, dark entity creeping beside us in the shadows," William stated.

"And I believe that this is that same entity!" Menashe confirmed.

Snapping his head back over to the side of the ship, Rich frantically searched the coastline to try and locate the shadowy vapor.

"Where is it?!" he fretted.

"Over there!" Menashe exclaimed, pointing at the sandbar.

As Rich and William both looked, they observed the black mist was now crawling and twisting over the surface of the sand, heading directly towards the stone figure, which now lay only a couple hundred yards in front of their vessel. Within a matter of seconds, the undulating murk reached the statue, at which point, it immediately started to ooze into the effigy itself. After a brief moment, the harrowing apparition had completely disappeared.

All three men stared expectantly at the sculpture as their transport slowly glided along the calm surface of the canal, until they were situated directly alongside the monument. From their vantage point on the deck, they towered at a height of one hundred and fifty feet above the ground, and despite the high elevation, they could easily make out specific details of the large statue.

The figure of a woman stood on top of a wide, blocky base, about four feet above the ground. She was clothed in long, draping robes that completely covered her feet, hanging onto the foundation. The sleeves of the stone garment completely concealed her arms, which were held above her head, with only the hands slightly extending out through the ends. A large, circular emblem was centered on her torso, just beneath her chest, and a simple hood adorned her almost featureless face, dangling back behind her neck and shoulders. The head of a serpent extended out from the center of her forehead, sitting atop the plain mantle in a pose that suggested it was ready to strike. Branching out from the sides of both arms, an enormous pair of wings arched upward, with the tips almost touching five feet over the top of her head. Situated directly behind the figure, a large obelisk rose to nearly the same height as her airfoils, and sitting at either side of her feet, two ancient, bearded sphinxes were crouched on the ground.

From the side of the ship, William stared intently into the face of this carved stone, arduously searching for some sign of the murky fog that had dissolved into its surface just moments earlier. And then, he witnessed a site that would have chilled any person's blood to ice.

Painstakingly, both wings of the female effigy began to slide downward, accompanied by a distinct creaking and crackling sound, as if one massive boulder was being ground across another. As the appendages extended downward, the feathers appeared to shift in their position, seemingly ruffled by the light breeze. Finally, the edges of the outermost plumes looked as if they paused for a moment above the heads of the two flanking Egyptian creatures, and then began to gently stroke them as one would scratch behind the ears of a dog. Seemingly in response, the heads of both Sphinxes lifted upward and began to nuzzle the feathered ends.

Shifting his gaze to regard the mostly featureless face, William's breath caught. In the very instant he stared into the lifeless eyes of the figure, both sockets erupted into flames, casting a palpable heat onto the surface of his skin. The next moment, a ruinous grin split the evil creature's maw, and an earsplitting shriek pierced the night sky. Ostensibly responding to the command of their master, both the kneeling fiends sprang up from their crouched positions, accompanied by the grating noise of crumbling concrete. A pair of wings extended from the backs of both Sphinxes, who then launched themselves into the air, snarling and snapping as they climbed up into the sky.

As they soared past William and his companions, the stone crumbled off their bodies, revealing two dark, sinewy hellions with tough, leathery skin. Their forms resembled those of wolflike, wild dogs that roamed the plains of Africa, scavenging for meat. Their hind legs were like lions', but their forward limbs looked as if they belonged to men. Powerful hands were situated at the ends of both front legs, culminating in four-inch jagged black nails. Short, matted hair covered almost the entire body of each beast, except for a broad, almost man-like chest, which was situated in between two hulking shoulders. On each identical creature, an elongated neck protruded from the upper torso, supporting a narrow, jackal like face with wolf-like ears, and an elongated snout housing razor sharp teeth.

As the three men stared in amazement at the two flying monsters, who had begun to circle above the oil tanker at a height of roughly fifty feet, they could hear shouts of alarm and screams coming from a few passengers as they frantically scrambled to make it below deck.

"We're not the only ones who can see them!" William shouted. "This hasn't ever happened before!"

The next moment, another hideous, high-pitched scream was projected from the sandy shore, and all three men peered over the side to locate the source. Gazing down, they immediately perceived a frightening entity standing atop the concrete platform where the statue was located.

With her head angled sharply upward, she stared defiantly at what she likely perceived to be her prey. The mantle which had previously covered her head, was now lying across the back of her neck, revealing short, tightly cropped black hair that protruded from her skull in virtually every possible direction. Her face was pale, and despite her hideous sneer, William and Rich observed the potential for beauty. Magnificent white wings were connected along the back edge of her lengthy arms, flowing elegantly downward, with the tips barely touching the surface of the ground. She was a sight to behold, and upon first glance, one could have easily mistaken her to be a winged guardian.

"We need to get out of here!" William barked.

"But to where?!" Rich thundered.

"Let's go beneath! At least we'll be able to hide."

As the three men turned, readying themselves to run back across the length of the deck, a massive hand firmly gripped Rich's shoulder from behind, causing him to literally squawk in response. They all turned in unison to see who, or what, was clutching him. What they saw could only be described as glorious.

Standing on the deck before them was a magnificent man, at least seven feet tall, with an exquisitely dark complexion and naturally short, closely cropped hair. He wore a maroon Arabian-style robe, which extended down to the tops of his thighs. The front of his attire displayed a beautiful, symmetric gold pattern across his powerful chest, with a similar arrangement embroidered down the outside of the full-length sleeves that covered his brawny forearms. His enormous biceps lay beneath the fabric of his clothes, appearing as if they would split the material in two with little effort. A thick, black leather belt was wrapped around his waist, supporting a gargantuan broadsword that lay sheathed, with its end extending down four feet, almost touching the ground, as well as a golden horn with a long neck. His legs were covered by a pair of very plain, almost pure white, baggy trousers, and he wore a pair of equally drab brown sandals on his feet. William immediately realized that he had seen this individual at least twice before. The first time, during their escape from the hospital, he had protected them from a murderous security guard, and the second time, he had appeared during the battle at the Cenetics laboratory. Besides the fact that he wasn't wearing the brilliant protective armor that had clad him previously, there was one very obvious feature that was completely lacking – his wings. As the behemoth stared at the three men, a grim look crossed his face, which strangely brought a sense of reassurance.

"We should seek safety, gentlemen," he casually commented in a deep, baritone voice.

Without waiting for them to respond, he turned away from the group and started making his way over to the opposite side of the ship.

"But what about those flying beasts?" William blurted out. "And that, that..." he struggled to find the right words, "...abominable *woman?*"

Turning back with a sidelong glance, the stern smile he had flashed previously, shifted into an ominous, shockingly gruesome smirk.

"Seraphina will take care of them," he vowed in a dangerous tone.

Both William and Rich immediately followed the colossal man to the other side of the ship, leaving Menashe standing next to the railing, staring at the heinous winged succubus that still stood on the platform below. Locking eyes with the trembling man, a gruesome sneer split the malignant spirit's face, transforming her from a thing of beauty to one that reflected vile ugliness. The next instant, she raised one of her arms up into the air, extending her clawed fingers toward the circling beasts.

"*Devour him!*" Aosoth howled.

A moment later, both the jackal-like fiends circling the ship simultaneously dove toward their prey, their curved talons extended. But having plunged roughly half the distance to their objective, a blinding light erupted from behind Menashe, followed almost immediately by a high-pitched whizzing sound ripping through the air above his head. Glancing upward, he caught a glimpse of an almost glowing trail of blinding white light angling upward at one of the creatures. The next second, a screech of horrific pain burst out of the lungs of one of the winged hellions. Casting his eyes toward the source, he could clearly see a large, silver arrow penetrating through its chest, with a two-foot length of the shaft protruding out the other side, ending in a ghastly barbed head. The demon immediately burst into flames and disintegrated into thin air. The next moment, another shrill noise tore through the sky above him, immediately followed by a deathly howl as the second brute withered and disappeared. The female entity on the shore screamed in fury, and the air immediately around her person shimmered from the sheer intensity of her cry.

"Seraphina! I will end you!"

Menashe turned around quickly and was astounded by the spectacle he witnessed.

Poised in the air, roughly twenty feet above the deck of the ship, hovered an angelic winged warrior, emanating authority and determination. While it was impossible to estimate accurately, she had to be at least ten feet tall, with a pair of extraordinary, reddish-orange wings reaching out to either side of her person at least twelve feet in either direction. Vibrant, fiery-red hair flowed back five to six inches from her head, and a deep emerald-green elven tiara adorned her forehead. Her arms and torso were shielded by malachite armor resembling the vine-like foliage that covered the walls of ancient castles. Similarly, her upper legs were enclosed by protective coverings of the same material, as well as ornately designed boots extending from her toes to just beneath the knees. Slung across her back was a quiver of silver arrows, and she held a glorious golden bow with a shimmering bowstring.

Looking down at the vile succubus, a side-long smirk appeared on the face of the ethereal being.

"Aosoth," she flatly relayed, "you will try."

Instantly, the vile she-devil ascended into the air to the same level as her enemy, positioning herself roughly fifty feet away. While hovering in the sky, the creature brought both of her hands together in front of her abdomen to make a sphere, from which flames immediately spewed and began to swirl. In rapid succession, Aosoth then launched two fiery orbs directly at Seraphina, who simply brushed aside both strikes with the back of her hand.

Locking eyes with her adversary, Aosoth threw her head back roaring in anger. Then, with two powerful thrashings of her airfoils, she thrust herself upward an additional thirty feet and glared down menacingly at Seraphina. Both her wings then spread outward, and flames began to seethe out from her chest, building into an immense roiling ball of fire, easily five feet across. The next instant, a high-pitched shriek pierced the atmosphere, and the succubus launched the meteoric strike down upon her opponent.

Slinging her bow across her back, Seraphina readied herself for the fiery onslaught. As the flaming projectile reached her position, she caught the roiling ball and nonchalantly cradled it in her arms.

"How cute," she taunted.

Then, without further hesitation, she compressed the fireball between her hands, condensing it into a flaming sphere no more than six inches in diameter, and the energy emanating from the orb intensified into a vibrant, blinding blue light. She then casually shifted the burning ball into one hand and glanced upward at Aosoth.

"Your turn!"

With a thrust of her hand, she hurled the gleaming projectile at her foe with tremendous speed. Without any time to react, the powerful attack slammed into Aosoth, exploding in a blinding flash of light, shattering her form into thousands of shards of obsidian glass. The amount of energy released from the explosion was so immense that Menashe was thrown backwards, sliding across the deck almost ten feet. Still prostrated across the flooring, he looked back up to Seraphina, who gave him a knowing nod and a welcoming smile. Then, with a shimmer, she completely disappeared.

After getting back to his feet, Menashe sprinted to the other side of the boat to join his companions. Rich and

William were standing next to the herculean man, who was casually leaning up against the side railing with an amused expression on his face.

"What do you find so funny?" Menashe almost accused.

"Seraphina nearly ignited the whole ship!" he chortled. "I'll have to ask her to be a little more careful next time."

"Who are you?" Menashe pressed.

"My name is Gabriel."

CHAPTER 16

Instruction

The expression on William's face reflected awe and respect for the glorious man as he leant on the side railing of their transport. It now seemed evident to him that this being had played a part in saving his life at least *three* times now. But before he even had a chance to open his mouth to thank him, his father-in-law jumped in.

"Gabriel?!" he exclaimed. "You don't mean *the* Gabriel? As in the left hand of God? As in the messenger of God? As in..."

"As in he who will hold aloft his trumpet and pierce the earth with a triumphant blare, announcing to the world that the Day of Judgement has come," he threw out indifferently. "Yes, I guess that would be me."

As Rich stood staring at the gargantuan man with his mouth fully agape, William seized on the moment to speak.

"Thank you," he genuinely expressed. "I owe you a great debt, not just for saving our lives, but for saving me from that creature in the garage. And then at Cenetics, when..." his voice froze as his heart reminded him how much he missed his wife.

An expression of deep sorrow appeared on the face of the colossal being. He then walked over to William and, while placing his hand on his shoulder, he leveled his gaze to look directly into his eyes.

"I'm truly sorry," he expressed sympathetically. "I wish I could have saved her."

With tears welling up in his eyes, William reached up and grasped the enormous hand cradling his shoulder. He didn't say a word, but simply gave him an appreciative nod.

Menashe, who had been silently watching the interaction, glanced down at the enormous broadsword that hung at Gabriel's waist. Then, his eyes caught a glint of a golden object lying just behind the hilt and his breath caught.

"Is that…" his voice trailed off, unable to finish his sentence.

"It certainly is," Gabriel cheerfully announced. "Would you like to hear me play a tune?" he proposed as he lifted the instrument toward his lips.

"No!" Menashe literally shouted. "Wouldn't that…"

"…Bring an end to the world? I guess it would. Maybe I should hold off on that for a bit," he jested.

"Oh, I think I'm going to like this guy," Rich chortled.

Walking back to the railing, Gabriel turned to face the three men, once again propping himself up against it in an unpretentious manner. As he stared at them, a broad grin arose on his face.

"I guess you probably have a lot of questions," he stated. "Go ahead, fire away."

Perplexed by his ordinary mannerisms and language, William found himself staring at the sizable man, and suddenly became aware that he was staring right back at him.

"Why don't we start with you, William?" he suggested.

William's cheeks reddened in response, but he was able to quickly regain his composure.

"Why are you here?" he began.

"Ah, a great question to start. Do you not remember your vision, in which Ariel visited you after she had ascended? Do you not recall the words she spoke to you?"

"She said that things were going to get worse," he recalled despondently.

"True," Gabriel agreed, "but she also spoke of hope, and of a peace that would last for one thousand years. And she spoke of work you needed to complete. A task that you, and only you, would be able to accomplish. I am here to help facilitate that."

While squeezing his lips tightly together, William rapidly inhaled through his nostrils, holding his breath momentarily, before noisily blasting the air back out with a frustrated expression on his face.

"Alright then," he declared, "what exactly can *I* do that is going to benefit humankind?" What can *I* possibly do in the face of demons and destruction, pestilence and death, that will have any impact on anything?!"

Gabriel contemplated the question as he gazed peacefully into William's eyes, until a knowing smile appeared on his lips.

"My dear man," he gently reproved, "have a little faith. You may not believe you can do anything of significance, but the reality is quite to the contrary. Your role was established before the beginning of the world, and the fate of all humanity lies in your hands."

Lowering his head, William's shoulders slumped in a disheartened manner.

Sensing the mood needed to be lightened, Rich walked over to his son-in-law and wrapped his burly arm around his shoulders, squeezing him tightly.

"Don't worry, son. I'll be with you every step of the way."

"As will I," Menashe chimed in.

Looking at both his companions, William forced an appreciative smile, then turned back to Gabriel with an inquisitive expression on his face.

"You sacrificed your divinity in the same way that Ariel gave up hers, in order to join us, didn't you?"

"Yes," the hulking man calmly replied.

"Why?"

"I don't think I made a sacrifice. Rather, I believe I have seized an opportunity. You see, angels are beings of pure intellect, without physical form."

"Wait a second," Rich interjected, "during the battle at the Cenetics facility, those legions of angels seemed real enough to me."

"Well, that's because they were…at least for a short period of time. You see, angels, and demons for that matter, do not exist in your reality. We live in what I guess could be described as a *different* actuality."

"Life a different dimension?" William probed.

"Yes, I believe that's a fair description. Let me try to explain. There are a total of ten different *dimensions* as you call them, coexisting separately and simultaneously. They are among and around us, much in the same way that we are among and around them. However, things endure in them in different states. The first dimension, which has no beginning and no end, is the realm of God. It is here where God created all things."

"Like our world," Rich threw in.

"Exactly. But this world, and your existence, do not reside in a single dimension. There are a total of four different dimensions intertwined with one another, all of which constitute your reality."

"I don't understand," Rich admitted.

"Space is comprised of length, width and height, right?" Each of these are a unique and separate dimension, and it is the combination of these three which create what you perceive as your reality. Individually, they are very impressive…but combined, they comprise what you refer to as the expansive and endless universe. And, in fact, there is no end to it."

"Ok, so what's the fourth dimension then?" Rich pressed.

"Time!" Menashe called out.

"Exactly," Gabriel agreed. "Without time, your reality of three-dimensional space would have no meaning. Time gives you a sense of direction, and the ability to experience your reality in a way that allows you to learn and grow from experiences."

"Ok, I don't totally follow you," Rich reluctantly admitted, but let's pretend I do. That describes five of the ten dimensions. What are the other five?"

"The next three actualities," Gabriel professed, "are places that exist for all humankind to dwell once they depart from this world into the next."

"You're talking about the verse from first Corinthians, right?" Rich asserted. "If I remember correctly, it states, 'There is one glory of the Sun, and another glory of the Moon, and another glory of the stars: for one star differeth from another star in glory.'"

"You are correct. These realms, or dimensions, are in fact the place where all humanity will ascend after mortality. Depending on the sincerity of their hope and effort, each individual accepts how and where they will spend immortality."

"Alright, this is making a little bit more sense," Rich enthusiastically stated. "That covers eight of the ten. What about the other two?"

"The ninth and tenth dimensions are closely related. The first is the dimension of hell. This is the location that was prepared for the Hosts of Heaven that rebelled against God's plan."

"You're talking about where the Devil and his followers were cast after the Great War in Heaven, right?" William asked.

"Now you're catching on!" Gabriel enthusiastically commented. "Of course, I'm not surprised. You were there."

William visibly shuddered as he was reminded of the vision he had had over three years before, and how he himself had somehow been one of those fighting on the side of good during that war.

"Believe it or not," Gabriel continued, "hell is all around us. It exists outside of space and time. If you were able to peer through the barrier separating these realities, you would see endless lakes of unquenchable fire roiling up to the surface, with countless miserable creatures enduring never-ending torment."

Shifting his head upward, William immediately felt as if a puzzle piece had snapped into place in his mind.

"So, when demons come into our world to attack us, they are able to break through the barrier you were just talking about, right?"

"That's correct. But, as you can probably imagine, it is not an easy thing to do. It takes a tremendous amount of energy to breach the boundary separating the dimensions. Under normal circumstances, nothing physical is able to pass through."

"So, if it's so hard," Menashe interjected, "why do they do it?"

"Hatred," Gabriel flatly replied.

"But why do they despise us so much?"

"Because you have something they don't…a physical body. Before coming to Earth, every individual in existence was fairly similar to angels - you were pure intelligence. You had personality, you made decisions, and you learned. But your ability to learn was limited by the fact that you didn't have a physical body. There was no way for you to experience things directly; rather, you had to conceptualize them. It is the combination of space and time that enables you to learn and progress to something you can't even fathom."

"And the only way for us to exist in space and time is by having a physical body," William postulated.

"Exactly. Lucifer and his followers were cast out during the War in Heaven, and never received physical bodies. This is why they abhor you, and why they are trying to destroy all of humankind. The fact you have a body gives you power over them, and in their disembodied forms, the amount of strength they have is limited."

A thought suddenly occurred to William.

"When the demons possessed their cloned bodies, didn't that essentially give them tangible bodies?"

Gabriel raised an eyebrow, but otherwise, didn't acknowledge the question. Rather, he seemed to be almost analyzing William for a few moments. When he finally did respond, he was full of caution.

"That is correct," he said.

"Then, if occupying the clones allowed them to have a physical body, wouldn't that also make them more powerful?"

An expression of understanding swept over Rich's countenance as he immediately connected the logical path William was detailing, to what they had experienced over the past few years.

"They are making an army," Rich asserted matter-of-factly. "But not just any army; a battalion is being forged to win the Final Battle. They are getting ready for Armageddon!"

William's eyes immediately darted to those of Gabriel to confirm what he already knew was true, and with a slight nod, their new companion endorsed his father-in-law's hypothesis.

"Ok, so what you're telling me is that I still have some role to play in all of this. But I don't just have to deal with the *weak* demons who can destroy me without barely beating an eyelash. No, now I have to worry about even more powerful hellions who are preparing to destroy the world and all of humankind."

"That about sums it up," Gabriel agreed in almost a jovial tone of voice.

Luckily, William was able to see the humor in the situation, and he broke out in a light chuckle.

"Well, I guess I might have guessed it. So, exactly what role am I supposed to play in this horrific drama? How will I influence the outcome of this impending war?"

"Unfortunately, even I don't know what's going to happen, or exactly how you will factor into events. But what I do know is that the fate of all humanity is teetering on the edge of annihilation, and without you, there is a chance the adversary will be successful in his final onslaught. The path before you will reveal itself, as will the task that you, and only you, can complete."

"Figures," complained William with a weary smile.

Rich once again wrapped his thick arm around the man as a show of support.

"Don't worry. We're with you to the very end," he promised.

William shot him an appreciative smile, then returned his attention back to Gabriel.

"Alright, so that's nine of the ten dimensions. What's the tenth?"

"A place of solitude and misery. It is a realm of existence reserved for those who have known the truth and made a conscious decision to fight against it. While it is similar to hell, it is a little different. Hell is the holding place for those that initially rebelled, where Outer Darkness, as this reality is known, will be the final dwelling place for all who knowingly defy God and seek to overthrow Him. Hell will cease to exist, and this will become their everlasting reality. There will be no reprieve, and hope for anyone in this actuality will be lost forever."

"Good to know," William joked. "Let's avoid the tenth dimension at all costs then, yes?"

"Well," Gabriel nodded, looking off to the west, "we'd better go and try to get some sleep. We've got a long journey ahead of us, but we can't head out until we stop at Mecca."

"How did you know we're heading to Mecca?" Menashe asked incredulously.

"Why…that's where your friend Widad lives, isn't it? She has a part to play in this story as well."

CHAPTER 17

Retribution

(Later That Evening)

The faint light flickering from torches mounted on the perimeter walls did very little to illuminate the massive subterranean chamber located deep beneath the Cenetics facility. The chandelier hanging above the enormous stone table remained dark, allowing for long, eerie shadows to dance across the rocky surface, adding to the gloomy mood permeating the room. An oversized concrete throne was positioned just off to the side of the table, occupied by a man with an indignant expression on his face. With an audible huff, he pushed himself up and walked a few steps over to a charred carcass that lay prostrate across the surface of the ground.

"Your apology is accepted, Sephtis. I'm certain it will never happen again."

Turning on his heels, Schmidt began to walk toward the far side of the chamber, when he suddenly froze. Standing motionless, he silently reconsidered his course of action, and as he did, the look on his face slowly shifted from embittered outrage to one that reflected extreme apprehension. Pursing his lips together, he exhaled once more through his nostrils, spun around, and made his way back the chair he had just vacated. After pausing for a brief moment, he retook his seat and gazed over to the ancient mirror that stood on the surface of the table with an expression of trepidation. Reaching forward, he grasped the archaic blade, and without hesitating, he roughly sliced open the palm of his hand and began the vile incantation.

"Audi vocem meam..."[60]

A bright flame accompanied by a burst of heat radiated from the reflective surface, causing Schmidt to abruptly cut off his enchantment. Peering at the glass, he observed multiple conflagrations shimmering across the very surface, rather than appearing as if they were only viewable through the portal the mirror provided. The next instant, burning embers appeared to float into the air above the stone table, along with tendrils of black smoke. As Schmidt continued to stare at the mirrored surface, he realized that the images were no longer contained within the aperture. Rather, they were expanding outward from the opening, consuming the very chamber he was occupying. Looking around the room, he saw that the confining limitations of exterior walls and a ceiling were completely gone, replaced by an expansive, desolate landscape covered by deep fissures and boiling pools of lava. Massive rock formations protruded upward to a staggering height, along with great billowing clouds of vile gas spewing from the ground. Craggy formations protruded at abnormal angles from all surfaces, and a deep reddish-black hue bathed the entire area with a sickening stain. Schmidt began to frantically search the landscape for something recognizable that would let him know where he was...and then, he found it.

Positioned on a raised bluff roughly one hundred yards away, a colossal throne of obsidian glass sat vacant. The base of the chair was positioned a good fifteen feet above the ground, and enormous arm rests ending in gnarled fists flanked the broad seat's sides. An immense, blocky backing extended forty feet into the air, topped by twisted black horns curving upward along the topmost edge. It

[60] Hear my voice...

immediately became clear to the trembling man that he had somehow been transported not only into the very depths of hell, but was in fact standing directly within the abominable throne room of the Prince of Darkness.

Schmidt began to clumsily stumble backward, as if distancing himself from the evil seat of authority would somehow protect him from the reckoning that would soon befall him. The next moment, the discordant sound of steel cutting through solid stone pierced the air, stopping him in his tracks, and as he peered off to the right side of the massive chair, he spotted the source of the noise.

Slowly marching around a stony cliff rising out of the ground, the Father of All Lies came into view. He was truly immense, looming over the desolate landscape by at least a hundred feet. Gnarled, skeletal feet resembling those of a vicious dinosaur supported his enormous frame, ending in five-foot-long jagged nails. Thick, sinewy tendons reached up and around two bony ankles, continuing the full length of heavily muscled calves that bent awkwardly backward, before wrapping behind angular knees. Thick, powerful thighs rippled rhythmically, and each stride left broken rocks and debris in their wake. A broad, sharp pelvic bone protruded grossly outward from both sides as if it might split through the repulsive black, leathery skin covering this creature at any moment. Heavily defined abdominal muscles heaved in and out with each breath, along with mammoth pectorals, framed between equally imposing shoulders. Thick, tubular veins crisscrossed the entirety of the upper torso, extending out and across impressive biceps, and down into substantially muscled forearms. A broad, disgusting neck revealed thick, nodular tendons reaching up to a dreadful, monstrous head. Black, sickening bile-like liquid freely oozed from the corners of Its lipless maw, which seemed frozen in a horrific sneer, revealing dozens of razor-sharp fangs. Two slits sat squarely on the middle of Its face, and deep-sunken eye sockets belched forth liquid fire capable of consuming the soul. Two pairs of massive, gnarled horns curled back from the jawline and temple on either side of Its head, ending in razor sharp points, and a pair of colossal, leathery wings with black hooks at the ends were pulled in closely to Its back, with the tips dragging across the rocky earth as It walked.

Shifting his eyes to the side of this creature, the source of the ear-splitting sound was revealed. Gripped tightly in Its herculean fist was the hilt of a ghastly weapon at least fifty feet in length. The jagged blade was so heavy that it dragged straight through the ground, with the tip of the sword piercing the rocky surface at least three feet down into stone. All Schmidt could do was watch in awe.

Satan did not acknowledge, or even so much as glance at, the quivering man standing less than sixty feet from His throne. Rather, He simply made his way over to His evil seat, and roughly sat down. Calmly, He started to look out across His dominion, taking in the various features, until finally, his gaze rested squarely on the shaking frame of His servant. His eyes immediately erupted into a violent inferno, and He drove the tip of His sword ten feet down through solid rock.

"You!" His voice exploded, reverberating across the landscape.

Schmidt immediately scampered his away across the uneven surface until he fell upon his knees ten feet in front of Lucifer's throne, bowing his head in absolute deference.

"My Master," he whimpered.

"You have failed me for the last time! Do you not realize you are insignificant without me?"

"Forgive me, Master!" he cried as he abased himself. "I should have counseled with you before taking action."

"Moving against the enemy too early has reinforced in his mind the significance of his role. Do you not realize that he is the key?"

"I am truly sorry. It will never happen again."

"Yes, I know."

Pausing for a moment to seemingly consider his plea, the Great Deceiver refocused his attention at the cowering man before him.

"You are forgiven," he hissed. *"Isn't that what you said to Sephtis, just after obliterating him for your failing?"*

Absolute terror swept across the face of Schmidt, as the realization sunk in that his end was near.

"No, Master! Please! I beg you!"

Ignoring the trembling man's petition, the Devil pulled his sword clear from the rocky surface, and it immediately burst into flames as he held it menacingly over His head, ready to obliterate Schmidt from existence. But instead of casting the deathly blow, Beelzebub's visage seemed to slight shift, and he gradually lowered the flaming weapon to one side.

"I may still have a use for you," he contemptuously spat. Realizing that he wasn't going to be destroyed, Schmidt clasped his hands together, and began to bow repeatedly before his ruler.

"Thank you, Master! Thank you! I promise I will never disobey you again!"

"I know you won't," He seethed in a menacing manner. *"But let me leave you with a reminder of what will happen to you if you ever falter again."*

Releasing his hand from the hilt of his sword, the Adversary reached toward the still kneeling man, extending his thumb from his fist, and placed it squarely on the left side of his face. Immediately, Schmidt shrieked in outright agony as intense heat and flames dissolved his flesh, turning half his face into a deformed disfiguration of liquefied skin and bone.

Finally relenting, the Beast released the howling man, who fell convulsing onto the ground, and a hideous grin appeared on His lipless maw.

"Never put yourself above me again. Never think for yourself. You only exist to serve me."

Fighting to control the pain, Schmidt regained enough composure to get back upon his knees, and with his one remaining eye, he gazed up at his Lord and Master with a grotesque, misshapen smile that would haunt any living soul with eternal nightmares.

CHAPTER 18

Ally

(Two Days Later)

At seven o'clock in the morning, the Jeddah Islamic Seaport would typically be bustling with a well-coordinated ballet of workers, ships, cargo, and equipment, all focused on moving goods in and out of the harbor in a complex, but well-organized choreography. Recent events, however, had created an almost chaotic environment in which ships, normally laden with only goods, were now being transformed into carriers of refugees seeking shelter from poisonous clouds of anthrax. Hundreds of thousands of evacuees had already made their way south through the Suez Canal seeking protection, and no end was in sight for the seemingly endless flood of humanity.

Standing behind half a dozen other passengers, William and his companions anxiously waited to disembark the tanker. At the end of the short gangway, two customs agents stood at a podium, talking with individuals, and checking paperwork before allowing them to freely enter Saudi Arabia. William, who would be the first to approach the checkpoint, turned around with an anxious expression on his face.

"Do you think they're requiring proof of vaccination to enter the country?" he whispered in a cautious tone. "If so, our journey is going to be over before we even start."

Standing directly behind him, Gabriel reached forward and rested his gargantuan hand reassuringly on William's shoulder.

"Why don't you let me speak with them first?" he offered ominously.

Without a word, William stepped to one side and ushered the herculean man forward with a grand flourishing of his arms. Roughly sixty seconds later, one of the officers motioned to Gabriel to approach his workstation and present his credentials. The guard's eyes nearly bulged out of his head as the immense man stepped down the ramp and approached the stand. The next moment, Gabriel was easily standing a full eighteen inches above the smaller man, looking down at him with a grim expression.

"Ah…'awraq min fadlika,"[61] he stammered.

"Excuse me, I don't speak Arabic," Gabriel admitted.

"Oh, sorry," the guard apologized. "May I see your papers please?"

Narrowing his eyes, the towering man stared at the significantly shorter man, who gulped in response.

"You see, my companions and I had to leave rather abruptly, and we neglected to bring them," he recounted while motioning for his three friends to join him.

"I…well…you need to show proof that you've been vaccinated in order to enter Saudi Arabia. We can't make any exceptions."

After tightly clenching his teeth, causing his jaw bones to protrude half an inch on either side of his broad head, Gabriel leaned toward to the border agent, who was visibly shaken by his imposing presence.

"Don't you think you can just take our word for it?" he whispered.

Clearly understanding the gravity of the situation, the guard took a half step backward, uncontrollably swallowing for a second time.

"Umm…yes. I see," he confirmed. "Let me get your paperwork in order and you can be on your way."

[61] Ah…papers please.

Fumbling awkwardly, the customs agent retrieved four pieces of scrap paper from the counter, randomly imprinted them with authorization stamps, and handed the sheets to the hulking man.

"Everything looks to be in order," he squawked. "Welcome to Saudi Arabia."

Looking back at his companions, Gabriel flashed a sly grin, then proceeded to walk through customs without so much as a glance at the trembling officer. William, Rich, and Menashe immediately fell in behind the colossal man and started making their way further into the docks.

"That was amazing!" Rich exulted.

"I have my moments," Gabriel grinned.

"Well, we got into the country, but how are we going to get into the Great Mosque, let alone find Widad?" William doubted.

"Remember what I said about having a little faith?" their massive companion cheerfully reminded them. "Besides, *we're* not going to go find Widad…*I* am."

"What do you mean?" William argued. "We're in this together."

"We definitely are. But there's no way *you*," he continued while motioned to them collectively, "are going to pass for Muslims. I, on the other hand, shouldn't have a problem."

"He's got a point," Rich agreed.

"And besides… 'ana 'atahadath alearabiat bitalaqa."[62]

A broad smile appeared on William's face, as all three of the men nodded their heads.

"It sounds like we're in agreement then. What's the plan?"

"After we travel to Mecca, the three of you can rest at a hotel close by, and I'll make my way into the Great Mosque

[62] I happen to speak fluent Arabic.

to locate Widad. Once I've found her, I'll *convince* her that she needs to come and speak with you, but she'll have to venture outside the sacred edifices."

"Convince?" William hesitated. "What exactly do you mean by that?"

"Don't worry," Gabriel chuckled. "I can be quite persuasive, even without the threat of deadly force."

Roughly two hours later, Gabriel found himself walking down a broad hallway inside the Holy Mosque, where several Muslim practitioners were having hushed conversations with one another. Beautiful marble and tile adorned the towering corridor, decorated with artistic borders along the floor and up just over half the distance to the lofty ceiling overhead. Smooth, alabaster stone covered the full length of the hall with a dark, ornamental pattern bound along the edges. Coming to the end of the wide passage, the flooring changed from stone to smaller tiles, which began to gently slope upwards, opening into an enormous circular room. Three massive pillars were situated in the center, supporting a large circular aperture that revealed the balconies of additional floors above the first level. Certain of the direction he needed to go, Gabriel purposely traversed the annular chamber and exited through ornate glass, double doors leading to a colossal atrium.

The open-air courtyard was truly a sight to behold. The shape of the area was mostly round, with dimensions from one side to the other varying from four hundred fifty to five hundred feet across. Thousands of faithful Muslims surrounding the Kaaba walked in a counterclockwise direction, ensuring to keep it on their left side. The colossal man stood for a moment, watching worshippers advancing around the monument before he, too, joined in the manifestation of faith by beginning his first of seven revolutions.

As Gabriel commenced in his circumambulation, or *Tawaf*, of the Kaaba, he clearly stood out amongst all the faithful Muslims, standing over sixteen inches taller than the average Arabian man. The tradition dictated that the men would walk at a brisk pace for the first three rotations, then at a normal speed for the final four circuits. Given Gabriel's lengthy stride, though, it took just over six minutes for the man to complete three rotations, and as he began his fourth, a dark-skinned woman, nearly two feet shorter than him, silently fell in next to him.

"tasa'alt mataa satandamu 'iilay,"[63] the behemoth gently spoke without turning his head. "kayf ealimt anani huna?"[64]

"'ant la tandamij bialdabt,"[65] she whispered in reply. "daena natahadath fi alshurfa."[66]

Nodding his head in reply, the large man walked slightly ahead of her as he continued to circle the Kaaba.

Roughly thirty minutes later, he found himself on the second level of the building overlooking the courtyard, where thousands of pilgrims continued to walk counterclockwise around the shrine. As he stood at the railing, he heard the quiet footsteps of someone coming up from behind him.

[63] I was wondering when you would join me.

[64] How did you know I was here?

[65] You don't exactly blend in.

[66] Let's speak on the balcony.

"You are *Jibreel,* are you not?" the woman asked in English. "I mean, Gabriel?"

Turning around, the enormous man gazed down on her with a broad grin on his face. Standing at five feet, two inches tall, Widad would have been considered normal height for a Saudi Arabian woman. She wore a long, brown *abaya* that extended down to just above a pair of black sandals covering her feet, with a light tan pattern embroidered down the full length of her robe and adorning the edges of each sleeve. Her head was covered with a similar beige burka that wrapped around her neck and settled loosely around her shoulders. Her face was smooth, and a serene expression exuded from her eyes, along with wisdom and maturity.

"You are very perceptive, Widad. How did you know?"

"Oh please," she jested with a light huff of her breath. "You know the second pillar of our faith is belief in angels. And of *all* the guardians serving the One God, you are one of the easiest to recognize."

A deep chuckle rumbled inside Gabriel's chest.

"I guess you're right."

"So, why have you come?" she pressed with almost a stern expression.

"Cut right to the chase? Alright then, I guess I'll get right to it. I need you to accompany me to a hotel close by to meet my friends."

"Why didn't you simply bring them here to speak with me?" she challenged.

"I think you know the answer to that."

Furrowing her brow, Widad turned away from the man and gazed out across the expansive area.

"And why would I want to go and meet with these infi..." she caught herself short before continuing, "with these *non-believers*?"

The smile on Gabriel's face broadened even further as he audibly exhaled through his nostrils.

"You know I wouldn't be here if *He* had not asked me to do so. I am here on *His* command, and it is urgent that you come with me, now. The destiny of all humankind hangs in the balance."

Turning to her left, Widad looked back up into the eyes of the extraordinary man, an abashed look on her face. She then shifted her gaze down to the small golden horn hanging from the man's leather belt, and her eyes widened. The next moment, her countenance shifted to one of serious determination.

"Of course," she agreed. "Take me to them at once."

Having reached the apex of its path, the sun was just starting the second half of its journey down to the horizon in the West. While the streets in this part of the city were nearly devoid of traffic, scores of people were dashing here and there on foot, going about their business in the middle of the day. Small carts lined the sidewalk adjacent to a small, two-story hotel, with long lines of patrons talking animatedly with one another while they waited to order food.

It had been almost two hours since Widad and Gabriel had left the Kaaba, and as they made their way in between all of the people, dozens of locals turned and gawked at the towering man.

"It's just right over there," Gabriel advised, pointing at the entrance to the inn.

"This should be interesting," Widad grumbled.

"Come now," he lightly chided her. "Let's have a positive attitude."

"I agreed to come and listen to them. I didn't say I was going to be cheerful about it."

The large man chuckled in response as he escorted Widad into the open-air lobby of the establishment. Sitting on a maroon couch against the far wall of the foyer, William, Rich, and Menashe were engaged in a conversation, which abruptly stopped when they were approached.

"Menashe!" Widad exclaimed. "Gabriel didn't tell me it was *you* that wanted to meet."

"Asalam alikom,"[67] Menashe replied.

"And upon you, my friend."

Stopping short of the furniture, Widad glanced over at William and Rich, who sat expectantly on the edges of their cushions. Then, she glanced back at Menashe.

"Well, you should probably introduce me to your companions," she instructed.

"Umm…yes," Menashe stammered. "This is William Mears and Rich Cline. William is…"

"I know who *this* is," Widad nearly spat. "This is the man that created an abomination in the sight of Allah. He created a perversion of nature!"

"Widad, please!" Menashe implored. "You know me, and you trust me. Please, give him a chance. When I first met William, I had the same reaction. But then I had, well…an experience that truly opened my eyes. And I met someone who changed my life forever. You see, I met a woman…well, not exactly a woman, she was…well…"

[67] Peace be upon you.

"He met Ariel," Gabriel relayed matter-of-factly, "the Archangel who assisted the One God in the creation of the universe."

The expression on Widad's face reflected absolute wonderment as she began to connect the dots between Gabriel's appearance and the reference to the creation of the cosmos. Turning to face the angel, she asked the only question which made sense.

"Is the end near?"

"It is," he replied. "And that is why it is critical you listen to these gentlemen. They need your insight and, frankly, your help."

As she turned to face William, her countenance now reflected curiosity rather than disgust.

"Well?" she encouraged as she took a seat. "Get on with it."

After taking a deep breath, William began recounting to Widad everything that had transpired since the beginning of his research up until their present situation.

As he detailed everything, a quizzical expression arose on her face, as she seemed perplexed. When he had finished, she walked over to him and stared silently into his eyes for almost thirty seconds, as if she was trying to read his mind. With a slight pursing of her lips, she nodded her head as if she had been able to solidify the question nagging at her brain.

"Why do you think this all started with your research?"

"I guess it's because when my ex-associate, Don, created actual clones from our research, demonic entities possessed the nefarious duplicates."

With her mouth falling slightly agape, an incredulous expression swept across Widad's face as she was able to finally put two and two together.

"What is it?" William pressed.

"As you were detailing everything that occurred up until this point, something didn't quite sit right with me…the *why*. And I believe that your guess is exactly correct."

"I don't think I follow you."

"Let me try and explain. You see, in Islam, we believe every soul on Earth which has lived, and will live, was created by Allah. Angels were also created by the One God. We all resided with him in the preexistence, and we all endure as intelligences."

William cast a quick glance over to Gabriel, who raised an eyebrow and gave a knowing smile in response. Then, he refocused his attention on Widad, who went on.

"But there's a key difference between these two groups. Humankind was given free will, and angels were not. When God presented His plan of sending humans to Earth, that choice was not given to angels, and it angered some of them. In particular, it greatly angered Iblis, or the one you refer to as Satan. Iblis was a very persuasive angel and He convinced one third of every intelligence to follow Him, angels and humans alike, and they openly rebelled against the One God. Ultimately, they were all cast out, and they became Jinn, destined never to receive physical bodies. Now, the Jinn hate us, vehemently. They do everything in their power to try and hurt and deceive us by whispering in our ears. With that said, the thing that gives us power over them is our physical bodies, which ultimately allows us to triumph."

"The intellects you refer to as Jinn, are those who we refer to as demons in our faith, correct?" William postulated.

"Yes, you've got it," Widad agreed. "And I believe in my heart that Iblis has perverted your scientific advance for His own benefit. I believe Satan's goal is to build an actual army to destroy all of humankind."

"That's exactly what I thought!" Rich blurted out. "I mean, maybe not in so many words, but it's essentially what we discussed. You see, we were watching a documentary about paranormal experiences, and they hypothesized that the Large Hadron Collider might be creating a breach to another dimension, where demonic entities live."

"If that's true," Widad asserted, "then the Jinn would be able to come into our world at a significantly higher rate."

"But that wouldn't do them any good. Not unless there were thousands of clone bodies waiting to be receptacles to house each horrific fiend," Rich suggested.

"Millions of receptacles," Gabriel attested. "Not thousands...*millions.*"

A look of alarm immediately appeared on William's face.

"In the vision I had after the trial, when they locked me up in that nut house, I saw hundreds of thousands of clones being created beneath the Cenetics facility in Germany. That's when I knew I had to escape, and why we tried so desperately to destroy it."

"But that would mean..." Widad's voice abruptly cut off.

The next moment, she sprung up from the couch, with fear and panic filling her visage. Turning to face William, she grasped one of his hands tightly between both of hers, looking seriously into his eyes.

"We must stop this evil work. If Iblis succeeds, it will mean the end of the world, and all of humankind will suffer interminably. I understand now why Gabriel brought you to me. I must join you and do everything in my power to help you achieve victory."

CHAPTER 19

Acknowledgement

(Later That Same Day)

At just past nine o'clock in the evening, the area surrounding the Great Mosque was dark and eerily quiet, with few cars out on the roads, and only a smattering of people walking through the city streets. Light emanated through the glass windows of a local restaurant, illuminating the sidewalk and spilling out onto the narrow lane that ran adjacent to the establishment. The dining area contained eight small circular tables, all of which were empty, except for one located in the back corner with five people seated around it, engaged in a quiet conversation. Each diner had a single plate covered with multiple delicious looking foods in front of them, except for the hulking patron, who was seated in front of four different dishes, each heaped with enough cuisine to feed a family of four.

"Now, Gabriel, are you sure you've had enough food?" Rich joked. "I'm certain we can get the waiter to bring you a half rack of lamb, or maybe a full kettle of lentil soup."

"My dear sir," the herculean man mumbled around a mouthful of food, "I've only been in human form for about a week, and up until recently, food hasn't been much of a necessity. However, now that it has become a requirement, I have learned to greatly appreciate it."

"I'm sure you've come to the same conclusion about myself," Rich chortled, patting both sides of his ample belly.

"Gentleman, if we can please get back to the matter at hand," Widad more than lightly chastised. "There will be more than sufficient time to discuss dietary needs after we are on our way."

"You're right," Gabriel apologized. "Gentlemen, please go on describing what you experienced after the battle at Cenetics."

"Certainly," Menashe replied. "William, Rich and I just narrowly escaped the encounter with our lives, thanks in large part to Gabriel, and we made our way a few miles from the facility. At this point, we set up a small camp for the rest of the night to try and grab some much-needed rest. I don't think any of us really believed we would be able to actually sleep…least of all William."

Lightly pursing his lips, Menashe reached over and laid a comforting hand on top of his friends.

"I am truly sorry for your loss," he offered empathetically. "Tara was a wonderful woman, and I greatly miss her."

"Thank you," William smiled. "I've come to terms with losing her, but it still makes my heart ache every time I think about it."

Widad's face expressed pure compassion as a single tear rolled down her cheek.

"I am so sorry," she offered. "I was not aware you lost your wife. I hope you know her sacrifice was not meaningless."

William gave an appreciative nod in response, then audibly inhaled through his nostrils before speaking.

"Alright then, let's get on with the story," he suggested.

"Of course," Menashe agreed. "Well, we were all dozing around the campfire when a brilliant flash of light, accompanied by a resounding rumble of thunder, ripped through the night. All three of us jumped up to stare at the sky above our makeshift campsite, and we observed a dreadful event. Directly above our location, we saw an incandescent swirling of colors rotating in a clockwise motion, accompanied by numerous jagged bolts of electricity shooting out from the nebulous cloud in every direction. Then, suddenly, a thin, brilliantly white line appeared across the disturbance and instantly split in two, each part racing away from each other in opposite directions. As each boundary retreated, a massive, murky void was revealed over the earth and dreadful, hair-raising howls emanated from the dark aperture."

"That's horrifying!" she exclaimed.

"That's not even the half of it!" Rich chimed in.

"As you can imagine," Menashe continued, "we were pretty much scared out of our minds. And then, things got worse. As we gaped at this eerie fissure in the sky, hundreds of thousands of terrifying entities erupted from the dark rift, plummeting through the atmosphere toward the earth. When the first group of vile creatures vanished behind the treetops, the sound of an enormous explosion ripped through the forest, violently shaking the ground. An interminable stream of monsters flowed through the fissure in space for more than ten minutes, and then, as the last of the creatures entered into our world, the portal immediately vanished."

"At this point, all three of us started to run in the direction the hellions had fallen, and after about fifteen minutes, we paused at the edge of a clearing in the woods. Looking out across the open area, we saw the outline of a dark, vile pit, filled with a putrid, oil-like black liquid. Suddenly, a deep rumble started to emanate from deep within the earth, and the ground started to shake. As the sound intensified, the murky abyss began to gurgle and bubble, until it resembled a roiling pot of boiling water. Then, a dark arm literally reached up out of the pit, flailing around until it grasped some low-lying grass close by, and began pulling itself up and out of the burbling ooze. While we watched this creature struggle to get completely out of the pit, it seemed as if its body was fluctuating between a solid and specter-like state. Finally, once it had completely emerged from the abyss, it began to laborious crawl across the earth in the direction of the Cenetics campus."

Leaning back in her chair, Widad silently glanced upward at the ceiling for a full thirty seconds, a thoughtful expression on her face. The next moment, her eyes slightly widened, and she looked directly at William.

"Tell me, the direction the vile creature began to crawl, was that toward the same building from your shared dream?"

"It was," William acknowledged.

"And you are certain that in your vision, there were thousands of these *clones*," she nearly spat, "sitting inside glass cylinders, waiting to be possessed?"

"Absolutely. Hundreds of thousands."

Shaking her head back and forth, Widad's expression reflected extreme disquiet.

"Based on what I know about the Jinn, and their ambition to acquire physical bodies, I can come to no other conclusion. We must return to Germany and destroy Iblis's ability to assemble an unholy army of Jinn. If He were to succeed, their forces would bring about the utter end of the world and bring unrelenting misery to every soul."

"But we've already tried," Rich grumbled, "and failed miserably."

Staring at the rotund man's face, Widad's eyes narrowed momentarily, then widened again as something dawned on her.

"What is it?" William probed.

"We don't need to destroy Cenetics to win…just their ability to create clones. Rather than trying to demolish such an obvious target, we should go after something they don't even know we are aware of. We go after the source. I believe the pit is their gateway into this world, and that by destroying it, we can prevent them from bringing any other demons into our reality."

Roughly thirty minutes later, the small group exited the restaurant and began walking away, with Widad leading.

"Alright everyone, you will stay at my home this evening. I can only offer you a floor to sleep on, but it won't be too bad. It should take us about ten minutes to walk there."

"That would be greatly appreciated," thanked Menashe as he inclined his head.

"I'll join you later," advised Gabriel. "I need to tend to a couple things this evening."

"Of course. I'm certain you know this city better than I do. You've been visiting it for thousands of years."

Gabriel simply smiled in response and turned down a side street, walking away from his friends at a quickened pace.

After about thirty seconds, the enormous man turned down a narrow alleyway, then peered around to confirm that no unwanted eyes were watching him. Satisfied he was alone, he closed his eyes and brought both his hands together in front of his chest, pressing the palms firmly against one another. Then, with a slight inclination of his head, his body began to shimmer and he completely disappeared.

The next moment, he was standing back inside the inner courtyard of the Masjid al-Haram, next to the Kaaba, in near-complete darkness. In almost a casual manner, he glanced around the atrium to confirm no one else was present, and then began to circle the holy shrine seven times in a counterclockwise manner. Given the lack of any other person, he was able to accomplish this tradition in less than two minutes, after which he knelt down on the ground and bowed his head.

"I serve Thee and only Thee," he reverently spoke in a hushed tone. "I have accomplished the task You gave unto me, and Widad has agreed to join our crusade."

For the next few moments, he continued to kneel without saying a word.

"Yes, Father," he finally responded to an unheard voice. "The Ulama believes that by destroying the pit in which the outcast souls reside, we will be able to frustrate the plans of the adversary. Is this not Thy will?"

Continuing to prostrate himself on the ground, Gabriel meekly abided, seemingly listening to instructions for several moments.

"But if that is true, then why strike against it at all?"

This time, as he hearkened to instructions, the solemn man's eyes widened, and he tilted his head to stare up into the night sky at the stars in the firmament.

"I understand," he finally said.

The expression on Gabriel's face now exuded consternation, rather than acknowledgment of the words being spoken into his mind.

"I'm sorry," he broke down, "I knew this day would finally come, but now that it is near, I grieve for the millions of souls that will be lost forever."

Again, he bowed his head in respect, nodding in concurrence with his instructions.

A moment later, the massive man pushed himself back up into a standing position, with an exultant expression shining from his countenance. Reaching down to his waist, he placed his hand confidently on the golden horn strapped to his belt and gazed upward to the heavens.

"Thy will be done!"

CHAPTER 20

Incubation

(Fourteen Months Earlier)

A tremendous round of applause ensued as Doctor Koenraad Schmidt traversed the raised area in front of the entrance to the Holy of Holies at the recently dedicated Temple of Solomon. Standing in front of the podium, he gazed out across the crowd for a full thirty seconds, soaking in the adulation from everyone in attendance. Finally, he raised both of his hands slightly above his shoulders as a signal for the audience to quiet down and take their seats, so he could proceed with his speech.

"Thank you, thank you everyone," he proclaimed. "I am thrilled to have even been a participant in the events leading up to such a momentous day in the history of the world. If you will please take your seats, I have prepared a statement for this occasion."

Everyone in attendance promptly sat down as Schmidt readied himself to deliver his message to the world.

"As you all know, we have been faced with difficult times recently. Cowardly acts of hatred and violence have dominated the headlines, impacting many members of the human race throughout the entire world. Dramatic natural disasters have abruptly ended the lives of millions of individuals the world over. It would have been easy to lose hope when facing such dire circumstances. But did we? No! We did not give in to the fear gripping the world. We pulled together, and through unprecedented cooperation, we faced these challenges head on.

"Our differences have always been a source of contention, especially here in the Middle East, where brothers have fought against brothers over differences in theology and pieces of land. We have been mired in continuous war and strife for countless centuries, based on the traditions of our fathers. And to what end? Nothing has been resolved until this point in time, when you decided to set your opposing views aside and appoint a single individual to lead us all forward...together.

"The world is recovering, and we *are* rebuilding. Nations affected by global disaster have received immeasurable amounts of humanitarian aid. Different people of separate nationalities, with different beliefs, have banded together, unified behind a single cause, with a single purpose...to save the human race. We will once again flourish, not just to the level of success that we previously achieved, but we will surpass and accomplish more than we ever thought possible."

Applause and praise immediately arose from the audience, as Schmidt scrutinized the crowd with a more-than-pleased expression emanating from his visage.

"How have we been able to successfully navigate our way through all of the turmoil and strife?" he questioned. "I believe you all know the answer. If it were not for *me*, you would have continued to squabble in your petty arguments and skirmishes, while millions of men, women and children suffered.

Multiple jeers erupted from the audience in response to the toxicity that had just sprung forth from the speaker's mouth.

"Now, now," he chided, "you know I only speak the truth. The only possible explanation that exists for the world recovering, is me! Peace in the Middle East? *I* am the master puppeteer that brought all the different nations together, manipulating them in such a way as to allow for this absurd construction project to move forward. I know it has required sacrifice by all of you, and I thank you for everything you have given on my behalf. Trust me, you will be required to sacrifice even more moving forward."

As additional scoffs and shouts of hatred arose from the congregation, several men in obsidian black combat uniforms, carrying automatic machine guns, flowed in from the rear of the courtyard, taking up position around the entire perimeter of the space. Several of the religious leaders and dignitaries became visibly alarmed by the show of force, with many of them standing up, suggesting they were going to try and exit the gathering.

"Please," he dictated, with more than a note of antipathy in his voice, "sit down. No harm will come to any of you. With your full cooperation, you, and the people you represent, will not be harmed."

Directly behind Schmidt, the figure of a woman could be seen walking out of the entrance of the temple within the Holiest of Holies. She approached the main entryway to the sacred edifice wearing a less-than-modest black silk dress, cut uncomfortably low down the front, along with a long slit up the front of her gown that revealed most of her upper thigh, stopping only two inches from her groin.

As she walked closer to the broad opening, it became evident that she was holding a large, silver platter in her hand, almost like a food server bringing out the evening's feast. Just before crossing the threshold into the Court of Women, she lowered the plate to her waist and spat directly onto the disc in a show of absolute revulsion. The next instant, she upturned the tray onto the stone tiles beneath her feet, and the small remnants of flesh that had just been provided as a burnt offering within the temple, dropped roughly to the ground. Gasps immediately broke out from the crowd, as the woman made her way up to the podium and stood directly next to Schmidt.

"Thank you, Mania," he extolled.

Turning to face directly into the camera, the loathsome man prepared to address the world again.

"This is a time to celebrate. To honor those we have lost, and most importantly, to honor the one that has brought us to where we are at this moment. It is now time…to honor *me*!"

Kim descended the stairs to the right of the platform and approached the enormous object lying beneath the dark charcoal blanket. Casually grabbing a corner of the drape, she gave it a violent jerk downward, resulting in the black covering sliding down to the floor.

"Blasphemy!" someone shouted.

"Bdelygma erēmōsis!"[68] shouted another.

Standing at least thirty feet in height within the walls of the Third Temple of Jerusalem, was a profane statue that completely dishonored the sacred structure. Carved out of a huge single piece of black onyx, stood a life-like statue of Koenraad Schmidt. The all-black effigy showed a man clothed in robes, standing defiantly with his arms folded tightly across its chest. Different symbols had been carved into an apron that hung loosely over his upper legs, and a thick belt was tied at the waist. The realistic visage of the monument was so strikingly similar to that of the actual man, it almost looked like a mold had been taken from his face. Emotion poured out of small, squinting eyes, spilling hatred onto all those gazing upon it, and a vile, thin smile

[68] Abomination of Desolation!

had been chiseled for a mouth. A long, black robe carved out of the stone itself was draped behind the massive figure and looked as if it was rippling in the afternoon breeze. Finally, two long horns extended back from the temples, curving down for several inches, until they unnaturally twisted back upward and ended in sharpened points.

"You have long worshipped your own, imaginary God. It is now time you worship the one and only, *true* God. I declare to you this day, that I am the Chosen One. I am the King, not just of Israel, but of the entire world. I am your God!"

Roughly one hour had passed since Schmidt had made his appalling communication to the audience at the Temple dedication, as well as to the entire world watching the broadcast. Formidable looking soldiers, attired completely in black, were now ushering the remaining officials to the exit. As the final leaders were escorted from the Court of Women, the last guard looked back at Schmidt, who simply nodded in response, after which the military officer exited the Temple, closing a massive bronze door behind him.

Standing in front of the opening leading to the Court of the Israelites, where the Holy of Holies resided, Schmidt gazed out across the empty rows of chairs that now lay scattered haphazardly about the place, following the hurried departure of most of the audience. As he shifted his stare from one end of the space to the other, his eyes finally came to rest on the blasphemous likeness looming over the entire area, and a sinister grin appeared on his face.

From next to the statue, Mania simply stared back at the man, with almost an amused expression on her face. The next moment, she ascended the stairs and walked past Schmidt without so much as even glancing in his direction. Somewhat perplexed, Schmidt simply fell in behind the cold-blooded women as she walked through the entrance into the inner atrium.

"You're quite pleased with yourself, aren't you?" she stated venomously as she neared the stairs to the inner sanctuary of the Tabernacle.

Surprised by her outspokenness, Schmidt stopped momentarily, but quickly moved forward again, not wanting to show that she had him off balance.

"And why shouldn't I be?" he countered. "All of this transpired from my doing!"

This time, Mania was the one to pause, and she spun back around to face the arrogant man.

"Not too pretentious, are we?" she goaded with a sneer. "You're too quick to forget who actually raised you to the position that you currently occupy, and without whom you'd be absolutely nothing!"

Angered by her words, Schmidt scowled at the woman, who simply spun back around and climbed the steps with an almost buoyant attitude.

As Mania entered the Holiest of Holies, she glanced upward to the ornate vaulted ceiling. She then shifted her eyes across the length of the chamber to a large, golden podium sitting directly in front of a colorful curtain that stretched from the ceiling to the floor. Without pausing, she walked across the open area toward the podium. Schmidt, who had quickened his step, almost caught up to the woman as she flung the partition aside, revealing another section of the interior room.

On the other side of the drapery, a golden replica of the ornate Ark of the Covenant sat on the ground in the center of the space. The only other object in the room was a massive black mirror surrounded by a silver frame, with multiple symbols etched into the surface. As Mania and Schmidt approached the reflective glass, a luminous glow began to emanate from the surface. The next moment, flickers of fire could be seen on the other side of the mirror, along with the sensation of heat.

Stopping roughly five feet short of it, Schmidt dropped to one knee and bowed his head low in veneration for his master. In stark contrast, Mania, continued to walk toward to the speculum with her head held high, and as she approached it, an enormous hand materialized on the other side out of nothingness. Reaching forward, her hand penetrated the surface, and as she grasped a single massive finger, she was somehow transported into the very realm of Hell.

Standing on the other side of the mystical portal, Mania looked around at the barren landscape. Immense features of stone and rock loomed overhead from a cavernous ceiling, with more still protruding upward from uneven craggy surfaces. Large lakes of boiling fire were distributed about the place, and the putrid stench of brimstone and burning flesh were carried within endless flows of polluted smoke. Standing immediately beside her, the Father of All Lies soared to a height of one hundred feet. As she gazed up at Him from the ground, her own form appeared to become hazy, and something began undulating directly beneath her skin. The next instant, she began to physically increase in size, until she exceeded fifty feet in height. As her frame enlarged, so too did her appearance. She was now clothed in an oppressive obsidian armor from head to toe, highlighted with golden accents at the boundaries between plates. Her complexion seemed to have become even more pale, accentuating the gauntness of her cheeks, and a pair of twisted black horns curled upward from her head. Hanging from her waist was a ghastly looking, jagged sword at least twenty feet in length.

She continued to stare into the fiery soulless pits of Satan's eyes for what seemed to be a full thirty seconds, and then, she shifted her gaze back through the supernatural aperture connecting the two worlds. On the other side, Schmidt could still be seen, kneeling on the ground, almost frozen in time.

"Time progresses forward so slowly in their reality," she thought to herself. "It only seems to emphasize the grotesqueness of that repugnant parasite."

"Your affliction is only for a season, my love," a grizzly voice whispered in her mind. *"And then, you'll be free, and able to enjoy the bounty of your efforts."*

Turning her head sideways, she gazed up at the Angel of Darkness with affection radiating from her eyes.

"My husband…we were dealt a substantial blow by the enemy. Our assault against the gates of Heaven was an utter failure."

A disgusting smile creased the face of Satan as His brow furrowed tightly together.

"This is all part of My plan to ensure victory at Armageddon. Our apparent failure brings us one step closer to the successful execution of My design. With all My sycophants cast down into the lowest levels of Hell, they are but a stone's throw from entering their world. The truth of it is that we needed Him to permanently exile us from His presence for our strategy to work. And work it will!"

"Forgive me for questioning you, but the dark abyss outside Cenetics only allows for a small number of Your followers to enter their reality. And then, they have to make their way to the facility to possess a clone. Wouldn't it have been more efficient to have simply constructed Your building directly on top of the pit itself?"

"That would have ultimately led to failure," He chastised. *"I have foreseen that their assault against the fissure will be successful, which is why I located the laboratory elsewhere. They will waste time and effort on a meaningless target, thus protecting our true prize."*

"I understand," she acquiesced.

Consternation then crept across her visage as a thought occurred to her.

"What is troubling you?"

"With the pit destroyed, the only way to bring demons into Earth's realm will be with antimatter, and our ability to create that element at scale is nonexistent. Even with the Hadron, it would take us centuries to create a sufficient amount."

A deep rumbling laugh loudly echoed within her mind as the Father of All Lies gazed at Mania almost compassionately.

"I have bigger plans for the Collider. I will turn their scientific innovation against them, enabling Me to bring forth the entirety of My armies. Trust me...I have accounted for everything."

Glancing back through the portal at Schmidt prostrated on the ground, a hideous sneer swept across Mania's face.

"How much longer must I deal with him?" she seethed.

"Not for much longer. He still serves a purpose, and his work is accelerating. Soon, I will not need him at all, and then..."

"And then, I get to take his life?"

"Yes, my love. You can do with him as you please."

In a move that almost resembled a show of outward affection, the Prince of Darkness then gently brushed Mania's hair with the backside of his hand.

Suddenly, the landscape around them began to swirl in a counterclockwise direction, and when it came back into focus, the two of them were floating in the sky over the Cenetics facility. They then began to descend through the air, directly through the roof of the facility, and finally through the bottom of the structure. For a moment, they passed through rock and stone, and as they emerged on the other side, they found themselves in a large subterranean cavity, at least five stories tall and five hundred feet across. It resembled the hub of a massive cave system, with a pentagram carved into the floor of the primary space. Lines of blood were running from the points of the shape back to considerably sized openings in the walls, which led back into dark tunnels. A series of ledges were situated around the perimeter of the hub, covering the walls from the floor to the ceiling, on which an almost innumerable number of large, glass cylinders were located. Several of the containers possessed a pink, fleshy mass of tissue, which seemed to writhe and wriggle randomly, where others enclosed the form of fully developed human clones.

Now hovering a few feet above the floor, they began to advance toward one of the bleak hallways located at each apex of the unholy star. As they approached the large opening, it became apparent that the tunnel expanded up into a much larger passageway, three stories in height. Similar to the central chamber, the walls were lined with thousands upon thousands of clear cylinders, each containing vessels that appeared to be human. As they moved outward through the passageway, the appearance of each clone began to shift, almost as if they were evolving over time. It wasn't a forward-developing process, though, such as would be seen in the progression from Cro-Magnon man to modern humans, but a backward evolution, from a human to a more primal-looking creature. Looking down the tunnels, it was evident that the bodies of the duplicative vessels were purposely being changed to allow for much more massive and hideous monstrosities, the likes of which could never inhabit the smaller human form. This was a hatchery, an incubator for demonic souls, where hundreds of thousands of fleshy hollow receptables lay lifeless, waiting for their new hosts to take control.

CHAPTER 21

Decimation

(One Month After Arriving in Mecca)

It was nearly twilight as a massive cargo ship slowly cruised north through the Red Sea, heading to the southern entrance of the Suez Canal. In sharp contrast to the accommodations enjoyed on their initial journey to Mecca, this time, William and his companions were afforded a little more space. While the dimensions of the space were virtually identical, demand was very low for passengers wanting to travel toward the quarantine zone, which meant their party of five had the entire cabin to themselves. Several beds were scattered across the floor, and a small area was sectioned off in one corner by two large white sheets hanging from the ceiling, in order to give Widad more privacy. A rectangular table was located next to the wall opposite the doorway, with several chairs situated around it, upon which various members of the group were now sitting.

"So, I'd like to mention again how great it is to have Widad joining us on our adventure," Rich beamed as he looked around their room. "We've definitely been treated much differently on this trip given your standing."

"I don't know if I deserve all the credit," she countered with a smile. "To be honest, I think we're the only passengers on the ship."

"True," the hefty man agreed, "but they weren't going to allow any travelers at all, until you spoke with them."

"I think Gabriel had a much greater influence on their decision than you know," she giggled.

"How so?" probed Rich.

"Well, they weren't willing to help us initially. And then I used my *influence* to persuade them."

"What did you say?"

"In not so many words, I told them that unless they granted us permission to travel back to the Port of Haifa, our herculean friend here would be happy to impress upon them how cooperating would be in their best interests."

"You didn't!" Rich guffawed. "That's hilarious!"

Gabriel, who had been quietly listening to the conversation, reached both arms above his shoulders, interlacing his enormous fingers behind his head.

"Sometimes, all it takes is a little encouragement to coax people into compliance," he grinned.

"More like the threat of bodily harm!" interjected William.

"Persuasion…intimidation…they're just different sides of the same coin."

The entire group broke out into laughter for a few moments, then Widad raised her hand.

"Alright," she snickered, "let's talk through our plans a bit more. It's imperative that we successfully dismantle Iblis's ability to transport jinn into our world. We will need to act quickly and decisively to ensure victory."

"What are you thinking?" Gabriel wondered.

"For starters, I recommend we get Seraphina to join the fray," Rich suggested. "She made easy work of…what was that thing's name?"

"Aosoth," their massive guardian enunciated. "She was a powerful adversary."

"Exactly! I bet if we bring Seraphina, along with a whole contingent of angels, we'll be able to destroy the portal in no time."

"I don't think I'd recommend that," Gabriel cautioned.

"Why not?" pressed Rich.

"Well, for starters, they don't know that we are even aware of the corrupt reservoir bridging the depths of hell with Earth. If we march in there with four legions of heavenly hosts at our backs, it's pretty much a given that they will know we are coming."

"What do you suggest, then?" asked Widad.

"I'm thinking a stealthier incursion will serve us better."

A troubled expression flashed across William's face. He tried to immediately conceal it, but pretty much everyone in the room noticed anyway.

"Do you have something to share?" inquired Gabriel.

"Well…it's just that we were extremely secretive when we attacked Cenetics. We planned for several months, and only a very small group of us made up the assault team. But when we attacked, it was like they were waiting for us."

"They *were* waiting for you," Gabriel flatly stated. "The adversary foresaw your attack, and he positioned his vile soldiers to meet you on the battlefield. It was an obvious target to strike, and if you had been successful, it would have thwarted his plans. He would have been foolish not to have anticipated your attempt."

Exhaling loudly through his nostrils, William pursed his lips in deep thought for a few moments. Then, with a renewed expression of hope, he stood up from his chair.

"Do you believe we will be successful in this attempt?"

In response, Gabriel pushed himself up to a standing position and he turned to face William. With a slight inclination of his head, he placed both of his hands heavily on the other man's shoulders, and his visage exuded grim confidence.

"I am certain of it!"

"Then that's good enough for me," William confirmed.

"One thing that *I'm* certain of," Rich interjected, "is that the rumbling you've been hearing for the past ten minutes isn't thunder. If we don't get some food, and soon, I think I'm going to pass out."

Turning to his father-in-law, William smirked.

"Always thinking with your stomach?"

"Of course, I do," he laughed. "How else did you think I crafted this svelte physique?"

The entire group laughed again for a few moments, until Menashe stood up from his chair.

"It's definitely dinner time," he suggested. "Why don't we make our way to the dining hall and grab a bite?"

The entire group stood up from the table in silent agreement. A few moments later, they were making their way down one of the ship's interior hallways, and the smell of freshly cooked vegetables wafted through the air. As they approached a doorway situated on the side of the passageway, Gabriel stopped short of entering the kitchen and faced the rest of his companions.

"You all go ahead and grab something," he suggested. "I need to take care of a couple of things first. I'll get some food a little later."

"Did you want some help?" William asked.

"I'll be fine. This is something I need to take care of on my own."

"We'll see you back in the room then?"

"Absolutely," he agreed.

As William and the rest of his companions entered the mess hall, Gabriel found himself standing alone in the hallway. The next moment, he turned on his heels and backtracked down the corridor until he spotted a doorway leading to a flight of stairs. Within a matter of a few seconds, the colossal man had ascended three flights and exited the stairwell, where he walked out onto the deck of the ship. With conscious resolve, he made his way to the very bow of the ship and looked out across the Red Sea in front of their vessel. The next moment, he looked at the shoreline of Saudi Arabia as it slowly slid by on the starboard of their ship.

While it was still early in the evening, the Sun had already set thirty minutes before, resulting in a landscape illuminated only by the dwindling twilight. The coast immediately adjacent to the ship was bathed in darkness, with only a few dim lights peeking through from small towns, and out toward the eastern horizon, the glow of a larger city was barely visible.

After staring at the horizon for a few moments, Gabriel closed his eyes tightly, then as he exhaled through his mouth, he opened them again.

"Itinerantur!"[69] he whispered.

The outline of his body immediately started to become less distinct, and his entire form began to shimmer until he completely vanished from the deck of the ship.

The next instant, the heavenly messenger was soaring over the desert landscape at a dizzying speed, racing toward the skyline in the distance. In a matter of seconds, he traveled over one hundred miles until he abruptly halted, floating two hundred and fifty feet above the Al Masjid an Nabawi in the city of Medina.

This ancient pilgrimage site, built by Muhammad, also served as the final resting place for the Prophet, with his tomb lying beneath the Green Dome. From his current

[69] Travel!

altitude, Gabriel was able to see almost all of the impressive grounds that comprised the sacred complex. Large, spacious courtyards with ornate, highly polished stone covering the surface, reflected the brightness of the surrounding lights, bringing the exteriors of most buildings into view.

With a somber expression on his face, Gabriel began to descend slowly toward a large white tower adjacent to the Green Dome itself. A few moments later, he found himself standing on the uppermost balcony of the lookout, easily eighty feet above the ground level, gazing out across an immense open space completely devoid of any other person. Leaning on the railing encircling the deck, he stared out across the city and a single tear rolled down his broad cheek.

The next moment, he gazed upward at the firmament gleaming in the night sky and closed his eyes. Finally, with a deep sigh, he reached down and grasped the golden trumpet dangling from his belt, and with resolute purpose, he lifted it to his lips and blasted a pure tone that pierced through the atmosphere and reverberated around the world.

Early the next morning, all five members of the party were soundly sleeping in their beds in their cabin, as the transport carrying them continued its journey northward through the Red Sea. Suddenly, an earsplitting alarm shattered the silence, immediately jolting everyone awake.

"What's going on?!" Menashe blurted out. "Did we hit something?"

"I don't know!" William exclaimed. "Let's head up on deck to see if we can figure out what's happening."

With adrenaline coursing through their veins, they all ran out of the room, down the hallway, and up three flights of stairs, until they reached the top level of the ship. Dashing out onto the deck, it became obvious that the massive vessel was sharply turning to the port.

"What are they doing? They're turning around!" shouted Rich.

The next moment, one of the shipmen burst out of a doorway on the opposite side of the boat and started running toward the small group, with a wild look in his eyes. Upon reaching their location, he leaned over heavily on his knees, trying to catch his breath.

"Madha yahduth huna!"[70] demanded Widad.

"The sea is death!" he panted. "The Mediterranean has turned to blood! Every creature that comes into contact with it is met with ruin and destruction!"

With a look of absolute horror, Widad turned and faced their heavenly companion, who stood off to the side with an anguished expression on his face.

"What have you *done?!*"

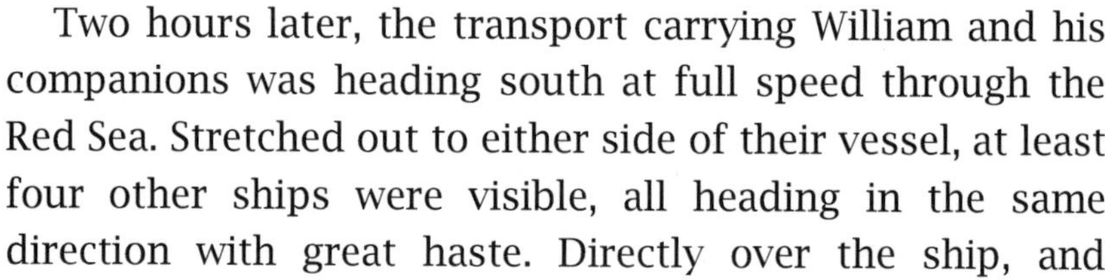

Two hours later, the transport carrying William and his companions was heading south at full speed through the Red Sea. Stretched out to either side of their vessel, at least four other ships were visible, all heading in the same direction with great haste. Directly over the ship, and

[70] What's going on?

heading in the opposite direction, a twin-propeller plane flew north, several hundred feet above the surface of the water.

The aircraft continued on its course for the next three hours until, finally, the southern entrance of the Suez Canal could be clearly seen through the front windows. As the airplane drew closer to the entryway, the pilot could see dozens of ships had collided as they tried to maneuver around one another in an attempt to flee south. As she then gazed up the Suez Canal, her breath caught at the sight unfolding beneath her.

A thick, blood-red fluid twisted its way along the surface of the waterway, leaving in its wake a scene of complete devastation. Strewn out along the surface of the canal, hundreds, if not thousands of dead and dying sea creatures littered the water. Scattered here and there, various ships and other sea vessels had capsized, and it was apparent that the lifeless bodies of their passengers were floating aimlessly amongst the rest of the carnage. Everything that came into contact with the crimson liquid had been destroyed.

"thuma sakab almalak althaani jamah ealaa albahra. wasar kadam mit. wamatat kulu nafs hayatan fi albahri."[71]

With tears streaming down her cheeks, the pilot slowly started to turn her plane around.

[71] And the second angel poured out his vial upon the sea; and it became as the blood of a dead man: and every living soul died in the sea.

CHAPTER 22

Indicative

(Three Weeks Later)

Despite the mid-afternoon sun beaming down through a nearly cloudless sky, very little warmth seemed to reach the surface. For the time of year, average temperatures would usually hover between eighty-two and eighty-four degrees Fahrenheit, but that day, it had barely climbed into the sixties. The cargo ship carrying William and his companions had departed Mecca a little less than three weeks earlier, and it now sat stationary in the Arabian Sea, just east of the Gulf of Aden, except for the occasional rolling waves gently rocking it back and forth. Given the emergency that had gripped the region a few weeks earlier, each port of entry from Saudi Arabia to Sudan had been closed, forcing all ships fleeing south from the contaminated Suez Canal to exit the Red Sea through the Bab al-Mandab Strait. A flotilla of no fewer than fifty vessels drifted peacefully in the waters off the island coast of Socotra, one of the largest in the Socotra archipelago south of Yemen. The mood on the ship was decidedly somber, given the dramatic calamity that had killed several thousands of people caught in the advancing water-borne plague, not to mention what appeared to have been every living creature in the depths below.

The mess hall on the cargo carrier was occupied virtually twenty-four-seven, serving both as a dining area and a centralized meeting place for passengers. Fortunately, the number of people on board the vessel was significantly beneath its capacity, and thanks to a replenishment of food before departing Mecca, there was easily a sufficiency for each patron. This, however, was not the case for most of the other crafts sailing nearby, and it had become a common occurrence for ships to pull up alongside their massive vessel in an attempt to barter for food and water.

Small clusters of people were spread throughout the large room, with an empty table usually separating each one. Seated in the corner furthest from the kitchen, William and his friends occupied a small, rectangular table they had selected for its close proximity to a flat-panel television occupying the wall less than ten feet away. The video on the screen depicted various images of the lingering carnage after the horrific scourge had transformed the Red Sea with a dark hue that befitted its name. Every member of their party, except for Gabriel, sat facing into the common area, with their herculean companion located on the opposite side of the table, his back to the room. With the audio on the television muted, they were actively engaged in a discussion about what their next steps should be.

"Well, we can't stay here forever," Widad pointed out. "Every day we spend drifting around aimlessly, just means we are one day further away from our destination in Germany."

"I totally agree with you," debated Menashe, "but we need to have a plan in place before taking off too hastily. We have no idea what security measures have been put in place between here and Germany, and heaven knows what new safety controls have been implemented at the Cenetics campus. It's just too risky to charge forward blindly."

"I fear the danger associated with not taking action is far greater," she countered. "It's not just the lives of every man, woman and child that are in jeopardy; it's their very souls!"

Menashe let out a gruff sigh while scratching at his hairline, thinking for a moment about the course of action they should take. After a few seconds, he focused his attention on the gargantuan man, who was sitting silently on the opposite side of the table.

"What do you think?" he posed.

Gabriel remained quiet, simply staring at the surface of the table immediately in front of his clasped hands.

"Gabriel," Menashe called again. *"Gabriel!"*

The next instant, their enormous companion snapped his head upward with a startled expression on his face.

"I'm sorry," he apologized, "were you talking to me?"

"Talking to you?" Menashe almost squawked. "Haven't you been listening to the conversation?"

"I was thinking about everything going on," he admitted in a heartbroken tone. "What was your question?"

Sensing their normally staunch companion was having a difficult time coping with the current situation, Widad reached across the table and rested her hand atop his. Tilting his head sideways, Gabriel responded with an appreciative half-smile.

"What's troubling you?" she empathetically probed. "I mean, we are all greatly saddened by everything going on, but it seems to be weighing even heavier on your shoulders."

Taking a deep breath, the massive man looked squarely into the eyes of the caring woman.

"I've always known what the future held in store for all of humankind, but it doesn't make it any easier. And to some extent, I feel partly responsible. The evening before the scourge began to circulate through the Mediterranean, when everyone went to eat some dinner, I slipped away to..."

Before Gabriel finished his sentence, Widad fiercely gripped his hand with a surprising amount of force, causing him to abruptly stop.

"Nonsense!" she insisted. "You of all people should know it wasn't you that caused this catastrophe. You were only following the orders of Allah. It's your role to communicate messages from the One God to all of humanity, so don't think for an instant that you are in any way to blame. The very fact you are here with us now, illustrates how much you love humankind. So much so, you were willing to sacrifice your divine status to join our crusade and fight alongside us to prevent Iblis from succeeding. So, push that idea completely out of your head, and let's focus on what we need to do next."

As Widad delivered her pep talk, William, Rich, and Menashe's faces expressed great concern, bordering on incredulity. However, and much to their relief, their enormous companion took Widad's advice in the spirit it was meant, and a broad grin began to crease his visage.

"You are a wonderful woman!" he rumbled with a deep laugh. "Thank you!"

Widad simply smiled in response and released Gabriel's sizable hand.

"Ok then, what was the question you had for me?"

"We wanted to know what our next move should be," Widad repeated. "I feel that we need to move quickly, or we'll lose valuable time. Menashe, however, thinks we need to get more information about what lies in front of us."

"You're both right," he pronounced, leaning backward in his chair.

"But how can we both be right?" insisted Menashe.

"From a strategic perspective, it *would* be foolish to move forward without information about what to expect. And from an urgency perspective, we *do* need to move quickly."

"But what do we do then?" Menashe questioned.

"We take comfort in the knowledge that everything is moving forward as it should, and nothing will transpire before its time. Since our role is inextricably tied to future events, we move forward with the intent of figuring out what information we can, but doing so as quickly as possible."

Everyone on the opposite side of the table stared at Gabriel with dumbfounded expressions on their faces for a full ten seconds before simultaneously bursting into laughter. A couple of moments later, Rich raised his hand to try and calm the group.

"So, what you're saying is, don't worry?"

"Exactly!" he emphatically agreed.

Shifting his weight, the large man looked back over his shoulder at the television, which now displayed a female commentator sitting at a desk with the words 'Breaking News' scrolling across the bottom of the screen.

"I think we should pay attention to this," he casually suggested.

Without any hesitation, William immediately hopped from his seat, walked over to the flat panel, and turned the volume up on the set.

"We have breaking news at this hour, related to the horrible pestilence that has been spreading throughout the Mediterranean and Red Sea," she announced. "As of thirty minutes ago, the deathly contamination seems to have halted its advance. While it hasn't shown any signs of retreating, the affected area is no longer growing, which is the first positive piece of news we have received in the last few days. While several authorities and experts have been quick to reassure the public that this is just a natural disaster, there is a rising belief among many religious leaders around the world that this event is biblical in nature, signifying that the End of Days is near. We're going to cut over now to our correspondent at the Vatican to get an update on..."

Both the audio and video abruptly cut off, as a large man with a dark complexion and thick black beard unplugged the power cord from the outlet.

"Excuse me!" Rich objected. "We were listening to that."

Without responding, the other man simply started walking back to his table on the other side of the room.

"Excuse me!" Rich called out even louder.

Stopping in his tracks, the man with the heavy beard turned around and stalked back toward Rich with a threatening expression on his face, halting just short of the table.

"limadha la tahtamu bishuuwnik ya rajul simin?"[72] he growled in a gruff tone.

Gabriel, who had been sitting with his back to the room facing Rich, didn't so much as move a muscle.

"limadha la tashghal maqeadak baynama la tazal tastatieu?"[73] Gabriel spoke in a quiet, controlled voice.

Shifting his gaze, the bearded assailant looked down at the man who was seated directly in front of him with a sneer on his face.

"man sayajealuni 'ajlisu? 'anti?"[74] he demanded while thrusting his forefinger sharply into his back.

[72] Why don't you mind your own business, fat man?

[73] Why don't you take your seat, while you still can?

[74] Who's going to make me sit down? You?

Without saying a word, Gabriel slowly stood up from his chair and turned around to face his aggressor. After he had risen to the height of the other man, he paused for a moment to glare directly into his eyes, then continued to stand fully upright, a full eight inches taller.

For a brief moment, the Arabian man stared up at the towering giant with a flicker of apprehension on his face, but quickly pushed that sensation to the periphery as he gritted his teeth. The next instant, the bearded rival swung a clenched fist with tremendous speed and power, connecting solidly with the broad jaw of his adversary. A second later, his mouth agape, he stared down at his injured hand, which had literally crumpled after impacting with the uncompromising chin of Gabriel. A mischievous, almost playful grin emerged on the face of the heavenly messenger.

"My turn!" he warned.

With a fluid motion, Gabriel lifted his attacker nine inches off the floor with one hand, and immediately threw him backward across the room, sending him crashing into the table where his two companions remained seated. The other two men then helped the bearded man up off of the floor and out of the room as he cradled his crushed hand.

Walking over to the television set, Gabriel plugged it back into the outlet and tuned it to the previous broadcast.

"Can you hear that ok?" he asked nonchalantly, as if nothing had happened.

"Just fine!" Rich grinned. "Everything is just fine."

After walking back to the table, Gabriel turned his chair to face the screen and took his seat.

"I think we'll want to listen to this," he suggested.

"...that hasn't been seen since the days of Moses. Different plagues..." the newscaster cut off as a sheet of paper was slid in front of her on the desk. She paused for a moment to read it, then she looked straight back into the camera. "I have breaking news to report. The United Nations has just announced a shift in their global vaccination passport program. We are going to cut over live to join a news conference that is already in progress."

William immediately glanced over to his father-in-law, clearly concerned, before looking up again at the television screen, which now reflected a substantially-sized podium covered with half a dozen microphones from various news organizations. Standing behind the podium, an Asian man with styled black hair and black-rimmed glasses was addressing the audience. On the bottom of the screen, the words 'Dr. Fen Zhao – Chinese Center for Disease Control' identified who was speaking.

"...it has become apparent that efforts to slow the transmission of COVID-21 through the implementation of a global digital passport, has fallen short of containing the epidemic. As a result, the United Nations has just unanimously approved resolution two-seven-one-six, which will require the immediate implementation of an implantable vaccination tracker into the arms of the entire population across the planet. Through the use of Radio-Frequency Identification, or RFID, we will be able to efficiently monitor every person's movement for effective contact tracing in the event of exposure. This is a compulsory requirement that will be enforced without exception. Any person refusing to report to a local center at their designated appointment time will be subject to arrest, confinement, and monetary penalty. Our goal is to have one of these new RFID chips embedded into every man, woman, and child in three months' time.

"In preparation for this massive undertaking, we have already created over three billion implantable tracking chips and have plans to complete production by the end of February. Every citizen on the planet will receive notification within the next two weeks of their scheduled appointment to receive their new tracker. If you are not contacted, please make every effort to reach out to local authorities, who will assist you with setting a date. Your cooperation will help to ensure the safety and health of every member of our society the world over."

Slightly lifting his chair up off of the floor, Gabriel turned his seat back around to face the table. With a serious expression and a somber tone of voice, he addressed his companions.

"Let him that hath understanding count the number of the beast: for it is the number of a man; and his number is six hundred threescore and six."

CHAPTER 23

Elucidation

(Six Days Later)

The early morning sun had just fully cleared the eastern horizon, with the entirety of its sphere beginning its slow ascent into the sky. The sound of seagulls and lapping waves caressing the shoreline filled the air, along with the sporadic clunking of heavy machinery moving pallets of cargo across the docks. Temperatures had already reached the low nineties, and it was set up to be a scorching day, without a single scrap of cloud cover visible in any direction. Adding to the intensity of the heat, the lack of any sort of breeze seemed to emphasize the strength of every ray of sunshine beating down upon exposed skin.

"This heat is going to be the death of me," Rich bemoaned. "I'm either going to die from second-degree burns or dehydration. Whose idea was it to steal a rowboat and paddle our way to the coastline?"

"It's not that bad, my friend," Gabriel chuckled. "And besides, we needed to find alternate transportation. If we had stayed onboard the ship, it's likely we'd still be floating in that same spot six months from now."

"Easy for you to say! Your complexion stands up much more easily to these brutal rays than mine."

"Don't worry," William interjected. "We'll make landfall in a couple of minutes, then you'll be able to find some shade."

"We're just lucky that Widad knew where the Socotra Port was located. Otherwise, we might have landed in the middle of a desert," Rich complained.

"I think we should steer to the right of the port and go ashore on the beach about a quarter of a mile from the docks," Menashe suggested. "No need to draw unnecessary attention to ourselves."

Simply grunting in response, Gabriel began to guide their small craft with powerful strokes of the oars. Five minutes later, the small boat ran aground, embedding itself into the sandy shore of the island. Gabriel immediately leapt out onto the sand and dragged the small vessel, along with its four remaining passengers, ten feet up onto the beach.

"Alright folks," he announced, "time to disembark."

After everyone had hopped onto the sand, they made their way to the two-lane road one hundred feet away, and started walking toward the docks.

"So, what's the plan again?" Rich prodded.

"Once we get to the port, we're going to *negotiate* with one of the fishermen to transport us to Kuwait City, and from there, we'll make our way to the Euphrates River and find a boat to take us all the way to Turkey."

"You do realize that Kuwait is over two thousand miles away?" grumbled Rich.

"You're sure in a *great* mood today," chuckled Menashe sarcastically.

"I'm sorry," he apologized. "I just wish I was about fifty pounds lighter, that's all."

"No worries," William assured him. "Besides, it could be worse. You could weigh four hundred pounds like Gabriel here."

"Four hundred and twenty-five," their herculean friend corrected with a grin.

Everyone laughed for a brief moment, then they started to make their way out onto the wharf, where a number of various-sized vessels were moored.

"I think that you should let Gabriel and I handle the negotiations to secure transport," Widad announced.

Without waiting for a response, she turned around and began gliding across the dock. Gabriel threw a quick look of surprise at the other three men before quickening his pace to catch up to the determined woman.

"That's a quite a sight," chortled Rich. "Widad's got to weigh at least three hundred pounds less than Gabriel, and he's got at least two feet of height on her."

"So, what do we do in the meantime?" William asked.

"I'd like to find some of the shade, and maybe something cool to drink," Rich urged while wiping his brow.

The three men made their way over to a small, open-air café close to the water and promptly sat down on some wooden stools situated at a counter. The only person in the establishment was an elderly man with a dark complexion and heavily weathered skin, who eyed them wearily from behind the bar.

"assalaam 'alaikum,"[75] he greeted in a raspy voice.

"assalaam 'alaikum," Menashe cheerly replied.

"madha yumkin 'an 'uhdir lika?"[76]

"thalathat 'akwab min alma' min fadlika."[77]

The older barkeep simply grunted in reply, reached down beneath the counter to retrieve three tall, clear glasses, which he set on the top of the bar. After placing a generous amount of ice in each cup, he filled them to the brim with water. Each of the three visitors nodded in appreciation and promptly gulped down all the liquid. Without waiting for a request, the bartender refilled each container and slid them

[75] May peace be upon you.

[76] What can I get you?

[77] Three glasses of water, please.

back across the counter. This time, the three sipped them more casually.

"That's gotta be one of the most refreshing drinks I've ever had," Rich cheerfully announced.

"Definitely," William agreed. "How long do you think we'll need to wait for them to return?"

"If I know Widad, and I definitely do, she'll get something arranged in short order," advised Menashe. "I'd bet they'll be back in less than an hour."

"E-excuse me," the older gentlemen interrupted, "are you American?"

"We are," Rich announced. "You speak English?"

"A little bit, yes. How you on Socotra?"

"It's a long story," Menashe cautiously offered.

"I-I sorry," the older man stuttered. "No offense."

"No, I'm sorry," he apologized. "I didn't mean to be so distrustful. It's been a very difficult couple of weeks."

"Y-yes. I no see any boats come this morning. How you arrive?"

"We were on a large fishing vessel out in the Gulf, which wasn't able to take us to our destination. So, we traveled by a smaller boat, landing just this morning."

"I-I see," he replied. "And where you going?"

William threw Menashe a weary expression, along with a slightly raised eyebrow.

"We're heading to Mumbai," Menashe lied. "I have some colleagues that we're going to meet there in a couple weeks. We're working with the United Nations to help assess humanitarian needs."

"Y-Yes. I see. L-Lots of help needed," he replied while glancing out to the wharf. "Your friends return."

Simultaneously, all three men turned and looked up the dock at Widad and Gabriel, who were triumphantly walking toward them.

"Looks like they arranged transportation," Rich surmised.

"What do we owe you?" Menashe asked, turning back to their host.

"O-Oh, you no need to pay. You help people in hard times. No charge."

"Well, thank you..." Menashe paused. "We never got to know your name."

"Nadim. My name is Nadim."

"Thank you for your generosity. ila-liqaa' my friend."[78]

"ila-liqaa'" Nadim replied with a slight bow.

Rich, William, and Menashe then hopped up from their seats and made their way back out onto the dock to join their friends.

"So?" Menashe prodded. "What were you able to find out?"

"All I can say is that this woman can get anyone to agree to anything," their enormous friend chuckled. "Not only did she find out that a small boat headed to Kuwait is leaving in thirty minutes, but she was able to convince the captain to give us accommodation."

"What can I say?" Widad joked, shrugging her shoulders. "I think I just got lucky."

"Thirty minutes?" William stressed. "We've better get a move on."

"Absolutely," Gabriel concurred. "The vessel is just at the end of the dock."

As the small party of five turned and started walking down the wharf, the elderly barkeeper watched them

[78] Until we meet again.

vigilantly from inside his café. Just as they were about to disappear behind a large cargo ship moored to the dock, Gabriel glanced back and locked eyes momentarily with the storekeeper. The next instant, they completely vanished behind the large boat.

Immediately, the barkeep reached beneath the counter and retrieved an old-fashioned rotary phone. After lifting the receiver to his ear, to carefully entered multiple numbers into the dial and waited silently as the call was connected.

"Hello," he responded, his stumbling English immediately becoming noticeably more fluent, "it's Nadim. I found them."

For a moment, he listened quietly as the person on the other end of the call spoke.

"Yes, they made up a lie about working for the United Nations and said they were heading to Mumbai."

Another moment of silence passed.

"I believe they're heading to the Persian Gulf, but I'm not one hundred percent certain. Once their ship leaves, I'll go and speak with the harbormaster to find out."

He listened for a few more seconds.

"Of course, I'll call you as soon as I get confirmation."

Another moment of silence passed.

"Thank you, Miss Dyson. It's my pleasure to serve you. Just let me know if you need anything else."

CHAPTER 24

Leviathan

(Ten Days Later)

One-and-a-half hours after sunset, William and the other male companions of his party were sitting in a semicircle in the front deck section of a small fishing trawler, facing the bow. While the surface of the Arabian Sea was mostly calm, conditions hinted toward a potential storm, with wind speeds starting to increase and an intermittent sprinkling of rain failing from the sky. Far off on the north-western horizon, sporadic flashes of light indicated their time above deck might be limited, and more importantly, that they might be in for an unpleasant evening of rough seas.

"Where exactly are we?" inquired Rich with a somewhat sour expression on his face.

Taking a moment to gaze off the port side of the ship, Gabriel seemed to be getting his bearings from an unseen shoreline lying hidden in complete darkness.

"We should be rounding the easternmost edge of Oman in the next half hour or so," he estimated.

"How can you possibly know that?" Menashe doubted as he looked skeptically out into the night.

"I have my ways," their herculean companion maintained with a sly grin. "While I did give up many angelic traits in becoming human, I retained most of the supernatural capabilities with which I was endowed."

"Fair enough," Rich shrugged. "What else can you tell us about our current location?"

Gabriel took a moment to look out over the murky waters, squinting his eyes slightly as if he was trying to focus on something.

"Well, for starters, if we were a bird, we'd only have about five hundred miles until we pulled into the port at Kuwait City. Regrettably, though, we don't have wings, which means we'll need to wind our way through the Gulf of Oman and across the Persian Gulf."

"How long is that going to take?" complained Rich.

"Let me see...based on our current speed, it should take us about another ten days to travel the remaining one thousand miles."

"A thousand miles?!" Menashe blurted out. "This is going to be a long ride."

"It's definitely going to feel like a long journey," their enormous navigator announced. "Those flickers of light out in the distance are going to hit us head on in about two hours' time."

"How bad is it going to be?" William pressed.

"Let's just say we'll be joining Widad beneath deck in about thirty minutes.

"Ugh!" William declared while rolling his eyes. "I thought you said you'd secured a spot on a small transport ship, not a fishing boat."

"Well, it *is* transporting...fish," Rich joked sarcastically. "They just have to catch them first, that's all."

Lightly chuckling, each of the four men silently looked back out over the bow at the looming storm ahead. About one minute later, Rich leaned forward, tapping Gabriel on his broad shoulders to get his attention.

"Yes?" he casually replied in his deep voice.

"What about in that direction? What's over there?"

Looking off of the starboard side of the ship, their angelic navigator gazed into the darkness for a moment before replying.

"If you head due north for about one hundred and sixty miles, you'll bump into Iran."

"And over there?" he asked motioning to the East.

"That would be five hundred miles until you hit the coast of India."

"Here's one for you," William interjected. "What about directly beneath us?"

Standing up from his chair, the gigantic man strolled over to the side of the vessel and quietly peered down through the water for a few moments. William, Menashe, and Rich had also risen up from their seats, joining their companion at the railing.

"I think you'll find this interesting. We are almost directly over the deepest section of the Oman Abyssal Plain in the Arabian Sea."

"How far down is it?" he wondered.

"Nearly twenty thousand feet down to the bottom of the ocean."

"That's almost four miles!" Rich exclaimed. "I'd hate for my boat to sink here...no one would ever find it!"

"Assuming that Gabriel wasn't part of the salvage team," jested William.

"That's true," his rotund father-in-law agreed. "Gabriel, can you actually see the shipwrecks of different boats on the sea bottom?"

"I guess I *could,"* he postulated, "but why would that be of any value?"

"Treasure, my friend. Treasure!"

"I see," he smiled. "Would you like me to locate some sunken galleons for you?"

"Why not?" Rich encouraged. "Besides, it will help pass the time."

With a broad smile, Gabriel leaned back out over the side of the ship and began intensely surveying the darkness of the depths below. After about sixty seconds of searching, he finally spotted something.

"There we go!" he called out. "I just spotted a fairly large ship, and by the looks of it, it must have gone down at least three hundred years ago."

"Are there any chests full of gold and silver?"

"It doesn't work that way," their immense friend commented, still peering down into the water. "You see, I can see over vast distances through air and water, but I can't see through physical objects. For example, I can perceive that most of thc hull of the vessel is buried in sediment on the ocean floor, but I can't see anything on the inside of the exterior."

"So, I guess angels weren't blessed with x-ray vision," joked Rich.

"Not in the sense you're thinking. While we are able to see into the heart of a man or woman, we don't have the ability to…"

He then paused for a moment, squinting silently down through the surface of the water.

"Don't have the ability to what?" Rich prodded.

"Quiet for a second!" Gabriel barked.

"What is it?" William exclaimed.

"Shh!"

For the next few moments, their angelic friend peered fixedly at an unseen location far in the depths below the vessel. As he closely surveyed the sea bottom, his eyes suddenly widened, and an expression of alarm swept across his visage.

Thousands of feet beneath the surface, a massive fissure, over six hundred feet long and one hundred feet wide, fractured up through the bottom of the ocean. Immediately, sediment, sand, and large pieces of rock began to shoot up through the water at high speed. The next moment, a crimson hue emanated from deep within the breach, becoming gradually brighter, until liquid magma abruptly spewed out of the broad crevice. As rivers of lava were belched out of the abyss, it looked as if an enormous object was squeezing through the opening, shrouded within the volcanic slag. Twisting his head toward his companions, Gabriel's face reflected what could only be described as absolute panic.

"Grab onto something!" he yelled. *"Hurry!"*

Each of the three men frantically wrapped their arms and legs around the exterior railings and braced themselves for the unknown. The next moment, the ship wildly lurched upward at least twenty-five feet and was thrown sideways by an enormous displacement of water emanating from the seabed. The ocean retreated nearly as fast as it had surged upward, and the sixty-foot long fishing boat crashed down, slamming into the surface of the sea.

"What the hell was that?!" exclaimed William with a bewildered expression.

"Leviathan!" Gabriel uttered.

A few moments later, Widad burst through one of the main accommodation doors and ran up to the small group. Blood was freely flowing from a gash on the side of her head, undoubtedly sustained from the sudden upheaval of their ship.

"What's going on?!" she demanded, wiping blood from her brow.

"We are being hunted by an ancient demonic titan," their herculean colleague warned. "And it's about to attack!"

"By a what?!"

Menashe rushed over, taking Widad's hands firmly within his, and stared into her eyes.

"It's the Leviathan! The dragon that will be delivered to the righteous at the end of time. And it almost certainly will be the end of us."

A raucous gurgling suddenly erupted off the starboard side of the ship, somewhere out in the darkness. One of the ship hands standing on a small balcony encircling the wheelhouse, directed a powerful spotlight affixed to the railing out into the black night. As the powerful beam searched for the source of the noise, it fell upon a sizable disturbance on the surface of the water roughly three hundred yards to the side of the ship. Tremendous amounts of roiling watering churned and bubbled along with silt, debris, and various sediment on the surface of the ocean. Suddenly, an enormous, triangular formation ripped precipitously through the surface, rising to a height of ten feet, with the tip of the structure angling sharply back. As the three-cornered shape continued to rise, two sharp, pointed horns appeared roughly eight feet to either side of the initial structure, rising in unison to a height of nearly twenty feet. The horns were easily five feet in circumference and had deep gouges and pock marks along their full length.

A broad, flat form emerged from the water, at least twenty feet in width, appearing to angle slightly downward. As it emerged further, feather-like structures fanned backward from a dark green, leathery, scale-like skin, which covered both sides of the creature's face. Two hideous, loathsome eyes sat within sunken sockets, casting a neon-green glow from deep within. At the front of the monster's face, a flat nose with two large slits for nostrils sat atop a gaping maw with rows of three-foot-long razor-sharp teeth. The same radiant hue emanating from the beast's eyes also emerged from deep within the hellion's throat. Next, two massive wings breached the surface a full fifty feet to either side of the fiend's horrific skull and extended upward into the sky. Each was covered by the same dark leathery skin that enveloped the creature's head, with sharp hooks reaching outward from the outer frame.

As the leviathan continued to materialize, a long, thick, sinewy neck lifted the massive head to a height of almost twenty feet before expansive, muscular shoulders appeared. Additional triangular-shaped plates flowed down, back from the head along its neck, reaching up from the skeletal spine at least ten feet in height. Rising up further, powerful arms extended out from the broad shoulders, ending with long, gnarled fingers and jagged blade-like nails, and as the rippling chest emerged from the water, the creature's upward motion ceased. At this point, the beast had risen to at least eighty feet above the surface of the sea, literally towering over the diminutive trawler. However, the materialization of this abominable beast was not yet complete. One hundred feet to its side, a thick, snake-like coil, easily thirty feet in diameter, emerged from the surface and curved back down beneath the water. Seventy-five feet further, another writhing tendril was exposed, and the final tail of the horrific colossus protruded twenty feet across and thirty feet high, ending in a sharp, barbed tail.

To make matters worse, the distant flashes of lightning they had previously seen were practically upon them, with bolts detonating in the clouds directly above their location. A strong gust began blowing from the east, spraying everyone on deck with cold seawater and causing the boat to rock in an unpredictable manner. Along with the wind, sizeable waves began to batter the ship, amplifying the convulsing motion.

"What do we do?!" Widad shouted.

But before anyone could respond, a brilliant electrical discharge illuminated the gargantuan leviathan floating in the ocean less than one thousand feet away. Almost as if sensing her stare, the vile creature turned its head and glared directly at the horrified woman. The next moment, it arched its head upward and an ear-splitting screech burst from its jaws as it lurched forward, closing the distance to the ship.

Without hesitating, Gabriel got down on one knee, held his trumpet to his lips, and fiercely blew into the mouthpiece of his golden clarion. A pure, inspiring note rang out from the instrument and reverberated across the ocean in every direction. The next instant, an intense spark of light exploded one hundred feet over the surface of the water between the ship and the beast, creating a rupture in the air and a portal to the heavenly realm. As light continued to emanate from the fracture in the sky, the familiar outline of a guardian flew through the opening and into reality. It was Seraphina.

Despite the near-complete darkness of the night, the persistent bursts of lightning, which were easily approaching one hundred strikes a minute, illuminated the entire region as if a strobe light was firing over and over again. With the constant flashing lighting up the entire area, their angelic champion could be seen hovering in the air with powerful thrusts of her reddish-hued wings. Without any delay, she reached back, drawing one of her silver arrows from her quiver, and fired a flaming dart at her target, faster than the blink of an eye. As soon as the first projectile left her bow, she repeated the motion three more times with such nimbleness that four flaming shafts soared through the air in a perfect cluster.

Completely ignorant of the new combatant who had joined the fray, the serpentine miscreation continued to advance toward the vessel. The next instant, each of the flaming missiles slammed into the creature's neck before ricocheting harmlessly down to the water below. While the attack didn't so much as scratch the spiny exterior of the leviathan, it definitely caught its attention.

The repugnant beast changed its course, plummeting directly toward their winged protector. Realizing her arrows were having no effect on the creature, Seraphina brought her hands in front of her chest and began creating an intense fireball. The next moment, one of the herculean wings of the vicious behemoth slammed into her body, flinging her backward over one hundred feet, causing her to crash into the side of the fishing boat. As a result of the impact, the entire ship violently trembled and Widad lost her balance. As she did, she stepped backward and fell overboard into the ocean.

"Widad!" Menashe screamed. *"I'm coming!"*

The next instant, he jumped over the side of the boat and into the water. A couple of seconds later, he resurfaced roughly ten feet away from the flailing woman and swam over to her.

"I've got you!" he yelled, as he came up behind her.

"Look out!" Rich roared as he threw a lifebuoy down from the ship.

Having collected herself, Seraphina soared back up into the air and headed directly for the monstrous demon, grasping a gleaming sword. As she drew closer to the beast, an almost guttural sound ripped through the air as the hellion widened its mouth. The next moment, a brilliant flash of vibrant green burst from the gullet of the serpent as intense, malachite-colored flames shot through the air, engulfing their protector.

Fortunately, Seraphina seemed unaffected by the fiery bombardment and almost casually embraced the conflagration, cradling it in her hands. As she compressed the fireball, the energy radiating from the sphere intensified to the point at which everyone standing on the deck of the ship had to shield their faces from the intense heat. The next moment, she hurled the blazing orb back into the chest of the immense titan and a fantastic explosion instantly rang through the air, along with a burst of fire. As the smoke cleared, it became obvious Seraphina's strike had had absolutely no effect on the creature, except for enraging it even further.

"Gabriel!" William cried. *"What do we do? Nothing is going to stop this beast!"*

Closing his eyes, Gabriel knelt down on the deck of the careening ship and bowed his head. A bright aura began to emanate vertically around his head, and an ancient-looking halo was visible, similar to that of a Renaissance painting. As he knelt in silence, an intense rumbling of thunder started to resound through the stratosphere. The next instant, he lifted his head and gazed up into the sky, his own eyes ablaze with electricity. Instantly, a brilliant flash of light discharged from the atmosphere, illuminating all the clouds in the sky. As another burst of light lit up the scene, the outline of an enormous, robed figure appeared, highlighted against the walls of the gloomy storm.

Unaffected by everything that was going on, the leviathan surged along the surface of the roiling sea, headed straight for its helpless victims, who were clinging desperately to the lifebuoy. As it approached its prey, it stopped twenty feet short, raising its head up above the water, ready to deliver a death stroke. The next instant, it thrust its gaping maw forward to devour its target.

A bluish-white bolt of electricity immediately burst out of the sky above, coming directly from the shadowed figure in the clouds. A deafening clap of thunder followed and in response, Gabriel jumped up just in time to catch a golden, burnished shield that Seraphina had launched toward him. Bracing himself for impact, he lifted the massive shield above his head just as the balefire reached his location. Instantly, the powerful lightning was redirected by the armor, discharging directly into the gaping mouth of the savage attacker. The effect on the leviathan was immediate and complete. Entering through its gaping maw, it surged throughout the entire body of the creature, leaving absolute destruction in its wake. Fire and electricity surged through every internal organ and tissue and erupted from every orifice, leaving a burnt, lifeless husk behind.

Lowering the shield, Gabriel looked up into the air and spotted Seraphina gliding by, a huge smile on her face.

"Not bad for a human," she teased.

Gabriel simply inclined his head and smiled in response, before turning his attention back to Rich and William, who were busy directing members of the ship's crew to retrieve their companions.

Still holding onto the lifebuoy, Menashe and Widad patiently waited while the crew started to lower a smaller boat to pull them from the sea.

"What were you thinking?" Widad berated him. "You could have killed yourself!"

"I wasn't thinking," he admitted. "All I knew was that I needed to save you."

In spite of the near darkness that had returned, as Widad gazed into Menashe's eyes, the bright crimson hue emanating from his cheeks seemed to illuminate their immediate area. With an almost timid smile, she placed her hand on top of his, and with a little effort, planted a soft kiss on his cheek. For a brief moment, even the onlookers from the ship above caught a glimpse of a red glow on the surface of the water.

CHAPTER 25

Animus

(Eleven Days Later)

It was early in the afternoon, and the entire skyline was filled with multiple billowy, cumulus clouds, casting enormous shadows on the earth as they temporarily concealed the sun. A light sea breeze was blowing onto the shore, providing a much-appreciated cooling of temperatures, which were certain to climb into the mid-nineties before the end of the day. Alongside the fishing trawler that had provided transportation to Shuwaikh Port, seven other vessels of various sizes were moored on either side of the five-hundred-foot dock of Kuwait City. Strewn across the entire length of the pier was a line of no fewer than two hundred individuals waiting to be processed through customs. William, along with each of his companions, had been standing in line for the past fifteen minutes, slowly progressing forward to the checkpoint.

"How long do you think this is going to take?" Rich complained.

"Well, based on the fact we only moved ten feet in the past quarter hour, I'm thinking we'll clear customs just after midnight," William joked.

"Seriously though, why do you think this is taking so long?"

"I'm not sure," he commented. "Why don't you and I make our way to the head of the line to see what we can see?"

Rich nodded in agreement, and he and William casually started walking away from the rest of their group.

"Be careful," warned Gabriel.

"Don't worry," William called back, "I'm always careful."

About two minutes later, both men had made their way up the crowded wharf and found themselves roughly thirty feet away from a makeshift processing kiosk, where three border control agents with grim expressions were positioned. Two of the guards looked to be just over six feet tall, with the third towering above them, at least seven feet in height. Each was dressed all in black and carried an automatic machine slung around their shoulders. Despite being so far away, the men were able to easily hear the intense conversation between the border control agents and the individual trying to gain access.

"Where are your papers?" one of the smaller guards demanded of a man wearing a cream-colored robe.

"My wife has them," he responded pointing at a woman standing about five feet behind him at the front of the line.

"Come here!" the agent growled.

Hesitantly, the woman complied and approached the security booth, the passports held tightly in her hand.

"Here you go," she nearly squeaked.

The massive agent roughly grabbed both sets of credentials, mulling over them silently for a few moments. The next instant, he thrust them back at the woman, who nearly dropped them on the ground.

"These look to be in order," bellowed the massive officer, "but they're not enough to get you access into Kuwait!"

Reaching over to the counter, he grabbed a rectangular-shaped rod, which he then pointed directly at the woman's husband.

"We've got to scan your vaccine tracker before you enter the country."

"But...but we haven't received ours yet," the man squawked.

"That's not going to be a problem," snickered the first agent in an ominous tone.

The third officer, who had remained silent up until this point, retrieved what looked to be a stainless-steel gun from the desk, and approached the couple with a menacing expression. Without any warning, the defender firmly seized hold of the man's arm, sharply twisting his wrist so as to face his palm upwards. The next instant, he harshly shoved the pointed end of the gun-like apparatus into the man's forearm and pulled the trigger. Immediately, a loud clicking noise could be heard as the RFI tracker was injected into his arm, just beneath the inside of his elbow.

"What are you doing?" demanded the shocked immigrant.

"If you want to enter, you must be tracked," the guard replied flippantly.

Shocked at what had just transpired, both Rich and William quickly turned around, almost slamming into the enormous frame of Gabriel, who somehow had snuck up directly behind them.

"Don't draw attention to yourselves," he whispered. "Let's just head casually head back down to the dock and rejoin the others."

Without a word, both men silently complied. A few moments later, they had walked far enough that they were completely out of sight of the security booth and stepped over to the side of the pier.

"What are we going to do?!" Rich fretted. "Did you see the size of that man? He's nearly as large as you!"

"That isn't a man," warned Gabriel. "The work at Cenetics has progressed significantly over the past few months. They are creating much larger clones to house some of the ancient abominable souls of the adversary."

"You mean that was a demon?" William shuddered.

"Yes, a demon that has possessed a clone's body."

"But wouldn't that make him extremely powerful?" worried Rich. "I mean, we were talking about how demons lacked human form, which made them weaker. But now, wouldn't he be able to…"

"…be able to destroy me? Yes. That's exactly what it means."

"And the other two guards?" whimpered Rich.

"They would be demons as well."

"What are we going to do?" William demanded. "We can't fight our way through the checkpoint – there are three of them. And we can't just casually walk up to them and present our passports. At worst, they would recognize us and kill us on the spot. At best, they would inject us with one of those trackers, and then they would know exactly where we were at all times. There's no way we'd be able to even get close to the portal outside Cenetics."

Pursing his lips, Gabriel quietly contemplated the situation for a few moments until a devious grin cross his face.

"I think I've got an idea."

"What?" pressed Rich.

"Both of you go back and get in line with Menashe and Widad. When you get closer to the checkpoint, I'm going to create a distraction," he emphasized, motioning over to an oil tanker moored two thousand feet across the harbor.

Rich and William turned to look at the ship, but when they returned their gaze to their herculean friend, he had vanished.

"I've got a bad feeling about this," Rich warned, a concerned expression writ large across his face.

"Let's just go back to the others and let them know what's going on."

Roughly three hours later, William and his small party had traversed almost the entire length of the pier, and now found themselves only fifteen feet away from the security booth. Two of black-clad border control agents were verbally abusing another group of travelers, while the gargantuan officer was physically dragging one man to a police van on the other side of a narrow road.

"This isn't going to work!" Menashe softly whined. "Where'd Gabriel go? If he doesn't do something soon, we're going to get caught for sure."

"Don't worry," Widad insisted. "He isn't going to let anything happen to us."

The next instant, the sound of a small explosion echoed across the bay from directly behind the line of petitioners, and each member of their party, along with everyone else, rushed over to the side of the wharf to see where the sound had come from. On the other side of the inlet, a small plume of black smoke had climbed about twenty feet up into the air from the deck of the vessel.

"I don't know if *that's* going to be enough of a distraction," Widad worried.

The next instant, a second, much more massive explosion burst out from the side of the ship, launching a fireball over one hundred feet up into the sky. The shockwave from the blast visibly raced across the water and as the turbulence from the explosion reached the dock, half the people standing on the edge were knocked roughly to the ground.

"I guess I didn't need to be concerned," Widad tartly offered, pushing herself up off the ground.

Pandemonium immediately broke out on the pier, with hundreds of people, who had been waiting patiently to enter Kuwait, now charging at full speed to get away from the destruction. As the crowd started rushing through the security gate, the two remaining border control agents fruitlessly tried to stop them in their tracks.

"This is our chance!" William announced. "Let's go!"

Joining the human stampede, there entire party easily passed through the checkpoint and made their way into the warehouse area adjacent to the docks. As they crossed over to the other side of the first street, they noticed a large frame of a man casually leaning up against the side of one of the buildings with an enormous grin on his face.

"Don't you think you went a little overboard with your *distraction?"* accused Widad.

"Means to an end, my dear. Means to an end."

As the entire group turned back to survey the chaos enveloping the entire waterfront, the smile on Gabriel's face suddenly disappeared and his breath caught. The next moment, he started searching through the crowd to try and locate the source of his apprehension.

"I haven't felt this presence for thousands of years," he silently considered. *"Not before the great war in..."*

"We should get as far away from the docks as possible," Gabriel quickly advised his party. "Start heading down this street and I'll join you shortly."

Everyone nodded in agreement and began walking with haste away from the commotion.

Gabriel again searched the crowd for almost thirty seconds, until his gaze fell upon the same colossal police officer he had initially seen at the border crossing. This time, however, he clearly saw the vile creature lying beneath the surface. Protruding from either side of his broad forehead were two gnarled horns that twisted and turned in all directions. He had a prominent brow, which jutted out from his skull by at least two inches, providing the upper frame to his fiery eye sockets, which lay sunken in its face. He had a flat, wide nose resting on top of what appeared to be an almost human smile, except for the four-inch fangs extending out from his lower jaw. Two enormous ears lay on either side of the creature's head, each with at least five golden rings pierced through the lower lobes. He had a broad, thick neck, with an ornate golden necklace hanging around it. The shoulders, torso and waist of the beast were both hefty and muscular, exuding gluttony and power. He had massive arms with enormous biceps extending down to powerful forearms, and large golden bracelets encircled each wrist. A segmented, golden belt, at least four inches in width, surrounded his waist, with a symbol of a pentacle inscribed on a large circular buckle on the front. A crimson-colored, pleated skirt hung from his waist to just above his knees, and two thick golden straps were wrapped around the tops of muscular calves. The appalling fiend simply stared at Gabriel with a sinister expression that exuded pure hatred.

"Mammon," Gabriel spoke in his head.

"Gabriel," the hellish fiend returned. *"We will meet again."*

"I look forward to it!" the archangel growled before turning to follow his friends.

CHAPTER 26

Confrontation

(The Next Day)

Within the subterranean antechamber beneath the Cenetics campus, it was impossible to know whether it was night or day, with the only illumination being provided by flickering torches positioned along the outer edge of the circular hall. While two individuals were seated relatively close to one another, next to the massive, circular stone table, it was obvious that neither of them appreciated the other's company to any degree. Occupying an excessively large stone throne, Koenraad Schmidt sat almost at an awkward position, with one leg lazily draped over the arm rail, while leaning at an angle back into the opposite corner of the seat. Dressed in his normal business attire of slacks and a white, buttoned shirt that lay open at the collar, he looked as he normally did, except for the large patch situated over his left eye. Despite the hefty size of the covering, it didn't fully conceal the hideous disfigurement he had sustained at the hands of his Master, with dark pink, freshly-scarred tissue creeping out from beneath the sides.

Located roughly ten feet to the side, Kim Dyson was perched on a stone bench, back squarely oriented to demonstrate the absolute disdain she held for her companion. In an attempt to further emphasize her lack of interest in the other man, she was actively engaged in navigating her smartphone to access something of perceived importance. She wore a relatively immodest gown with a low-cut neckline and an almost entirely translucent bodice that left little to the imagination.

"So, how soon until we hear from your errand boy? I mean, he should have been back hours ago…if everything went as smoothly as you predicted," Schmidt mocked.

"Oh, don't you worry," she retorted, "he'll be back soon enough!"

Mania paused for a moment, surveying the appearance of the man.

"Why do you even have that thing? You look absurd on that throne!" she ridiculed. "The only additional stature you get from sitting on it, is in your own mind. The Master thinks you're a fool!"

"Our leader knows my worth and my capabilities. That's why he entrusted *me* with the most critical tasks from the very beginning. The only purpose *you* serve is to appease his more carnal needs."

"Oh, I agree that He values your contribution," attested Kim. "That's why He gave you such a nice parting gift during your last interaction," she smirked, motioning toward her own cheek.

Angered at her disrespect, Schmidt leapt up from his seat, advancing toward his rival in a menacing manner before pausing just a couple feet from her.

"Oh, this is rich," she taunted, flinging her long black hair over her shoulders. "Do you actually think I could even feel remotely threatened by you? I'm surprised you've lasted this long."

With rage seething through every ounce of his frame, Schmidt visibly began to shake as a deep, red flush flared across his entire visage. Encouraged by his visceral reaction, Kim casually stood up from her chair and silently stared into his eyes for a full five seconds before finally walking away, cackling in delight.

As Schmidt prepared to launch into a verbal assault on his antagonist, he caught a slight shimmering in the air directly overhead. Shifting his gaze, he spotted the loathsome messenger returning to report on events. Gliding down from the four-story ceiling, the vile imp noiselessly landed off to the side of the room and stared expectantly at his female master.

"Well!" demanded Mania. "Out with it!"

"I bring you word, Mistress," he hissed. "For your ears alone."

Shaking her head in disgust, she stomped over to the winged creature, crouching down to quietly converse.

As Schmidt silently regarded the interaction, he could sense things hadn't gone as smoothly as Mania had predicted. With her body language clearly showing disbelief and anger, the devilish imp visibly recoiled back from her dangerous glare.

"What?" she finally exclaimed in anger. *"He failed?!"*

Unable to contain his euphoria, a broad smile split Schmidt's face in two as he deliberately stepped closer to the pair in order to clearly hear the conversation.

"I apologize mistress," the small fiend blubbered. "I am simply bringing you word as to what transpired."

"The Leviathan should have been able to easily destroy all of them. Nothing on this earth has the ability to destroy that behemoth!"

Extreme apprehension swept across the contorted face of the jinn, whose eyes darted around the chamber, looking anywhere other than in the eyes of his assailant. Unable to contain her anger, Mania energetically grabbed either side of the demon's skull, forcing him to focus on her.

"Tell me what happened," she slowly enunciated.

"The giant serpent was clearly winning," he panted. "There was nothing they could do to stop him. Not even Seraphina could inflict so much as a scratch."

Clearly exasperated by his inability to answer her questions, Mania violently swung her fist, striking the little hellion across the face, sending him careening back across the floor in a clatter.

"Let's try this again," she threatened. "What happened?"

"It was Father!" cried the brute, prostrating itself on the ground.

Mania's eyes instantly widened as disbelief pervaded her visage. Wordlessly, she took two steps backward, staring blankly into the air over the abject servant, and after a few moments, she audibly swallowed.

"Father intervened?" she incredulously shuddered.

Unable to contain his amusement any longer, Schmidt erupted in a howl of laughter, to which Mania responded with a glare before refocusing her attention on the cowering beast.

"How?"

"The Leviathan was about to destroy the ship, killing everyone, and then...then..." he stammered, "a bolt of electricity erupted from the heavens, directly striking Gabriel."

"He attacked His own archangel?" she demanded incredulously.

"Not exactly. He had Seraphina's shield for protection. When the balefire struck him, it reflected off the armor and obliterated the colossus."

Overwhelmed by this revelation, Mania staggered backward until she fell clumsily onto her stone bench. The next moment, Schmidt gleefully bounded to her side, gently resting his hand on her shoulder.

"I guess your *sure-fire* plan wasn't so certain after all," he viciously mocked.

With a violent thrust, Mania jumped back into a standing position, squarely up to the vile man.

"I would have been successful if it weren't for Father," her mouth twisted.

"You should have foreseen that as a possibility," he goaded maliciously. "I guess you're not as good as you thought!"

"You'd better watch yourself!" she threatened. "I'll…I'll…"

"You'll what?"

"If you're not careful, I'll make sure you depart this earthly existence sooner rather than later."

A sinister sneer appeared on Schmidt's face as he chuckled through closed lips.

"Master would never allow you to!" he taunted. "I am vital to His success. He can't achieve his plans without me! And after we succeed, I've been promised I will rule large areas of the world as a reward for my efforts. I will be a king!"

"Do you really think that He will ever allow you to rule anything? He will control everything and everyone. You mean absolutely nothing to Him. And I will rule by His side. Who do you think He's going to listen to? You? Don't fool yourself. As soon as He's squeezed every last bit of value from you, you'll be cast aside and forgotten."

"You've got things backwards," scoffed Schmidt. "As soon as He's achieved His objective, it is you that He'll have no further use for. My election is certain!"

And with that, he turned on his heels, leaving the fuming woman to stare at his back as made his way to the rear of the underground chamber.

CHAPTER 27

Hardship

(Two Weeks After Arriving in Shuwaikh Port)

At eleven o'clock in the morning, the thermometer had already broken above one hundred and ten degrees with no sign of slowing. Just ten days before, William, Rich, Menashe, Widad, and Gabriel had secured passage on a small fishing boat to take them up the Euphrates River as far north as possible. But given the limited space, sleeping on the vessel was an impossibility, so they had been forced to camp on the shore each evening before resuming their travels the next day. The lack of accommodation on the barge also meant there was little-to-no respite from the blazing heat as it relentlessly beat down on them from above. This left William and his four companions with the privilege of taking turns to sit beneath the small canopy positioned directed over the captain's seat, while the others tried to cover up any exposed skin and avoid passing out from heatstroke.

Roughly two hours earlier, they had floated beyond the north-western edge of the city of Baghdad and were now flanked on both sides by a barren, desert landscape, which seemed to amplify their abhorrent conditions. And as the vessel trudged forward on the river, time itself seemed to slow down, stretching out their torturous experience.

"And I thought the heat was unbearable when we rowed to that small island in the Arabian Sea," Rich swore. "This is truly going to be the death of me."

"Cheer up. You said you've been wanting to lose some weight. This could be the perfect opportunity for you," jested William.

"Easy for you to say while you're enjoying that shade. I think it would be less painful to saw off an arm or a leg, than to contend with this misery. Why are the temperatures so blazing hot?! This can't just be global warming!"

"It isn't," grumbled Gabriel, who himself sat shirtless on the starboard side of the boat. "There's more at work here than just rising temperatures. These are a sign of the times."

"Things are going to just keep getting worse, aren't they?" asked Menashe.

"I'm afraid so," the massive man stated. "As we approach the final days, the frequency of calamities will increase dramatically. And all we can do is to keep pressing forward."

"I think you're all getting a bit too negative," declared Widad. "Why don't we listen to some music? It should help pass the time more quickly and take our minds off of our circumstances."

Without waiting for any agreement, Widad walked over and spun the dial on the radio on the dashboard of the boat. The next moment, the sound of eighties music started to emanate from two small speakers located on either side of the craft.

"There we go," continued the diminutive woman, "that should do just perfectly."

For the next fifteen or so minutes, everyone sat silently as various popular songs echoed out over the water. Even Rich seemed to be less depressed as he lightly tapped his foot to the baseline of the song.

After a couple of minutes, he grinned with relief. "Your thirty minutes are up and, if I remember correctly, it's my turn to sit in the shade."

With a grimace, William pushed himself up into a standing position and he and Rich exchanged seats, being careful not shift weight in the boat too quickly. Just as William started to lower himself on the bench next to Widad and Menashe, something caught his eye on the shoreline over the massive shoulders of their protector. As he took his seat, he continued to stare out across the waterway and onto the shoreline, with a perplexed expression on his face.

"Did you see them?" Gabriel asked.

"See what?" Widad stated with a note of concern.

"The observers. They've been following us since we boarded the ship ten days ago."

"Why didn't you say something earlier?" she demanded.

"It wouldn't have made a difference," he flatly replied. "They are only here to monitor our progress, not hurt us."

Furrowing her brow in dismay, Widad stood up and glared down at Gabriel, who was now holding up his shirt to provide some shade.

"And who are they reporting our progress to?" she demanded.

"My guess is they report to Mania, or possibly Schmidt. In any case, there's nothing we need to immediately worry about, at least not presently," he casually commented.

"Presently!" she demanded. "Nothing to worry about *presently!* And when, I hate to ask, should we begin being concerned about our safety?"

But before Gabriel could reply, the upbeat music coming out of the speakers was abruptly cut off, and the sound of an emergency tone started to blare from the radio. The attention signal lasted for about twenty seconds and then cut off just as suddenly as it had begun. Then, the voice of a woman speaking in English crackled through.

"This is an emergency message being broadcast to all inhabitants of Earth," she stated. "Over the past few years, we have been experiencing an increase in global temperatures, which has been attributed to global warming. However, the last two weeks have provided an unprecedented increase in conditions, threatening the safety of millions across every continent and in every nation. On average, temperatures are between twenty and forty degrees hotter than normal, and climatologists have been unable to accurately determine the root cause. More importantly, there is no end in sight to this dangerous heatwave. We recommend everyone take shelter whenever possible and stay indoors, ideally where air conditioning is available."

"Perfect!" Rich scowled.

"Quiet!" William insisted. "Let's see what else they have to say."

"While we are just in the early stages of this calamity, thousands of our global citizens have already lost their lives due to the extreme heat. In particular, nations in central Africa, all countries in South and Central America, and the continent of Australia, have been hit particularly hard. Furthermore, livestock and many forms of sea life have been affected, impacting vital food sources with drastic consequences. The United Nations has declared a global state of emergency, and will be coordinating the distribution of water and other necessities to those nations and communities in greatest need."

From his seated position on the starboard side of the boat, Gabriel reached into the water and retrieved the lifeless form of a fish, which had been simmered to death in the hot waters of the Euphrates. With a sad expression on his face, he gazed into the eyes of each of his companions before speaking.

"And the fourth angel poured out his vial upon the sun; and power was given unto him to scorch men with fire. And men were scorched with great heat, and blasphemed the name of God."

As they looked back across the river in the direction from which they had just come, they all gasped as they saw hundreds of deceased fish floating aimlessly on the surface of the water.

CHAPTER 28

Oblivion

(April 30, 2022)

At just past three o'clock in the afternoon, the sun was already well on its way toward the western skyline. It had been three weeks since William and his companions boarded their transport in Kuwait City, and everyone was almost as sick of the cramped accommodations on the boat as they were of the ceaseless heat. While temperatures had been roughly ten degrees lower over the past couple of days, they had only dipped beneath one hundred in the evenings, making each day's journey a blistering experience for everyone. Having covered nearly one thousand miles in total, the fishing vessel was nearing the northern border between Syria and Turkey, where the river ranged in width between one-and-a-half and two miles across.

"Either my eyes are deceiving me, or I'm seeing lush, fertile farmland in front of me?" called William in disbelief, pointing directly in front of their path.

"That's not a mirage, it's the northern bend of the Fertile Crescent," Menashe answered. "This area is commonly referred to as the cradle of civilization. Believe it or not, some of the world's most important innovations occurred here, such as writing, the wheel, and irrigation."

"It's amazing how the landscape can transform so quickly from a harsh, barren desert, to one so burgeoning with verdant crops and plants."

"Not only that," Widad interrupted, "but it should probably give us a little respite from this oppressive heat."

"Oh, count me in for that," Rich joked, as he looked up into the sky, squinting at the sunlight. "Quick question," he tentatively threw out after a brief moment. "Is it just me, or have you noticed it's gotten somewhat darker over the past few minutes?"

"Now that you mention it," Menashe remarked, "it does seem to be slightly dimmer."

Sheltering his eyes with his hand, he peeked up into the air, scrutinizing the sky.

"It almost looks like there's a shadow starting to creep in front of the Sun?" he speculated.

"That's strange," Gabriel commented. "There *is* supposed to be a solar eclipse early tomorrow morning, but it shouldn't be occurring until twelve hours from now."

"Why didn't you mention this earlier?" puzzled Widad.

"Well, it's only supposed to be viewable from the western hemisphere, and even then, only from the west coast of South America and Antarctica. Otherwise, I would have let you know days ago so no one would start to worry."

"Well, now I'm even *more* concerned!" the diminutive woman exclaimed. "How is this even possible?"

Placing his hand on top of his chest where the amulet was positioned beneath his shirt, William looked at Gabriel with an alarmed expression.

"What is it?" their herculean protector demanded.

"My talisman is burning!" he exclaimed. "I think something horrible is about to happen!"

Abruptly spinning to his side, Gabriel began to scan the shoreline as an increasingly bleak expression spread across his visage.

"I can't believe I didn't anticipate this!"

"Anticipate what?" Rich shuddered.

"An ambush!"

"Where? By whom? I don't see anything!" William worried.

"By the looks of things, from pretty much everywhere," the massive man lamented. "And I think we are going to be in for quite the battle."

After examining the shoreline for a few moments, William looked at their enormous companion with a perplexed expression.

"Are you sure they're there?" he questioned. "I'm not seeing anything."

"Oh, they're there," he affirmed. "They're just secluding themselves in the shadows, probably because they're in physical form."

"Why would they do that?" Rich huffed.

"My guess is they recently possessed clone bodies created at Cenetics, and they are still getting accustomed to their new forms. Until they do so, they will be weaker and more susceptible to injury from weapons or divine power. I presume Lucifer is exerting His power to conceal the Sun, allowing for His minions to attack us once He has bathed the earth in complete darkness. Once the divine light from the heavens is fully cloaked, their attack will commence."

"Well, I'm glad you don't sugar coat things," Rich wryly replied. "What can we do?"

Looking up at the sky, Gabriel assessed the advance of the shadow creeping across sun.

"Most likely, we have fewer than thirty minutes before the solar eclipse is complete. Probably less for initial incursions."

He paused for a moment and a grim smile of satisfaction began to form on his lips as he surveyed the landscape.

"This should actually work to our advantage," his deep voice rumbled. "In fact, I don't think we could have asked for a better defensive position."

"Seriously?!" Menashe exclaimed. "We're an easy target in the middle of the Euphrates. They'll be able to flank us from a higher elevation on both sides of the river, let alone from the air, if any of them can fly. And then, of course, they could strike us from the water itself!"

"This is all true," their angelic protector agreed, "but I have a few tricks up my sleeve, which will play to our advantage."

Gabriel then looked at the navigator of their vessel, who was visibly shaking as he listened to the conversation unfold between his passengers.

"My friend, would you mind steering us into the center of the river, then keeping us there?"

"kulukum majanin!"[79] he exclaimed as he leapt over the side of the boat and began swimming to the shoreline three hundred feet off the port side.

"Alright then," Gabriel casually commented, "we're going to need a new navigator. Widad, would you do me the honor of taking up position behind the wheel?"

"I'll...I'll do my best," she faltered.

"Excellent. Go ahead and start steering us as near to the center of the river as possible. Gentlemen, will you excuse me for a moment?"

Without waiting for a reply, their herculean companion then made his way around to the bow of the vessel as Widad began guiding them to the middle of the waterway. Upon reaching the front of the boat, he kneeled down on the deck and solemnly bowed his head. After a few moments he reached down off the side of the boat, scooping up water from the river, then carefully cradled the liquid directly in front of his chest.

[79] You're all crazy!

"O aqua creatura Dei sal exorcizatum in nomine Dei Patris omnipotentis, et in nomine Iesu Christum eius Filium, adoremus Dominum, et in virtute Spiritus. Exorcizo te, ut potes exorcizata ad effugandam omnem potestatem inimici, et possit eradicare et explantare valeas, qui hostes cum angelis suis apostaticis, per virtutem ejusdem Domini nostri Jesu Christi, qui venturus est judicare vivos et mórtuos, et sæculum per ignem."[80]

As Gabriel uttered the last words, he rose to his feet, gently poured the water back into the Euphrates, and turned to face his companions, who all stood silently watching.

"That should be good for starters," he declared with a broad smile.

"What exactly did you just do?" Rich pressed.

But before he could respond, a horrific shriek erupted from the water off the side of the boat, and they all rushed to the railing to discover the source. Struggling in the water, a mere ten feet from their craft, a floundering demon struggled to keep its head above the surface as it gasped for air. The skin covering the creature was dissolving off its form, almost as if it had been submerged in a vat of acid, and a cruel gurgling sound crept out of the fiend's maw as the soft tissue within its throat liquified and it drowned in its own flesh.

Rich turned around with a look of admiration on his face as he gazed at their guardian.

[80] O water, creature of God, I exorcize you in the name of God the Father Almighty, and in the name of Jesus Christ His Son, our Lord, and in the power of the Holy Spirit. I exorcize you so that you may put to flight all the power of the enemy, and be able to root out and supplant that enemy with his apostate angels, through the power of our Lord Jesus Christ, who will come to judge the living and the dead and the world by fire.

"You blessed the entire river!" he exclaimed. "I don't know how you did it, but you turned the entire Euphrates into holy water."

Wearing a stern expression, Gabriel simply nodded as he looked out across the river, where countless scenes of misery and pain were taking place. Within a matter of two minutes, hundreds of lifeless corpses floated aimlessly on the surface, while a putrid black oily liquid trailed from the vanishing remains of their would-be assailants, until they sluggishly disappeared beneath the water.

The next moment, their ethereal companion grasped the golden trumpet hanging on his side, and in one fluid movement, he held it to his lips and a glorious vibration resounded across the landscape. Instantly, a brilliant light appeared directly above the ship and thousands of winged angels rushed out of the breach and into Earth's reality. As the heavenly protectors flew into the air, they took up a defensive position at varying heights directly above and around the ship. In total, nearly four thousand angels formed a protective sphere reaching nearly one-and-a-half miles over the full breath of the river. Each of the winged guardians was clad in radiant silver armor from head to toe, adorned with raised golden borders, ornate etchings covering their shields and breastplates. Both male and female guardians wielded enormous broadswords or spears, and wore large, nearly solid helmets with small slits in the visors to allow for vision. Almost effortlessly, the entirety of the angelic force beat their wings rhythmically, enabling them to hover in their specific positions as they prepared for defense.

A small group of supernatural beings, totaling nine in number, glided down to the fishing vessel, landing at even intervals around the perimeter of the ship, and after sheathing their swords, each bowed deeply toward Gabriel. The next moment, the angels turned to face the water and interlocked hands with one another until they had encircled the passengers behind a radiant barrier. As the area known as the Fertile Crescent continued to be swallowed up by abysmal shadows, horrible snarls and growls from unseen beasts drifted across the water. Still situated at the bow, Gabriel gazed up at the sky just as the final edges of the Sun were shrouded by the heavenly satellite, and Earth was engulfed in complete gloom.

"And the fifth angel poured out his vial upon the seat of the beast; and his kingdom was full of darkness; and they gnawed their tongues for pain," he said in a hushed voice.

Almost immediately, the sound of cleft hooves erupted from both sides of the river as indistinct shapes began galloping toward the waterway. As the vague forms drew closer to the shore, each of the nine angels circumscribing the vessel bowed their heads in what appeared to be a silent prayer. The next instant, Gabriel, who had remained standing on the bow of the ship, raised both of his hands high above his head and uttered the following words:

"O Deus, auribus percipe verba oris mei."[81]

A flash of lightning instantly burst from the sky directly above the ship, and thunder reverberated across the ground. The brilliance cast by the electricity temporarily illuminated the horrific creatures converging on the river, sharpening the hazy outline of the indistinct hordes.

"ya 'iilhi!"[82] Widad shuddered. "There are so many of them!"

[81] Oh God, give Your ear to the words of my mouth.

[82] Oh, my God!

As bursts of light continued to strike in the sky above, the deformed shapes of nearly one thousand infernal beasts could be seen, bounding across the fields in the darkness. Even from this distance, the hellions were considerably larger than the demons they had previously encountered, with several easily towering over twenty feet in height. And, unlike the monstrosities they had fought before, each vile creature was covered from head to toe in a thick, obsidian black armor, which served not only the purpose of protecting the wearer, but also of inspiring fear. Large numbers of the attackers wielded blunt, machete-like swords, covered with a thick, vile tar, and others carried almost archaic looking spears, each as tall as a man. The heavenly guardians at the edge of the small boat then released their grasp and held their hands high over their head in unison

"O Deus, auribus percipe verba oris mei," they spoke as one.

Clasping his hands in front of his chest, Gabriel dropped to both knees and cried mightily to the heavens.

"Per fiat voluntas tua, defendat per lumen tuum!"[83]

The next moment, the angels raised their swords high above their heads and tremendous beams of light emanated from their collective being, rising up through the air intersecting with one another at a point one hundred feet above them. At the same instant the rays converged, the sound of shattering glass ripped through the air and a protective, dome-shaped shield slowly descended to the surface, fully enveloping the boat.

As the front wave of the demonic swarm neared the coastline, roughly half of the raiders leapt up from the

[83] By Thy will, protect us with Thy light!

surface and soared into the air on large, leathery wings to engage their enemy, and the other half jumped headlong into the Euphrates. Shrieks of pain and suffering immediately swept across the surface of the water as dozens of jinn were met with an ignominious death as their skins dissolved and entirely disintegrated from their unholy frames. Realizing the waters meant certain death, the remaining ground troops stopped short of the river's edge, screaming curses and guttural slurs in an incomprehensible language.

The dreadful winged battalions climbing into the air, were met by the fierce resistance of an overwhelmingly larger force of heavenly soldiers. However, what happened next would cause the most indomitable warrior to flee in terror. Despite being outnumbered more than four to one, the appalling fiends began slaying angels by the dozens. Hacked, disfigured, and otherwise mutilated bodies of celestial champions began to drop from the sky at an alarming rate. It seemed as if angels fell by the spear of each demon at a rate of ten to one.

"How can this be happening?!" Rich shrieked in horror.

"The malignant spirits of the adversary have possessed the physical forms of clones," grunted Gabriel. "Despite our greater numbers, they are considerably more powerful. We are at a significant disadvantage in this battle."

"But if that's the case, there's no way that we can win this fight!"

"It's not about winning. It's about surviving long enough."

The next moment, one of the angels standing on the port side of the vessel let out a rough grunt as he fell down to one knee, the thick shaft of a four-foot-long arrow protruding from his side. For a moment, he struggled to hold his sword above his head, but as a second and third projectile pierced his chest, he faltered, dropping his weapon noisily onto the deck. The radiance of the protective shield surrounding the boat began to lessen, and it was obvious its strength had been weakened.

Gabriel quickly leapt over and knelt down beside his fallen comrade, firmly gripping his gauntleted hand.

"You're sacrifice will not go unrewarded," he solemnly whispered.

The next moment, the fatally wounded warrior passed and slid soundlessly into the river.

Roughly pushing himself up to a standing position, Gabriel held his own sword above his head and joined the remaining angels to strengthen the defensive barrier, just before another barrage of half a dozen arrows impacted the obstruction and fell harmlessly into the river. After watching the last of the darts disappear beneath the surface, Gabriel looked at the battle ensuing in the sky above, almost as if he was searching for someone.

"Dadrail, te requiro!"[84] he boomed.

Located directly above the ship, a glorious seraph, engaged in combat with a winged hellion, paused for a moment to acknowledge Gabriel's cry, then returned her attention to her enemy. With a deft lunge forward, she easily parried a clumsy attack from her assailant and thrust the end of her sword just beneath its collar bone and up through the base of its skull. The body of the monstrous incubus immediately stiffened, then lifelessly fell down until it collided with the heavenly impediment surrounding the boat and slowly slid sideways into the river. With a satisfied nod, she pulled both her wings tightly to her sides

[84] Dadrail, I need you!

and dove directly through the protective barrier at high speed. At the last moment, she opened her wings to arrest her descent, alighting on the bow of the vessel adjacent to Gabriel.

"Jibreel," she greeted while bringing her fist across her chest with a slight bow. "Things are looking bleak."

"Aren't they always?" he quipped with a slight grin. "I find myself in need of a *Virtuous* angel. Are you busy?"

"I have a few things going on, but I can make myself available," she replied with a wry smile.

Without another word, Dadrail glided over to the position the last angel had occupied and held her sword firmly above her head.

"Per fiat voluntas tua, defendat per lumen tuum," she called out.

A brilliant beam immediately burst out of her entire being, merging with the light emanating from the other protectors, and the protective shield blazed power and strength anew. Convinced the barrier was sufficiently hardened, Gabriel lowered his sword and turned to face the shoreline.

Arrayed on both sides of the river, disgusting creatures launched multiple barrages of arrows and spears at the vessel. While the luminous barrier arrested virtually every attack, a few of the projectiles did manage to pierce the safeguard, dangerously plummeting toward the occupants on the ship as they did.

"Gabriel!" Rich shouted. "Why did you say you were in need of a *Virtuous* angel? Aren't all angels virtuous?"

"Indeed, they are," he agreed, "but there are nine different types of angels. Seraphim, Cherubim, Thrones, Dominions, Principalities, Powers, Virtues, Archangels and

Angels. Combining the powers from each different type creates an almost impenetrable shield. Israfil, who was destroyed, was one of the Virtues Angels, and I needed to replace him with an equivalent partner."

"But what happens if there isn't one available?"

"Let's hope it doesn't come to that."

"Gabriel!" Widad shrieked, pointing to the river. "Look out!"

Shifting his gaze, the archangel caught glimpse of a ghastly looking barb at the end of an enormous wooden pole, which was hurtling directly upon his location. Without a second to lose, he threw himself back and down toward the deck of the boat as the putrid spike sliced deeply through the tip of his shoulder. Roughly pushing himself back up to his knees, he turned to face Widad.

"Thank you!" he declared with an appreciative nod. "We had all better pay closer attention."

Now back on his feet, Gabriel searched the shoreline until he spotted the origin of his near destruction. Perched on a slightly elevated bluff, three contemptible brutes were hurriedly reloading a medieval looking ballista with another deadly projectile. Pursing his lips in dismay, he lifted his golden trumpet to his lips and another sublime blast filled the air, echoing throughout the area.

Instantly, an enormous burst of light appeared to the side of the ship and a flaming chariot burst through the breach, pulled by two magnificently feathered horses. The carriage itself was easily half the size of their boat and contained a winged female warrior, standing at least fifteen feet tall. As it raced across the surface of the water, the woman gritted her teeth, narrowed her eyes ominously, and gripped her lines tightly to spur the stallions forward. Surging ahead, she steered the vehicle directly at the enemy, who had just refilled their ammunition and were in the process of aiming their weapon for another attack. At the last minute before she fell directly upon their location, the driver shifted her wagon so the wheels would just avoid colliding with the target, allowing the ten-foot-long steel blades that protruded perpendicularly from the axle, to strike their target. Flesh, bone, and steel provided no resistance to the savage destruction inflicted by these swords, which swiftly cleaved demons and armament in two, assuring their permanent and complete departure from this world. Having completely its lethal attack, the chariot pulled up short and shimmered out of reality.

"Why don't you call in a few more reserves like that one?" Rich coaxed. "Very effective!"

"I wish I could, but unfortunately, I've already used up most of the energy in my horn. It will take at least a day to recharge it enough to muster another chariot, and this battle will be over by then."

Over the next several hours, the conflict continued with similar scenes playing out. Hundreds of winged succubi clashed in the air with thousands of angelic hosts, both sides sustaining heavy casualties. As Gabriel had foretold, the demonic forces were slowly gaining an advantage, despite their markedly lower numbers, and the sheer total of guardians had visibly dwindled. Several times, one of the nine angelic protectors supporting the luminous shield fell by arrow or spear, resulting in Gabriel summoning a comparable substitute from the remaining warriors in the sky above. Dawn should have been drawing close, but given the unnatural darkness overwhelming the planet, it was impossible to tell.

As the battle raged in the air, one of the larger winged demons managed to navigate its way to the top of the shield unscathed, and was now standing directly atop of the barrier. Lifting a substantial weapon high over its head, it drove the sharpened end directly into the protective sphere, sending bolts of electricity along the surface in all directions. With significant effort, the horrific creature began to slowly twist the shaft of its javelin, driving the blade further and further through the surface, until it finally broke through to the other side. For a moment, the shield failed, allowing the malignant devil to enter the interior before coalescing back into a virtually impervious boundary. With a jubilant shriek, the appalling fiend threw its head back and dove at breakneck speed to the exposed ship below. In one fluid action, it vigorously landed on the aft, causing the bow to rise nearly eight feet in the air. Before any of the guardians on the ship had a chance to react, the depraved succubus wildly swung an enormous sickle and the five-foot long blade easily split two angelic guardian bodies in half, just above the waist.

The barrier protecting the ship immediately disintegrated and each of the angels turned to face the enemy at the gate. With a sickly grimace, the hellion shifted its gaze across each foe, until it paused, staring at the diminutive form of Widad, who was cowering in the center of the boat. Without any hesitation, the demon leapt forward with an ancient, dripping dagger and thrust it through her shoulder, pinning her soundly to the floor.

"Widad!" screamed Menashe. "I'll kill you!" he spat, lunging at the creature.

Without any concern, the noxious fiend viciously knocked Menashe sidelong into the railing with the end of his sickle, then turned to stare directly at William. But before he had a chance to react, Gabriel stepped directly in front of him, lowering his sword so the point was oriented directly into the demon's face.

"Cur non colligunt aliquis in magnitudine tua?"[85] he challenged.

With a snarl, the disgusting beast stepped toward the archangel with its unholy scythe gripped tightly in one claw, and the vile dagger in the other. As it advanced on its prey, Gabriel swiftly turned to his side, launching an aggressive attack with his broadsword. Much to his surprise, however, the demon almost casually deflected his strike and swiftly stuck the archangel's hip with its knife. Before Gabriel could even react, the fiend struck again with the razor-sharp edge of its cutlass, inflicting a deep gash into his thigh. Falling backward, Gabriel's visage clearly exuded both fear and surprise.

One of the angels to the side of the boat jumped forward to protect his leader, but she was quickly struck down too, landing flat out on the deck of the ship. The six remaining angels swiftly encircled William and his companions, as the horrific archfiend began to cackle, seemingly amused by scene unfolding before it.

As the repugnant being started to take a purposeful step forward, several high-pitched whooshes ripped through the air in nearly instant succession, and the creature fell backward, leaning heavily onto the railing of the vessel. Shifting his gaze to the bow of the ship, Gabriel spotted the familiar sight of his angelic comrade Seraphina hovering effortlessly over the water. Without a word, she forcefully flapped her wings and rejoined the few angelic guardians still fighting in the air.

[85] Why don't you pick on someone your own size?

Gabriel pushed himself back to his feet and lumbered across the boat, until he was standing directly in front of the gasping demon as it lay on the deck. Reaching down, he roughly grabbed the jaw of the hideous beast, forcing it to stand upright for a brief moment. The next instant, he brutally swung his sword from the ground up through the base of the creature pelvis, directly through its torso, and out the side of its neck. After the two halves of the demon had slid noisily to the ground, he kicked them over the side of the craft and redirected his gaze toward the horizon.

"Get back in position!" he huffed. "We need to endure just a bit longer."

Straight away, each of the six remaining angels retook their positions on the side of the boat and began to reform the protective barrier. As Gabriel searched the still-darkened sky, he realized there were only a couple of dozen warriors remaining, and he didn't have the specific reinforcements to build the shield successfully.

"Seraphina," he called out, "non opus est tibi!"[86]

The red-haired angel spiraled down from high above the river, landing gracefully on the bow of the ship alongside Gabriel.

"I was wondering when you'd ask," she jokingly chided him.

"Even at the end, you continue to amaze me," he smiled.

"Will you gather additional guardians to replace the others?" she wondered.

"There isn't time. You and I will attempt to make up the difference."

Seraphina then set her sword on the ground, and as Gabriel held his aloft, she wrapped her hands tightly around

[86] I need you now!

his as the two of them jointly clutched the hilt of his massive sword. A tremendous flash of light immediately burst out from the blade and the protective sphere enclosing the boat brightly shimmered, almost appearing to solidify into translucent steel.

Standing in the middle of the vessel, William and his companions watched helplessly as the final remaining guardians were vanquished in the sky, leaving nearly fifty depraved jinn warriors either hovering above the Euphrates or scampering along the shoreline.

“So, what happens next?” shuddered Rich.

“They will burrow through the barrier until they breach it, and then lay waste to all that stand against them,” spat Seraphina.

Almost as if in response to her statement, two of the winged demons in the sky touched down on the shield directly above the ship, and immediately began thrusting their spears into the exterior. In a similar manner to the massive succubus who had broken through the boundary, electric bolts began crackling along the surface. Meanwhile, several of the flying creatures swooped down to the river’s edge, each grabbing one of the hellions stranded on shore and carrying them up to the faltering impediment. The instant their cloven hooves made contact with the invisible safeguard, they began ferociously hacking at it, creating even more streaks of electrical currents. As the onslaught continued, the toll on their angelic protectors started to become obvious, as each of them visibly labored to maintain their focus. Large beads of sweat rolled off the brow of each champion as every muscle in their bodies twitched beneath the strain.

"Kerubiel!" Gabriel shouted to the sentinel on his left. "Momenta pauca tenere!"[87]

But it was too late. The magnificent Cherubim buckled beneath the burden, falling loudly to his knees. Immediately, the strength of the barrier appeared to falter, then completely shattered inward upon itself. The winged hellions jabbing at the shield instinctively flapped their wings to hover in the air, while the five flightless fiends plummeted downward. Luckily, three of the vile creatures plunged directly into the river where the consecrated waters immediately deprived them of their lives. Seraphina, who had been anticipating the breach, reacted quickly, sinking two of her arrows deep within the eye sockets of another. The fifth succubus, however, managed to hit the side of the boat, where it desperately clung to the railing. An angel located next to the suspended creature began to swing his sword in an attempt to send the beast to its watery grave, but the demon nimbly dodged the strike. Without hesitation, the hellion then flung itself onto the deck, clambered onto its enemy, and began slicing through his protective armor with razor-sharp claws. Screaming in agony, the heavenly guardian wrapped his arms tightly around his assailant, and jumped into the water, carrying the vile imp down into the depths, and its assured destruction.

"Para bellum!"[88] Gabriel yelled.

Each of the surviving protectors warily eyed the sky as the nearly twenty winged evildoers launched themselves downward at great velocity. Standing in a protective stance, the angelic warriors braced themselves for what they knew

[87] Hold on a few more moments!

[88] Prepare for battle!

would be their final act, and one which they would courageously face head on. As the imminent assault drew closer, an almost sinister smirk appeared on the face of Gabriel, who lowered his sword and turned to the east.

"Fiat lux!"[89] he whispered.

Instantly, the most pristine shaft of sunlight peeked around the side of the moon for the first time in fifteen hours. As the glorious rays illuminated the nearly pitch-black landscape, the horrific minions of the Devil shrieked in pain. Skin, flesh, and bone were immediately incinerated as each of the winged demons were vaporized in mid-air. The exuberant imps on the shoreline tried to take cover, but they had no chance of outrunning the sublime radiance that had begun to spread across the earth. As the splendid light ushered in the beginning of a new day, it swept every malicious creature before it, cleansing the battleground completely.

Exhausted from the lengthy battle and suffering from multiple injuries, Gabriel finally fell backward onto the deck and drifted off into oblivion.

[89] Let there be light!

CHAPTER 29

Desiccation

(Three Days Later)

Almost as if he were dead, Gabriel lay motionless on a mattress that looked miniature in comparison to his massive frame, with both legs extending over the edge just below the knee. While his cheeks appeared completely devoid of life, in comparison to when they had dragged him into the cramped hotel room just three days earlier, they were now flush with color. The only indication he had not given up the ghost was the gentle rising and falling of his chest supporting his shallow breathing.

Situated on a cushioned chair adjacent to the bed, Widad tenderly patted his broad brow with a cool washcloth. Other than the thick, white bandage tightly wrapped around her shoulder, she showed no physical indication that she had nearly been killed during the skirmish. Across from the bed, William, Rich, and Menashe sat around a small circular table, engaged in a serious conversation about how best to continue on their journey to Germany.

"I believe his fever has broken," Widad breathed. "At least, I can't feel the heat radiating through the dampened cloth anymore. Hopefully, he'll be conscious soon."

"I certainly hope so," Rich wearily vented. "We can't just sit around doing nothing, and we need his input on how best to proceed. And even if we decide on what to do next, we won't get very far trying to transport a comatose giant. Virtually no one is walking on the streets, except for those damn U.N. soldiers dressed in black, badgering everyone they come in contact with about their vaccination passports. We'd be captured in no time."

Pursing his lips, Menashe audibly exhaled through his nostrils.

"Rich is right," he concurred. "I think we need to come up with a strategy that assumes Gabriel never wakes up."

"Don't count me out just yet," a hoarse voice rumbled on the side of the room.

The three men's heads immediately snapped in the direction of the sound, where they found their Herculean companion propped up on his elbow with a weary smile creasing his face.

"Gabriel!" William exclaimed as he leapt up from his seat. "It's so good to see you…" he faltered.

"Alive?" he rasped.

"To put it mildly, yes! How do you feel?"

Hoisting his body backward, he situated himself so he could sit completely upright with his back heavily leaning against the headboard. Even in this adjusted position, his feet lay a mere six inches from the end of the mattress.

"Well, my muscles are a bit sore, and my head is pounding. But other than that, I'm no worse for wear. How long was I out for?"

"Three days," William replied.

Shocked by this revelation, Gabriel swung his legs to the side of the bed and tried to push himself up into a standing position, before collapsing backward again.

"Oh no you don't!" chastised Widad. "You're not going anywhere!"

Ignoring her command, their angelic protector once again tried to push himself up into a standing position, but this time, it was the surprisingly strong hand of the diminutive woman that prevented him from rising.

"Like I said," she continued, "you need to rest. At least for a little while."

Relenting to her wishes, Gabriel settled himself back into a seated position and regarded William with a serious expression.

"The clock continues to tick, and it doesn't care if I'm injured or dead. We all still have a consequential part to play in this tale, and if the Adversary is successful in preventing just one of us from our completing our part, He will be victorious at the Final Battle."

Twisting his lips, Gabriel sat silently for a moment before continuing.

"What's the situation?" he finally asked.

"Well, when the solar eclipse ended and light returned to the world, the demons were completely destroyed," Menashe began. "With Widad injured, and you knocked out cold, we decided we needed a safer place to nurse our wounds. So, we traveled up the Euphrates a couple of kilometers and tied up on a dock outside the city of Jarabulus. Luckily, we found a dilapidated hotel not far from the river and were able to convince the owner to give us a room."

"Over the past few days," William interjected, "virtually no one has been out walking on the streets, except for Schmidt's soldiers, who are actively abusing citizens. And that's pretty much it."

Without any warning, Gabriel hefted his body up from the bed once more and, after pausing for a moment to calm his swirling head, he grasped his gigantic broadsword from against the wall and faced his companions with a determined expression.

"Let's head back to the boat. It's imperative that we don't lose any more time."

"But what about the guards?" Rich pressed.

A thin smile appeared on Gabriel's face, before giving way to a much more dreadful expression.

"Leave them to me."

Roughly ten minutes later, the small party emerged from the run-down inn and made their way onto a small side street, where the sidewalks appeared completely abandoned. The group walked down the short alleyway until it intersected with what appeared to be a main thoroughfare, despite it barely yielding enough space for two cars to squeeze past each other. As they turned onto the bisecting roadway, they could see the edge of the Euphrates lying less than one mile away, and after looking in both directions to confirm they were still alone, they began to walk down the center of the avenue.

"It looks like we might be in luck," hoped Rich.

The next moment, however, the shape of two darkly dressed persons stepped around a corner approximately one hundred yards away.

"What do we do?" Widad fretted.

"Just keep moving," exhorted Gabriel. "This shouldn't be a problem."

As the group made their way down the street, their enormous chaperone took the lead, walking purposefully toward the two soldiers dressed in all black. After standing for a moment staring at the advancing party, both the commandos began walking precisely down the center of the road on an intercept course. Within thirty seconds, both groups of people halted their advance, stopping roughly ten feet from one another, and stood staring silently for a seeming eternity. Finally, one of the troopers stepped forward.

"madha tafeal bialkhariji?"[90] the taller of the two challenged. "qadam 'awraqak ealaa alfawr 'aw..."[91]

But before the officer could finish his sentence, Gabriel unsheathed his colossal sword and delivered a vicious strike across the abdomen of the man, spilling his innards out onto the pavement. Despite his face being completely shrouded by a black Shemagh, you could clearly see surprise in the soldier's eyes just before he slid lifelessly to the ground.

Even with Gabriel's swift attack, the other militant had already unslung the automatic machine gun from his shoulder, and was in the process of readying himself to shoot. As he began to raise the barrel of his gun, a single shot erupted immediately behind Gabriel, and the security agent collapsed in a heap.

As Gabriel turned around, he saw Menashe standing squarely in the roadway, both feet more than shoulder-width apart and both hands extended in front of him. He was holding a smoking pistol.

"I was hoping you'd have my back!" he attested.

"Always," Menashe confirmed with a slight nod.

Standing motionless, Widad simply gawked at Menashe as he silently holstered his weapon.

"It had to be done," he lamented. "And now that it is, let's make our way down to the water as quickly as possible. I'm sure that's going to draw some attention."

[90] What are you doing outside?

[91] Present your papers immediately or...

Quietly, the group made their way down to the Euphrates, where they were able to board and launch their vessel without any further incident.

The blistering heat of the late afternoon relentlessly beat down on the travelers as they continued their journey along the Euphrates. Three hours earlier, they had cast off from their berth close to Jarabulus, crossed the border, and sailed nearly twenty miles into Turkey. As the day lingered longer, the oppressive temperatures seemingly continued to increase and even as the night was beginning to approach, there was no respite was in sight.

"Would you look at that?" Rich marveled. "You can almost see the river evaporating right before our eyes."

"You're not too far from the truth," Gabriel grumbled.

The next moment, the deck of the ship strongly lurched to the starboard, accompanied by the grating sound of rock scraping against the bottom of the boat.

"Did we just hit land?" Menashe blurt out. "This part of the river should be at least thirty feet deep."

"Look!" William exclaimed, pointing to the river's edge.

Off the starboard side of the ship, the discoloration on the shoreline clearly marked where the normal water level should have been located, and where it actually was, a full fifteen feet lower. Even more alarming, though, was the appearance of a few sporadic rocks and ridges poking up through the surface of the river, revealing, beyond any doubt, that the level of the Euphrates was dropping. Rich slowly began to shake his head as he took a deep breath through his nostrils.

"And the sixth angel poured out his vial upon the great river Euphrates; and the water thereof was dried up, that the way of the kings of the east might be prepared."

"That's one of the final signs, isn't it?" probed Menashe. "What exactly does it mean?"

"The river provides the eastern boundary to the land of Israel's inheritance. This prophecy essentially foretells that during the last days, the armies of the east will cross the Euphrates to join in the Final Battle against Israel."

"Well, we definitely need to keep moving then," William urged. "And I think we need to get off the river before we get stranded, or worse.

With a nod, Rich began to steer the boat toward the shore on the starboard side of the ship.

"Stop!" Menashe blurted out. "Head over to that inlet on the western side. There should be a small airport just west of here, where we should be able to charter a private plane."

"How do you know all these things?" Rich puzzled.

"You forget, I was in the Israeli Army. The Gaziantep Airport in Turkey is one we frequently used as a base of operations when embarking on incursions into Syria."

"Ok, so how do you know we'll be able to secure a flight?"

"About ten years ago, the Turkish government returned the airfield to their citizens, and we had to find another staging area. Since then, it's pretty much only been used by local pilots. I don't know for certain, but I'm hoping one of them will take us where we need to go."

"And where is it we'll be flying to?" Widad interjected.

"Vienna," Gabriel advised. "Austria is about as far north as we are going to be able to travel by air without raising too much attention. And from there, we will make our way into Germany, to the despicable pit from which the vile creatures of the Adversary are spewing forth."

CHAPTER 30

Breakout

(Two Days Later)

Strong crosswinds made the descent down to the Bad Voslau Airport, thirty minutes outside of Vienna, more turbulent than most passengers on the small prop airplane would have desired. This was especially true for Menashe, who was turning three different shades of green as the aircraft lurched about abruptly. The small white sick bag he was tightly gripping, seemed to be serving a double purpose, both as a means to fend off hyperventilation, and as a potential repository for the contents of his stomach. Widad, who appeared to be the least affected, was trying to hide her amusement at the queasiness the rest of her party was exhibiting.

"Are you certain you served in the Israeli Defense Force, my friend?" she jested. "I would have thought you'd be more used to this sort of thing."

"I was a combat engineer, not in the Air Force!" he scowled from behind the sack. "We rarely left the ground."

Giggling, Widad shifted her gaze out the window for a moment, then returned an empathetic look to Menashe.

"It looks like your prayers have been answered; we're nearly on the ground."

A few moments later, the plane touched down on the runway with a distinct thud, before bouncing back up into the air for a few more seconds.

"Oof!" Menashe exclaimed. "I think I'm going to lose it."

"Hang in there!" William pleaded.

The next instant, the wheels of the plane contacted the surface in a more controlled manner, and the craft began to rumble down the short runway. As the aircraft slowed, it began turning toward a sizeable area for private planes to park, situated a couple hundred feet from the control tower, before finally coming to a complete stop in one of the designated spaces. Without any hesitation, Menashe unbuckled himself, made his way to the door, and quickly descending the stairs to the tarmac.

"I guess he really wanted to get off this flight!" Widad joked.

Looking out of the window, she could clearly see her ailing friend kneeling on all fours, heaving up what was most likely their breakfast from earlier that same day.

"Poor man. Hopefully, he'll..." she abruptly cut off.

"What's wrong?" worried Rich.

"We've got company," Gabriel warned. "Everybody sit tight while I look into things."

Struggling to fit through the comparatively small opening, their enormous companion made his way down the short flight of steps to the runway and approached his recuperating companion.

"You'd better get back on the plane," he asserted.

Still crouching on the pavement, Menashe's eyes suddenly widened as he looked at the contingent of eight armed soldiers marching directly to their location. The next moment, he hopped back up to his feet with a serious expression on his face.

"What do we do?"

"I'm not certain," Gabriel apologized with a slight shaking of his head. "But one thing I do know for sure is that we can't fight. There are too many of them, and I'm confident that if we try, at least one of us will be killed."

Biting his lip, Menashe nodded in affirmation and briskly made his way back up into the aircraft. The next moment,

Gabriel took a deep, cleansing breath, and turned to watch the security forces cross the remainder of the concrete, stopping just a few feet away.

Four of the men confronting him appeared to be normal police officers, dressed in navy blue uniforms with gold patches displaying the word "POLIZEI" on the left breast. Each had a walkie-talkie and handgun holstered on their sides. The other four guards were dressed in the jet-black uniforms of the U.N. Security Forces, and had automatic rifles slung over their shoulders.

"Warum bist du hier?!"[92] one of the Austrian officers demanded in German, in a thick accent. "Die österreichische Grenze ist geschlossen!"[93]

"Ich entschuldige mich, aber unser Navigationsgerät ist ausgefallen,"[94] Gabriel replied in perfect German.

While he was speaking, one of the U.N. soldiers eyed the herculean man with skepticism. Sensing he was staring, Gabriel shifted his gaze to meet his, attempting to appear as benign as possible, notwithstanding his enormous stature. Unfortunately, the soldier's suspicion wasn't lessened as he glared hatefully at the larger man through narrowed eyes.

"Do you speak English?" the mistrustful officer challenged.

"Yes," he cautiously replied.

"Excellent. Please have everyone exit the aircraft and present themselves for inspection."

Gabriel nodded in compliance, then turned and stuck his head back into the doorway of the plane.

[92] Why are you here?

[93] The Austrian border is closed!

[94] I apologize, but our navigation equipment failed.

"Everyone needs to come outside. Try not to be too alarmed, but I'm pretty certain we're going to be arrested."

"But if we're detained, Schmidt's going to find us," fretted William. "And if that happens..."

"Let's take this one step at a time," Gabriel interrupted. "All of the guards are *human*, which means they have no idea who we really are. We'll just have to figure this out as we go."

Arching a speculative brow, William climbed out of the plane along with his three other companions and the pilot. A moment later, all six of them were standing on the tarmac facing the soldiers.

"Which one of you is the pilot?!" barked one of the policemen.

"Ah ... th-th-that would be me," stammered the aviator.

Without a word, the officer marched over to him and grasped his right wrist.

"I assume you have your vaccination chip, yes?"

"Ah...yes," he whimpered.

The next instant, one of the other officers stepped forward holding a metal wand in one hand, connected by a red wire to a digital display he was grasping in his other. Silently, he passed the wand up and down the shaking man's arm until the device emitted a high-pitched chirp. Reading the display, the officer briefly nodded and looked directly his suspect.

"It says here your name is Ihsan Demir of Turkey?"

"Yes, that's me."

"Fully vaccinated the end of last year?"

"Yes."

"Please come with us. We have a few questions for you."

Without any additional formality, the two police officers escorted Ihsan away from the aircraft and toward the main structure of the airport, leaving only two Austrian agents, along with the four U.N. guards.

"Alright then," the suspicious soldier challenged, "we need to scan each of your vaccination trackers."

"Ahh...that's going to be a problem. None of us have received them yet," confessed Gabriel.

Taking a step forward, the eyes of the agent narrowed even further.

"Present yourselves for scanning!" the man demanded.

"Suit yourself," shrugged Gabriel, exasperated, while holding both of his enormous hands outward.

The eyes of the police officer holding the electronic device nearly bulged out of his skull as he hesitantly reached forward and attempted to grasp Gabriel's wrist. After discovering he could only wrap his hand halfway around the gigantic limb, though, he tilted his head backward to look up at the mighty man who simply smiled back at him with an amused expression on his face. He then began waving the wand up and down his massive forearm searching for the implanted chip, and after a few failed attempts, he quickly backed away.

"He doesn't seem to have one," he blurted out.

"Check the others!" ordered the U.N. soldier.

After a few moments, the constable had scanned each member of the small group with the same results.

"How can it be that not a single one of you has an RFI tracker?" the trooper proclaimed in an incredulous tone. "That's just a little bit too convenient, don't you think? Everyone get out your passports and we'll do this the old-fashioned way."

"Umm...I think that might be a bit of an issue as well," divulged Gabriel. "You see, we all lost our passports a few weeks ago."

"So, let me see if I have this straight. You flew into Austria unannounced when the border is completely closed, you have no papers, *and* none of you have received a vaccination implant. Have I missed anything?"

"No, I think that about sums it up," the herculean man smiled.

"This isn't a laughing matter!" one of the other U.N. soldiers growled. "Given the situation, we don't have any alternative than to take you into custody until you can be properly identified."

Two of the troopers then took position on either side of Gabriel, grasping him by his elbows, and attempted to move his arms backward in order to cuff him. They quickly realized, however, that no matter how hard they tried, they couldn't budge him even a fraction of an inch. With a crooked eyebrow, the massive man glanced at both of the soldiers and his expression shifted to one exuding pure delight.

"Maybe you should just ask me to place my hands behind my back."

"Ahh…yes…umm…would you put your hands…"

"Ahem," the large man coughed, "would you *please* put your hands behind your back."

The visage of the soldier immediately shifted to one of irritation, but he quickly changed his mind when Gabriel leveled a menacing glare down at him.

"I…umm…yes…would you *please* place your hands behind your back?"

Without any resistance, Gabriel complied, touching his wrists together just above his buttocks.

"There, wasn't that easier?"

Without responding, the annoyed policeman removed a pair of handcuffs from his belt and attempted to wrap the single strand of steel around his captive's forearms.

"Really?!" he sighed in irritation.

"Is there an issue?" one of the U.N. soldiers barked.

"They don't fit!"

"Maybe you should try a set of zip ties?" chuckled Gabriel.

For a second, the officer was about to respond, but he then though better of it. A brief moment later, he retrieved a pair of restraints and firmly applied them to the prisoner. Satisfied the gargantuan man was bound in some manner, the officers then proceeded to handcuff the other members of the party and escort them toward the main building. When they had almost made it to a pair of double doors leading inside, one of them swung outward and a large U.N. soldier exited the building with an ominous expression on his face.

"We've just received new orders," he barked. "Take them to the secure transport. We'll interrogate them offsite."

Gabriel threw a concerned sidelong glance at William, who then turned to face the officer who had just spoken.

"Where are you taking us?" he asked with concern.

"You'll see," was the only response he received.

Roughly forty-five minutes later, the recently detained group were all seated in the back of a large, armored security van, speeding to an unknown destination. Gabriel and Menashe sat on a metal bench located on one side, with their other three companions seated directly across from them. No one knew exactly where they were heading and, due to the lack of windows, they had no idea of where they even were. For the first part of their journey, they merely sped along a roadway without so much as a slowdown, which was pretty much expected given the location of the airstrip south of Vienna. However, for the last ten minutes or so, the van had slowed significantly and seemed to be frequently stopping. William thought to himself that it could only be traffic lights halting their progress, so he surmised that they had to be in the city.

"I think they're taking us to the United Nations Office in Vienna," Menashe finally hypothesized. "At least, that's where I'd take someone to be *interviewed*."

"Well, if that's where we're going, it's only a matter of time before they determine who we actually are," Rich surmised.

"So, now what?" Widad directed toward Gabriel.

"I don't know yet," their herculean companion sighed. "But don't worry, we'll figure something out."

"If we don't come up with something, and fast, our quest ends here," William complained. "There's no way they will keep us together. Even before they determine who we really are, they're going to put us in separate rooms. And once they find out, they'll probably take us to completely different locations. And after Schmidt gets involved, they'll kill us!"

Pausing for a moment, he silently fumed about their entire situation until a thought occurred to him.

"Gabriel, when we were back at the airfield, about to enter the facility, you became...how should I say...extremely anxious for a moment when that soldier walked out of the airport. Why?"

"Remember when I said the four United Nations forces that met us at the plane were human? Well, the guard that came out from the terminal wasn't."

"Do you mean..."

"Yes," he interrupted. "It was a clone, and it was possessed."

"Did it..."

"Recognize me? Of course. That's why it wanted to whisk us away to another location where it would have reinforcements. Luckily, it's a fairly low-level demon...and not a very smart one."

"So, why didn't it attack us on the spot?"

"Like I said, it's pretty dumb, and more concerned about its own welfare than the overall strategy of the Adversary. If it had killed just one of you, then everything that had transpired up until this point would have been for naught, and the Final Battle at Megiddo would have been lost, along with all of humankind."

"Megiddo?" Widad wondered.

"That's the prophesized location where Armageddon will take place," Rich offered. "On the day of the great and Final Battle, Megiddo is where good and evil will engage in determinative combat."

Exhaling audibly through her nostrils, Widad drew her eyebrows downward and stared angrily at their angelic protector.

"That was quite a gamble you took!" she accused. "Or should I say, that you're still taking! We are firmly in enemy hands and if they so much as catch a hint of who we are, they'll execute us immediately."

For a brief moment, Gabriel looked up toward the roof of the van in deep thought, then returned his gaze to his friends with a broad smile.

"What are you so happy about?" pressed Widad.

"Oh, it's nothing," he commented nonchalantly.

The next moment, the forward motion of the vehicle abruptly came to a halt, along with the screeching sound of tire tread on the pavement.

"What's going on?!" yelled Menashe.

"That would be the calvary," Gabriel smiled.

Suddenly, gunfire could be heard outside of the van, along with the sharp sound of bullets ricocheting off the armored vehicle.

"Calvary?! More like executioners if whomever is outside isn't more careful."

"Everyone just sit tight for moment," Gabriel advised.

For the next several minutes, multiple gunshots echoed outside and men could be heard frantically yelling in German. Then, the chaotic noise ceased entirely and Gabriel stood up facing the rear of the vehicle. The next instant, he booted both of the doors cleanly off their hinges and peered around the opening.

Immediately outside the vehicle, the scene was horrific. Several police officers lay motionless on the roadway, blood pooling on the pavement immediately next to their fallen bodies. About twenty feet directly behind them, a police cruiser was fully engulfed in flames, and the burnt remains of the patrolmen were hanging out of an open window, where they had tried to unsuccessfully escape the burning vehicle.

Gabriel jumped out onto the street and turned back to face his companions.

"Let's get going," he coaxed firmly.

"What about these?" William asked, motioning toward the restraints holding his hands tightly behind his back.

“Oh yes, sorry.”

The next instant, both of Gabriel’s hand popped out from behind his back as he easily snapped the plastic zip ties that had been securing him. Then, after quickly darting over to his companions, he effortlessly twisted the metal cuffs off their wrists.

“Alright then, we need to be very careful,” he finally instructed.

“Where are we?” Menashe prodded.

“By the looks of it, we’re on a bridge crossing over the Danube. Ok, let’s go.”

Everyone exited onto the roadway, staying very close to the vehicle, and stared expectantly at their guardian.

“Who attacked the caravan?” William asked.

“My guess is some sort of militant group that doesn’t like the ridiculous mandates being forced on the world.”

“But why did they save *us?”* Menashe pleaded.

“Maybe you should just ask them,” offered Gabriel.

The next moment, several armed men appeared from around both sides of the van, wearing camouflaged fatigues and brandishing automatic machine guns.

“Sie alle müssen sofort mit uns kommen!”[95]

[95] All of you need to come with us, immediately!

CHAPTER 31

Confidant

(Fifteen Minutes Later)

Once again, William and his companions found themselves sitting in the rear of a large passenger van, but this time they were not restrained, and could look outside through the heavily tinted windows. A woman with black hair was driving the vehicle, and a small man with a stern expression sat in the passenger seat. William didn't recognize either of them. For several minutes, they had been riding in near silence as the van wound its way through the city streets of Vienna and entered what appeared to be an industrial district. Several warehouses flanked either side of the road, and they were quickly approaching what looked to be a rough railroad crossing. As the vehicle sped over the tracks, everyone inside was jostled around, and the man seated next to the driver threw an irritated glance at his companion.

"Hannah, was ist los mit dir? Langsamer!"[96] he snapped.

"Benutz keine Namen, du Idiot!"[97] she retorted.

"Sie werden sowieso lernen, wer wir sind! Außerdem sind sie auf unserer Seite."[98]

"Das wissen wir noch nicht genau!"[99] she huffed in exasperation.

"Verzeihung,"[100] Gabriel interjected. "We are definitely on your side, and we understand German. Do you speak English?"

[96] Hannah, what's wrong with you? Slow down!

[97] Don't use names, you idiot!

[98] They're going to learn who we are anyway! Besides, they are on our side.

[99] We don't know that for you sure yet!

[100] Excuse me.

"Of course we do," the driver scoffed.

"Excellent, then why don't we start with where you're taking us?"

"That will be answered quickly enough," she replied as she turned into a rough gravel lot located next to a small warehouse.

A few moments later, the vehicle came to an abrupt stop next to the entrance of the building and she threw the engine into park.

"Alright, everyone out!" she commanded.

Without waiting for a response, both Hannah and the passenger jumped out of the vehicle and started making their way to the front door.

"I guess we follow," Menashe offered with a shrug.

They got out and trailed after their escorts. A few moments later, they were all standing inside what looked to be the front office of a manufacturing facility, comprised of multiple desks, computers, and at least a dozen personnel actively working on tasks. The driver of the van was talking to a six-foot woman with a dark complexion and closely cropped black hair. Realizing their guests had joined them, she shifted her attention and greeted everyone with a smile.

"Welcome!" she offered in a French accent. "We're grateful that you have joined us."

"No, it is us who are grateful," Menashe coolly replied. "If you hadn't intervened, our captors would likely be driving wooden splinters under our fingernails at this point. Thank you for rescuing us."

"Don't think anything of it. Please, take a seat," she encouraged while motioning to a series of chairs against the wall.

The towering woman then shifted her gaze to Gabriel, who was standing with his arms firmly folded across his massive chest. Then, she glanced over at the small chairs and hesitated.

"In your case, maybe you should remain standing."

"That might be better for your furniture," he chuckled.

After everyone else had taken their seats, the woman addressed the group.

"I'm certain you have several questions," she began.

"We do," Widad responded. "Let's start with who are you and why did you save us?"

"Fair enough. My name is Mia Garnier and I'm the local leader of an international organization fighting to ensure right to privacy for everyone man, woman and child on the planet. We have been working against the global mandate that every person on the planet receive an injectable vaccination passport, as we see this as just another means by which the government can control our lives."

"And why did you rescue us?"

"We regularly monitor the airstrip you landed at, and Hannah happened to be there when you arrived today. We probably wouldn't have intervened, but when she realized that none of you had RFI trackers, she felt compelled to free you by any means possible."

Shifting her gaze, Widad smiled in appreciation at the woman who had orchestrated their liberation, to which she rolled her eyes and shook her head in annoyance.

"Why is your organization taking such a violent approach?" Menashe probed.

"Because of the means by which they are going about enforcing *their* rule of law. The United Nations have taken over distribution of food and other critical resources and are using this as leverage to *force* people to be vaccinated so they can track them wherever they go. Millions of people are starving because they object to submitting to the worldwide mandate. Peaceful protests haven't improved anything, and things are getting worse. Unfortunately, violence seems to be the only thing that gets their attention."

Mia paused for a moment, analyzing each of their guests, then slowly walked up to Gabriel. Stopping just a few inches short, she leaned in and whispered in his ear.

"Can I speak with you for a moment?" she said.

"Of course."

"I don't know why I'm telling you this, but there's something about you that gives me comfort. I believe the end of the world is coming. And I'm not talking about the common belief that the end is near...no, I think we really are in the end times. Most people I know just think of this as a fairytale, something made up a long time ago to give people a reason to behave in a specific, morally agreeable way. But my heart tells me this isn't the case."

Pausing for a moment, she looked around the room to confirm no one would be able to hear her, then she leaned in even closer to Gabriel.

"None of this is random!" she breathed. "I believe everything that has transpired, and that will occur, is part of a strategy that..." she faltered.

"That the Devil himself has put in motion to achieve victory at the great and Final Battle? Your hypothesis is actually pretty much spot on," he breathed.

Mia leant back, her face exuding surprise and relief at the same time.

"How do know all of this? I mean, what role do you and your friends have in it?"

Glancing over at his companions for a moment, Gabriel then looked Mia squarely in the eye to ensure she heard and understood every word he was about to say.

"We play an integral part in this story, and it is crucial that we continue to do so, as the fate of humankind is truly teetering in the balance. I can't tell you much more than that, except that if it were not for your team's efforts today, the Adversary might have succeeded, and all would have been lost."

"Then it's true?" she offered. "The RFI trackers *are* the *Mark of the Beast*?"

Gabriel simply nodded in response.

"I knew it," she exclaimed more loudly than she had intended.

Blushing at the realization, she grasped Gabriel's hands and stared into his eyes.

"What can I do to help?"

"We need a vehicle and safe passage to Germany."

"The car is easy, but the safe passage might be a little tougher. Let me reach out to my network to see which border crossings are most likely not being closely watched at the moment. Is there anything else you need?"

"I'm sure my friend would like to talk with one of your colleagues," he replied, motioning to Menashe. "We'll likely need access to some firearms and explosives to help us achieve our next objective. Oh, and information. If there's anything else you've heard recently, which might be relevant, I'd love to hear it."

Pausing for a moment, Mia mused silently until a flash of inspiration hit her.

"The only thing I can think of is a recent rumor."

"About what?" he pressed.

"I don't know how accurate this is, but just yesterday, we picked up some chatter about four military leaders who have started to raise a large army, supposedly tens of millions, off to the East somewhere. I don't know how that would even be possible."

Gabriel's eyebrows shot up in response.

"And the number of the army of the horsemen were two hundred thousand thousand: and I heard the number of them," he spoke in a hushed voice. "Time is running out."

CHAPTER 32

Infiltrator

(The Early Hours of the Morning, The Next Day)

A couple of hours after midnight, a solitary vehicle made its way down a rural road near the border of Austria and Germany, just north of the city of Salzburg, in near darkness. Rain had been falling for the past several hours, and as the tires rolled over the pavement, the soothing sound of water splashing off of the tread added to the somber mood. In order to draw as little attention as possible, the headlights remained off so as to hide their presence from any unknown eyes that might be watching the roads. The large van carried numerous boxes and cases containing various equipment, weaponry, and explosives, all of which would be required in order to have a chance at succeeding in their objective. With one hand on the steering wheel and the other leaning heavily on the arm rest, Gabriel gazed out into the darkness, seemingly unaffected by the severely limited visibility.

"Are you sure you can see the road clearly?" Widad quavered. "I mean, if you need to turn on the headlamps, I'm sure it would be ok."

"Don't you worry," Gabriel loudly chuckled. "I can see everything just as if it was the middle of the day."

"Well, maybe you could slow down just a bit?" she sighed. "You're going to give me a heart attack."

"I'll ease off the gas a bit if it will make you feel better. But there's nothing to worry about," he reassured her, "I can see perfectly fine."

"How much longer until we cross over the German border?" Menashe posed.

"About fifteen more minutes," Gabriel responded. "It's taking a little longer than I had hoped, but we need to avoid the city of Salzburg. These country backroads are ideal for concealment, but we can't drive nearly as quickly as we could if we were able to take paved highways."

"And how confident are you that the information Mia provided on where best to enter Germany is accurate? Based on what you said, we should be able to completely trust her. But what I'm worried about is whomever supplied her with the information."

Glancing over to the passenger's seat, Gabriel flashed Menashe a friendly smile, along with a slight nod.

"I'm not concerned at all with us safely getting to that vile abyss. What troubles me is what we do when we get there. How exactly do you plan on destroying it?"

This time, Menashe was the one to flash a reassuring smile.

"While I only *formally* spent four years with the Israeli Defense Forces, I have maintained contact with them over the past two decades. In the short time I was on active duty, people regarded me as an expert in my field."

"And what exactly did you do?"

"I specialized in blowing stuff up," he jested. "Several times, I entered into foreign states to oversee the destruction of specific facilities our government believed to be a threat to our national security. And since I left the service, I have worked more or less on a contract basis with the military to develop strategies on how best to demolish enemy structures."

"You are full of surprises," their angelic guardian laughed with a crooked eyebrow. "And here I thought you were only a Tzaddik."

"Looks can be deceiving!"

Returning his attention to the road for a moment, Gabriel silently began searching the darkness.

"What are you looking for?" Rich questioned from the back seat.

"That, right there!" he exclaimed, pointing off to the side of the road.

"I don't see anything?"

"Oh, my apologies," he grinned. "We just passed a small sign declaring that we've crossed into the country of Germany. Now, Menashe, if you would be so kind as to..."

Abruptly stopping midsentence, he quietly stared out of the top right corner of the windshield.

"What's wrong?" William probed.

"Nothing, I think," he replied. "For a second, I thought I saw something, but it probably isn't anything."

After another moment, he shook his head slightly and continued his discussion.

"As I was saying, Menashe, if you could detail for us the plan of attack you devised, it would be helpful to get everyone on the same page. That way, we won't have too many surprises."

"Of course. Our friends from Vienna have set us up with all the tools we will need to successfully pull off this operation. It's imperative that everyone dress in black so as to conceal our presence as much as possible. We have dark pants, jackets and boots which should fit everyone...well, hopefully everyone," he commented while smirking at Gabriel. "Since we will be infiltrating the facility in the early hours of the morning the day after tomorrow, I brought enough night vision goggles to ensure no one hurts themselves moving through the forest."

"Well, as our speed *angel* here has demonstrated, I don't think he'll be needing a pair to see," Widad joked.

"Good point," Menashe commented. "And actually, that should work out better for us, in case one of the devices fails. In addition to the goggles, we have ballistic helmets with wireless headsets so we can easily communicate with one another, and flak jackets to protect us from any attacks."

"Let's just hope we won't be needing those," she advised.

"With any luck. But we need to be prepared for anything," their strategist replied. "Now, the only people infiltrating the facility will be myself, Gabriel and William. Rich and Widad, you will remain at the tree line and warn us if anyone, or anything, is headed our direction. We will run a reconnaissance just after midnight to identify the best point to access the interior of the dome, and to ascertain whether or not they have any security guards on patrol."

"What if trouble finds us?" Rich worried.

"The two of you are going to be pretty much on your own until we have placed the charges inside. Mia provided us with multiple AR-15s and ammunition, which are in the crates," he explained, pointing to the rear of the vehicle. "Again, my hope is that we won't have to use them, but just in case, I'm going to show everyone how to safely operate these weapons. If you feel threatened, or are attacked, you will need to defend yourselves until we return."

"I'm not looking forward to this," Widad fretted.

"Don't worry," Rich assured, "between the two of us we'll be fine."

"So, that covers all of the logistics and monitoring. Now, how exactly do you intend to obliterate the gateway?" William questioned.

"That's what the C4 and detonators are for. Once inside the dome, we will place multiple charges along the based on the exterior wall."

"Why can't you just plant them on the outside of the structure?" Rich challenged.

"They won't be as effective," Menashe replied. "One of the most destructive components of this explosion will be detonating the devices in a confined space. If they're set off outside, next to the concrete base, a significant amount of energy from the blast will simply be redirected out into the forest. But blowing them within the building will transfer destructive energy out through the protective barrier and the enclosed space will actually amplify the damage."

"Alright, that should definitely demolish the protective structure covering the pit, but it probably won't do much damage to the gateway itself," Gabriel cautioned. "How exactly do you plan on destroying, or at least obstructing, the entryway into the world?"

"I assume dropping a couple hundred pounds of explosive into the pit won't seal the rift, will it?"

"Unfortunately, not even a couple thousand pounds of explosive will do that. It took a tremendous amount of energy to form the portal, and it takes even more to keep it that way. The best way to describe it is that the Adversary used a powerful form of black magic, and nothing of this world can hamper it."

"That's a bit outside my area of expertise," Menashe laughed. "Do you have any ideas on how, even if only temporarily, we can seal it?"

"Actually," their massive friend responded, "I believe I might just have an idea. If we can't stop or destroy the supernatural power maintaining the aperture, maybe we can simply redirect it."

"I don't understand what you mean?" puzzled William.

"To maintain a breach in our reality, the incantation would have to be extraordinarily strong. The only way to make one powerful enough would be to tie it to a physical object. In our case, that's the dark pit in the earth. But if we were able to alter the focus of this energy somewhere else, the pit would cease to function. At least, for a period of time. And this interruption just might cause enough of a delay to ensure that Beelzebub can't marshal all his forces for the Final Battle. That might give us just enough of an advantage to win."

Menashe sighed, then a broad grin appeared on his face.

"I think this just might work!" he exclaimed. "It has a lot of moving parts, but it's sound enough."

"I'm glad you agree," Gabriel declared. "Let's make our way to the staging location so we can get everything ready for our offensive. Even with a solid strategy, we need to..."

Suddenly, the tires of the vehicle screeched as he slammed on the breaks, bringing it to an unexpected stop. While the seatbelts kept everyone secure, Rich still managed to smack the side of his head solidly on the window.

"Son of a..." he blurted out, catching himself just in time. "What the hell was that for?" he exclaimed, holding his temple.

"I'm sorry," Gabriel expressed. "I saw an animal in the road, and I didn't want to strike it. Unfortunately, though, I think the back side of the van still impacted the creature. You all sit here for a second and let me check it out."

"I don't think you hit anything," William said. "And I didn't feel any..."

"No!" Gabriel sternly interrupted. "I'm certain something hit the car. Just stay here."

The next instant, the large man jumped out of the driver's seat and made his way around to the rear of the vehicle on the passenger's side. Suddenly, the back door of the cargo van was violently jerked open and Gabriel leapt into the rear space.

"What are you doing?" Rich complained. "You scared the…"

Stopping midsentence, he stared back through the interior of the van with a look of astonishment and terror at the scene before him. With his arm extended in front of his chest, Gabriel's massive fist was tightly clenched around the sickly neck of a gruesome-looking demon, who was wildly flailing its arms and legs and screaming. With a stern look on his face, their angelic protector walked back from the rear of the vehicle and stood at the side of the roadway. Each of the four passengers quickly exited the vehicle and gathered around Gabriel to witness the incident.

"Stop your squirming," the enormous man bellowed, "or I'll snap your neck!"

As the imp continued to thrash, the powerful muscles in Gabriel's forearm began to flex as he slowly increased the pressure being exerted on the throat of the vile creature. Within a few seconds, the succubus stopped struggling and hung motionless from its captor's grip.

"That's better," he growled. "Now tell me, Sammael, why are you spying on us?"

"Gabriel" the hellion hissed, "you know my name?"

"I know *all* the names of those that rebelled," he boomed. "Now, why are you spying on us?"

"I only do what my Master commands," he squawked.

"And who are you presently serving?"

"He will kill me if I utter his name!"

"*I* will kill you, here and now, if you don't!" Gabriel threatened, narrowing his eyes.

"Please, have mercy!" the demon pleaded.

"Tell me!" Gabriel shouted, increasing his vice-like grip once more.

"I…ack…I…" the demon choked. "I serve the Archfiend. He that makes the way for my Lord!"

"Your master is Schmidt!" he spat.

"Yes," he seethed. "He has been empowered by my Lord to oversee the final events that will announce His coming."

Furrowing his brow, Gabriel stared directly into the eyes of his prisoner.

"So, after hearing our plans, you were going to disclose them to your master?"

"Yes. But now your stench is upon my skin, and Master will know I have been caught and will kill me. If you set me free, I promise I will not inform him…"

"Promise?" Gabriel thundered while increasing the amount of pressure on his captive's throat.

"Please!" Sammael gurgled. "Have mercy!"

"I *am* showing you mercy," Gabriel replied, "by making your death quick and painless!"

The sound of bone crushing, accompanied by the sickly sight of flesh and blood percolating between Gabriel's powerful fingers, clearly indicated that the herculean guardian had wrung the life out of the loathsome form. The next moment, he simply opened up hand and the lifeless body slid down to the pavement.

Aghast at what she had just witnessed, Widad turned and ran to the side of the road, emptying the contents of her stomach onto the ground.

"I apologize," he softly lamented, "but if I had let him go, he would have reported everything he heard to the enemy."

Still standing hunched over position, Widad gazed at the Archangel with tears in her eyes.

"I'm not sure I can do this!" she sobbed. "I know what we are doing is right, but I don't think I'm strong enough."

Gabriel's expression exuded empathy as he offered a small smile of reassurance.

"You are far stronger than you give yourself credit for," he announced. "And while I don't know exactly how, I do know that before this is all over, your actions will help save all of humankind."

Menashe wrapped a comforting arm around Widad's shoulders, to which she immediately responded by burying her face in his chest, crying uncontrollably. While soothing the tearful woman, he looked at Gabriel with an expectant look on his face.

"Circumstances have changed, yes?" he asked.

"Yes, they have changed substantially," responded Gabriel.

"What do you mean?" Rich pressed.

"This demon, Sammael, is a spy. If he doesn't report to Schmidt, he will know something is wrong, and he will likely increase security tenfold, not just at Cenetics, but at the gateway as well. If that happens, there's no way we'll be able to succeed in our efforts."

"So, what does that mean?" wondered William.

"It means we attack tonight!" Gabriel announced, while making his way back to the vehicle. "It should take us two hours to drive to Cenetics, leaving us just over two hours before sunrise. I know I'm asking a lot from you all, but time is not on our side. We need to depart immediately!"

CHAPTER 33

Entombed

(Two-and-a-Half Hours Later)

Just after four o'clock in the morning, the small company of five made their way through the thickly wooded Hofoldinger Forest lying over eleven miles to the south of Munich. A thick layer of clouds enshrouded the landscape in near darkness, and the rain from earlier had slowed to a sporadic drizzle. While the damp, mostly dirt surface didn't present an ideal situation for hiking, it did help to minimize the sound their boots created as they quickly navigated through the woods. In spite of the relatively chill temperature, a thin film of perspiration had formed on the foreheads of each person, due to both the physical exertion and the anxiety at events to come.

Cresting the top of a knoll, their angelic guardian held up his hand, signifying that everyone should freeze where they stood. Situated approximately twenty feet in front of their current location, the dense forest opened up into a large, flat clearing. After motioning for them to follow, Gabriel began to cautiously creep forward, stopping at the boundary behind a few low-lying bushes. Glancing to confirm everyone was close by, he silently pointed out the large, dome-shaped structure occupying the center of the expanse.

"This is it!" William whispered. "When we were here last time, the concrete barrier was missing, but I'm positive this is the same place where we found that abominable pit."

William quickly glanced at Rich and Menashe, who nodded in silent affirmation.

“Alright then,” Gabriel breathed, “you all stay here for a few minutes while I search for the entrance.”

Without any delay, the enormous man sprinted across the field and began combing the entire perimeter. William and his companions silently watched him until he disappeared out of sight around the curve of the barrier.

“I hope he finds something quickly,” Widad squeaked. “I feel like we’re sitting swans.”

A quick grin flashed across Menashe’s face.

“I think you mean sitting ducks,” he gently corrected.

“Ducks, swans…who cares?! We’re exposed out here, and I don’t like it one bit!”

Suddenly, the sound of an engine broke the stillness of the night and a pair of bright headlights swung into view. A few moments later, a silver sedan passed their location, continued for almost one hundred yards before abruptly stopping adjacent to the dome. The door of the vehicle immediately swung open, allowing the driver to step out into the cold night. Luckily, the clouds that had previously blanketed the entire sky had somewhat dissipated, and the waxing crescent Moon provided enough illumination for them to discern who the individual was.

“Schmidt!” William hissed.

“What’s he doing here?” Menashe fumed.

“I’m not sure, but maybe this is a blessing in disguise,” Widad offered. “Maybe he’ll show us where the entrance is.”

Twisting his head sideways, Menashe threw an appreciative smirk at the woman.

“That’s actually a great thought,” he praised.

“Glad to know I can contribute something,” she grumbled. “Now, everyone shut up and let’s see what he does next.”

Almost as if on cue, Schmidt immediately walked over to the dome and proceeded to get down on all fours, meticulously searching the ground.

"What's he doing?" Rich wondered.

The next moment, he turned over what looked like a flat stone and reached down beneath the surface. Immediately, the faint sound of metal clanking could be heard, and a small area close to where he was kneeling looked as if it was sinking into the earth. Roughly pushing himself back up to a standing position, the man walked a few feet, paused for a moment by the sinking ground, then proceeded to descend into the earth itself.

"What the hell?!" Rich quietly exclaimed.

"I think we found our entrance," William exulted.

A few moments later, they saw a large shadow making its way along the tree line toward their location. Quickly donning his night-vision goggles, Menashe strained to identify who or what was approaching, but after a brief moment, he audibly exhaled and removed his goggles.

"It's just Gabriel," he announced.

The gargantuan man trotted up to the small group, pausing for a moment as he looked in the direction of the automobile. Shifting his gaze slightly, his eyebrows shot upward in recognition.

"I guess that explains why I couldn't find the entrance," he huffed. "We're fortunate our unexpected visitor offered to show us the way."

"It's Schmidt!" William spat.

"Fortuitous indeed. Maybe we'll be able to kill two birds with one stone," Gabriel grinned.

A perplexed expression appeared on Widad's face and Menashe had to struggle to contain his laughter.

"Why do all your metaphors involve birds?" she complained.

"I'm not certain," smiled their angelic guardian, "but we'd better get a move on. The early bird catches the worm!"

Rolling her eyes, Widad caught Menashe laughing more noticeably, and sharply elbowed him in the ribs.

"Ok, you and Rich head on down the timberline, while William, Menashe and I follow Schmidt," Gabriel directed. "Be sure to keep your weapons at the ready in case you need to defend yourselves."

Widad glanced at the AR-15 slung around her shoulder with an expression of disgust.

As the three men began making their way toward the gray automobile, Menashe paused and turned back to their other two companions.

"Be certain to keep an eye out and let us know over the headsets if you see or hear anything."

Having reached the side of the dome, they were able to clearly see how the person they were chasing had made his way beneath the surface. Lying roughly twenty feet from the sedan was a small, circular opening in the ground, with multiple earthen steps spiraling downward. Pausing briefly at the top of the passageway, William looked at their enormous companion.

"After you," he offered politely with a smirk.

With a quiet harumph, Gabriel began descending the stairs, and as he climbed lower, a dim glow began to emanate from the hilt of his sword, providing just enough light to illuminate the route. After making one complete rotation around the stairwell, the three men found themselves standing in a small rectangular room, and at the far end, an orange light could be seen flickering just inside a thin doorway.

"Stay here while I check it out," Gabriel ordered.

Once on the other side, he furtively stuck his head through the opening for a brief moment, then motioned for his two companions to join him. As they complied, Gabriel proceeded to walk directly through the opening into the next room.

The next chamber was a large circular room, easily twenty feet across, with four burning torches placed along the exterior wall casting a flickering illumination throughout the room. Gabriel was standing in the middle of the room, staring at a large, shard-like boulder that lay vertically in the middle of the room, adjacent to another downward-leading spiral staircase.

"I don't think we want to head in this direction," he announced. "That's not going to take us up inside the dome."

"Over there!" Menashe exclaimed, pointing behind their angelic defender. "There a stairway leading up."

"That's it," agreed Gabriel. "Hurry!"

Ascending the stairs proved to be more strenuous for William and Menashe, due mainly to the fact that they were both carrying fifty pounds of explosives, along with the firearms slung over their shoulders. As they neared the top of the steps, the distinct sensation of heat began to emanate from the amulet around William's neck.

"This is definitely the place," he announced. "My Talisman is going crazy."

Pausing at the top of the stairs, Gabriel turned to face both of his companions.

"We need to act quickly and decisively," he ordered. "I'm not exactly sure what we're going to see in there, but try not to get distracted. If anything, avert your eyes from the pit and focus on the exterior walls where you will be placing the explosives."

"What will you be doing?" Menashe asked.

"I'll be figuring out how to disrupt the enchantment linking the demonic realm to this reality. With Armageddon so close, even if I can just temporarily pause the flow of minions, it should tip the scales in our favor."

He then paused for a moment and took a deep breath.

"Ok, let's go!"

The next instant, all three men ascended the final stairs and stepped out into the space where the portal was housed. Despite the area being completely enclosed by a concrete dome, the interior was illuminated by reddish-green hues that appeared to swirl along the surface of the concave ceiling. Vibrant shades of light emanated from thick, undulating tendrils dancing along the roof, and a smoke-like haze seemed to congregate at the apex of the structure. Despite the warning their angelic escort had given them, William and Menashe's attention was immediately drawn to the vile, bubbling pit lying on the ground before them. A thick, gurgling stew of oil-like liquid roiled on the surface of the trench, stretching over fifty feet from one side to the other. As they stared in amazement, indistinct shapes of hideous creatures could be seen struggling to make their way along the top of the pit to the sides, where they endeavored to pull themselves up and out of their despicable quagmire. Dumbfounded, both men stood motionless, staring at the unbelievable scene.

"Guys!" Gabriel barked. *"Move it! Now!"*

Shaken back to the task at hand, both William and Rich headed off in opposite direction to place charges at even intervals along the perimeter of the dome. As they quickly dashed to complete their task, Gabriel purposely walked to the edge of the noxious pit and knelt on the ground. With light shining forth from his visage, he bowed his head in humility.

"Father, I implore Thee," he spoke powerfully in his mind. *"The time is at hand for the return of Thy Son. Give me the ability to perceive how best to prepare the way for His return. I beg Thee, help me to see how to impede the actions of the Adversary. Bless me with the discernment and knowledge to protect humankind."*

As the Archangel opened his eyes, he looked up toward the writhing colors shifting along the surface of the dome, searching for an indication of how to accomplish his task. Sitting motionless, he focused intently, examining every deviation of color and motion as he strained to identify a weakness. Then, suddenly, inspiration struck and he leapt up from his feet and stepped back from the edge of the pit. Raising both hands high above his head, he stretched his fingers outward, focusing all the energy of his soul.

"Let the light shineth in the darkness, and the darkness comprehendeth it not!" he triumphantly declared.

The next instant, he drew his tightly clenched fists to his chest, and as every muscle in his body strained, a brilliant light began to emanate directly from his torso. As he held this position, the light continued to intensify, and it appeared as if it was concentrating on the space between his closed hands. Droplets of sweat beaded profusely down his forehead as he labored, building up to what would undoubtedly be a tremendous release of energy. And then, when it looked as if he would be utterly consumed by the radiating light, he thrust both his hands upward to the ceiling and directed a tremendous bolt of balefire up into the simmering coils of luminesce. Instantly, the braids of curling light, along with the sickly haze, fractured into thousands of tiny particles that showered down from the ceiling into the gurgling pit. As soon as the fragments hit the surface, the roiling fluid seemed to slow in speed, as if it was solidifying, until finally, all motion ceased and it was suspended in a petrified state.

Exhausted from his exertion, Gabriel struggled to get back to his feet, just as William and Menashe were returning from their tasks. After fully standing upright, he stumbled, and both of his companions rushed over to help him maintain his balance. With his head hung low, he looked up into William's eyes and a weak smile appeared on his face.

"Thank you," was all he could muster.

"What just happened?" William pressed.

"I figured it out," he sluggishly replied. "Darkness cannot exist in the presence of light. So, I figured I'd introduce as much light as I could muster, and it worked."

"We need to get out of here," Menashe warned. "The charges are going to detonate in fifteen minutes and we don't want to be anywhere near this place when they do."

"Can you walk?" William asked.

"Yes, but I might need a little help. Let's get moving!"

A couple minutes later, the three men emerged from the earthen staircase and readied themselves to run across the clearing to Rich and Widad.

"Something's wrong!" Gabriel cautioned.

The three men sprinted across the field toward the tree line, and as they drew with a few feet of the forest's edge, William realized why Gabriel was so concerned. Lying on the ground in a pool of blood, he was able to make out enough details to see a lifeless body on the ground. It didn't take long to realize that it belonged to an armed security guard with a bullet wound to his chest. Situated a few feet from the deceased man, Rich lay unconscious with blood flowing from a head wound above his temple. And, kneeling on the ground directly next to his father-in-law, Widad was blankly staring ahead, holding an AR-15 in her shaking hands.

"Are you ok?" William called out. "Widad, are you ok? What happened?"

Completely unresponsive to his pleas, tears started to roll freely down her cheeks.

As Gabriel drew closer to the scene, he quietly kneeled down next to Widad, placing his enormous hand on her shoulder.

"Are you hurt?"

"No," she listlessly replied.

"What happened?"

"The guard surprised us," she recounted in monotone. "He hit Rich over the head with his rifle, and I thought he had killed him. I didn't know what to do, so I closed my eyes and pulled the trigger."

She paused for a moment and glanced over at the dead man, who lay prostrate on the ground.

"I didn't mean to kill him, but I had to protect Rich."

"It's ok," Gabriel advised, "you did the right thing. What's important is that you're ok. And by the looks of things, Rich is going to be alright too. But we need to get out of here as quickly as possible. The explosives will go off any second now."

Nodding her head in the affirmative, Widad got to her feet and looked sympathetically at Rich.

"Don't worry about him," Gabriel announced as he easily lifted the rotund man and slung him over his shoulder. "I've got him."

The next moment, shouts could be heard coming from the forest in every direction, and the beams of multiple lights converging on their location gave them a clear indication that they were going to have company very soon.

“What do we do?” William cried.

“We can’t stay here,” Menashe advised, “but we can’t escape either. We’ll be shot for sure.”

“So, what are you thinking?” Gabriel asked.

“We need to go back to the larger room under the dome. But this time, we need to take the spiral staircase further down beneath the surface. There should be enough rock and dirt to protect us from the blast.”

“But we have no idea what’s down there!” William doubted. “What if we get trapped?”

“We don’t have any other option. Let’s go!”

With Gabriel carrying Rich, their small group sprinted back across the clearing and descended once more into the darkness. When they reached the large circular chamber, they spotted the entrance to the stairs toward the middle of the room.

“Keep moving!” Menashe encouraged as he grabbed the woman’s hand.

Leading the way, William began climbing down the staircase, further into the ground. As the seconds ticked away, they dashed downward, spiraling round and round until, about sixty seconds later, they finally arrived at the bottom of the stairway. Walking out onto the stony surface, they began looking around the immense chamber to see if they could figure out where they were. Suddenly, the earth itself began to shake, along with the deafening sound of rock and stone fracturing. As pieces of earth and dirt began to shower down from the ceiling above, the support of the staircase gave way.

"Look out!" Gabriel shouted.

The next moment, the grating noise of twisted and torn steel reverberated throughout the chamber and crashed noisily to the ground. The few torches lining the exterior walls were immediately extinguished, and the small group of comrades were cast into complete darkness, buried alive.

CHAPTER 34

Confiscation

(Twenty Minutes Earlier)

A light drizzle fell from the sky as a silver sports sedan broke through the edge of a thickly wooded area into a large clearing. After pulling up alongside a sizable structure located in the center of the expanse, the engine cut out and the driver stepped out into the dark, chill night. Without hesitating, he began walking toward the concrete building, and after a few moments, he knelt down on the ground and began searching for something. Grasping the edge of flat stone, he lifted it up and over, until the top of the rock was lying flat on the ground. Then, he immediately thrust his hand beneath the surface. A moment later, an audible click, accompanied by the sound of sprockets churning, sounded from the ground, and a circular section adjacent to his location began sinking into the earth. After pushing himself back into a standing position, he approached the newly-revealed stairway and descended downward, until he had completely disappeared from sight.

Roughly five minutes later, the man found himself traversing the last steps of a large, circular stairway, leading into an enormous underground chamber. The cavern itself was easily one hundred feet across, with a ceiling looming four stories overhead. Multiple torches placed along the exterior walls at uneven intervals cast long shadows across the entire area, and at the far end of the cave, a circular opening lay in the side wall, extending backward and deep into the earth. Immediately in front of the aperture, a large, silver platform, with multiple symbols engraved into the border, lay on the ground.

With a satisfied grunt, the man purposely walked forward until he came to a stop only a few inches from the edge of the mysterious-looking platform. The next instant, he took a single step onto the shiny gray surface, and as he did, a deep greenish hue began to radiate from the surface of the disk, casting a dull illumination throughout the entire chamber. Raising his hand to a position directly in front of his chin, he began tracing an elaborate symbol in the air which, when completed, formed almost a tangible object suspended in front of him. Almost immediately, several of the runes on the outer edge of the circle on which he stood, began to glow crimson red, and a low rumble sounded throughout the cave. Then, a very faint light appeared in the distance at the center of the tunnel, growing in intensity as it drew closer and closer. Suddenly, the beam split into five distinct rays, which raced along the perimeter of the shaft until they collided with the outer edge of the circular opening, equally spaced from one another. Bright red beams began to reach outward from each point of light until they intersected with one another, creating a perfect pentagram along an invisible surface. With an expression of determination, Schmidt walked forward and placed his hand directly onto the shimmering face of the shape.

"Ideo indigas imperfectasque spatio et tempore!"[101]

Schmidt's entire form oscillated back and forth between a solid and translucent state, and his hand began to be absorbed into the fluctuating barrier. Over the next few moments, his entire body was drawn into the glowing gateway until it was completely absorbed by the surface. Having completely passed through the entrance, the despicable man hurtled along the enormous passageway at

[101] Traverse space and time!

a tremendous speed, racing toward the light's genesis for several minutes. Finally, as the end of the lengthy corridor came into view, his velocity began to slow until, as all motion stopped, he found himself standing in front of an identical pentacle, through which he initially entered. Placing his hand on the surface of the exit, he exhaled through his nostrils and instantly began passing through the pulsating door. The next moment, he found himself standing a top of an identical silver disk inside a gargantuan underground chamber, easily ten times the size of the previous one.

Gazing around the subterranean hall, a contemptable smirk appeared on his face as he took in the scene playing out in front of him. Hundreds of heavily armed, heinous-looking demons were standing around the entire border of the room. Upon noticing him, they immediately stood at attention and started to chant.

"Ave fili domini nostri! Salve, ductor interitus! Laudate nomen eius!"[102] they intoned in unison, shaking their armaments above their heads. "Ave fili domini nostri! Salve, ductor interitus! Laudate nomen eius!"

As they uttered these words, he slowly turned around and looked across the entirety of his unholy legion. After completing one full revolution, he thrust both his fists directly over his head, to which his minions roared in response and began banging their weapons against their shields noisily. Reveling in ecstasy for a few seconds, Schmidt finally gestured for his demonic warriors to fall silent so he could address them.

"Brother and sisters, the day has finally come for us to rise up and claim our glory! For thousands of years, you

[102] Hail, son of our Lord! Welcome, bringer of destruction! Praise his name!

have been cast out, spit upon, and denied your right to greatness. That ends now! Today, we will secure this *human* innovation and turn it against them. Here and now, we will forcefully take possession of their *so-called* Super Collider and turn it into a portal through which all of your brothers and sisters will be brought across space and time into this reality. Today, we will secure our victory in the great and Final Battle. Today, we begin ushering in the interminable rule of our dark Lord! Prepare yourselves!"

The resounding roar of the demonic warriors caused the entire chamber to shake, and pieces of rock and earth started to fall from above. As all the repugnant creatures continued their rally cry, two of the largest demons walked up an incline on the far side of the chamber, leading to a point at which the cavernous wall met the ceiling. Upon reaching the end of the ramp, they both started battering the roof with gargantuan war hammers. After only a few swings, the vault of the cave gave way, and several tons of earth fell downward, burying the two beasts that had caused the collapse. The next instant, several stars in the early morning sky came into view, and the fresh night air rushed into the chamber.

"It has begun!" Schmidt screamed with a hideous sneer.

Just over three hours later, Schmidt found himself standing directly in front of several monitors covering the wall of the control room at the C.E.R.N. The image on the primary display reflected thick gold wires protruding from two metal prongs, which were connected to a large glass tube with silver caps on either end. Abruptly, he turned around, stalked over to a cowering male scientist, and struck him squarely in the face with a closed fist.

"If you value your life, you will recalibrate the system to the specifications you were given!"

Visibly shaking, the researcher looked to his side and immediately gagged at the sight of two physicists whose lifeless bodies laid on the floor in a slowly spreading pool of blood.

"How...how...how do I know you won't just kill me if I help you?" he stammered.

"You don't!" Schmidt fumed. "But one thing is for certain, you *will* be executed if you fail to comply!"

Uncertain of his decision, the frightened scientist glanced again at his murdered colleagues and bit his lip in consternation.

Schmidt then nodded at the horrific creature towering just behind the prisoner, and without any warning, the beast wrapped one of its massive claws around the man's throat and started applying pressure.

"Wa...wait!" he choked. "I'll do it! I'll do it! Just *please,* don't kill me!"

With a satisfied grin creasing his face, Schmidt signaled the fiend, who reluctantly released him.

"Get on with it!" he commanded.

Stepping over the sanguine fluid, the researcher pulled himself up to a table and began furiously inputting commands into the laptop. The screen flickered and a high-level schematic of the twenty-seven-kilometer ring of the collider was reflected on the display, including directional arrows indicating how subatomic particles entered and flowed through the apparatus. After a few more keystrokes, the scientist hesitated and glanced at the man looming over him.

"If I do this, it could theoretically create a spatial anomaly in the space-time continuum. You have no idea..."

Schmidt once again struck the man on the side of his skull with an open hand, sending him reeling onto the floor.

"This is your last chance!" he screamed.

Without a word, the man pulled himself back up off of the carpet, reached over, and entered a final keystroke into the computer.

Almost immediately, the sound of a rhythmic pounding could be heard echoing throughout the facility, as the Hadron powered up. The directional arrows shown on the screen now pointed in the opposite direction, and the glass tube reflected on the primary display began to glow bright red. With Schmidt beaming at the screen, the researcher started slowly backing away in an attempt to flee. After a few steps, though, he turned around and crashed headlong into the hulking fiend, who wrapped his enormous hand around the man's throat once again. Hearing the man's gurgling struggle, Schmidt turned around with an annoyed expression on his face.

"Dominum?"[103] the fiend inquired.

"Disponere eum!"[104]

A disgusting sneer appeared on the demon's maw, and he tightened his grip, decapitating the helpless man in an instant. The lifeless body collapsed on to the floor with a thud, joining the others.

[103] Master?

[104] Dispose of him!

CHAPTER 35

Passageway

(Three Hours After the Explosion)

An eerie silence permeated the still air, punctuated only by the occasional sound of droplets falling into a dank-smelling, shallow pool of water. Along with the near absence of sound, the entire subterranean chamber was engulfed in complete darkness, making it impossible to know if anyone had survived the cave-in. Suddenly, the sound of rocks clattering over the stony floor echoed throughout the cave, indicating someone, or something, was still alive.

"Is anyone there?" a male voice groaned as he continued to push himself to a seated position. "Hello? Can anyone hear me?"

Dead silence was the only response.

Reaching into his pocket, his hand wrapped around a cold cylindrical object.

"Thank goodness it's still here!" he exclaimed in relief.

The next moment, illumination shined brightly from a small flashlight he was clutching tightly in his hand, and he began searching around the chamber for any sign that his companions were still alive.

"William!" he blurted out. "Rich! Gabriel! Widad!"

With a distinct grunt, he finally pushed himself up into a standing position but nearly fell straight back to the ground as he stumbled over the loose rocks that were strewn out all over the place. A moment later, the glare of his handheld torch fell upon William and Rich, whose unconscious bodies were half covered by rocks and other debris. Kneeling by their side, he was able to confirm that both men were still breathing. After a few moments, he was able to clear away most of the rubble and he stood up to continue his search.

"Widad!" he called out anxiously. "Wi..."

His voice caught in his throat as he spotted the woman's diminutive hand protruding from a large pile of gravel. Rushing to her side, he dropped to the ground and immediately began digging. A few moments later, he had uncovered the majority of her frame and he leaned in closely to see if he could detect breathing. There was absolutely no indication of life.

"No!" he cried.

Frantically, he pulled the woman out from beneath the remaining rubble placed her on a relatively flat surface, knelt down at her side, and began to conduct CPR. For a seeming eternity, he administered thirty chest compressions followed quickly by two rescue breaths, in an attempt to bring her back to consciousness. Then, after a few more moments, he stopped and gazed through tear-filled eyes at the lifeless body lying on the ground.

"Widad, you can't die!" he sobbed.

The next moment, he raised both his hands over his head and emotionally pleaded for some divine intervention.

"Please, save this woman! We still need her...*I* need her," he wept.

Suddenly, the sound of coughing came from the lips of the woman lying on the ground, and Menashe's heart leapt inside of his chest in jubilation.

"Widad! Widad!" he wailed. "Can you hear me?"

"I..." she coughed, "I can hear you."

Elated by this revelation, he leaned forward, tightly wrapped his arms around the woman and buried his face into the side of her neck.

"But I won't be able to keep breathing unless you loosen your grip!" she wheezed.

"Sorry," he quickly apologized, leaning back slightly onto his heels. "I thought you were..."

His voice caught again in his throat as he gazed compassionately at her.

"Dead?" she laughed. "It's going to take more than that to kill me."

Looking up at Menashe, she could tell that the man was struggling to keep it together. As she sat up from the ground, the ambient light being cast from the flashlight allowed her to gaze into his tear-soaked eyes. Suddenly, it struck her why the man was so emotional about the prospect of her passing from this world. Reaching toward him, she cradled his face between both her hands, and stared into his eyes as she pressed her forehead against his.

"Thank you," she whispered. "Thank you for saving my life, and for your love."

As the two silently gazed into one another's eyes, they were startled by the sound of large stones falling to the ground.

"Well, shall I give you two a moment alone?" laughed Gabriel from the darkness.

The flushing in Menashe's cheeks was so severe that they could have turned off the flashlight and still had enough illumination for the entire cave.

"I'm sorry," he chuckled again, "I couldn't resist. Looks like the two of you are alright."

"And I think that Rich and I will pull through as well," William coughed, as he helped his father-in-law to a standing position. "You ok?"

"I think so," he replied. "What happened? How did we get here?"

"You were knocked unconscious by one of the guards. And then, we were about to be overrun by a small army, so Gabriel threw you over his shoulder and we headed back down beneath the dome."

"Is that why my ribs ache?" he complained, staring at the massive man.

"Desperate times," the angelic guardian chuckled.

"The best I can tell, the explosives caused more damage than I had anticipated," admitted Menashe sheepishly.

"Let's get an accurate assessment of our situation," Gabriel announced, raising his hands back above his head.

A bright aura of light immediately erupted outward from his entire form, casting enough radiance to illuminate the entire underground cavity. As their eyes adjusted, they were able to take in the wreckage that was strewn out across the entire chamber. Earth, dirt, and large rocks covered the majority of the ground inside the enormous hall. The spiral staircase that had provided them with their path to safety from four stories above, now lay in a pile of twisted steel. At first glance, they appeared to be completely trapped.

"Go ahead and start looking around," Gabriel sighed. "Maybe we'll find something that will help us escape."

The group of five began to methodically walk around the gigantic cavern, searching for something, anything, that would help them to find a way out of their predicament. As they were probing the debris, William paused, a curious expression on his face.

"Widad, did you ever see Schmidt come back up the stairs after we entered?"

"He never did," she commented. "At least, not while we were watching. After that security guard knocked Rich out, I was a little preoccupied. Besides, after we decided to head back down, his vehicle was still parked by the stairway."

"Is that why my head is pounding?" Rich grunted while rubbing the side of his skull.

"Then if Schmidt never came back up, maybe he's still down here!" William noted in a hopeful tone. "Maybe he's buried beneath all of this."

At that very moment, Gabriel stood upright and closed his eyes for a few seconds, almost as if he were in some sort of hypnotic state. Suddenly, his body convulsed and he reopened his eyes.

"What was all that about?" Rich pressed.

"I was reaching out with my mind to locate Schmidt and I believe I found him."

"Well! Where is he?"

"He's just over two hundred and fifty miles southwest of our current location," he advised. "But that's not the whole story. When I found him, I sensed a disturbance in the space-time continuum."

"The space what?" Widad asked.

"The spacetime continuum. We talked about this previously when I was describing how your reality is formed."

"That's right," agreed Rich. "Our world consists of the dimensions of length, width and height, and a fourth dimension of time. But what do you mean that there was a disruption? Is that bad?"

"It's actually worse than bad. It means that my assumption was completely wrong," Gabriel conceded.

"Your assumption of what?"

"That destroying the pit for demonic entities to enter into this reality would have frustrated Beelzebub's plans. How could I be so foolish? This was only a distraction from His real strategy!"

"I don't understand," Rich admitted.

"He never intended to use this small portal to bring *all* His minions into this world. Instead, He is going to create a colossal gateway through which he can bring his entire army to Earth in one fell swoop."

"That *is* bad," admitted Menashe, "but how will he achieve this?"

"On the border between France and Switzerland, there's a large scientific facility for advanced research."

"The Hadron Collider?" suggested Rich.

"Exactly. How did you know about this?"

"A few months ago, William, Menashe and I watched a program about supernatural events occurring at the Hadron. I guess that was just a prelude for what's to come."

"You could say that," Gabriel replied sourly. "And that's exactly where Schmidt currently is!"

"But how is that possible?" Widad challenged. "There's no way that he could have gotten from here to there…unless he teleported."

Pausing for a moment, Gabriel ruminated on the situation until suddenly, his eyebrows shot upward in a moment of recognition.

"You are exactly right, Widad! There *is* no way for Schmidt to have journeyed all the way to Meyrin, Switzerland, unless it was by, shall we say, *supernatural* means. And that explains how the Adversary will transport all of his legions from that remote location to Cenetics, where all the clones are housed. Schmidt must have used a mystical portal to traverse the distance almost instantaneously. And that's exactly how all the vile minions will be brought back here to claim their physical bodies before the battle of Armageddon."

"So, what do we do now?" William pressed.

"Everyone spread out and start looking for something that resembles a portal."

"How exactly are we going to know it when we see it?" questioned Rich.

"Oh, I'm pretty certain you'll know!"

For the next few minutes, everyone in their party began diligently searching around the cavern for a gateway, but after about ten minutes, the frustration level was palpable.

"I'm not finding anything!" exasperated William. "We're never going to find it!"

"Keep looking!" encouraged Rich.

The next moment, Widad spotted a shiny piece of metal on the ground, almost completely obscured by chunks of rock and stone. After taking a deep breath, she hesitantly placed the tip of her foot on top. Immediately, a dark green light radiated up through the wreckage immediately beneath her location, casting a verdant brilliance across the entire chamber.

"I think I've got something!" she exclaimed.

The others rushed over to her location and clustered tightly around the small woman, staring at the smooth surface beneath her.

"Go ahead and lift your foot up off of the ground," Gabriel instructed.

As Widad removed her foot, the vibrant light dissipated, leaving only the radiance emanating from Gabriel to light the cavern.

"I see," Gabriel announced. "There must be a large platform beneath all of this rubble. Everyone move outward and try to find the edge."

Over the next few minutes, each member of their party began slowly making their way back from Widad's discovery in all directions, until they each stopped at varying distances. With each individual standing at the outermost edge, it was obvious that the strange silver surface was circular in shape.

"Excellent. Now, begin removing the debris from the area. We need to get it completely cleared before we can use the device."

"What are *you* going to do?" asked Widad.

"I'm going to clear away the huge boulders blocking the entrance to the passageway that we'll be using."

"What entrance?" asked William.

Walking to the side of the chamber, Gabriel dislodged a tremendous rock from a large pile and casually heaved it to one side, revealing a large opening bored into the side of the cave.

"This one!"

One hour later, all the debris had been completely cleared away from the silver platform, as well as all the rubble that had been hiding the passageway back through the side of the cavern wall, deep into the earth. While the center of the shiny disk was completely smooth and devoid of any markings, the border circumscribing it contained a total of thirty-three ancient runes engraved on the surface. Standing close to the edge of the area, Menashe stared at the markings with a quizzical expression.

"What are these for?" he posed.

"They're used for navigation," Gabriel announced. "If you know the proper sequence, they allow you to transport yourself to any location, as long as there is a functioning gateway on the other side."

"Do you mean *teleport?"* Rich asked.

"No, not teleportation. This is called translocation."

"What's the difference?"

"With teleportation, an object is physically deconstructed and moved from one location to another. As you can probably imagine, this wouldn't work so well with a living being. If you were to teleport a person, it would literally rip their soul from their body, and when the body materialized on the other side, it would be dead. Translocation, on the other hand, allows physical objects to be conveyed over great distances, as long as there is an open pathway that connects the two together."

"So, this *hole,"* suggested William motioning to the side wall, "is dug straight through the earth to the Hadron?"

"Exactly!" their angelic companion agreed. "All we need to do is to activate the portal, and we'll go exactly where Schmidt went."

"Sounds pretty straightforward," Rich attested. "Shall we get started?"

"It's not quite that easy," Gabriel noted, creasing his brow. "First of all, we have no idea what's waiting for us on the other side. And secondly, the runes that you see on the edge are unhallowed and corrupt. When Lucifer was cast out of heaven, he took these sacred symbols and altered them to be used in unholy rites. Only those who are truly committed to following the Father of All Lies can handle them with impunity."

"So, what happens if you work with them?" questioned Widad.

"I'm not entirely certain. They might not do anything at all, or they could possibly kill us."

A look of consternation unfolded on William's face as he slowly started to shake his head.

"It's too risky," he advised. "Not knowing if we'd be transporting ourselves into the middle of a battle is bad enough. But if we arrived at the Hadron and our greatest defender was injured, or worse, that would be game over."

With his hands behind his back, Gabriel began walking silently around the perimeter of the disk, deep in thought. A few moments later, he had made his way around the entire circle and rejoined his companions.

"I believe this is our only choice," he finally announced.

"No," disagreed Widad. "If this tunnel goes straight to our destination, we should just start making our way on foot."

"That's not going to work," Menashe disagreed. "We'd have to travel two hundred fifty miles to get there, and by the time we had, the Final Battle would already have occurred."

As Widad spun to look at Gabriel for affirmation, she was met with a nod of the head.

"This is our only option," he insisted. "With that said, we're going to be smart about how we approach this. After I initiate the portal, I will be the first to pass through to the other side. Once I get there, I'll ensure that everything is safe and secure so when you come through, you won't be in danger."

"How long should we wait?" probed William.

"Once I leave, give me ten minutes before you enter."

"But what if the portal closes before then?"

"As long as you are standing on the disk, the gateway will remain open."

Pausing for a moment, Gabriel took a deep breath and closed his eyes. Then, without any hesitation, he approached the silver disk and confidently stepped onto the platform. The same greenish hue that had filled the room previously, once again radiated from the uncovered surface.

"Please, join me," he encouraged, turning back to his companions.

With their entire group standing on the disk, Gabriel raised his right hand in front of his face and began drawing an elaborate design in the air with his forefinger. Immediately, the amulet hanging around William's neck began to burn, and a look of alarm flashed across his face.

"Gabriel, my..."

Abruptly, Gabriel held up his other hand to silence his companion.

"I need to concentrate," he snapped. "This is extremely dangerous."

The next moment, several runes on the outer edge of the platform began to glow red, and a faint pinpoint of light appeared in the distance of the horizontal shaft cut into the rock. Gradually, the brightness increased as the beam grew closer and closer to their location, until it finally split into five distinct rays, intersecting with the outer edge of the mineshaft. Immediately, crimson threads of light crept across the surface of the opening, connecting with each other to form the figure of a pentagram. Then, it began to undulate over an invisible barrier covering the entrance.

With the enchantment complete, Gabriel staggered and nearly fell to the ground. He had turned pale and looked as if he might empty the contents of his stomach. Instinctively, Widad rush over to the herculean man's side.

"I'll be alright," he assured her. "Just give me a moment to collect myself."

Roughly ten seconds later, he stood back up, a determined expression on his face.

"Alright then, what happens next is very important. I am going to initiate the portal and translocate to the other end. You will all need to do this, so it's critical that you carefully watch and listen, then do exactly as I do when it's your turn to pass through. When the time has come, you each need to stand directly next to the entrance, placing your hand flat on the surface at the same moment. Once you do this, it will feel like your body is being pulled forward. Don't fight it! You must allow yourself to be drawn into and through the surface. And then, just enjoy the ride. It will take a couple minutes for you to traverse the distance, and once you do, you will be standing directly in front of an identical gateway.

"Now, this part is critical. Once you arrive, you will be able to see through the barrier and into the room, where an identical silver disk will be on the ground. Do not place your hand on the surface until you know it is safe! The instant you touch it, you will be pulled through to the other side. As long as you remain in the tunnel, the gateway will remain open and you will be protected. Does anyone have any questions?"

"What if when we get there, you're...umm..." William paused.

"Don't worry," the enormous man vowed, "I can hold my own."

After pausing for a moment to confirm there were no other questions, Gabriel audibly exhaled through his nostrils and nodded his head.

"Let's get going!"

Turning to face the glowing portal, he stepped up to the rolling barrier and placed his hand solidly on the surface. The next instant, he completely disappeared.

After hurtling along the lengthy tunnel, the passengers came to an abrupt stop and found themselves standing in front of a transparent barrier with a glowing pentacle dancing over it. Looking through to the other side, they were able to see a massive chamber, easily ten times the size of the one they had just left. Enormous stalactites hung down from the ceiling over two hundred feet high, and the cave itself had to be at least five hundred feet across. While they couldn't hear any sound, they knew that the confrontation they could see in front of them could only be referred to as an epic battle.

Gabriel was engaged in grievous combat with a demon that loomed over the massive man by at least ten feet. The vile creature looked strikingly familiar to the contemptible serpent that had confronted them in Saint Peter's Square in the Vatican. It had deep-set, glowing eyes that sat squarely on its broad, snakelike head, directly above two large slits where its nose should have been located. Its gaping maw possessed four ghastly fangs, dripping a black putrid liquid from their jagged points, with an oddly slender tongue that darted in and out as it concentrated on the combat. Two large wings stretched out to either side of the thick, cylindrical body, along with two short, powerful looking arms, each ending with four fingers tipped with five-inch-long, sharpened nails. And while the horrific being had no legs, it was easily keeping itself upright on its mighty coils. Standing in front of this monstrosity, Gabriel fought ferociously, wielding his mighty broadsword.

As the two were engaged in a deadly struggle, his companions silently watched and held their collective breath. While the battle raged back and forth, it was clear that Gabriel had the distinct advantage. No matter how the serpent-like succubus varied its attack, he anticipated and easily countered each strike. Seemingly frustrated by its inability to gain the upper hand, the hellion shrieked in anger and launched itself upward with powerful flaps of its wings. However, before it could get away, Gabriel managed to grasp the tail of his enemy, and with a mighty downward jerk, he changed its trajectory and propelled it solidly into the ground, directly on top of the silver disk. Before his opponent could recover, he spun in a clockwise direction, swinging his sword above his head, then directed it down and through the creature, completely severing one of its wings. Without wasting any time, Gabriel then placed his foot on the writhing fiend's body and raised his blade high above his head, ready to deliver a death strike.

Meanwhile, Menashe had become so enthralled by the skirmish that he leaned forward too far, pressing his cheek up against the shimmering doorway. The next moment, his body was conveyed through the barrier and he found himself standing on the same platform as the two warriors.

Startled by his sudden appearance, Gabriel paused for a fraction of a second as his eyes darted over to his dear friend. That slight hesitation was ruthlessly exploited.

Before he could even react, the repugnant demon thrashed its tail directly at the unarmed man and the razor-like scales covering its form sliced directly into Menashe's body.

"No!" screamed Widad, instantly placing both of her hands on the barrier.

As the distraught woman rushed to the injured man's side, Gabriel narrowed his eyes and struck true with his sword, cleanly severing the head of the serpent. Then, turning to assess the damage, the reality of the situation crushed the mighty archangel's heart.

Sitting on the ground, Widad lovingly cradled the mortally wounded man's head in her lap. The injury inflicted was clearly too great. Blood flowed out of a deep gash that had cut sideways through Menashe's body, up through his shoulder, and directly across his neck. As the tears freely rolled down her cheeks, William and Rich entered the cavern with bleak expressions covering their faces.

With the last moments of light and consciousness departing from him, Menashe managed to look into the eyes of the woman that he had come to love, and a pure smile appeared on his lips. And as his eyes shut for the last time, that simple expression of affection remained, testament to the genuine connection they had formed.

<u>CHAPTER 36</u>

Devastation

Standing with his arms tightly folded across his chest, Schmidt closely monitored the energy levels of the Hadron as protons whizzed around the seventeen-mile pathway at close to the speed of light. Each revolution of the infinitesimal particles amplified both the speed at which they were traveling, and the consequential collision energy they would convey the moment they struck another object. Powerful magnets dispersed along the entire length of the circular pipeline ensured the molecules did not interact with any other matter within the vacuum, allowing them to continually accelerate until maximum velocity was finally achieved. It was at that point when Schmidt intended to unleash a chain reaction that would literally tear a hole in the fabric of space-time, creating a high-speed thoroughfare between Earth's reality and the dwelling of the condemned.

"It is nearly time!" he announced jubilantly. "Ready yourselves. We will need to move with haste once the rift has been formed, to open up the portal."

Three armored demonic guards, who stood at attention at the rear of the room, simply grunted in response to the proclamation.

Ignoring the tepid reaction, Schmidt leaned forward, holding a now-trembling hand over a large red button, and anxiously stared at the images reflected on the monitor.

"Finally!" he resounded.

Immediately, he slammed his hand down onto the button, and the mechanical thumping noise that had been echoing throughout the facility for the past thirty minutes suddenly ceased. Multiple red warning lights mounted in the ceiling began to spin, and a warning siren burst from the speakers. With a maniacal expression on his face, he spun around to face his infernal companions.

"Follow me!" he announced.

As he stalked out of the rear of the room, the three hellions silently fell in behind him, following him down the tunnel leading back to the gateway.

Still cradling Menashe in her arms, Widad rocked back and forth, large tears streaming down her cheeks. As she agonized over her loss, Rich quietly knelt down next to her, wrapping his arms around her shoulders.

"I'm so sorry, Widad," he consoled. "I will miss him too."

"I…I…" she stammered. "I'm in so much pain! Why did such a wonderful man have to die? It just doesn't make sense."

"Things don't…"

"Someone is coming!" Gabriel interrupted. "I'm sorry Widad, but we need to hide."

Realizing the woman was in no condition to spring into action, he scooped her up, along with Menashe's lifeless form, and carried both of them to a large pile of rubble resting on the side of the cavern. After reaching the location, they all concealed themselves behind the debris, ducking out of sight just as the unanticipated intruders burst into the cavern.

Peeking out from around the boulders, William spotted a man dressed in slacks and a white dress shirt charging toward the silver platform, followed closely by three hellish fiends.

"What's he up to?"

"He's completed the transformation of the Hadron into the portal for all of Satan's warriors to enter into this reality," Gabriel replied. "Now, he just needs to open the gateway to Cenetics, so when the endless hordes begin flowing into this world, they will be able to occupy the soulless clones housed beneath the laboratories."

"And then what?" Rich whispered.

"War!" Gabriel growled.

"Why don't we just destroy the platform controlling the gateway?" William suggested.

"The platform is inextricably connected to the Hadron now, and if we destroy it, it will obliterate us, along with all of Europe."

"But wouldn't that stop the battle from occurring?"

"Unfortunately, it would not. Armageddon would only be delayed, and in order for Lucifer to be defeated, the battle must occur at the preordained time."

"So, what do we do then?" grumbled Rich. "Just sit back and watch the largest army ever formed march off to battle?"

"That's exactly what we need to do."

"Gabriel, I hope you know what you're doing!"

Glancing back into the chamber, Schmidt stood directly at the edge of the platform, while his vile defenders took up position at three different points around the circumference. As the demons paused to look at their master, he gestured for them to step onto the disk. Immediately, a brilliant light radiated from the surface, casting a green hue throughout the entire cavern. Then, Schmidt purposefully stepped up onto the platform and walked to the center, facing the aperture in the cave wall. Glancing down, he noticed the fresh puddle of blood congealing on the surface, but summarily dismissed it as nothing of note.

"Great Lord of Darkness," he formally intoned, "the time has come for You to enter this reality and claim what is rightfully Yours. For millennia, You have been unjustly shackled in the bowels of hell. And for what reason? Because You had the strength to stand up against Father's plan, and protest what You knew was wrong, rather than to just blindly follow. Today is the day You and Your followers are set free from Your chains, enter into this reality, and receive the physical bodies You have been denied. Brothers and sisters, I call you to come forth from purgatory and stand together in a victorious battle that will usher in endless torment and misery for all those that oppose us!"

"Victoria contra eos qui nobis adversantur!"[105] the devilish slaves roared in response.

Schmidt began tracing a complex series of symbols in the air and when he had finished, the shimmering figure wavered for a moment, then began to glow a vibrant crimson red. Immediately, the earth began to violently shake and a deafening thunder resounded throughout the entire area. Then, without any warning, thousands upon thousands of ghoulish apparitions began flowing into the colossal cave, all racing toward the passageway bored into the side wall. The instant before they entered the shaft, a flaming pentagram materialized at the opening, and the seemingly endless horde of devilish souls blasted through the barrier. Horrific beasts of all sizes and forms flowed through the portal in an endless stream. Some creatures were half human, half beast, while others were serpents, winged succubi, dragons, imps, and all manner of other

[105] Victory against those that oppose us!

indescribable creatures. Over the next hour, they all made their way through the gateway at such a rapid velocity, and so tightly packed together, that it was impossible to even venture a guess as to how many malignant spirits had moved through the breach. And then, just as fast as it had begun, the torrent of demons abruptly stopped, leaving only Schmidt and his three protectors in the chamber.

"You two," he barked, "make your way through the portal and join the battle. And you!" he commanded. "Come with me!"

Quickly spinning on his heels, Schmidt then strode back down the hallway leading away from the portal, followed closely by one of the horrific guards. The two remaining fiends then approached the undulating pentagram, and after passing through, the gateway collapsed on itself and the light emanating from the platform ceased altogether.

Confirming they were completely alone, Gabriel squatted down beside Widad and gazed sympathetically into her eyes. While her sobbing had ceased, the anguish manifest in her countenance was palpable. She was truly heartbroken.

"Everything is lost," she whimpered. "All of our efforts have been for nothing. Satan's army has entered into the world, and right now, they are possessing clones and preparing for war. Nothing we have done matters!"

"Widad," Gabriel comforted, "don't you know the One God knows the beginning from the end? Everything that has occurred has served a purpose, and nothing has been for naught. Your heart is broken, but it will heal. Your sacrifice will be rewarded. In the depths of your devastation, peace awaits you and Menashe. There must be an opposite in all things. Without evil, there can be no good. Without darkness, there can be no light. And without your desolation, salvation would have no meaning. Sacrifice is the truest sign of love and devotion, and the sacrifice you have made here today, can serve no higher purpose."

As his message sunk in, tears began to once again flow freely from her eyes. But as she buried her face into his shoulder, gratitude at his words overshadowed the grief, and her spirit seemed to be whole once more.

After another moment, Gabriel released his embrace and stood up.

"I'm afraid I have to leave you now," he lamented.

"What are you talking about?!" shouted William.

"I have to travel to Israel to make way for The Son to return to Earth."

"We can't do this without you!" protested Rich. "You're joking, right?"

"I'm afraid not," he apologized. "But rest assured, you will know what it is that each of you must do. In your moment of need, you will be inspired to take the action you must. Trust your heart."

Gabriel paused for a moment and a single tear rolled down his cheek, where it hung from the edge of his chin.

"I have greatly enjoyed your company," he continued, "and I love each and every one of you. I will see each of you again, but our paths must part here. Much like you, I have a specific task that only I can complete."

Without any additional words, all four companions fiercely embraced him, who then took a few steps back and raised his hand in farewell. The next instant, light began to emanate from his being until it fully consumed his body. When the light completely dissipated, he was gone.

CHAPTER 37

Onslaught

(Two Hours Later)

A light breeze from the east blew across the predominately rural landscape of northern Israel. With temperatures registering at least fifteen degrees above normal for several weeks, conditions that morning seemed fairly typical and would even have been perceived by many as a bit chilly. While the small village of Megido had a population of just under one thousand residents, it now had the appearance of being completely abandoned, and not a single individual could be detected. Indeed, not a solitary bird, or any other creature was present, and a strange silence permeated the entire area.

Situated just over eight hundred feet to the northeast of the town, the archeological site of the ancient city of Tel Megiddo sat on top of a hill overlooking the fertile Jezreel Valley. A total of twenty cities had been built on this fifteen-acre location over the course of five thousand years, until it was finally abandoned in the fifth century before the birth of Christ. To the east, vast farms lands were sprawled out as far as the eye could see, and the Megido Forest lay directly to the west, on a series of low-lying hills.

As the deafening silence continued to pervade the entire area, the shape of a man suddenly appeared on a narrow dirt walkway on the excavation site, moving in an easterly direction. A few minutes later, he arrived at the outermost edge of the city ruins, where he paused and silently stared at the countryside from his elevated position, a stoic expression across his face. As his chest slowly expanded and contracted with each breath, he closed his eyes, allowing himself to be lost in the moment. The sensation of wind gently swept over his face as he stood motionless, relishing what he knew might be his last experience of peace and serenity.

Then, without any hesitation, Gabriel opened his eyes, held his mighty golden clarion to his lips, and powerfully blew into the mouthpiece of his trumpet. A forceful, pure blast, erupted from the bell of his horn, and resounded throughout the landscape, echoing across land and water, sweeping over mountains and plains, until it had traversed the entirety of the planet and reached upward into the very heavens. As the celestial vibration continued to resonate through the air, light began to emanate from all corners of the planet, until the entire Earth was bathed in a glorious meridian light, and it was perceived by all the inhabitants of the world.

A deep, low rumbling noise, began to rise beneath Gabriel's feet, becoming louder and louder, until an almost deafening roar echoed across every continent and nation. As the sound intensified, the terrain began to convulse as tremors caused great fissures to appear in diverse places the world over. Mountains were laid low and valleys raised, while thunder and lightning enveloped the globe and the entire Earth was in tumult. This continued for a period of thirty minutes, until finally, Earth ceased its heaving and an eerie stillness swept across the planet.

In the distant sky, just over fifty miles south from Megido, a series of brilliant beams of light suddenly burst out from large alabaster clouds in the stratosphere, and thousands upon thousands of angelic, winged beings began flooding into reality. Located in the very center of the luminous burst, the outline of a robed figure began to advance as if He were walking on an invisible path through the sky.

With his trumpet still tightly clutched in his hand, Gabriel peered toward the glimmering horizon with respect and devotion on his visage, and deeply bowed his head.

"My Lord!" he solemnly proclaimed.

As the silhouette began to slowly lower to the earth, the radiant light surrounding Him descended along with it, until it completely disappeared beyond the horizon. Although he couldn't see it directly, Gabriel knew what was transpiring beyond the skyline, and what would ensue once it was complete. Closing his eyes, he was able to envision the King of Kings descending from the clouds to the city of Jerusalem, with multitudes of angels accompanying him. Every man, woman, and child in the city, along with every human soul on the planet, would be fixated on the event, as it was broadcast in real time everywhere. A hush, the type of which hadn't occurred since the world began, permeated the entire globe as everyone stopped to witness what was most assuredly the greatest moment in history. Finally, after having traversed down through the air, His feet finally touched upon the Mount of Olives, and the prophecy was fulfilled. The ground beneath His feet immediately split in two, with half of the earth shifting to the north and the other to the south, forming a considerable valley.

The next instant, a great voice echoed from the heavens, reaching the ear of every living soul.

"It is done."

Lifting his horn once again, Gabriel sounded another blast from his trumpet, and an intense flash of light appeared directly over his head. Immediately, hundreds of thousands of angelic hosts, clad from head to toe in brilliant gold and silver armor, began streaming into reality. Many of them held protective shields and they were all armed with divine swords, spears, pikes, halberds, and golden bows. After entering the realm of Earth, they began arraying themselves in a highly organized manner around the Hill of Megiddo in immense rows of legions, stretching out to the north and south beyond the edge of the horizon for at least ten miles. Enormous pikemen comprised the first few rows of the front line, each of them armed with weapons at least twice the size of their own bodies. Positioned directly behind them, at least ten rows of foot soldiers, equipped with either swords, spears or halberds, stood at the ready. Gaps appeared at periodic points along the front line, where large groups of angelic cavalries on top of winged horses staged themselves to provide offensive thrusts to divide the enemy, and to quickly reinforce the ground troops. A space of at least thirty feet separated the initial line from a colossal body of archers at least twenty rows deep. Each had a quiver slung across their back, housing an innumerable number of golden-tipped arrows. Another empty zone of fifty feet lay behind this immense group of champions, then five rows of catapults, ballistae, and trebuchets, operated by additional heavenly guardians, were staged to rain down destruction upon the enemy. And, finally, the rear of the tremendous army contained thirty rows of winged archangels sitting atop armored winged horses, brandishing divine weapons of every sort. After a period of almost one hour, the seemingly never-ending flow of celestial guardians ceased, creating a military formation the likes of which the world had never seen, standing at least one hundred million strong.

Still in the same location where he had initially sounded

his trumpet, Gabriel gazed out to either side of the massive throng and grunted in approval. The next moment, a greenish blur in the sky caught his eye as it approached at high speed, and after a brief moment, he was able to identify it as Seraphina.

Effortlessly gliding down from above, she landed gracefully in front of Gabriel, and after slightly inclining her head, she gazed into his eyes with a serious expression.

"The enemy has been spotted, and they are many," she informed him.

"How large would you estimate their forces to be?" he inquired.

After pursing her lips for a moment, she replied.

"At least two million."

"Only two million?" he puzzled. "That means we outnumber them fifty to one. Lucifer will be sorely mistaken if he thinks he'll win the day with so few."

"That's two million physical entities," she clarified. "There are at least ten times that amount in bodiless fiends."

Obviously shaken by the revelation, Gabriel furrowed his brow as he audibly exhaled through his nostrils.

"They have been far too busy at Cenetics," he fumed. "With that many corporeal demons, we're going to be hard pressed to destroy them all."

"It would have been even more if you hadn't sounded your trumpet when you did. There are probably another three million clones housed in the chambers beneath the laboratories. If they had possessed all of them…"

Her voice trailed off as she considered the unthinkable.

"But they didn't," Gabriel affirmed. "Even so, we will have quite the battle to fight, if we are to end up victorious today. How soon until they reach our front lines?"

"No more than thirty minutes," Seraphina replied.

"Then we'd better get the troops ready for war," he boomed.

Spinning to his left, Gabriel hopped onto the back of a winged horse and soared up into the air as the stallion flapped its mighty wings. After taking up position a few hundred feet above the earth, he prodded the winged gelding to hold position, then he stood up in his stirrups to address the troops.

"Brother and sisters!" he roared in a voice so loud it echoed across the landscape and reverberated off the hills behind the troops. "The Great Battle is finally here. After multiple millennia, the day that we have been preparing for since the beginning of time, has come. As we counseled in the beginning with Father, we knew His plan for humankind required choice, and we witnessed firsthand, one third of the host of heaven reject that plan in outright rebellion. Those we once loved so dearly are now advancing on our position, and their only goal is to completely annihilate each and every one of you. They have fallen so far, they believe evil can triumph over righteousness. *However, they don't know your strength*!" he enunciated.

"Ooh-rah!" echoed the troops.

"They don't know your devotion!"

"Ooh-rah!" they resounded again.

"Today, we make a final stand against the Adversary himself, the former Son of the Morning, who has fallen so far that He believes he will be victorious. But we will show him here today, that he is wrong. *Light will prevail against darkness, and evil will be cast out, ushering in one thousand years of peace and tranquility!"*

"Ooh-rah! Ooh-rah! Ooh-rah!" they chanted in unison.

Raising his fist over his head, Gabriel reared his feathered stallion in a show of jubilance, before encouraging the steed to glide back down to his position on the front line. After hopping out of the saddle, he turned to face Seraphina, who faced him with an idiotic smirk on her face.

"That was *quite* the speech!" she quietly jested. "I mean, I nearly teared up!"

"Oh, just keep your mouth shut!" he grinned.

"No, seriously. You've got quite the talent for public speaking. Maybe after this is all said and done, you should run for office or something."

"Yeah, yeah, enough already. Sometimes, you drive me absolutely crazy."

"Keep talking like *that*, and maybe I'll ask the Big Guy if he'll make me mortal too," she expressed with a fluttering of her eyelids. "*Then*, I'll make you follow up on your threats!"

For the first time in his existence, Gabriel felt a flushing in his cheeks so profound that he thought the troops on the fringes of his battalion would likely have seen the reddish glow radiating from his cheeks. Abruptly turning to face forward, he began to search the horizon for any movement. A few moments later, his investigation was rewarded.

"Over there!" he called out, pointing at the skyline.

"That just looks like wispy clouds," Seraphina countered.

But as the indistinct shadows in the air grew closer, Gabriel began to slowly shake his head.

"Nope. That's a winged battalion of incubi. There are just so many of them that you can't make out any detail, especially at this distance."

After another moment, Seraphina began to glumly nod her head in acknowledgement.

"That's an understatement," she observed. "There have to be at least ten thousand fiends in that *so-called* formation. What do you think they're doing? They've got to be at least ten minutes ahead of the main body of their army."

"It's probably a scouting party to ascertain our strength."

A grim smile appeared on Seraphina's face in response to Gabriel's hypothesis.

"Well, I'd be happy to oblige them. With your permission of course,"

Turning to face his companion, Gabriel gave a brief smile and a quick nod.

A few moments later, the massive group of winged demons were no more than one thousand yards away from the angelic front line, and the hideous features of the enemy became clear.

The body of each creature was roughly the size of a man, possessing thin, leathery wings, stretching out to either side by at least six feet. Their faces were angular in shape, with a set of deeply sunken eyes set in their bony skulls. Small slits on the front of their faces were located where noses should have been, and sat directly on top of broad, almost bird-like mouths, were razor-sharp beaks. Long ears reached back from either side of their skulls, slightly flapping in the breeze as they flew through the air. Elongated necks sat atop unnaturally narrow frames, with bones showing through gaunt leathery skin, tightly stretched across their forms. Reaching out from bony shoulders, long sinewy arms with small fists tightly grasped horrific battle axes dripping in vile, black liquid. And, dangling beneath those small waistlines, thin, muscular legs swung back and forth with each beating of their wings.

With a quick thrashing of her own, Seraphina flew up into the sky and once she had climbed high enough to be seen, she held her arm high over her head. A small section of archers, only one hundred feet in width, drew their bow strings back in response and held position, waiting for the signal to unleash their deadly projectiles. The next moment, Seraphina swung her arm sharply downward, and a barrage of nearly one thousand darts whizzed through the air, striking directly into their targets just a few moments later. Despite only firing a small number of arrows in comparison with the total number of targets approaching, nearly every single enemy was completely destroyed. As soon as the arrows impacted, a bright flash erupted in the sky, with each detonating in a small explosion.

"You didn't tell me you were using explosive balefire tips!" Gabriel shouted.

"Only the best!" replied Seraphina.

With their ranks nearly decimated, the nearly fifty remaining flying beasts began a nosedive, directly toward the front line of pikemen. As they neared the ground, Seraphina unleased another bombardment of projectiles, which destroyed all but two of the leftover attackers, who immediately crashed into the front line. The next instant, screams and shrieks erupted from the heavenly ranks, as two dozen soldiers fell down to the ground, having received fatal wounds at the hands of the invaders. One of the winged succubi lay lifeless on the earth in a pool of black, tar-like liquid, but the other remained, wildly swinging its weapons as it snarled at the warriors. The next instant, a female fighter stepped directly in front of the assailant, motioning for it to attack her. Without any warning, the beast ferociously lunged through the air wielding both axes, in an attempt to wipe her from existence. But at the last second, she easily parried his attack and as he clumsily fell to the ground, the stabbed him right through the chest with her pike.

With a grim look on her face, Seraphina glided back to the ground, landing next to her commander.

"How did one of those creatures do so much damage?" she exclaimed with a shudder.

"After possessing a physical body, their power is magnified," he snorted.

"I know, but that's ridiculous."

Glancing off to the horizon, the expression on Seraphina's face shifted from one of concern, to one that exuded outright fear. While they had been engaged in battle with the initial attack, the entirety of the enemy's armies had taken up position across the battlefield, their front lines sprawled over three miles, less than four thousand feet away. While Gabriel and his forces had an advantage of nearly five to one, the physical disposition of a vast number of warriors provided them with an unknown advantage, which would only be determined as the battle played out.

Shifting her gaze to the center of the horrific legions, Seraphina's breath caught in her chest at the scene unfolding. Advancing directly through the troops, the Father of All Lies marched forward with complete disregard for their safety, crushing His soldiers with each step. A few moments later, He stood at the front of his unholy army, accompanied by his abominable queen, Mania. Thrusting a dreadful looking sword into the sky, a horrific shriek erupted from His maw as He belched fire into to the air, signaling the final advance of His depraved campaign.

CHAPTER 38

Divination

(Immediately After Gabriel's Departure)

Widad sat on the rough stone floor for several moments after the archangel left, quietly mourning the passing of her dear friend. Kneeling next to her, Rich wrapped his arm around her shoulders and provided consoling words of comfort to try and ease her grief. After a few minutes had passed, she roughly wiped her teary eyes with the back of her hand and looked up at William, who was anxiously pacing back and forth.

"You're going to drive me crazy if you don't stay still," she sniffled. "What's on your mind?"

"It's the last words Gabriel spoke to us," he exasperated. "That we have a specific task only we can complete. I've been racking my brain, and I can't think of anything that we can possible do from the Hadron that would help out."

Pursing her lips, Widad sat for a moment, puzzling through the problem.

"Well, it's obvious we aren't meant to participate in the battle itself," Rich offered. "I mean, we'd be more of a detriment than a benefit. They would have to assign multiple warriors just to protect us."

"Agreed," grumbled William, "we don't have any powers or abilities that would be useful."

Just then, Widad's face lit up.

"What if that's exactly it?" she exclaimed.

"What do you mean?" William probed.

"What if we *do* have abilities that would be suitable to the task? What if our presence here at the Super Collider isn't just by chance, but an essential component of what will ultimately play out in good triumphing over evil?"

"Alright," William conceded, "let's follow that train of thought. What are you thinking?"

After pausing for a brief moment to collect her thoughts, she continued with her conjecture.

"The Hadron is a massive power source, right? Why did they need to place their gateway so close to it?"

"I guess because the portal requires an enormous amount of energy to function," Rich guessed.

"Correct. And what is its function?"

"To open up a fissure in the space-time continuum, allowing Schmidt to bring all the vile souls from hell into our reality," William chimed in.

"Correct again. Now, if we think about this logically, wouldn't you conclude that if it could be used to open the doorway between our reality and purgatory, we could…"

"…Use the portal to create a bridge between Earth and the heavenly realm?!" William interrupted with a broad grin.

"That's precisely what I was thinking!" she agreed.

"So how do we do that?" Rich challenged.

"Well, going back to Gabriel's comments, he said we have a specific task only we can complete. William is a brilliant scientist, and here we are, sitting in one of the most advanced laboratories in the world. Don't you think William's knowledge *might* allow us to leverage the Hadron to accomplish a specific task?"

Rich's face nearly split in two as he grinned in response.

"I think I understand where you're going with this. If William can figure out how to activate the Collider, we might be able to bring in angelic reinforcements."

"And that's what Gabriel was probably hinting at. If we can figure out how to bring the entirety of the hosts of heaven to the fight, we will win the battle!" exclaimed William. "We need to find the control room!"

Five minutes later, the small group found themselves at the end of the short hallway dug through solid rock, standing in front of an open doorway that led into an operations center. Just as William was about to enter into the room, Widad grasped his hand, jerking him backward.

"Stop for a minute!" she whispered. "We have no idea what's in there."

"One thing we know for sure is this is where Schmidt went," he replied.

"Yes, as well as that intimidating demon. If we run into that creature, it will kill us for certain."

"I don't know what other choice we have," he countered. "We're not going to be able to turn on the gateway unless we power up the Hadron. And in order activate the Collider, we've got to get in there!"

"He's right," Rich agreed, "but that doesn't mean we run rashly into an unknown situation. Let's be a bit more *discreet*," he cautioned.

Nodding his head in agreement, William leaned forward into the opening, trying to peer around the corner to see if there was anyone, or anything, waiting on the inside. As he edged his way inside, the air in the entrance began to undulate, as if he had bumped into an invisible barrier. Instinctively, he immediately pulled himself backward and held his breath, and after a brief moment, he expelled the contents of his lungs in a soft *whoosh*.

"What was that?" hissed Rich.

"Probably some sort of camouflage, meant to hide this hallway."

"Did you see anyone?" pleaded Widad.

"The room was completely empty. I think it's safe for us to go inside."

Without any further discussion, William stepped tentatively into the next room, sliding through the invisible boundary. Once on the inside, he turned back to the opening to motion for the others to follow and was astounded by the fact that the doorway was vanished. Instead, he only saw the surface of an ordinary wall.

"Should we come through?" he heard Rich breathe.

"I can't see you!" William responded. "Schmidt has somehow been able to completely conceal the door."

"That's great!" Rich spouted. "Do you want us to come through or not?!"

"Oh, sorry. Yes!"

The next moment, the forms of Rich and Widad materialized as they entered through the imperceptible boundary.

"I hope we can get back through," worried William.

Turning back to the wall, Widad extended her hand, which immediately disappeared as it passed through the surface.

"Satisfied?" she smirked.

"Yes, thank you. Now we just have to remember this specific spot."

"Well, it's not like we can draw a mark on the surface," joked Rich.

"Just make a mental note of where it is located," he advised.

William made a quick assessment of the equipment strewn across the room, and after a brief moment, he turned back to his companions.

"This is it! I'm sure of it!"

"Great. Let's get to work," Rich announced.

Walking over to one of the desks, William took a seat and began examining the information represented on the screen. As he was doing so, the image coming through a television mounted on the wall caught his attention, and after glancing up at the screen, his expression shifted to one of great anxiety and horror.

A tremendous battle was being broadcast on the display, and without the text indicating that it was live from Israel, one would have likely concluded that it was a special effects scene from a blockbuster movie. Apparently, multiple news organizations were using drones to provide aerial shots of the horrific conflict as it occurred. Thousands upon thousands of dead or dying bodies were strewn out over vast areas of ground. The angle being broadcast predominantly showed a massacre of demonic creatures, their bodies heaped one upon the another, sometimes three or four high. But then, as the camera began to pull back to show a wider shot, it was clear that the evil hellions were not losing.

As more of the battlefield was displayed, the number of heavily armored winged combatants that had been slain easily outnumbered the heinous soldiers three to one. With the drone ascending further in the sky, the death and devastation sustained by the heavenly forces was almost too much to bear. Tens of thousands of angelic protectors lay lifeless on the blood-soaked ground. Many of them were missing limbs or had large gashes that had gone right through their protective armor and inflicted mortal wounds to their bodies. Glorious wings had been torn off ethereal soldiers and were fitfully fluttering downward from the sky, littering the landscape as they landed. The carnage was strewn out across the battleground, traversing at least two miles in length and several hundred feet in width.

As the camera shifted off to the side, a whole battalion of mounted calvary could be seen charging directly into a group of no more than one hundred succubi wearing little to no protective gear. Just before impacting with the enemy, several of the demons jumped into the air, and after barely clearing the stallions, they savagely swung their deadly weapons into glorious seraph warriors, sending nearly every mounted soldier at the front of the charge crashing to the ground. Then, the second row of disgusting creatures leapt on top of the wounded guardians, repeatedly stabbing them with jagged blades, until their bodies lay motionless on the ground. Without any hesitation, the heinous beasts then launched another attack into the next row of celestial champions, with almost identical effect. While some of the horrible incubi were slain in the onslaught, a very disproportionate number of divine combatants were slaughtered. It appeared a very one-sided battle.

Suddenly, the image of a single, massive demonic entity, wielding an enormous, jagged sword, began to creep into view from the corner of the screen. The next moment, the screen was filled with static and was then replaced with text stating that the drone had been destroyed, and to please wait while they work to get another feed.

A disheartened expression swept across Rich's face as he shook his head in disbelief.

"I just don't understand," he lamented. "This isn't the way it should be happening. Good always triumphs against evil. But that isn't what's happening. They are easily slaughtering all of God's warriors. How is this possible?"

"I don't know," William cried. "It's almost as if the demons have some sort of supernatural power giving them an unfair edge."

Shock and excitement suddenly erupted from Widad's visage, and she reached over and punched William squarely in the shoulder.

"What was that for?!" William yelled.

"That's exactly it!" she exclaimed. "That's exactly why we're losing!"

"What are you talking about?"

"They *do* have an advantage over the armies of heaven. They have physical bodies. We can't just bring all the angelic hosts of heaven into this reality to wage war with the Adversary; we have to enable them to be victorious. If they try to fight them without bodies, they will be easily annihilated. They must have tangible forms in order to defeat the enemy."

"There's only one problem. How do we do that?"

"Cenetics!" Widad blurted out. "You said there were millions of clones being grown beneath their facility. There's no way each and every one of those soulless shells was possessed by a demonic entity. If we could figure out how to send the heavenly army through the gateway, all they would need to do is to make their way to the Cenetics facility, which isn't too far from the other end of the portal."

"I think we're missing a piece," Rich speculated. "Just turning the gateway on should allow us to easily transport an army to Cenetics, and turning on the Hadron gives us the energy required to open up a rift connecting our world with another realm. But we haven't figured out how to direct that energy specifically toward the heavenly dimension. If we just turn on the Collider, for all we know, we're just going to transport another couple of million demonic souls into our reality."

"There must be a way of locking the coordinates into the Hadron, so it knows where to direct the energy once it has been generated. But I'm at a complete loss as to where to even start looking. Turning on the Hadron should be relatively simple, but Rich is right. As of right now, it's aimed squarely at the depths of hell."

Sitting down roughly in one of the swivel chairs, William buried his face into his palms as he silently tried to solve the puzzle. A moment later, he lifted his head and looked at his companions in despair.

"I'm racking my brain, but I can't figure it out. Even if we determined how to input coordinates, I wouldn't know which ones to..."

Suddenly, all sight and sound vanished, and William felt as if he was being transported to a different location. The dreary darkness was gradually replaced by a dim light, which grew in intensity as the seconds ticked away, until he found himself standing on a distant, pure-white landscape. As he shifted his gaze, he was unable to identify any features or landmarks other than the overpowering illumination that not only filled his vision, but saturated his very soul. The next instant, something caught his attention out of the corner of his vision, and as he turned to identify the source, his breath caught in his chest. It was Ariel.

She stood almost as if on an invisible platform in the air, slightly higher than his shoulders. She wore a modest, alabaster silk dress which covered her body, except her hands and feet, both of which were bare. Peace emanated from her visage and a simple smile expressed such love and emotion, that he nearly wept.

"William," she intoned, "it is so good to see you. You have accomplished so much, and your journey is nearly complete."

"Ariel," he gasped, "how is this possible?"

A serene smile crept across her face and the corners of her eyes slightly wrinkled.

"Don't you know that nothing is impossible? You can accomplish anything if you simply have faith."

"But why are you here?"

"I am here in your time of need. I am here to answer your questions."

"How do I direct the energy from the Hadron to create a portal to heaven?"

"You already have that knowledge, but you just don't realize you do. What do you remember about the silver disk that lay on the ground in front of the portal?" she questioned.

"That it illuminated when you stood on it."

"Is there anything else?"

"There were symbols engraved around the edge of the platform."

"That is correct. Was there anything about those symbols that seemed familiar?"

Closing his eyes for a moment, William envisioned the runes adorning the perimeter, and as he tried to focus on them, his mind wandered. The next instant, he thought back to the shared vision he and Rich had experienced together at the mental institution, and the different symbols reflected on the banners of the angelic forces on the battlefield.

"The symbols located on the edge of the disk resembled the ones the banner carriers brought with them when they cast Satan out of heaven. But they were different somehow...modified, perverted in some way."

"That is correct. All the souls waging war against heaven were once good. Everything they knew and believed in was true. However, much like the symbols you recall occupying the platform, their minds were corrupted. If you are able to return them to their original state, you will have found the answer to your question."

"*William! William!*" Widad shouted. "Are you ok?"

Opening his eyes, William found himself once again seated in the control room of the Hadron, and he instantly leapt up from his chair.

"I know what we need to do!"

CHAPTER 39

Redemption

"Well, out with it!" pleaded Widad.

"The symbols located around the perimeter of the silver platform are the key! The emblems *themselves* are the coordinates."

"How so?" Rich pressed.

"I'm not entirely sure," he admitted. "When you combine all the various figures together, it somehow pinpoints our position here on Earth, as well as the location of the supernatural realm. Do you remember when you visited me at the loony bin?"

"How could I forget?" shuddered Rich. "That's where we experienced the same vision of a massive battle between good and evil."

"Exactly! Do you remember the symbols on the pennants the angelic forces were carrying?"

"I think I see where you're going with this," he affirmed, "but the figures on their banners were different from the ones on the portal."

"They *are* different, but they're also *very* similar. So much so, that I believe, in my heart, the symbols on the gateway were once divine in nature, but were perverted by Lucifer. If we can just figure out how to return them to their original state, we'll be able to connect with the heavenly sphere."

"How can you be so certain?" Widad challenged.

"It'll take too long to explain. Let's just say I received a recommendation from an old friend."

After crooking a speculative eyebrow, Widad shrugged her shoulders.

"That's good enough for me!"

"So, what do we need to do?" asked Rich.

"We need to go back to the portal and figure out how to return each of the runes to their original state!"

After making their way back through the invisible barrier, the three of them rushed back into the enormous underground chamber and made their way over to the portal, which lay dormant on the ground.

"Everyone take a position around the platform and start fiddling with those symbols," William commanded.

"What exactly are we trying to do?" Rich asked.

"Again, I don't really know. Somehow, we need to try and reverse the pattern, almost as if we're creating a mirror image of the original design."

"You mean like if I hold up my right arm while looking in a mirror, it looks like my reflection is holding up its left?"

"Something like that!" William insisted. "Now, just start fiddling! We don't have much time!

For the next few minutes, they all attempted to figure out how to transform the engraved images, but to no avail. Nothing they did seemed to have any effect on their appearance.

"This isn't working!" grumbled Widad.

"Just keep trying!" William encouraged.

Struggling to get his fingers beneath the section of the disk where the runes were positioned, Rich identified what appeared to be a very slight seam. He immediately reached into his pocket, pulled out a set of keys, and started to force the edge of one into the joint. With a bit of effort, he was able to wedge them into the steel, and he began to lift it.

Suddenly, the section of the disk where the design was located started to float upward and levitated in the air directly in front of him. Without knowing why, he reached forward, touching the corner with his forefinger, and the rune started to brightly glow. The next instant, the entire section looked as if it was turning itself inside out, as the design folded inward upon itself, before shifting back out, revealing an entirely different symbol. The color of the design began to oscillate, until finally, there was a golden pattern sitting atop a brightly shining piece of silver steel. Having completed its transformation, the floating section descended back to the gateway, reattaching itself to the surface.

"That's it!" William exclaimed. "Show us how you did that!"

Shifting himself forward on the ground, Rich began picking at the next symbol with his keys, and after a few moments, he was able to duplicate the results, as the second section sealed itself to the surface.

"Brilliant!" he shouted. "You two stay here and convert the rest of the runes, while I go back into the control room and get everything ready to activate the Hadron. I'll be right back!"

Hopping up from the ground, William sprinted back down the tunnel, leapt through the imperceptible boundary into the operations center, and rushed over to the computer. After taking a seat, he began furiously tapping on the keyboard as he worked to navigate to the startup menu. Stopping for a moment, he glanced in the direction of a large monitor mounted on the front wall, and his heart sank into his stomach.

The image reflected on the screen showed the container that would collect antimatter created by the Collider. In addition, there were several rectangular cubes next to the apparatus, wrapped in a light brown paper with the words 'C4 – High Explosives' printed on it. A series of wires were sticking into the munitions, connected to a digital clock that had begun its countdown to zero. The display showed less than fifteen minutes to go.

As William stared in disbelief at the image on the monitor, the sound of clapping broke the silence from the corner of the room. Slowly turning his head in the direction of the noise, William's gaze fell upon the source. It was none other than Koenraad Schmidt.

"I see you have finally figured out how to tip the scales in your favor. Unfortunately, you are too late. I have set a bomb that will destroy everyone and everything in this facility, and there is no way to defuse it. I'm afraid you will be unable to bring reinforcements to fight in Armageddon. The clock will reach zero, and you will die!"

"Along with you!" William spat.

"I think not. You see, I will be taking an express ride back to Cenetics well before this facility is destroyed, along with you and you companions."

A devilish smirk suddenly appeared on William's face.

"You're talking about the gateway we took to travel here, right? I'm afraid we sabotaged your machine. You're not going to be leaving here anytime soon!"

"You didn't!" he exclaimed as panic swept across his visage. "You fool! Now both of us will die!"

"I hate to disappoint you again, but *you* are the only one that's going to die today!"

Without any warning, William darted directly at Schmidt, leapt through the air, and slammed into his body, sending him reeling onto the concrete floor. Before he could recover, William crawled on top of the surprised man, and began delivering blow after blow into his face, his fists tightly clenched with pure rage.

As he readied himself to deliver another blow, Schmidt forcefully turned onto his side, throwing his attacker into the legs of a nearby table. He instantly pushed himself up off the ground and began brutally kicking his assailant in the ribs. William took several of the kicks, then caught Schmidt's foot and violently twisted his ankle, sending him to the floor once again.

Having got to his knees, William then grabbed a flat screen off a desk, and sharply struck the other man's skull. A bright trickle of blood immediately sprung from Schmidt's split forehead, but he didn't appear to realize he had been injured. Jumping back to his feet, he took a few steps backward and stared menacingly at his opponent.

"Come on!" he heaved. "Try and kill me! You'll meet the same fate that your *poor wife* Tara did at the hands of Mania."

Suddenly, something inside William's head snapped and the hatred he was feeling turned to uncontrolled madness.

"Don't you *dare* say her name!"

"Your wife got *exactly* what she deserved. Death by a thousand obsidian shards of glass!"

A wicked sneer appeared on the evil man's face as he continued his harangue.

"There wasn't *anything* left of her body, was there? I mean, other than a red stain on the earth. You should have done something to protect her. *You failed her*, just as you are going to fail here today!"

A blood-curdling scream immediately erupted from William's mouth, and he leapt forward with the intent of tearing his enemy limb from limb. But just as he was about to crash into his opponent, Schmidt deftly sidestepped the assault and grabbed him by the back of his head. With his hands tightly clenched around his hair, he violently jerked William back off his feet, causing him to fall awkwardly onto his rear. Then, with his free hand, he pulled a long, ancient dagger out of a sheath affixed to his belt, and forcefully placed it along the side of William's neck, cutting through the first few layers of skin. Almost at the point of hyperventilating, William froze where he lay, realizing the other man could end his life without much effort.

A maniacal cackle crawled from Schmidt's throat, as he realized that William had failed and nothing was going to stop him.

"Like I was saying," he condemned, "you are about to suffer the same fate as your miserable wife."

A thought suddenly occurred to Schmidt and a disgusting expression of jubilance creased his visage.

"You didn't sabotage the gateway; you merely transformed it, didn't you? Changing those symbols doesn't affect the portal's ability to send me to Cenetics; it only modifies the dimension it is connected to. You have failed. I am going to slice your neck, destroy your friends, and then…"

Suddenly, a loud crack abruptly cut him off mid-sentence, and the knife slowly slid away from William's neck and onto the floor. William sat up in surprise and turned back to see what had happened.

Schmidt's lifeless head was turned awkwardly backward by almost one hundred and eighty degrees and enclosed almost entirely in the huge, trembling hands of his father-in-law. With a satisfied grunt, Rich released his prey and pushed himself back to a standing position, where he offered his hand to William with a simple smile.

"You didn't come back, so I went looking for you."

Firmly grasping his hand, Rich pulled him back to his feet and the two men fiercely hugged one another.

"You ok?"

"I think so," William replied, while touching his fingers to his neck.

Looking down at his hand, he examined the smeared blood on his palm.

"Is it bad?"

"I don't think so," Rich reassured. "He cut you for sure, but it shouldn't take long to heal."

The next moment, William spun his head back toward the front of the room with a panicked expression on his face.

"What's wrong?!"

"That!" he exclaimed, pointing at the monitor. "Schmidt hooked up an explosive to the Hadron."

"Can we diffuse it?"

"I don't know. Let's go take a look."

After a few moments, the two men found the explosive device through a doorway in the front of the control room. The clock on the apparatus showed just under eight minutes remaining before it reached zero.

"That isn't enough time for us to turn on the Hadron, bring the armies of heaven into our reality, and then escape ourselves," Rich lamented. "You're going to have to defuse it."

Looking at the web of wires, detonators, and plastic explosives, William started to shake his head slowly.

"I wouldn't even know where to begin," he sadly admitted. "If I just start pulling wires, it'll probably go off."

"What's that?" Rich inquired, pointing at a small button on the side of the display with the words 'Reset to Normal' next to it.

"Again, I'm not a bomb maker. I don't have a clue."

"Well, that's got to be better than just randomly cutting wires."

"Let me take a closer look at..."

The next instant, Rich reached over and depressed the button, and the numbers on the display changed and began counting down from twenty minutes.

"What the hell!" exclaimed William. "You could have blown us up!"

A huge smile creased the large man's face.

"Nothing ventured," he beamed.

Still shaking his head, William's expression shifted to one of extreme amusement.

"You're absolutely crazy. You know that, right?!"

"Ok, so we know that pressing the button resets the clock to twenty minutes. If we keep resetting the timer before it gets to zero, we can power the gateway for long enough to bring every divine warrior to Earth. They then use the portal to get to Cenetics, pick up a physical body, and we can..." Rich paused midsentence. "What's wrong?"

William's visage exuded extreme anxiety, and most of the color had drained from his cheeks.

"What is it?!"

"Someone has to stay here and keep resetting the timer."

"Yes, that's not a big deal. Once we've brought everyone through, we all just hop back through the gateway before the bomb goes off, and we're out of harm's way."

"The timer is located in the same room as the antimatter collector. Whoever goes into that room will be exposed to massive amounts of subatomic particles."

"And that's bad?"

"Yes, that's really bad. The tiny molecules, protons mostly, will start breaking down chemical bonds in human

DNA. Normally, even slight exposure can kill cells, stop them from dividing, or create cancerous mutations. But the number of particles bouncing around that room will be immense. It will have a traumatic effect almost immediately."

"Can't we all just take turns resetting the clock?"

"Unfortunately, that won't work. Getting bombarded just one single time will result in irreparable damage. Taking turns will simply kill all three of us, rather than just one person dying."

Rich's expression became very somber.

"If one person stays behind to reset the clock, they will probably be killed by the radiation before the bomb explodes, right?"

"Most likely," William uttered.

"Well, that's an easy answer then. I'll stay here and keep the clock running as long as I can. Once we get the gateway open, you and Widad take the portal, and…"

"No," interrupted William. "This is my responsibility. My initial research is what kicked off the whole series of events leading up to this point, so I should really be the one that sets everything right."

"You can't blame yourself for this. Armageddon was going to happen regardless of your research."

"I know, but I still feel as if I bear some of the blame. Gabriel said we each had a specific role to play, and this is mine."

With tears welling up in his eyes, Rich wrapped his brawny arms around William, embracing him roughly.

Just then, Widad came running into the room, where she paused for a moment, a quizzical expression on her face.

"I think we're all set," she announced. "As least, I hope we are. All we need to do now is turn on the Collider."

After releasing Rich, William gave Widad a slight nod, turned around, and clicked enter on the keyboard. Immediately, a low humming noise started to reverberate throughout the entire facility, and the clanging of electromagnets turning on could be heard. Glancing up at the monitor at the head of the room, the metallic cylinder began to glow, as a small, undulating particle of pure energy could be seen forming in the tube.

"Come with me. Hurry!" Widad implored.

A few moments later, they were all standing next to the inoperative portal once more. An angled dashboard, not present before, sat on top of a metal shaft, protruding up from the ground, with a series of symbols matching those on the silver disk represented on the surface.

"I figured out how to access this control panel while you were gone," she beamed. "All we need to do now is designate the correct symbols and turn on the gateway."

"I'm pretty certain I remember the symbols that were on the pennants from our vision," Rich announced.

"Are you positive?" William asked.

"I've got this," he replied simply. "This is *my* role."

Slightly furrowing her brow, Widad stared at the two men, wondering what unspoken message they were sending to each other.

"Now, if I remember correctly, there were ten symbols."

"*If* you remember correctly?!" William joked.

"Just kidding. Here we go."

Rich then designated the runes on the dashboard and a loud click emanated from beneath the silver surface.

"That should do it," he announced confidently.

"Now what?" Widad asked.

"Now, you and Rich stand on the platform and make your way back to Cenetics, where you will be safe."

"What about you?" Widad pressed.

"I need to stay behind."

"But why?" she complained.

"Schmidt set a bomb in the control room, which will detonate in less than ten minutes unless someone stays behind and keeps resetting the timer."

"What?!" she exclaimed. "Why didn't you say something sooner?"

"We just found out," Rich replied. "And there just wasn't time to explain."

"Well, if you're staying behind, I'm staying behind too," she announced defiantly.

"There's no reason for you to die as well," William counseled.

"But…but…but can't you just reset it a few times and then come through the gateway?" she stammered.

"I'm sorry, Widad. The levels of radiation I'll be exposed to will likely kill me before the bomb goes off. It's the only way."

Wiping tears from her eyes, Widad walked forward and wrapped her arms tightly around him. Glancing over at Rich, who was silently sobbing, she motioned for him to join them, and for the next thirty seconds, they quietly comforted one another in an emotional embrace. William then leaned back and looked into his father-in-law's eyes.

"You're the best person I know," William said.

"And you're the best son any man could have."

"You need to go. I've got this."

Rich tried to speak, but his voice caught in his throat.

"Besides," William continued with an affectionate smile, "the sooner I get this over with, the sooner I get to be with Tara again."

A large smile swept across Rich's face.

"You be sure to tell Tarz that I miss her. And that I love her more than she could ever know."

"She knows," William laughed. "But don't worry. I'll tell her."

After releasing one another, Rich and Widad stepped up onto the portal, and a deep greenish hue began to immediately emanate from the silver platform. A few moments later, the entry to the tunnel began to undulate, and both travelers walked up to the entrance. There, they stopped just short and turned to face William for a final time.

With tears streaming down his cheeks, William raised his hand in farewell to his companions, who returned the gesture. Finally, they both turned back to the portal and stepped into the barrier, disappearing altogether.

Now alone in the subterranean cavity, William became aware of a brilliant blaze radiating immediately behind him. As soon as he turned around to face the tunnel, a tremendous burst of light exploded through the aperture, and he found himself surrounded by concourses of angels. Thousands upon thousands of winged guardians, seraphs, divine messengers, and other supernatural beings, all flooded by and through him as they made their way onto and through the gateway leading back to Cenetics.

After a brief moment, he made his way back to the control room to restart the timer. As soon as he entered the chamber, he experienced extreme discomfort from the barrage of radiation besieging his body. Ignoring the pain, he reached forward and reset the clock to twenty minutes.

Taking a seat on the floor, William let his mind wander as he waited to start the timer once again. He thought of everything that had transpired and led up to this single moment in time. He thought of how much he would miss Rich, Menashe and Widad. He wondered if evil would be defeated, and if he would ever see Gabriel again. Finally, he reflected on the love of his life, and how he longed to be with Tara once more.

Glancing up at the clock, he noticed it showed less than one minute remaining. Struggling, he reached upward to try and reset the device, but was physically unable to accomplish the task. He closed his eyes and then, he felt as if someone else was in the room. As he slowly opened them again, he witnessed the magnificent image of a celestial archangel bowing before him in gratitude, with glorious light emanating from her visage. This time, when he closed his eyes, his soul was quickened as he passed onto the next life, never having to experience the sting of death.

CHAPTER 40

Restoration

A horrific scene of death and destruction was strewn across the entire landscape as far as the eye could see. Hundreds of thousands of mutilated, dying, and deceased warriors lay heaped upon the ground, sometimes as many as five bodies high. The once verdant acreage, burgeoning with its crops and other plant life, now lay decimated, completely trampled underfoot by skirmishing soldiers, charging horses and wheeled chariots. Littering the battlefield, innumerable weapons were scattered everywhere, some protruding from the bodies of combatants, and others still clutched in the lifeless hands of deceased champions. A blanket of thick, viscous mud, formed by the combination of dirt and copious amounts of blood, created a sludge-like hindrance to movement of any kind. The battle that had been fought - that was still being waged - was one that Earth had at no time ever seen, and would hopefully never experience again.

With nearly ninety percent of their warriors obliterated, Gabriel had just signaled for all the angelic armies to regroup and ready themselves for another onslaught of the enemy. Despite initially outnumbering the adversary by nearly five to one, there now remained an equal number of fighters, to a total of nearly ten million, on each side. Lucifer had sustained significant casualties in His ranks of physical demons, losing nearly eighty percent of those forces. However, the remaining four hundred thousand tangible hellions, along with the millions of accompanying demonic specters, gave Him more than enough strength to exterminate the surviving archangels. Momentum and strength clearly leaned in his favor, and it seemed as if He was now casually toying with how best to destroy the opposition, while bringing as much humiliation and disgrace to their commander as possible.

Swooping down from the sky, Seraphina landed roughly on the ground next to her leader, who was still sounding his glorious trumpet to rally his troops.

“Gabriel,” she heavily huffed, “how are we going to win against an enemy so strong? Although our numbers are equally matched, they have an unfair advantage. For the first time in my existence, I am fearful of losing a war.”

Biting his bottom lip, Gabriel placed his hand firmly on her shoulder and stared into her eyes.

“We need to remain strong and confident,” he whispered. “Our troops look to us for courage, and if they feel we are faltering, then they will as well. You need to have faith that we will triumph over evil, even in the face of seemingly unbeatable odds. Our conviction and belief will propel us to victory.”

“Forgive me,” she apologized.

“There is nothing to forgive. I too am fearful, and have anxiety over the outcome of this battle. But it is one thing to acknowledge concern, and another to give into panic. The trick is to turn your internal disquiet into a source of motivation, driving you to greater valor and stronger resolve.”

“Thank you, Gabriel,” she resounded. “I’ll do my best.”

After flashing him a broad grin, she soared back up into the air and rejoined her winged ranks.

With the bulk of their forces either covering or surrounding the countryside immediately around the Hill of Megiddo, Gabriel hopped onto his winged horse and soared into the air over his troops. From this height, he could see the outermost edge of his army, which lay not too far from the horizon on either side of the front. While his troops had been decimated to a large degree, they still formed an extensive battalion of heavenly warriors that would not go down without a courageous fight. Knowing his soldiers needed encouragement, he stood up in his stirrups as he readied himself to galvanize his troops.

"Brothers and Sisters!" he bellowed. "You have fought with mighty strength and valor today. You are stalwart warriors for righteousness, even in the face of a formidable enemy. I call on your indomitable spirits to continue pressing forward until we achieve nothing less than victory over evil. Our cause is just, as is our..."

Suddenly, an intense rumbling resonated across the landscape and the earth itself began to shake. The next moment, a long fissure in the ground appeared beneath the front lines of the angelic forces, nearly twenty feet wide and two miles long. Instantly, tens of thousands of demonic fiends sprung up from out of the breach and fell upon the astonished guardians with deadly effect. Thousands of angels immediately fell by the sword, as their attackers leveled a deadly incursion into the center of their forces.

Located directly above the attack, Seraphina rallied her winged battalion to engage with the adversary on the ground. The next instant, more than twice the number of ground invaders were met with a ferocious barrage from the sky, as feathered warriors swooped down to engage the enemy. Her troops response was so swift and fierce, that their opposition was virtually unable to respond in any meaningful way to defend themselves. Thousands upon thousands of evil creatures immediately perished, their vile, ink-like blood saturating the battlefield. Bolstered by their comrade's courage, the ethereal ground troops pressed forward with renewed vigor, inflicting equal damage and destruction upon their opponents. The adversary's attack was met with such resistance that one-third of the invading force began a full-speed retreat, racing across the landscape to rejoin their army.

A hair-raising howl suddenly erupted from enemy lines, and the next moment, the enormous form of Satan himself started making His way toward the cowardly troops. Outrage seethed from His lipless maw, as fire erupted from His sunken eye sockets. Stomping forward to intercept His retreating army, he trampled dozens of malignant spirits in a matter of seconds. He wielded His ghastly fifty-foot sword in one hand and swung it directly through the front edge of his escaping troops, not only cleaving several hundred of them in two but burying it solidly into the earth as he did.

"Fear me more than you fear them!" he shrieked. *"You kill, or you are killed! You have no other option!"*

Invigorated by their success, Seraphina leapt back up into the air, leading a charge of her winged contingent to hunt down and destroy the fleeing enemy. After reaching back to her quiver, she took an arrow and readied herself to launch a fiery dart immediately upon the Father of All Lies. The next instant, an enormous black harpoon tipped with a vile barb pierced her chest and protruded five feet out of her back. Incapable of continuing forward, she helplessly fell downward, impacting the earth a few moments later with a dreadful thud.

"Seraphina!" Gabriel cried as he rushed forward.

Within a few seconds, he had traversed nearly one hundred feet and was now kneeling sorrowfully at her side.

"Seraphina, can you hear me?!"

A brief fluttering of her eyes indicated she was still breathing, but it was obvious that life itself would leave her very shortly.

"My dear Gabriel," she choked, "I wish I could have been by your side after our burden was complete."

But before he could respond, the lifeforce housed within her magnificent angelic frame departed from her form and returned back to the heavens above.

With tears filling his eyes, Gabriel stood back up and glared menacingly across the battlefield, meeting Satan's stare head on. A wicked grimace appeared on Beelzebub's hideous face, as his disgusting laughter echoed across the landscape, obviously reflecting his pleasure at what had just transpired.

Passion and rage filling his soul, Gabriel began charging across the field to engage with the enemy. A bloodthirsty rage propelled him forward and he crushed any and all opposition in his way. Dozens of physical demons attempted to slow down his charge, but to no avail. Cleaving through bone and flesh, Gabriel left of path of destruction of amputated limbs and mutilated corpses. So great was his fury, that combatants on both sides stared in bewilderment as he fought his way through the enemy.

"I see you had feelings for that one," a repulsive female voice resounded over the field. "It's too bad really. The two of you would have made a good couple."

"Mania!" he screamed.

Standing a mere twenty feet away, the abominable Queen of the Devil stood in the flesh, directly between Gabriel and her beloved husband. Standing more than a full head shorter than Gabriel, she was clad from head to toe in an obsidian black armor that offered superior protection. A broad breastplate adorned with a winged dragon covered her torso, and ornate designs were encrusted on charcoal-colored steel plates covering her shins and knees. Hanging from her waist, a dark, multi-segmented tasset hung from a thick, black, leather belt to protect her upper thighs. To either side of her neck, black pauldrons rising up to razor-sharp tips protected both her shoulders, and defensive jointed plates flowed down from them, covering her arms to the top of steel gauntlets guarding her hands. A hardened collar was wrapped around the backside of her head, rising to just beneath her ears, and a long, black cape flowed behind her, ending just above her ankles. Long, black hair cascaded down from her head, framing her alabaster skin and almost attractive features. A maniacal expression exuded from her face as insanity poured out of her eyes.

"Gabriel," she replied in an almost offhand manner, "you knew this day would come. All I want to know, is if you are ready to be wiped from existence?"

"I am ready," he challenged, "but at the end of our combat, you will be staring at me through blood-filled eyes, with the end of my sword planted firmly in your skull."

With Mania and Gabriel racing toward each other, insane laughter rolled from Satan's maw.

The sound of steel meeting steel crashed through the air, signifying that the battle had begun, and lightning erupted from the edges of both of their swords. They each danced across the uneven surface as they launched and countered ferocious attacks with their two-handed weapons. As soon as one blocked the onslaught of the other's attack, they countered with a strike of their own. Back and forth the battle raged, with neither side obtaining a clear advantage, nor being able to inflict much damage. After a period of about five minutes, both fighters backed away from one another, struggling to bring in enough air to fill their oxygen-hungry lungs. Finally, a sly grimace crept across Mania's face as she narrowed her eyes.

"You're quite skilled," she mocked, "but I'm afraid that isn't going to help you here today. It is my destiny to kill you...Moloch has foreseen it, just as He has foreseen the end of your world, and the beginning of His."

Without any warning, she threw a thin dagger through the air, lodging it deep within Gabriel's thigh. Then, she charged forward, screaming with madness.

Ignoring the wound, Gabriel shifted his body and leaned heavily on to his rear foot, preparing to meet her attack. At the last second, she leapt up into the air, twisting her body as she began to swing her sword forcefully down toward her target. Sliding his foot in anticipation of her assault, Gabriel turned his shoulders in the opposite direction of her offensive and easily parried her strike with the side of his sword. Having missed its target, Mania's blade was buried solidly into the earth next to Gabriel's feet. Loosening his hold on the grip of his sword, he then grasped Mania by the hair of her head, hoisting her two feet off the ground. Forced to release her sword, she grasped his flexing hand with both of hers in an attempt to prevent him from tearing chunks from her scalp.

Holding her at this height, Gabriel was able to stare directly into the fear-stricken eyes of his enemy. The next moment, a condemning sneer appeared on his face as he leaned in to whisper in her ear.

"Mania, you really should study the book of Revelations," he breathed. "I don't know where your husband is getting His information, but according to *my* prophecy, you lose!"

The next moment, he placed the end of his enormous blade beneath Mania's chin, and without any hesitation, decisively slid it up through her head, piercing the bottom of her skull and burying it deep with her brain. As blood oozed from around her eyes, the last flicker of life fled from her frame as she stared into the eyes of her destroyer.

"My love!" shrieked Lucifer. *"You will suffer for eternity in the depths of hell!"*

Stalking forward, Satan raised his sword high above his head and the blade immediately burst into flames.

"All forces attack!" he demanded. *"We end this now!"*

Every single enemy combatant began to surge forward in a tumultuous charge that would have caused the bravest soul to question their resolve. However, rather than fleeing in response, all of the angelic champions arrayed themselves in perfect order, readying themselves for the great and final conflict, with Gabriel leading their orderly march.

Projectiles of seething fire launched from grotesque catapults, slammed into the advancing lines of celestial warriors, wiping dozens of soldiers from the battlefield. Barrage after barrage of golden tipped arrows flew over the heads of angelic soldiers, impacting with flying demons and advancing ground troops, killing them by the thousand. Armored cavalry charged forward at an extreme speed to meet head on with demonic, heavily clad beasts. As the front lines clashed together, the horrific sound of battle and death could be heard everywhere. Winged succubi fought feathered angels in the sky with swords and spears, and hundreds of lifeless bodies fell down to the earth. Across the entire two-mile long battlefront, death and carnage raged, and immense casualties were suffered by both sides.

However, the forces of evil had one distinct advantage in their favor. They had the Archfiend *himself* as the ultimate combatant.

Standing directly on the battlefront, dozens of angelic champions sliced their weapons at the Devil, attacking him with no effect. Even the mightiest swing of the sharpest sword could not so much as scratch the surface of His skin. Hundreds of spears and arrows glanced harmlessly off His impenetrable exterior.

Rearing his head toward the sky, a horrible shriek filled the air. The next instant, he opened his gaping maw, belching destructive fire that not only consumed enemy, but his own troops. He was mad with fury, consumed by a deep-seeded rancor that would destroy everyone and everything in His wake.

Pausing for a second, Lucifer surveyed the devastation being wreaked upon his enemy, and a horrible grimace emerged upon His face. He knew His forces were winning, and it was only a matter of time before all the angelic opposition was complete exterminated.

Almost at the same time, Gabriel fell back to the top of the Hill of Megiddo and held his ethereal horn to his lips one last time. A pure blast poured out from his trumpet, and all the remaining angelic hosts fell back to the hill and immediately around it, to mount one final defense against the enemy.

Seeing the end was nigh, Satan held his hand in the air, signifying for his troops to cease their attack. Immediately, all fighting halted, and an eerie silence fell over the battlefield. Taking a few steps forward, The Father of All Lies stood a mere twenty feet from the few hundred thousand remaining beleaguered angelic troops.

"Today is the not the end," he announced. *"This is the beginning of My sacred rule. I am not a vengeful God. In fact, it was My design to save each and every one of you. You all once knew and respected Me, and now, I give you this one final chance to join Me. Bow down and worship at my feet, and you will find a place in My kingdom. Otherwise, you will be destroyed here and now."*

Pausing for a moment, he stared triumphantly across the opposing forces, a proud expression emanating from his visage.

"What say you?!" he demanded.

As His voice reverberated across the land, it was met with absolute silence. Not a single soul offered allegiance.

"As I thought. You are all cowards, unwilling to stand up against the Creator. Prepare to die!"

Suddenly, directly above the remaining heavenly forces, a bright light appeared in the sky, growing in intensity until it completely blinded everyone in its presence. Then, as the strength of the illumination dissipated ever so slightly, the battlefield witnessed a figure descend down the clouds until it alighted softly on the very top of Megiddo. Standing in the midst of all this destruction and death, life itself was now present, bathing the entire earth in glory.

Glancing across the field, His eyes locked with those of the Adversary for at least thirty seconds, and not a single sound permeated the air. The next moment, a warm smile appeared on the Man's face, as he turned his head to look to the north.

Instantly, a brilliant flash of light erupted on the horizon, brighter than the explosion of a thousand suns. And then, hundreds of thousands of archangels with physical forms began flowing out of the light and flooding the landscape.

Rather than engaging the enemy, they simply encircled them, fully encompassing all the combatants so that not a single soul could flee. Standing there quietly, they all turned to face their Master on the hillside.

"Father," the robed Man spoke, *"it is finished."*

Immediately, a bright light filled the sky, seemingly exuding from the entire universe and bathing the world in its magnificent illumination. As it immersed the entire planet, every unclean and evil thing it rested upon was immediately destroyed. All the forces of evil were wiped from the face of the Earth, leaving the Devil standing alone.

"Thy works have condemned many," a voice boomed from the heavens. *"And by Thy works, Ye shall be judged. I command all My legions of angels to come forth, bind You, and cast You into prison for one thousand years. There, You will have no power or ability to tempt human souls. And there You will remain, in misery, until the time when all humankind will come forth from the grave and receive final judgement. And then, You will finally be cast into eternal darkness for all time."*

"No!" screamed Lucifer. *"This is not what I have foreseen! This is not possible!"*

The next moment, a large contingent of heavenly sentinels came forth from all sides to bind the Personification of Evil. As they surrounded Him, He was unable to move, as if He had been paralyzed by an unseen force. As they gripped His wrists and ankles, His face contorted and horrific shrieks burst out of His mouth. Once He was fully restrained, they stepped backward, leaving Him alone in the middle of the blood-soaked battleground. The ground itself began to waiver, as if a fissure was being ripped into the space-time continuum, and then, as He screamed in agony, Moloch...Diabolus...the Son of the Morning, drifted down through the undulating surface, until He had complete disappeared from Earth's reality.

Clouds immediately began to form in the sky and a pure, cleansing rain, fell down upon the ground, washing away all the taint and evil covering the land. Not since the beginning of time, when the Earth was newly formed, had it been in a more perfect and paradisical state. The eyes of the blind were opened and the ears of the deaf were unstopped. All manner of death and disease was completely eliminated, as humankind moved forward together, united in peace, and in every thought and deed.

CHAPTER 41

Exaltation

Brilliant, luminous light radiated through and across the entire landscape, carrying with it the promise of true happiness, and a hopeful future. Vast fields of pure white stretched out as far as the eye could see, as colossal billowing clouds ascended high into the sky. A single river wound its way across the plains, twisting and turning through pastures and broad meadows. In the distance, a beautiful white dogwood tree encased in blanched bark stood next to the stream, its branches reaching upward, dotted with delicate alabaster blossoms. A calm, rejuvenating breeze swept across the area, sending sporadic ivory blooms fluttering down to the surface of the water, where they were whisked away by gentle currents. Shifting breezes caused clouds to vacillate here and there, revealing vast swathes of newly formed galaxies and gaseous nebulas in the heavens above. A pristine silence permeated the land, as peace and tranquility flowed in every direction.

A man walked quietly across the purified landscape, gazing in awe at the majesty and grandeur of the setting. Making his way toward the solitary tree, he paused for a moment and dipped his hand into the cool stream flowing through the ground. Cupping his fingers, he dipped them into the life-giving water, and as he drank, his soul felt renewed. With a serene smile, he continued to walk forward until he came within twenty feet of the dogwood, where he suddenly froze, stricken with awe. There, located next to the shrub, an elegant woman stood clothed in an inculpable white gown, gazing at him with a genuine expression of love and respect. Hope and charity emanated from her visage, accompanied by a feeling of satisfied delight at the knowledge that William had finally made his way to the heavenly realm.

"Ariel," he breathed with deep respect.

"My dear William!" she nearly blurted out. "I am so very pleased to be the one to welcome you into immortality."

They both rushed forward and enveloped one another in a joyous embrace. A moment later, they released their hug, but still firmly gripped one another's hands.

"Does this mean…" he trailed off, apprehensive to ask the obvious question.

"That we were victorious?" Ariel completed his question. "Yes! Good has triumphed, and evil has been banished."

A tremendous sensation of relief washed over William, as every last ounce of anxiety and concern was consumed by the revelation that everything had been worth it.

"So, now what?" William asked.

"Well, you need finish your ascension," Ariel scolded him with a friendly smile. "But before you go, someone has been waiting for you."

With a knowing smile, she turned back toward the blossoming tree and a familiar figure stepped out from behind the shrub. Dressed in a simple, pure white gown, Tara stood radiant, love and joy emanating from her face.

"My dear Tara!" William cried as he rushed forward, wrapping his beloved wife in his arms. "I have missed you so much!"

"And I have missed you," she tearfully exclaimed. "I am so proud of everything you have done, and how you accomplished it."

After a long embrace, the two of them stood hand in hand, facing the angelic protector who had given her very life in defense of their souls. With a broad grin on her face, Ariel started to wave her hands in an ushering motion, signaling that they should move on.

"Alright you two, you'd better get going. There's a lot in store for you in the future, but you still have much to learn."

In response to her encouragement, a bright light began to radiate from behind the couple as an extravagant golden staircase appeared. After turning to face the steps, William looked back over his shoulder at Ariel, who stood with a fulfilled expression.

"Will we see you again?" he asked hopefully.

"Of course!" she laughed. "Who do you think is going to be leading your through your studies?"

After a simple nod of his head, William turned back to the gleaming stairway and, while holding Tara's hand, he dissolved into the light as they ascended the threshold.

Now, standing alone in the white fields of Elysium, Ariel looked up at the sky, and peered across space and time. Traversing the cosmos, her vision finally fell upon an Earth reborn, brightly glowing in the Milky Way and cleansed of every unrighteous and abominable act. With a peaceful smile, she turned back toward the entrance to paradise and entered the celestial realm.

Silence continued to permeate through the heavenly meadows, and as the vision of Earth in the cosmos above began to fade, a distinct shadow appeared on the left side of the planet. The obscurity split into three, claw-like appendages, which wrapped themselves around the planet, slowly dragging across the surface, like a predator caressing its prey, just before the kill.

My story comes to an end with the third and final installment of the Creation Abomination series. It has been quite a journey for me in completing this project over the past eleven years, and I have honestly enjoyed the process. I also hope that you enjoyed the characters, storyline, and overall experience! If you have loved this book, please consider writing a review on Amazon and Goodreads. And if you haven't already, be sure to follow me on Instagram and Facebook - @creationabomination. Finally, be sure to sign up for my newsletter on creationabominatino.com, where you will hear about everything Creation Abomination, as well as some new planned projects that I will be starting soon!

Best!
Alan W. Thompson

To purchase a fine art print of the illustrations included in this novel, or other unique Creation Abomination merchandise, visit my website:

creationabomination.com/merchandise